HOPE
DEFERRED

HOPE DEFERRED

An Amish Romance

Linda Byler

New York, New York

HOPE DEFERRED

TABLE OF CONTENTS

"Hope deferred makes the heart sick, but when longing is fulfilled, it is a tree of life."

Proverbs 13:12

CHAPTER 1

Everyone knew they were best friends.

In the Amish circle that was a bit unusual, but nothing ever changed, from that first day of school when they played a game of kickball and he told her she could kick better than any girl he knew. She looked into his sparkling blue eyes and checked out his white teeth in a smile that was as big as her world. He watched her step back, lower her brows, bite her tongue in determination, and place a direct kick that sent the ball flying in a wonderful arc.

They lived on neighboring farms in Lancaster County. They walked to school together with a gaggle of older siblings who hardly took notice of either one, except to yell at them to get off the road; didn't they see that car coming? They didn't.

David Stoltzfus was six years old, already tall and well built, with blue eyes that seemed lit with an inner light. His beaming enthusiasm endeared him to his teachers. Way ahead of his class, his hand waving wildly at every question, knowing all the answers, he was never left behind in any discussion, or sport.

Anna Fisher was no slacker, either, only a bit shy and unsure of her own answers. She was a small child, thin to the point of being skinny but able to run effortlessly, like a small deer, her legs propelling her forward with no strain, simply a seamless rhythm of arms and legs. Her blonde hair was the color of ripe wheat flecked with cream-colored strands where the sun bleached the rolls along the side of her head and where her mother twisted them according to the Amish *ordnung* for small girls. Every school day she wore colorful dresses with a black pinafore-style apron, her feet bare in warm weather.

When David learned to drive a pony, Anna was the first one he took for a ride. She sat beside him in the spring sunshine and allowed a giggle of pure joy to escape her mouth before turning to look at him to share the bubbly feeling of riding in a cart that swayed and bobbed. The pony arched its neck and trotted down the road, its small hooves beating out a staccato rhythm that caused the harness to flap and bounce, sending small puffs of dust from the thick hair on its rump. It was all right if the loose hair from the pony's winter coat floated back and clung to the sides of her mouth or stuck to her cheeks. It was all in the bargain of being allowed to sit beside David as he handled the reins, a competent driver, even if he took the turns too fast, causing her to lean over and grab the iron railing that curved around the wooden seat.

Their lives intertwined like the borders of their families' properties were joined by the Pequea Creek, each family's right to half of the water never disputed. It was a lovely little waterway, meandering through the countryside beneath overhanging willow branches that hung into the creek, the ends carried endlessly along by the current as it ran its riverward course. It separated rolling hills, deep-soiled corn fields, and verdant stands of soybeans and alfalfa.

In spring the water turned the color of caramel pie, a thick brown roiling sluice that was more dangerous than it appeared. Parents warned their children, "*Bleivat aus de grick.*" More than one drowning had cruelly taken loved ones when the Pequea was in flood, and well they remembered. But in summer, the creek was a pleasant place to play, cool, deep and green beneath overhanging maple and oak branches, the banks slick with mud and heavy green grass. Minnows darted beneath gnarled tree trunks, and the only way to catch them was with a net scooped in the proper area. The minnows were deposited in their mother's plastic scrub bucket, taken home, and dumped into the water trough in the barn, where they all met an untimely death. David and Anna never could figure out what caused them to become so dead so quickly, the white flash of their silver bellies the first thing they saw in the morning when they checked on them.

"*Dote. Sie sinn all dote.*" David said sadly.

His older brother gave him the oxygen statistics of a creek versus a water trough, but David shook his head in furious denial. "You don't know everything!" he shouted, then gathered up all the dead "minnies," put them in an old shoebox, gave them proper names, and then buried them behind the henhouse.

Melvin, Marcus, Mervin, Mary, Mattie, Marvin, and when he couldn't think of more names that started with M, he named the rest with names starting with N. Nancy, Naomi, Neil. He couldn't tell the boys from the girls, but that was all right; at least they had a proper burial if they could never grow up to be big fish.

Anna and David loved playing in the creek, with Abner and Isaac and Anna's sister MaryAnn, who were all older and wiser and tried to boss them around. The bossing resulted in the same passionate blow-up from the outraged David, Anna standing stoically beside him completely in awe of every word he said.

Where does childhood begin and end? No one can say, as each child is an individual and begins remembering at a different time than his or her peers.

David remembered being carried to the barn in his father's arms and deposited on a prickly bale of hay, his father hurrying to milk the cows. He never stayed on the bale of hay but slid off immediately, finding cows that couldn't reach their allotment of corn silage, which he quickly remedied by pushing it within the reach of the animal's long, sandpapery tongue. He wandered quietly around the barn like one of the cats, darting here and there in search of whatever interested him at the moment, usually the corn silage disposal, an empty bucket, a brush, or any empty feedbag he could throw at the cats that rubbed themselves against his trousers.

In summer, he played in the milk house, squirting water on the floor from the hose coiled on the cement block wall, then sliding across the slick painted floor, making an awful mess. Being the youngest boy, he was not scolded, simply put up with.

His life was inhabited by adults, his closest sibling being eight years his senior. MaryAnn was like a second mother, sent to keep an eye on him and make sure he didn't get into trouble. How was she supposed to keep him out of it if he turned into an outraged little Rumpelstiltskin the minute she tried to propel him away from yet another disaster? He would turn fire engine red, yell, wave his arms, and stomp his feet if he was not allowed to continue with whatever forbidden project he'd thought of now.

And this all before he turned five years old.

His mother, Rachel, a bowed and plump housewife of forty-seven years, was simply tired. She had been past what she considered childbearing age when she produced a nine-pound, twelve-ounce baby boy. The pregnancy had been rife with nausea and water retention, until she felt like a water balloon and resembled a hippopotamus.

After David entered the world, she was merely exhausted and stayed that way, her shoulders steadily rounding, her head tilted forward in a bowed stance of martyrdom and submission. The spark that had been reduced by the antics of Abner and Isaac had been extinguished completely by the youngest son's passionate outburst of rage.

His father, tall, slim, with energy that never waned, went full speed from sunup to sundown, his eyes bright with the zest of his life on the farm. If his wife seemed unenthused, it was all right; he loved her anyway. Chewing tobacco behind her back, he sat on the cultivator and sent streams of its juice across the corn rows. He lifted his old straw hat to scratch his head and consider ways to improve profits on the price of milk. Good-humored 90 percent of his life, easygoing, and never riled about much of anything, Eli Fisher was well liked and respected, always voting on one board or another. He'd done a good job with his boys, raising them to be hardworking and obedient. The girls, too, were good workers and sought after by the market-stand owners.

The farm itself was a testimony to hard work and good management, the buildings preserved through decades of use from one generation to the next. The gray limestone house was built in 1798 and set close to Hollander Road, a bank of Boston ivy keeping the weeds down on the north side beneath an oak tree.

The first impressions on anyone who turned into the homestead came from the wide front porch, the low windows, and a massive door that seemed to welcome visitors. A white barn appended with a new hip-roofed cow stable complemented the constant flowering of perennials and annuals such as petunia, marigold, begonia, and hot pink vinca. These were set off by a row of pine trees that separated the machine shed and horse barns from the garden, a row of lilac bushes along the south side of the lawn kept as neat as a green carpet, and edges dug in precise borders.

The Stoltzfus property was another picturesque Lancaster County farm built on fertile soil tilled for centuries and nurtured with animal waste, lime, and commercial fertilizer. Seasons came and went, babies were born, the elderly were laid to rest, the traditions carried on, a vein of teachings from the ordained ministers nourishing the lifeblood of the community.

Vass die alte trick glesst hen. An interwoven mixture of moral values and obedience to God and His word, submission to the *ordnung*, chaste, honest brotherly love, one caring for the other in humility, the wife's duty to her husband as keeper of the home.

Some more than others.

As in every culture, there was diversity. Liberals and conservatives strove to coexist in harmony, to allow each one his own prickling of conscience by standards as various as the colors on the earth, yet bound to God and each other through the very existence of the Amish faith. A simple life, without electricity and automobiles. In spite of this truth, modernity stabbed its fingers into the woven fabric of the ancient culture, rearranging, tweaking, and bringing small changes here and there. Solar panels on roofs powered washing machines and LED light bulbs positioned above a happy housewife's sink. Cell phones creeped into the fabric of the church, considered unwanted as sin by some folks, and the handiest of devices by the more liberal ones, gleefully Googling a world of knowledge. Either way, the youth slipped into the informational lure of the cell phone on the well-oiled slide of the world. The ministers and bishops repaired rents in the woven fabric of the church. They conferred among themselves, prayed for the wisdom to advise, admonish, discipline, and tread the tightrope of accepting small changes while preserving the old Amish lifestyle.

David Stoltzfus was born and raised in this world, where his story begins at the age of seven, when he attended Meadow Run School in New Holland township.

The windows were bitter cold. Autumn wind blew the leaves in nervous shades of dull orange and red as the gale tore at the tender stems, sending a great many of them swirling off into the woven wire fence surrounding the small parochial schoolhouse that was the color of sand. Cornfields had been reduced to stubble by the plodding teams of Belgians or mules that drew cutters along the rows, binding the immense stalks of corn that had grown all summer, nurtured in the excellent soil by sun and rain that seemed to arrive when and where it was needed. It truly was the garden spot of America.

David walked backward, his hat pulled down so far it hid his eyebrows and most of his eyes, so he could talk to Anna, his words hurled away on the howling wind.

He carried the same sensible red and white Rubbermaid lunch box he'd carried the year before, the bottom lined with a stiff Great Value paper towel from Walmart, a juice box, a bologna and cheese sandwich on a white roll with mayonnaise, a sour red apple he wouldn't eat but that would stay in his lunch all week, a bag of rippled potato chips, two molasses cookies sprinkled with sugar, and a packet of cheese crackers.

No granola bars. He'd eaten the last one in bed last night, waking up to find his pillow holding a raisin, which he popped into his mouth first thing.

David entered the schoolhouse, answered Naomi King's "good morning" with one of his own, smiling, jaunty, already organizing the game of kickball that would take place before the bell rang. Anna, Melinda, Marvin, and Sammy on his team; Ruthanna, Elvin, Christopher, Mark, and Emily on theirs.

The sound of the bell clapper atop the roof of the schoolhouse put an end to the game. Each child raced to the front door, eager to begin the day.

Naomi King was in her late twenties, a tall, slim, brown-haired brown-eyed girl with a pleasant but plain face. There was no outstanding feature, but no ugliness either, just a face that held no attraction, save an occasional smile that showed more of her gums than what was deemed conventional. She was kind, strict but fair, managing her classroom of eight grades efficiently. Twenty-four students and one sixteen-year-old helper who was more interested in the shape of her eyebrows and the gleam of oil on her nose than anything else.

Naomi thought wryly about having twenty-five students and no helper.

She stood to read the first chapter of Psalms in the Bible, watching for any movement, any rustling of paper from beneath lowered lashes. Students were expected to sit still while the Bible was read.

"David."

Guilty, David closed the tablet and put it away. Like a cornered rat, he glared back at the curious stares of his classmates, ready to hurl insults at accusing eyes.

They stood to repeat the Lord's prayer, all together in modulated tones and a certain reverence.

"Our Father which art in heaven, Hallowed be thy name."

After praying, they all surged forward and helped themselves to a handmade songbook, the pages filled with hymns the various teachers had taught them through the years. They raised their eyes expectantly.

"Sally, I believe it's your turn."

Sally whispered shyly, "Forty-three."

Naomi repeated it more loudly so the others could hear. Shuffling their songbooks, older children reached forward to help the first graders. Then the room was filled with the voices of twenty-four children who poured their hearts and efforts into the hymn. The clean bell-like tones of innocent children whose voices were unmarred by self-consciousness or strife rose and fell as the beauty of the song poured across the classroom.

"Father, I adore thee, Lay my life before thee."

Once singing was over, David found his Spunky the Donkey arithmetic book and opened it to the page to be worked on that day. He looked around furtively before clicking down on his lead pencil and proceeding to write. He knew he was supposed to wait till Naomi announced his class, but he was ambitious. By the time she got to second grade, he had finished more than half of his work, bringing a sigh from his teacher.

"David. You know you should wait till I explain your new lesson."

"I already know how."

"I know. But you need to wait."

"Why?"

"What will you do the rest of the period?"

"Read."

David held up a copy of *The Adventures of Tom Sawyer.*

Naomi shook her head. "Really, David? *Tom Sawyer?*"

"What's wrong with that?"

Nothing really, Naomi thought as she shrugged and gave him a small smile. But he was seven. Most of her students were reading Amish picture books. There was nothing really wrong with David's book, it was just, well, advanced for a seven-year-old.

But she knew he would be able to read and understand every word. He was just so ahead of his class, just so old for a second grader.

Too busy to be pondering the intellectual advancement of one small boy, she moved on to aid little stumbling Henry Esh. "Anna, would you give Henry these flas hcards after you're finished, please?"

Eagerly, the angelic blonde-haired girl nodded.

Naomi smiled, gave the class to her helper, and moved on to third grade.

His arithmetic completed in less than forty-five minutes, David slid down into his seat, opened *Tom Sawyer* where his bookmark was inserted, its black tassel swinging from the stiff cardboard, and began to read, entering Tom's world of a muddy brown Mississippi River, the villain Injun Joe, the blonde-haired Becky Thatcher, and all the crazy things that went on in that watery, steamy hot world in the antebellum South.

David sneezed, unexpectedly sending a spray of moisture across his desk and anointing the unkempt strands of brown hair directly in front of him. The hair turned into a furious white face, eyebrows lowered in true boyish outrage. David met the snapping black eyes with indifference, lifting a forefinger and twirling it slowly.

"Turn around," he mouthed silently.

And, of course, Henry did. In the unspoken pecking order among the children, David was the undisputed king of second grade.

Anna Fisher was the second child in a family of five. Her parents were in their early thirties, a slim ambitious mother with hair the color of new wheat and eyes bluer than robin's eggs.

Her husband, Elias, short, trim, and as light of hair and eyes as his wife, matched her energy with that of his own, driven to succeed on the farm handed down to him from his father.

Elias and Barbie Fisher were a model couple who'd been raised to be exactly what they were: hardworking, God-fearing young people who were an asset to the community and the church in numerous ways. They never missed a church service unless there was an illness or an emergency, or if they attended services in another district to show support for friends or family.

Die gmay nemma.

Every Amish family was responsible to take their turn hosting church services in the home, be it in a basement, shop, or shed, or perhaps in a garage or an empty upstairs apartment. Services are held every two weeks. If there were twenty-six households in a district, that meant each family's turn came once a year. Less than twenty-six meant every ten or eleven months. But all in all, roughly once a year, more than one hundred people descended on a home expecting to be seated according to tradition and fed lunch after the three-hour service.

Anna Fisher had the good fortune to be raised in an Amish home that upheld the highest standards. At daily devotions around the breakfast table, Elias read from the Bible in his well-rounded baritone. The family sung a hymn afterward, the melodious blending of man and wife, the sweet, celestial voices of the children chiming in.

Discipline was doled out in love, arguments were quiet, well-modulated discussions as each parent sought to be the example the children would come to see as the light of Christ's love. But they unknowingly developed a form of pride, secure in their position as leaders in the community, a perfection of character that slowly shifted into the realm of loftiness, of haughtiness.

They took notice of loose morals and loud voices, fancy dresses and youth with hair cut in the English style. They clipped their words short and compressed their lips when discussing the goings-on of the disobedient, saying, "Where are the parents?"

But sweet Anna remained as free as an unfettered butterfly, eating her healthy granola and singing her fervent hymn at the breakfast table, her world infused with the golden glow of her parents' love for her and for Christ. There was no ugliness in Anna's domain, no tension between her parents, never an angry word or a sharp slap given in anger, so she remained covered by the gossamer silk of a righteous, happy home.

She loved David, the way she loved everyone, expecting all those in her world to be as kind and sweet and loving as she was. She enjoyed spending time with David and his big sister MaryAnn, who had to accompany them to the creek and on pony rides.

From her seat in the long row of wooden desks at Meadow Run School, she could slant her gaze sideways to watch David finish his arithmetic with long, sure strokes of his pencil, seldom using an eraser, charging to the table with the finished work, twirling around to run back to his desk and slam into his seat. He looked up to give her one of his dazzling displays of white teeth, and sank into his seat with his book, while she bent over her work, agonizing over the correct answer of $6 + 4 + 2$.

Her family and the school taught her to do the utmost to her ability. Things done halfway were not acceptable, so each problem had to be correct. She checked and rechecked her work, resulting in high grades that brought flowering speeches of praise from both parents.

It puzzled her how David could fly through his work and still have scores of 100 percent almost every time. On the way home, when the cold autumnal wind was at their back, leaves skittering across the road like panicked children, she asked him how he could finish his lessons so fast then stick his nose into a book.

David shrugged. "I dunno. It isn't hard."

"You're smart, that's what."

He smiled his bright smile, swung his red-and-white lunch box in a wide arc, and pranced along like a long-legged colt. Her admiration for him was an accepted thing, a part of her living breath. She never thought about it, nor did she try *not* to think about it. She didn't know exactly why she waited to walk home until he was beside her so they could talk, or why she kept her pumpkin whoopie pie until they were on the way home so she could share it with him. She only knew that to be with David made her happy, and she could talk more easily and freely than she could with anyone else, including her own parents.

"You hungry?" she asked, holding out the whoopie pie.

"Oh, wow! Sure!"

Chapter 2

THEY WALKED SIDE BY SIDE THEN, THE SHARED PUMPKIN WHOOPIE PIE OPENing up a world that contained no other creatures except themselves.

"Your mam makes the best whoopie pies ever."

"I know. She makes blueberry ones too."

"Blueberry whoopie pies? Wow!"

His own overweight old mam was always too tired to make whoopie pies and just bought vanilla-cream cookies at the bulk food store, all crumpled together in a plastic bag with a red twisty on top. They were hardly worth eating.

"Should I bring you one?"

"Sure. If your mam doesn't mind?"

"She doesn't."

"Okay."

"When will you drive Rudy again?"

"Rudy? He has a loose shoe. Dat said I'm not allowed to drive him barefooted. His hooves will crack."

"That's too bad. I was hoping we could drive him before winter. At least once," Anna said, a hint of sadness in her voice.

"I'll ask my dat, okay?"

"I'll watch for you. Think MaryAnn will go?"

"She doesn't always have to. I can handle Rudy."

He had so much confidence. Her eyes shone as she ate the last of the pumpkin whoopie pie, carefully crumpled the Saran Wrap, and put it back in her lunch tote.

David watched her replace the Saran Wrap and asked why she didn't throw it in the weeds. Shocked, Anna shook her head.

"Never. That's littering."

"No one would see you, though."

Anna pursed her lips. "I suppose you're right. But just because no one sees you doesn't make it right, you know. God would see you. He sees everything."

"He doesn't care. God doesn't care about little things like that. He just cares about the big things, like lying and stealing and stuff like that."

No matter their differences, they always seemed to rectify the situation in a manner far beyond their years. Their complete love and admiration for each other was, of course, the reason their personalities blended so well. But neither one understood this. The only thing they both knew was how much they looked forward to being in one another's company.

David let the door slam behind him on the way into his house, letting in cold air and the smell of burnt leaves and dust, the residue of whoopie pie icing around his mouth.

"Hey!" he yelled.

"What? Oh, hi, David. Home from school so soon?"

His mother poked her head around the frame of the open bedroom door, her hair *allus schtruvvlich*, pinning her white covering hastily, jabbing the pins with a guilty look in her small blue eyes.

"I was napping. I shouldn't do it, but your dat is at the horse sale in New Holland, MaryAnn is helping Abner sie Ruth, and a nap just felt so good."

David watched her lumber out to the recliner and jerk the footrest into position, lifting the white legs and feet encased in a pair of ratty house slippers before flipping her skirt down over the sausage-like legs.

"Come give me a kiss, David."

She reached for him, her fat white fingers beckoning him to obey her, so he did, thinking it would help the pony situation, for sure.

Her cheek was soft and warm and silky. She smelled of her warm bed and laundry soap and the kitchen. He placed his lips on the softest part and made a smacking sound, then stepped back and smiled into his mother's eyes.

"Ach, David, you're growing up so fast. My baby boy. Next thing we know MaryAnn will be married and then you'll be almost out of school."

"Mam, me and Anna want to drive Rudy. Can I hitch him up?"

"Why not? Sure. Then I'll finish my nap on the recliner, okay?"

"Yeah, sure. Thanks, Mam."

Not a word about the missing shoe or his father's warning. David knew his father wouldn't be home for a while, not when he was at the horse sale, so he had plenty of time to hitch up Rudy and get down the road to Anna's house.

Rudy seemed as eager to go as David was to drive him. He had a hard time getting the prancing pony between the shafts, finally managing to secure the traces with a constant volley of loud whoas.

"Whoa! Whoa. Rudy! Whoa, now. Hold still till I'm in the cart. Seriously, you dumb pony. Hold it right there. Whoa!"

The last whoa was a bellow of frustration, followed by a hard tug on both reins, which lifted the pony's head as he strained to ease the pressure on the bit. David caught the cart with one leg hooked over the side and pulled in the rest of his body as Rudy took off, tearing down the driveway as fast as his short legs could take him. David leaned back on the reins as he fought to keep the pony under control.

Any mother that had not raised a bevy of boys and their many accidents would have been a bit more concerned. But as it was, she soon fell into another soft and fluffy nap as her youngest son careened out the drive at breakneck speed. David was barely able to slow the pony enough to turn right, taking the turn on one wheel, lurching in his seat, his feet sliding out from under him as he struggled to stay upright.

"Rudy! You slow down right this minute," he bellowed, his face beet red. The pony took no notice of the outraged instructions of his driver, merely running for the joy of it. He took the turn into Elias Fisher's lane as if he was in a sulky race, spitting gravel and dust and dirt as he lunged on.

David pulled him to a stop at the hitching rack by the barn and waited. Elias Fisher came around the corner of the barn, a smile lighting up his features.

"Why David! You drove over by yourself?"

"Sure. Of course. I can handle Rudy. I came to give Anna a ride."

"You sure?"

Always careful, Elias narrowed his eyes, assessing the spirited pony and the overconfident seven-year-old. The pony was small, not much larger than a miniature one, but still. . . He valued the safety of his daughters above many other things, the way a good, conservative parent normally does.

David fastened a bright stare on Elias's face, an unnerving look that made him feel as if he had done something wrong and should absolutely apologize. And what was he doing, standing there and not going to get Anna, the way he was supposed to?

"All right. I'll get her," he said, and went to the house.

Delighted, Anna came flying out the door, pulling on her coat and scarf and settling happily into the slippery upholstered seat as Rudy tossed his head, eager to go.

"Why don't you just take him out through the field lane?" Elias asked. "I'd rather you didn't take him on the road with Anna."

David looked at Anna.

"Are you scared?"

"No."

"We'll be back."

With that, David loosened the reins, turned the pony in the direction of the road, which was toward home, and the rest was pony history.

Every pony loves to return to its home. It will increase its energy and speed the minute its nose is turned in the direction it came from, a trait that is repeated constantly, especially in small Shetland ponies, which is what Rudy was.

There was a seven-year-old holding him back, but not a strong, muscular seven-year-old. A few yards out the driveway, and his speed increased by the second. David heard Elias shout, but he was too intent on getting Rudy under control to bother trying to answer. By the time they got to the end of the drive, Rudy turned left at a dead gallop. David and Anna were thrown right, sliding out of the cart to hit the macadam and roll. It all unfolded in front of the fast-running Elias, who felt the horror of what was happening long before he actually saw his beloved daughter fly off the cart and hit the ground like a rag doll.

His arms and legs pumped in unison. Elias reached the frightened children, their clothes torn and disheveled, their faces bleeding, sitting by the side of the road alternately yelping and crying.

Elias fell panting on his knees, gathered Anna into his arms, running his hands over her small arms and legs, asking if they were all right.

David stopped howling. His face turned burgundy with rage. He got to his feet, blood pouring out of his nose and a gash on his head excreting another stream of it. He shook his fist in the direction of the disappearing pony and yelled his wish for Rudy's improbable doom, his ineptitude at being a pony, and, above everything, he hoped his hooves would crack forever.

Shocked, the conservative Elias told him to sit and calm down.

"David, my goodness. Don't get so upset. Here, use my handkerchief."

"Get away from me. I don't need your stupid old *schnuppy*." David batted it away then took off running down the road, oblivious to the slowing vehicles with alarmed motorists at the wheel.

In his gentle way, Elias spoke to the worried drivers, then steered his quietly sobbing daughter into the safety of the drive and the arms of her hysterical mother. Then he went to make sure David and his pony got home safely.

Elias was glad to see that Eli was home. Watching his son David steaming up to the barn and unhitching Rudy, Elias panting after them, Eli greeted both of them.

"Well, looks like Rudy didn't want to be driven, huh?" he said with a barely concealed chuckle creasing his cheeks.

David was breathing hard, his face still bleeding, his eyes wild with rage and humiliation.

"He's a dumb, stupid pony!" he shouted.

When his father burst into a great bellow of laughter, David stamped his feet, balled his fists and slammed them into his father's side.

"Here. Here." Still chucking, Eli caught his son's fists with one hand, dug into his trouser pocket with the other, handing a wrinkled navy blue handkerchief to his irate son. David batted it away with one swift kick, then delivered a few more resounding kicks that his father expertly sidestepped.

"S'what happens, Sonny, when we disobey. Now go to your mother so I can talk to Elias."

David exited the barn. He was literally hopping mad, actually walking on the balls of his feet, his head jerking slightly as he stalked to the house, giving both men a baleful zinger from those bright eyes before he slammed the door with every ounce of his seven-year-old strength.

Eli chuckled softly, shook his head.

Elias was completely mystified. He'd never seen such a display of unprincipled anger. In a child so small, it was like the beginning of a small forest fire: dangerous and in need of special attention. All the child-rearing books he'd read, the hows and whys and methods of discipline, would certainly be helpful in a situation such as this. He didn't hesitate to come to his neighbor's assistance in raising his son, which was met with icy disapproval, much to the earnest Elias's surprise.

Lifting his chin, Eli pointed in the direction of the house. "That little act he just pulled off? That's classic David. He's a bundle of energy, with a quick temper to match. My father all over again. No use getting riled. It's healthy to let him blow off steam."

"But . . . but . . ." his neighbor stammered. "In Michael Stern's child-rearing book, a child should never ever be allowed to kick or hit a parent. That is a definite no-no. It portrays the undermining of authority and leaves the parent in a very vulnerable position."

Eli sent a stream of tobacco juice into the empty box stall to his left. Elias winced, watching in horror. He had no idea his good neighbor used the abominable tobacco. It was uncouth, low-classed, a vicious, addictive, low-down, dirty habit.

"You can read a thousand of those books, Elias, but none of them will know your children the way you do. David is strong-willed, angry, passionate about everything, and way too smart for his age. You can make or break someone like him quite easily."

"Maybe you're right, Eli. Maybe you are. You know, I haven't raised my family yet, the way you have, so I'll keep my advice to myself, huh?"

Eli smiled slowly and shook his head in his wise way. "I don't hold much account for one person telling another how to raise their children. You raise yours the way you see fit, and I'll do the same, and we'll see what happens. Okay?"

They parted after a few more words about the change in the weather, baling corn fodder, and the price of milk, no animosity between them.

Elias felt the need to pray for his neighbor, which he shared with his wife, who encouraged him to pray with her as they knelt side by side before retiring that night.

Eli talked to David and told his son the unvarnished truth: he could have been hurt worse or killed by an oncoming car, and by no means should he attempt anything like that ever again. Then he left it at that.

When David's mother woke from her nap, her husband related

the afternoon's mishap, but she merely shook her head and said, "*Lieve leut, voss doot eya sñeckst.*"

They both believed all was well that ended well. David cuffed Rudy a good one out of spite but forgave his pony after a few days. The worst part of the whole deal was feeling bad about Anna. But she said it was all right, her knee was healing and so was her face, and her mother said Jesus had sent his guardian angels to keep them safe.

David thought a lot about angels from that moment on, but not in the way Anna did. Something invisible wasn't there. How could she say stuff like that? It scared him so severely he didn't sleep well for a week, thinking about angels fluttering around the house like gigantic birds.

Nobody knew things like that, for sure. So why did they say it? He wasn't ever afraid of the dark until he thought of all the invisible stuff, like the devil for one thing. Where was he? The minister said the devil made people do bad stuff, but how exactly?

It was too creepy to think about. But being seven years old, eventually his old stability returned, restoring all his brash confidence until the next time something went awry, which was sure to happen with the *Old Farmer's Almanac* predicting one of the worst winters in ten years.

The Christmas program at school was underway the week after Thanksgiving, each child given their part in the German play, with instructions to outline their sections of the script with a yellow highlighter, which David did not own. He was Grandfather Yoder, and, in his own opinion, he had absolutely no right to be a grandfather, as small as he was. And besides, the lines he had to say were stupid. They made no sense. He told his mother, his teacher, and all his classmates, until the teacher gave the part to Andrew Lee in the third grade, which pleased him until he was given a long, serious poem about the birth of Jesus and the astounded shepherds in the fields to recite.

He told Anna on the way home from school that he wasn't too

sure about this shepherd thing. How were the sheep out grazing given all the snow on the ground most Christmases?

She looked at him with wide-eyed innocence and said the hills were green around Bethlehem; they had colored them like that in a picture on the wall. He agreed immediately, then went home and asked MaryAnn what she thought about the shepherds.

Mam heard them, and said Bethlehem was in a warm country, so of course Anna was right. Then she told him he shouldn't question things the way he did.

"Too young, David, you're too young," she said.

Voss Gebt mitt da boo? she thought.

On the night of the program he stood tall, fastened his eyes above the crowd, and recited the poem in a clean voice that carried well, making a huge impression on his teacher and everyone in the packed schoolhouse. Elias and Barbie thought of the prayers they had offered on his behalf and felt a deep abiding renewal of their faith. Surely David had changed after all. Thank God.

His father sat in the audience and wiped tears from his eyes, thinking what a talented young man he was and wondering how one was expected to know how to direct the energy to the greater good?

Anna simply smiled at him, a sweet warmth filling her chest.

By the time David was in fifth grade, he'd reached a level of intelligence seldom found in Amish parochial schools. He did his schoolwork out of necessity, then read anything he could manage to get his hands on.

His parents both read books, mostly history or true stories published by a variety of Christian publishers, believing all literature of the modern world contained teaching contrary to their belief. His mother enjoyed an occasional romance, and the magazine rack by her recliner held the "Reader's Digest" and "National Geographic," both of which David devoured like a starving little man. He read his father's hunting publications, including the ads not meant for a ten-year-old. With no one knowing, he pondered the mysteries of life. He read every book in the limited library at the small parochial schoolhouse, reading and rereading the dog-eared paperbacks. Even the girls' books *Little Women, Amelia Bedelia,* and *Heidi* were part of his world.

Teased unmercifully by the seventh grade girls for reading *Little Women,* he merely shrugged his shoulders and glared at them until their smiles slid sideways and they slunk away, feeling thoroughly punished by the light in those blue eyes.

He begged his mother to go to the Bookmobile, the large white bus emblazoned in green and blue that made regular stops at small towns throughout Lancaster County. She pursed her lips and shook her head, saying there were too many unfit books for boys his age.

Most Amish parents saw no good coming of a head swimming in nonsense, leading away from a simple, contented lifestyle. It's the reason cell phones and computers were so frowned on. Forbidden. *Verboten.*

David threw one of his classic fits of rage to the point of wiping tears after the tirade had lost steam. Why? Why not? What was wrong with reading books?

He read every Laura Ingalls book at least a dozen times, especially *Farmer Boy.* He lived and breathed Almanzo and his brother Royal, telling MaryAnn she reminded him of Eliza, the bossy older sister. He practiced eating copious amounts of food, including two slices of pie, the way Almanzo did.

All the reading, the comprehension of what he read, coupled with an extremely lively imagination, produced an interesting young man at the age of twelve, entering sixth grade but able to do eighth-grade work and beyond. Life on the farm and in school was the physical part, but what went on in his head traveled way beyond the simple life.

He still walked to school with Anna, but it felt different now. They had grown older, with the attached stigma of being boyfriend and girlfriend, though they both denied it adamantly, Anna's face flushing to a rosy hue, David's burning with the start of a temper fit.

A boy of twelve did not want to have a girlfriend. Boys were tough and cool and never noticed the group of giggling females who hardly ever contained one brilliant thought in their head.

But he knew, deep down, that Anna did. She was cute and funny and sincere, and she was smart, too. She knew about the galaxy, the stars, and many of their names. She knew about coyotes killing baby deer, and she knew the correct pronunciation of *gosling* was not "gooseling."

They no longer shared whoopie pies or plastic ziplock bags of cheese curls, knowing at a certain age that it was no longer proper. But they cared immensely when one hit a home run and wanted to be the first to smack a congratulatory high five. When their sparkling eyes met, they knew.

There was something there. It was the uplifting sensation he felt when Anna was in the same room, on the ballfield, along the same road. He knew the color of her dress, the gleam of her blonde hair, her smile when she was happy, and the frown of concentration that produced two fine lines between her eyebrows when she did arithmetic, her biggest challenge.

Every morning, he donned a clean shirt for her, he combed his hair just so for her. When most boys his age couldn't have cared less, David harassed his mother until she remedied torn suspenders, or replaced them with a new pair. He begged for red ones, like the *rumschpringa* wore.

He cut slits in his old sneakers, after the toes turned up and the laces became frayed, when he saw the new gray and yellow Adidas that Michael in eighth grade had on his feet. This appearance thing was very important to David, in spite of his mother's relaxed view on clothing and other apparel like shoes and coats and beanies.

Anna took to begging her mother to buy a package of wide barrettes, afraid that David would find Suzie attractive with gold in her dark hair.

Anna's mother was an expert on child rearing. Having read all the latest books on adolescence, she prepared herself for the coming years when her daughter would notice these things.

Now that she had done just that, Barbie Fisher shivered, thinking of her eldest daughter's innocence, her pure and unspoiled life, and the terrors of the world around her. Kidnappers, men with strange desires, traffic on the road, wild and unruly horses driven by wild and unruly youth who would stop at the yard gate to take her away on the weekends after she turned sixteen.

Well, there would be rules.

Fully aware of her daughter's blossoming beauty, she determined with a fierce, almost maniacal resolve to protect Anna from heartache, from sin in its various forms, and certainly from marriage to someone who would not meet the high standards her parents had set for her.

It was God's will that a daughter be raised to be chaste, a keeper at home, to love her husband, and raise children in willingness to follow God's teaching in all matters.

She sang hymns of praise as she worked in her bright gleaming kitchen, smiled with motherly benevolence as they baked cookies together, read Bible stories on most evenings in her quiet, well-modulated voice, listened to prayers with practiced ears, then discussed each child's strengths and weaknesses with her husband, listening to his wise counsel with an open mind.

CHAPTER 3

"Mom, Suzie has new barrettes from her older sister. They look really pretty in her hair."

Anna was taught to call her mother Mom, not the old-fashioned Mam. Barbie and Elias decided early on that Mom and Dad were just better, more in keeping with the facts in the Christian child-rearing books.

Barbie looked up from her pea shelling to search her daughter's face. There was no rebellion, no challenge, only a wish to have what a classmate wore in her hair. Barbie gave her daughter a smile of kind understanding. "And what do these hairpieces represent?"

Perplexed, Anna frowned, the two lines appearing. "Nothing, really."

"But of course they do, Anna. The Bible teaches us to stay away from outward adornment, from the hanging on of gold and jewels. What is good and humble in the sight of the Lord is an unadorned body, and a meek and quiet spirit within. So rather than having you strive to adorn the outside, you should be seeking a meek and quiet spirit, like Christ had while he was here on earth."

"But it's only two barrettes."

"No, Anna. It's much more than that. You are lusting after adornment that is not our *ordnung.*"

"But you wear them."

Quickly, Barbie's hand slid beneath her covering, finding the hard metal surface of the black barrettes.

"Black ones, Anna. No one can see them."

"But they are still barrettes."

Barbie searched the daughter's face and tried to stay calm in the face of the first display of questioning her parents' wishes. What had Debra Rissler spoken of in her latest book? Chapter 7, "How to Say No."

"We would not believe the barrettes are important. What is more important is for you to obey my words without question."

"But, why, if you wear them?"

There was no reply, merely a compression of the mouth and a sad shaking of the head. The conversation was ended.

That evening, parents and daughter held a long, difficult discussion, the parents elaborating with hand-picked verses from the Bible, explaining views on modesty and the inward adornment. That made it difficult for Anna, choking on a strong dose of spiritual meat that was hard for her young mind to comprehend. But she listened quietly, which was her way, then knelt obediently to ask God to cleanse her of the longings of the world.

Afterward, she lay with her hands crossed on her chest, her eyes wide open as the light from the neighboring pole and the movement of the leaves toyed with her mind.

She knew plain from fancy. Any twelve-year-old girl will know the difference between a large, conservative covering compared to the smaller heart-shaped version on the younger, more permissive women in the Amish church. It was normal, everyday variety, both acceptable.

So why was her mother's covering one of the smallest? Her dresses were bright colors cut in the latest trend, made of dimpled fabric, or fabric with small checks or raised bubbles. Why were those adornments ok, but not barrettes?

Far away in the night, a dog set up a mournful howl; another series of short yips followed it. Anna shivered, pulled up the quilt, and turned on her side to tuck both hands below her cheek, her eyes drifting shut as the questions faded away.

These days David wandered to the creek alone, fishing pole and bait bag slung over one shoulder. MaryAnn had no interest in accompanying him to the creek, and Anna never did, either. He often wondered when she lost interest but never got up the nerve to ask. He figured correctly that it had something to do with boyfriend-girlfriend stuff. If they went to the creek together it would mean they liked each other, which of course, they didn't.

He missed Anna to the point that he'd taken to sitting along the bank at a strategic angle, where he felt sure she could see him from her front kitchen window. He baited his hook with canned corn and caught two nice brown trout within a half hour. He kept watching Anna's house. Maybe, just maybe, this time she'd be down. School had been over for a month. The days were getting hot and summery, with corn stretching from the soil as the heat and wetness increased. A month was an awful long time to go without seeing Anna, and he was wondering how to signal her from the creek bank when he heard splashing and voices to his right.

He turned and peered around the swaying curtain of willow branches to find Anna and her twin little sisters wading along the edges of the creek, their skirts knotted in two fists, their legs bare to above their knees, hoisting a minnow net.

Anna was laughing, her blue dress like a portion of the sky.

"Hey, you!" she called.

David scrambled to his feet, tripped backward on a tree root, then righted himself before reeling in his hook.

"Hey."

"What are you doing?"

"Fishing."

"Catch anything?"

He held up two fingers, "Catch and release."

"You let them go?"

"Yeah."

She came to where the bank rose in front of David, stood still, and looked over to her sisters.

"*Velleta raus?*"

David reached for her extended hand and drew her up. She was as light and agile as a fawn. He reached for both sisters and drew them to the safety of the matted grass on level ground.

"There you go."

They looked at one another. Both were filled with infinite inadequacies. Floundering, David tried conversation.

"How's . . . you know, how's summer going?"

"Good."

A long silence, stiff with new and unresolved feeling.

"Um, Kathryn, you ready? Rachel Ann?"

She turned to her sisters and made as if to go.

David wanted her to stay but didn't know how to accomplish this. Desperate, he picked up his fishing rod and thrust it at one of the sisters.

"Would you like to fish? Do you know how?"

Hands clasped behind backs, their heads wagged in unison.

"No."

"You want to try?"

"No. Worms are icky," Kathryn griped.

"I'm not using worms. I'm using corn. See?"

He held up a green-labeled can of corn.

He baited the hook cleanly, piercing the large kernel with precision, then drew back, released the button on the reel, swung expertly, and watched as the hooked corn sailed through the air and plunked into the quiet waters of the creek.

Anna laughed, a sound he never tired of.

"You want to try?"

She nodded, "I do."

His hands on hers, he taught her proper technique.

She cast in short plunks, the corn barely skirting the grass. Over and over she cast, finally sending the bait to the middle of the creek. Her sisters whined that they were thirsty.

Did David understand his regret at not bringing his blue Coleman jug full of ice water? Did Anna realize the quick irritation that rose in her chest? At twelve years of age, they were possessed by a longing to be together, a happiness at being in one another's company, but now this pristine shyness, this scrambling to locate words that had never eluded them before.

Still a child in every sense of the word, having been taught well in the ways of kindness, Anna put a hand on Rachel's shoulder and said, "Okay, we'll go. I'm thirsty too."

Looking back once, she lifted a hand to say goodbye.

On the creek bank, David lifted a hand in answer, slowly, hesitantly, as if to prolong the leaving. A sigh escaped him. Two brown trout were enough. He reeled in his line, removed the soggy corn, shouldered his rod and bait bag, and moved off slowly.

And so it went for another summer. He gave himself to hard work in the broiling sun, unloading bales of hay and straw onto the rattling elevator, sweat dripping off the tip of his nose, tasting salt as it pooled in the corners of his mouth, his shirt stained dark with the sweat on his back.

His hands blistered and bled, then turned to thickened calluses. His legs became strong and sinewy with hours of walking, lifting, bending, and stretching. He mowed most of the grass in the large well-kept lawn and dug all of the borders around the flower beds.

He put up the wire of the pea vines and pounded the wooden stakes into the soil with the broad side of a hammer, the way he'd seen his father do it. He found his father's tobacco pouch, inserted two fingers and lifted a hefty chunk, placed it in his left cheek, waited for the taste, then threw up violently and never tried it again.

He ran the large wheeled cultivator up and down the rows of corn and beans, leaning into the bent, wooden handle, his elbows stuck out like wings, straining and puffing, his legs cramping as the bent teeth dug up the soil removing chickweed and redroot, thistle and dandelion.

He pushed wheelbarrow loads of mushroom soil, distributed it in wide curved flower beds filled with roses and hydrangea, boxwood and daylilies, MaryAnn scolding and shouting and telling him to slow down and stop ruining the coreopsis.

David couldn't tell one flower from another, so he went right ahead and dumped the mulch where he wanted, figuring she would yell, but she was lucky she had him to do all the hard work while she scuffed around in the bushes and shrubs. Until she got really mad and grasped his ear between her thumb and forefinger, and twisted till he thought she'd surely pulled it off. He grimaced and threatened before running off to tell his mother. "Ach my," she said, and went right on reading the mail.

Picking peas was the worst. Whoever heard of putting all that effort into raising a vegetable that wasn't edible in the first place? Peas were unhandy little green marbles that rolled around on your plate and that you were expected to stab with a fork and get to your mouth somehow. If macaroni and cheese grew on those crawly vines it would be different.

Peas ripened in June, when the mornings were wet and cold and the days turned broiling hot in a hurry. The peas hung thick and saggy in their shells, some of them ripe, some of them half-ripe, and some not ripe at all, so it was up to you to decide which to pick. The most depressing feeling came from leaving so many on the vine, knowing you'd have to go back and do this same soggy backbreaking work in about four or five days.

It was only him and his mother and MaryAnn. His mother wasn't worth that much, with all her stretching and groaning and exclaiming. She had a bad back and achy knees, she said, and nothing was worse than bending over halfway to pick peas off a wire.

"You can buy peas, Mam," David said, standing to open a long wet pad, extract the row of green peas neatly into his mouth.

Raw peas were good, it was the mushy cooked ones he had a problem with.

"Now, you know your Dat would have a fit. Those bought peas are just horrible," she answered.

"Well, if Dat likes his peas homegrown, he can pick them."

"David, you know you're way too big for your britches."

Unhandy, arrogant little know-it-all, she thought to herself.

"My britches fit just fine."

And so it went, picking peas. No one could say they really enjoyed it, not even holier-than-thou MaryAnn, and certainly not his fat, complaining mother. Pure misery for David.

"Mam?"

"Stop it. How old are you two? Three or four?"

She straightened her back, rubbed the palms of her wet hands over it, and said, "I'm quitting. I can't take this bending over."

"Seriously, Mam?"

"Yes, seriously. You can finish. There are only two more rows. I'll get the bowls and chairs ready. Daudy's are coming to help."

MaryAnn rolled her eyes.

"Why can't we shell peas by ourselves?"

"They mean well," Mam called over her shoulder as she left the pea patch, leaving MaryAnn and David to continue the work. The sun burned the surrounding fog into submission, becoming hot on their backs and creating a whole new level of discomfort.

MaryAnn's hands flashed in and out, grasping swollen pea pods, leaving flat underdeveloped ones, her mouth set in a determined line. David knew things would get ugly in a hurry without his mother, so he bent his back and picked peas.

"David, you're missing a whole pile of them."

"No, I'm not. You're just making that up."

"Yes, you are. Look here."

She parted the pea vines to show a cluster of ripe peas, her red face accusing him of treachery.

"It's not like I did it on purpose," he shouted.

"Oh, relax."

That did it. He yanked off pea pods and pelted her with them until she stalked off to tell Mam, who appeared on the porch as big as a bison and made him pick all those peas by himself. He disliked peas and everything to do with them, including his mother and sister. Muttering disparaging thoughts to himself, he slowly continued picking, the sun climbing high in the sky, pinning him into the earth with its heat.

He looked up to find the old, bent form of his grandfather, leaning heavily on his cane, his eyes as blue as a cornflower, twinkling with merriment.

"*Ganz allenich?*"

"*Ya.*"

"*Vell, vell.*"

He laid his cane aside, and made his way carefully down the row, his wide brimmed straw hat stained and torn, his beard long and full and white. His shirt had been blue years ago but had turned a grayish white with countless washings in homemade lye soap.

"So how is David?" he asked.

"Not good."

"I guess not, picking peas."

David braced for the usual boring account that started with, "Now when I was a boy," but nothing was forthcoming. He straightened to watch his grandfather's old gnarled hand search among the vines. His fingers were like small oak branches, so thin and misshapen, the veins on the backs of his hands like night crawlers, thick and discolored. David wondered what would happen if he accidentally punctured a vein. Would blood spurt out until he needed a tourniquet?

He blurted out this question.

Daddy Beiler lifted his two hands, turned them around, and peered through the lower half of his glasses.

"I doubt it. I don't know. Give me your pocketknife, and we'll make a hole in one of these veins, see what happens."

David looked alarmed, his eyes going to his grandfather's.

Daudy chuckled, his loose skin turning into a mass of wrinkled bread dough pushed together with both hands.

"You wouldn't hurt your old Daudy, would you?"

David shook his head.

"All right, let's get finished here. I think Rachel has warm cinnamon rolls cooling on the countertop."

Rachel being Mam, of course.

His grandfather's trousers were like a map of time. New denim patches on medium blue patches, down to faded gray His shoes were cracked and torn, revealing glimpses of white stockings along the top.

"You need new shoes, Daudy."

"Me?"

He bent to examine his shoes.

"Naw. Nothing wrong with these."

"They're torn."

"That's all right. There was a time when I had no shoes. I had to go to school barefooted late in the season. There was no money for shoes."

"No money at all?"

"No money. Everyone was the same. Poor as church mice. We ate a lot of beans, a lot of mush."

David listened to his grandfather's voice, carried away to another era, and thrilled to suddenly find the end of the row. The heat of the sun hadn't bothered him for the last hour, as his grandfather's voice rose and fell.

They carried buckets of peas to the porch, where his mother and grandmother were already seated, stainless steel bowls balanced on their knees, their skirts filled with peas. Mam and MaryAnn were smiling now, the good humor restored, sitting in comfortable lawn chairs in the shade of the porch roof in the company of someone they both adored.

Mammy was small and bent, her nose supporting a pair of round wireless glasses, the bifocals along the bottom of the lenses thicker than the top. Warts, moles, and brown spots sprouted out of her face wherever they felt like it. One of them clung to the side of her nose like moss, the color of an acorn; it waggled when she talked, which was just about all the time. David watched the growth move in and out of her glasses and thought that surely the thing should be shaved off by now.

"Mammy, why don't you have your warts removed?" he blurted out in his own typical style.

"Warts? Why, David, I don't have warts. Just moles. It would cost too much, that's why."

David watched her face and thought she didn't look very friendly after that. Surely he hadn't hurt her feelings. Did old people still think they were good looking or what? They certainly had seen their best days long before this one, he thought.

Old as the hills, he thought.

Well, now he had two things to look up in the *World Book Encyclopedia*: the Depression and facial growths. Abnormalities. Warts. Moles. Probably many more scientific names. Hopefully he could find out what caused them.

He ate three delicious sticky buns with caramel icing, drank a cup of coffee with French vanilla creamer despite MaryAnn's disapproval, and sat at the patio table defending himself when she tattled about the coffee, thinking how much she resembled an anteater with that pointy nose and big snout.

"Oh, coffee isn't going to hurt him. We were raised on coffee soup, right Daudy?"

"We sure were. No eggs for breakfast back then. No meat, either. We were lucky to have bread with coffee poured over it. It was hot and good, kept our stomachs filled till we ate what was in our tin lunch bucket, sometimes only lard bread and cornpone."

"Lard bread?" David screeched, letting his tongue hang out of his mouth. "Gross."

"It was good. Anything is good if you're hungry enough. And we were certainly hungry."

"Children nowadays have no idea. They would never eat the things we did."

Mammy lifted a finger. "Now, though, it's not their fault. Can any one of us help being born in the times we live in? Of course not."

And David felt better. Of all the thoughts that entered his head, that was one of the worst: the thought that everything that went on in your life was somehow your own fault, like you never did anything right, ever.

Depressing, that thought.

His grandfather winked at him when he pinched off another piece of the cinnamon roll, then pulled off an entire section and stuffed it into his mouth. He thought God probably looked a lot like his grandfather, all big and wide with a crown of white hair and a flowing beard.

And besides, someone had to have mercy on twelve-year-old boys, because none came from MaryAnn and Mam, that was sure.

CHAPTER 4

At the neighboring farm, the peas ripened the same week. Picking was viewed as a family get-together, an event long awaited and accepted with alacrity.

First, Mommy Esh arrived, trim and neat, not yet sixty years old, with Mom's sister Ruth by her side. They stabled the Friesian horse with the help of the son-in-law, who fairly glowed with their arrival. After greeting each other warmly, Anna stayed with the little ones, did the morning dishes, and swept the floor while the three women carried plastic totes to the pea patch, bent their strong backs, and picked peas, talking and laughing without one word of complaint.

They genuinely enjoyed it.

Strawberry season was the same. They thought nothing of bending their thin supple backs and picking box after box of strawberries for preserves and frozen desserts. They shared news of the community, discussed the sale days at the consignment shop in Strasburg as the sun climbed steadily in its great blue orb, bringing the usual heat and humidity.

Elias took time to help them pick a while, which was greatly appreciated by his wife, who did not hesitate to tell him, receiving a look of pure adoration from her beloved. They were a team, husband and wife molded together in the true sense of the word.

In the house, Anna sang as she worked, then took the children down to the pea patch after everything was finished.

"Oh, Anna, they'll get wet feet. Maybe you'd better take the little ones to the house, okay?"

Anna took them back, without resenting the order from her mother. She had been told the evening before what was to be expected of her, so she hadn't tried to change the schedule, accepting that her mother always knows best.

They did not sit around the porch to shell peas, but took them to the pea huller instead. After a bit of coffee, fruit, yogurt, and granola, her mother and sister left, leaving Anna to watch the children until her mother returned from the pea huller.

When all the peas were blanched, carefully measured into ziplock bags, and stored in the freezer, Anna's mother announced a surprise. They would all be going camping by the Susquehanna River for the weekend with Daniel's and Daddy's.

Anna was thrilled. She jumped up and down, clapped her hands, and squealed, Kathryn and Rachel Ann following her antics with the same motions. Baby Leon and four-year-old Micah merely looked up from their wooden toy barn and smiled before going back to their serious farming.

Later that evening, Anna asked her mother why they always went camping with Daniel's and Daddy's, and why not with their neighbors sometimes.

"Neighbors?" her mother asked, confused.

"You know, Eli and Rachel Stoltzfus."

An intake of breath, a careful release from her mother.

"Why would we do that?" in a well-harnessed voice.

"Oh, I don't know. I would enjoy it. Their David taught me how to fish."

Her mother's head snapped to the right, her eyes boring into hers.

"When?" she asked sharply.

"I told you, didn't I?"

"No. Where were you that he could possibly have taught you to catch a fish?"

"Down at the creek. When Kathryn, Rachel Ann, and I went to catch minnows."

"You did not tell me."

"But what's wrong with it?"

Catching herself quickly, her mother forced a smile.

"Nothing. Of course not."

"David helped me cast. He stood behind me and put his hand over mine, and we brought the line way up, then flung it out across the water. But you have to press a button on the reel or else it won't let go."

The mother gazed into her daughter's sparkling eyes and thought, *Oh no, no.*

A shot of unexpected anger was quickly quenched by the power of the Spirit. *I must not, must not,* she told herself calmly. She took a cleansing breath and thought rationally.

"You and David have always been friends, so perhaps it's good he was the one who taught you how to fish."

"Oh yes, Mom! David knows everything. He is so smart. He caught two brown trout before we came along. He catches them then throws them back. That is so kind to the fish, isn't it?"

"It surely is. Well, I'll talk to Daddy, and we'll decide whether that would be all right."

"Oh, goody! I would love to go camping with MaryAnn and David."

"We'll see."

The usual evening discussion brought a serious gathering of Elias's eyebrows, pursed lips, and a quiet, "Hmm."

"They're only twelve, Elias. But she seems to increase her admiration for that boy."

She could hardly contain the disapproval that started as a seed, thinking of his hand on Anna's. The arrogance.

A deep sigh from Elias.

"What is the best approach, do you think? Should we tell her things she should know pertaining to boys? Should we forbid her to go to the creek? Or should we shrug our shoulders and not overreact?"

"It is a serious thing. I totally agree. But for now, why don't we pray for answers? Anna is growing up so fast, and I do not understand her fascination with David. Her eyes shine when she talks about him."

"Well, one thing," she continued thoughtfully. "So often when there's an infatuation at school, it fizzles out by the time they join the youth. I cannot imagine David and Anna being in the same group, can you?"

"No. Oh no. Eli and Rachel are very liberal minded with those two youngest. I'm not saying they haven't raised a good family, but I don't know if they're just tired or uninterested, but seems as if they could use a shot of spirituality in that home."

His wife nodded, her eyes very dark and serious.

"The best thing, likely, would be for me to take her to Walmart, purchase a fishing rod, and teach her myself."

"Do you know how?"

"No. I've never fished."

They laughed, drained their tea, and headed for the shower and a good night's rest, after lengthy and meaningful prayer.

When school opened in the fall, there was so much to look forward to for both Anna and David. They did not walk to school together as in the past. David zipped to school on a brand-new silver scooter, careening recklessly down hills, cutting a wide arc at the crossroad, hoping to impress the serene Anna, who walked with her two sisters and a neighboring first-grade boy.

Shy glances, now, gladdened both their hearts. Secret smiles were strong enough to restore sunshine on a rain-splattered day. One was becoming a light to the other, a measurement of their days. She knew where he was every hour; he knew when she was at the blackboard, or out on the porch giving flash cards to lower graders, or simply seated at her desk.

Baseball games were a form of jubilance, a chance to be together to show one another their acquired skills. When the school purchased a volleyball net, they thrilled to the closeness of standing side by side, experiencing pride in each other's expertise and sportsmanship.

They thought, foolishly, that no one would notice, that no one would think anything was different between them than any of their other classmates. The teacher could tell, and thrilled secretly to the sight of young love, something she had always been denied, her cross to bear. The will of God was not always the will of man, she reasoned.

But she did her teacherly duty and discouraged any form of affection or untoward fondness of one pupil to another, especially in the upper grades.

She took David aside and asked for a bit of discretion, reminding him he was too young to be flirting. It caused his face to flame a deep red, ashamed at being called out like that.

The delicate Anna was let go, her winsome ways endearing her to her teacher. Plus, she had the upbringing everyone knew. She was taught the best Christian behavior and acted accordingly.

By the time David and Anna were officially "out of school," as the proper Amish term is pronounced, *aus de school*, there was no doubt in either one's mind with whom they wanted to spend the remainder of their lives.

Both lived all week to attend the three-hour vocational school, until they turned fifteen years of age and graduated to the labor force of all Amish children.

Boys were taught to work either at home on the farm, or more often now taken along on various construction jobs, or being an apprentice in some welding or woodworking shop. They learned to rise at five o'clock in the morning, eat breakfast, and spend all day becoming efficient at the line of work placed in their life by their parents. Choosing a vocation at that age was mostly out of the question. Young people normally took up the family business or worked for a construction company.

Farming was still the vocation of everyone's dream, but it became less viable as time went on. The high price of land, the low price of milk, and the rising costs of putting out an acre of corn—the spray, fertilizer, lime, all of it necessary—it all added up to a low margin of profit.

Competing in a world of large milking parlors and enormous machinery that could plant or harvest in a few hours seemed futile to some. Yet the love of the land and a willingness to work hard with no instant gratification kept many on the home farm, driving a team of plodding mules or Belgians, inspired by the clanking of harnesses and the squeak of steel-wheeled equipment, the sky overhead a blue dome of unlimited possibility.

All across America, the Plain people migrated to various states in search of affordable land and a good milk market, keeping the faith and the old ways in spite of the distance between the large communities.

Lancaster County was the hub of the wheel in Pennsylvania. The area burst with Amish farms and businesses, so David was assaulted by a diversity of possibilities and no idea what would be best for him.

Of course, his father needed him and planned on his help on the farm, with the niggling doubt about David bowing to the old way, given that energy and passion directed mostly to books.

He'd never seen anything like it. Mam scolded and riffled through books he picked up at yard sales and thrift shops, clucking her tongue and wondering who would be interested in all that stuff. Was it normal?

Anything from ancient hieroglyphics to Australia's Great Barrier Reef to an intimate account of President John F. Kennedy's life. What in the world? The pictures in some of those books were not meant for her son's eyes. So she waged a motherly war against the books of the world, carried a stack downstairs and showed the lot to her husband, wagged a finger under his nose, and said you better sit up and take notice of what is happening to your son.

Eli sighed and told her she was panicked about nothing. She

carried the stack back upstairs, thumped them down on his night-stand, and didn't talk to her husband for days.

How was a mother to raise up a boy in the way that he should go if she had no support from her husband? Look at Henry Zook's boys. Every one left the Amish, and they said that's what was wrong. She didn't support her husband, they said. She stood by her children, defied him, and look what happened. But they realized it was all the way of the flesh, of gossip and its sad consequences. Well, if Eli thought it was all right for David to stockpile all this unnecessary knowing of things that wouldn't be worth anything at all, then, she would support him.

So without restraint from either parent, David was free to accumulate a wealth of books on many different subjects.

He rode his scooter to every Saturday morning yard sale that was accessible within scootering distance and loaded up the front wire basket with the varied and colorful array of literature that piqued his interest and was probably unknown to his peers.

He spent his days on the farm, enjoying none of it, and lived to spend evenings with his books.

Every Monday afternoon, the vocational class met in Sarah Lapp's basement, a single girl who devoted her time to the three hours of instruction, enabling the fourteen-year-olds to have a bit of schooling before being thrust into the world of *rumschpringa*.

Every Monday, David took an hour to fine-tune his appearance, turning his head and liking the way his straight hair was cut above the ears. From another angle, he thought his nose and mouth were turning out quite fine, hoping he would yet take on a chiseled, masculine look. Only six inches away from the coveted six feet, he towered over most of his friends, his body honed by constant hard work on the farm.

He selected shirts with Anna in mind, blue to match his eyes, red to attract her attention, brown with a thin black stripe to be awesome.

He sprayed Shout on his gray Nike sneakers, scrubbed vigorously with an old terrycloth rag, wished there was more of a swoosh, the symbol of cool. He could hardly wait to wear white sneakers when he was sixteen.

He lived to see Anna at vocational class and believed she lived to see him. Always their eyes met, the same resounding gladness between them, the knowing of their secret attraction, their admiration.

And they were never disappointed.

On the last day before David's fifteenth birthday, vocational class was bittersweet. How would he manage to see her in the year before he turned sixteen? How could he be sure she would join the same group of youth? There were so many, and such a difference in the attitudes of the various parents and groups of young people.

David was old enough to know his parents were liberal, relaxed about rules, and figured the kids would pretty much learn on their own. So why not let them go out and sow some wild oats?

He stood beside Anna at recess, played volleyball knowing she was there. He leaped and bounded and smacked the ball across the net in various spikes, then looked for and received her admiration. When he scored an especially difficult return, her high five meant twice as much as anyone else's.

They parted that day with no chance to speak to one another, except for the usual backward glance, a raised hand lifted timidly so it would not attract any undue attention, aware of social expectations, of reserve and hidden feelings.

David waited till she came from the door of the basement. He stepped forward and handed her a folded piece of paper. Her eyes went to his, a bewildered look, followed by infinite happiness when she saw the adoration in his.

"Thanks," she whispered, her face suffused in a lovely blush.

She had no opportunity to read the paper until she changed clothes in the privacy of her own room. She bit her lip as she unfolded it, her heart beating quickly.

Dear Anna,

I wish we would have vocational class till we were sixteen. I will miss seeing you, and hope we can join the same group of youth.
Love,
David.

A hand to her heart, the paper clasped in trembling fingers.

Now she knew, for sure. He cared about her as deeply as she cared about him. The paper was pressed even harder to her racing heart.

Oh, precious world. Precious, lovely love that colored her days, that brought depth and meaning to her existence. She firmly believed he was her reason for being born, her destiny. God's will for her life.

She read her Bible and found every verse that instructed her in the way of a young man's love, of marriage.

Her mother provided her with an arsenal of Christian literature, inspirational writing by the best godly instructors. She was as lovely in the heart as she was in her outward appearance, the teachings of her parents paving the way for a solid foundation, making a sure young woman who would always be an asset to her husband.

Every morning she flipped the page of her daily devotional, pondering the words. Her soul drank from the well of her Christian provision in the form of good, sound inspirational writing. She had no reason to believe the writing wasn't true, living with parents who were daily examples of righteousness.

Her father never raised his voice to her mother, as she never did to him. They reveled in the happiness of one another, their days colored with kindness and thoughtful deeds, securing an atmosphere of happiness for their family.

There was, however, one flaw, one thorn in the mother's flesh: neighbor Eli Stoltzfus's son, David. Prayer had accomplished neither the cooling of his infatuation nor the dimming of the light in her daughter's eyes when she spoke of him. When she found the note while housecleaning, she literally ground her teeth, suffering the first stroke of pure rage in her otherwise unruffled existence.

It wasn't fair, this exploitation of her eldest. He was like a wolf waiting in the underbrush until her pure and innocent daughter walked by. Until he pounced on her.

She fought the evil of her anger with prayer. She stood at the curtained window in the light of early evening and asked for the power of the Holy Spirit. She received the gift of a calm and serene countenance, the boiling cauldron of her distaste for David and his family lidded and squelched—for now.

Rachel was just so slovenly, so tired and sloppy and outspoken. She was always the center of attention, bossing others around, having the answer for everyone's life, exactly like her son. Her covering strings were stained where they hung against her perspiring neck, her hair always adorned with flecks of white dandruff.

Ugh.

And that MaryAnn. She'd never seen anyone else with those ridiculous dresses. Her hem touched the floor, the sleeves so tight you could see the shape of her elbows, her black aprons always too short. What could you expect, with Rachel for her mother?

To think of her Anna being married to David brought a clenching to her chest, an irritation that brought a firm reprimand to her youngest daughter after she had only spilled a few drops of milk. The only solace she had was the firm belief that Anna was taught to obey, and this training would prove to be her saving grace. She could see nothing good come of her infatuation with David, and if she played her cards right, nothing would come of it.

"Anna, I accidentally found a note from David Stoltzfus."

Clashing cymbals of fear shot through Anna. She hid her face, turned her back.

"Look at me, Anna."

Obedience came naturally, so she did. She found her mother's eyes with a strange new look, one she had never seen and did not understand.

"Why did he write that note? Was it because of your encouragement? You are much too young to have your head filled with thoughts of boys. Anna, this is just wrong. God does not want you to be the recipient of someone's attention at such . . ."

"Mom!" Anna broke in, heartbroken.

She knew her mother's expectations and her disapproval. But she harbored the vain hope that she would change, would accept, perhaps bless.

"You are too young to know your own mind. What girl at fifteen knows what she wants? You don't. Anna, you can't."

"But . . . Mom!"

A wail of despair now, so deep and injurious, the color in her life was erased by the knowledge of her mother's firm ways and replaced by a bleak landscape of loss and grief.

"Anna, stop."

Anna sank into a chair, her lithe young frame rendered helpless in the face of matriarchal power.

Her mother lowered herself into a chair opposite her wilting daughter.

"It's not all about obedience. It's just that Daddy and I can see and understand so much more than you at your age and without experience. Your fascination with David is, indeed, immature and of the flesh. It is lustful. This love is not from God. It is the works of the flesh, Anna, and if we turn from it, you shall reap great rewards here on earth and later in heaven."

Here her mother drew in a deep, ragged breath, dabbed delicately at her eyes, blinked with an affected sadness.

"You are loved, Anna, very deeply. Accept your parental guidance now, at this young and tender age. It will never spite you."

And so began Anna's personal war between her own heart's desire and her parents' wishes, causing a battlefield of the mind and spirit that whittled away her health and well-being.

Unaware of any of the drama at the neighboring farm, David whistled and sang and lived his days in easy comradery with his easygoing father, filling his life with fascinating books, spending time with his best friend, Wayne, learning the ways of the farm, the ups and downs and whys of the untrustworthy milk market. He resolved to learn a skill somewhere, somehow, that had nothing to do with cows or horses.

He was happiest when he was fishing. His favorite spots included neighboring ponds, or any waterway within a twenty-mile radius, traveling with Wayne and one of his father's work truck drivers.

Wayne was tall, like David, with dark curls and a cherubic face, lacking any ambition except for volleyball, baseball, basketball, and fishing. He had never cracked open the pages of a book, so naturally the artesian flow of David's words were a constant source of fascination.

This was the basis for a long and lasting friendship.

Lounging on the banks of the Hess pond in Lampeter township, the swaying of the willow branches a hypnotic dance, they watched the antics of the water skates and the hovering of dragonflies, deciding this was not a good day for catching fish.

Wayne cast a glance at David. "I told you. It's not a good sign. Waning moon."

"You believe that crap?" David leaned sideways, grasped a stalk of grass, put it between his teeth, and felt very much like Huck Finn.

"Sure. I've proven it many times."

"How?"

"Duh. Went fishing."

"I guess."

"I'm starving. We should have thought to bring something."

"There's a Subway on 891."

"You got any money?"

"No. My wallet's at home."

They both remembered the roadside stand, lifted their rods, and laid them on the bank of the pond. They made their way to the stand containing bread, cookies, whoopie pies. A young girl came from the house, brown-eyed, friendly, waiting patiently while they chose the pastries that suited them.

"That it?" she asked.

"Yeah. Hey, we don't have any money. We're fishing across the field here."

Wayne jerked his thumb in the direction of the pond.

"So can we charge this? Maybe bring our money next week?" David asked, giving her his best wheedling tone.

"Yeah, you can. Sure."

A batting of her long eyelashes, a dimpled grin.

Stuffing themselves with chocolate whoopie pies and grinning, Wayne said she was cute.

"I can hardly wait to start chasing girls when I'm sixteen."

David laughed, but said nothing.

When Wayne questioned him, he shrugged. "Come on, man. You're so dead serious all of a sudden. You got a problem with that?"

"With what?"

"What I said about girls."

"No."

"Well, then. Lighten up."

David nodded and thought how he hadn't noticed that the girl was pretty, and how he had no plans of chasing anyone. He felt old, experienced, serious. He had found all he ever wanted in Anna, all he ever dreamed of. He knew with absolute certainty, his life was like an arrow's flight, straight and true to his fair and lovely Anna.

CHAPTER 5

B Y THE TIME HE WAS SIXTEEN, DAVID WAS WORKING FOR A ROOFER. MANNY Beiler was young, driven by a burning ambition to become wealthy, and to own the largest and fanciest house, the best Dutch harness horse, and finest brand-new carriage available.

David Stoltzfus was the best hire he'd ever made, he told his yawning wife late one evening. She fell asleep listening to him list the accomplishments of a guy so young he'd only started his time with the youth a month ago.

"He's worked for three weeks and I have never, mind you, Malinda, never seen anyone move the way he does. It's effortless. He's like a cat on the roof."

He only knew that he thrived on hard work and dangerous situations. He worked the steepest part of a roof, drove the nailer with lightning speed, and helped the others finish their sections. In summer, he sweat copiously, drank two gallons of water a day, and loved it. Shirtless, he turned a deep, dark, copper color, cut his hair in the English way, and acquired a cell phone that he carried in his trouser pocket as it became a part of his daily life.

After he discovered Google, there was no turning back. The Internet was a vast untapped panorama that stretched before him, one he could enter by the tap of a fingertip.

He joined a group of youth that were supervised, although many of them drove a vehicle after the age of eighteen, when they would not need a parent's signature. In a sense, he had joined a liberal group.

Wild. He was considered wild.

His father shrugged his shoulders, saying the other boys had gone through their time as well. So he looked at images on his son's cell phone, smiled, and took it as it came. It is what it is, he said. Let David be David for a while. No use panicking. Those cell phones weren't going away any time soon, so everyone may as well get used to them.

His mother fussed like a biddy hen, her words falling on deaf ears.

"Settle down, Mam. It's just like reading a book, but better."

And still she yapped, her strident voice as annoying as a small terrier.

David was Dave now. Dave was more mature, a better version of David.

His mother gave up, more or less. She brewed a pot of coffee and drowned her sorrows in coffee-soaked chocolate shoofly pie before collapsing on the recliner for a nap.

A month after turning sixteen, Anna still had not officially joined a group of youth. Many and varied, she could have easily chosen, settled in, belonged, but the compass of her heart always pointed true north to David. There was no doubt her parents would forbid her to join David's group.

There was no way, she told herself over and over. So why couldn't she give up?

Sitting in her bedroom, the exquisite curtains falling to the floor in expansive folds waving in the breeze, the sun creating patterns of light and shadow with leaves from the maple tree, she listened to her best friend Mandy tell her about joining the Cardinals.

Each specific group had a name as a form of identity, like a baseball team. The Cardinals were a decent group, one that many young parents hoped their youth would join.

No haircuts in the English way. No drinking or drugs. No vehicles. Curfews at 11:30. And so forth.

Mandy was small, petite, with curly brown hair and luminous eyes, which she fixed on Anna's dreamy gaze.

"I just don't get it, Anna. Why aren't you running around? This isn't normal, you know. I want you to go with me to the singing this evening, okay? You don't necessarily have to go to the supper crowd, but you can't just sit here weekend after weekend."

"I know."

"What are you waiting on?"

Wisely, after receiving Mandy's promise of secrecy, she told her why she wouldn't join, after which Mandy pursed her lips and said David knew where she was, and if he truly loved and wanted her, he'd join her group and they'd eventually begin to date.

Here is where Anna sighed, lifting her hands in helplessness.

"My parents don't approve of David and his family."

"What?" Mandy said in disbelief.

"My mother would not allow it. And I haven't come to accept the fact that we can never be together. So I'm planning my strategy. Maybe if I stay home, they'll begin to worry. Loosen up. I do not want to disobey, neither do I want to give up David."

Her words ended on a wail.

Mandy shook her head. "His group wouldn't be accepted by my parents, either. Those girls are really fancy."

"Not so much more than us."

"But still."

As true friends do, they sat gloomily, pondering the possibilities, the road ahead crosshatched with warnings. Parents forbidding anything was serious business in their protected world. To contemplate any form of disobedience meant a lava flow of guilt.

"I'm so young, Mandy. Too young to know what I want, and yet . . ." Her voice trailed off, lowered with shame, then resumed in a voice only a bit louder than a whisper. "I think I've always loved David."

The morning was soaked in dew, with the promise of another hot day. Anna and her mother were cooking tomatoes for spaghetti sauce and ketchup. At eighteen, Anna had acquired a rare quality of growing in grace and beauty, a tragic beauty, coupled with an inner sadness beyond her years.

She had joined the group her parents approved of, worked the jobs they thought were proper for a young lady, and very seldom, if ever, complained about her role in life. She was what her parents expected of her, a chaste and obedient young woman who was an example to all who encountered her.

For her mother to have the honor of achieving this upbringing meant more than anyone would know. It had been a goal, an objective, and by all accounts she had accomplished her heart's desire.

But there was something that bothered her mother more and more these days, in spite of her deep satisfaction in Anna's maturity and obedience. She seemed distant, withdrawn.

"Anna, the tomatoes are ready to be taken out to the stove in the laundry room."

"All right."

When she returned, her mother glanced at her, pondering the mask of serenity, the steady decline into quietness.

"How was your weekend?"

"Good."

"What were you doing?"

"We were at the supper and singing."

"Where was it?"

"Jonas Lapp's."

The short answers began to fluster her mother. Why couldn't they have a normal discussion, like they used to?

"So, is it true Mandy is dating?"

"Not yet."

"Who is her chappy?"

"Mom, no one says 'chappy' anymore."

"Oh, really? I'm sorry."

There was no reply.

She began again, valiantly picking up the threads of their fractured conversation.

"So she's not dating?"

"No."

"Well, you know the rules. You must be a member of the church to be allowed to date. I suppose she has given her life to Christ and will live accordingly?"

"Yes."

There was a long pause. The kitchen filled with the smell of cooking tomatoes, the windows reflecting the late morning sun, shining on the clean squares of heavy, recently installed flooring, the ferns in their shadowy corners lush and healthy. Everything around them spoke of good management, an enviable position of a properly maintained environment, with expensive taste and the funds to be able to acquire things of worth.

The walls were painted white with undertones of gray, accentuated by many framed pictures, plaques with various Bible verses imprinted in black calligraphy, and inspirational sayings everywhere. A daily devotional sat on the windowsill above the sink next to a wrought-iron book holder supporting the latest hymnbook. A small army of glistening glass canning jars stood on the countertop by a Tupperware container of rings and lids. Her mother's pale blue dress and black bib apron created a pleasing contrast to the surroundings.

Today, however, a small line of tension played between her eyebrows. A certain lift of her shoulders betrayed the niggling impression that something was not quite right. Her own daughter made her feel ill at ease, a stranger in her own kitchen.

What to do?

"Anna, is something wrong?" she asked, with a penetrating look, a sadness she hoped to convey.

"No."

"Are you sure?"

"Yes."

"But . . ."

And here she hesitated. To speak of the fact that she no longer confided in her mother was admitting it to herself, and to tell Anna how much this would hurt was relinquishing the control she had always exercised over her.

So she gave a small, self-conscious laugh.

"Oh, it's all right, Anna. I'm just so glad your life is going well and that you'll be joining church next year. We had always imagined you would make that commitment at sixteen years old, but we'll look forward to it for next year now."

There was no reply. In disbelief, her mother's head swiveled in Anna's direction and found her turning her back, opening a drawer to rearrange the contents, then closing it.

"I want to join another group, Mom."

The mother's heart plunged. She felt physically ill, reeled, caught the counter top with the back of both hands, her eyes large and frightened.

"Why?"

"I'm not happy with the Cardinals."

"What is wrong with them? It is a large, popular group. Surely there are many pleasant young men who would make a suitable companion for you. You are surrounded by fine young Christians, Anna. You are one yourself."

Anna traced the pattern on the linoleum with a bare toe, her face averted. How to tell her mother?

She could not begin to relate the chance meeting with David at Honeybrook Park. In the two years she had spent her weekends with the youth, it had all been a gray veneer of lost and hopeless feelings, watching the young men and knowing there was not a remote chance of wanting to start a relationship. The thought of marriage was incomprehensible. It was not that there was anything wrong with them, these fine young men with every good quality a girl could want.

They simply were not David. Dave, as he was now known.

How to explain to her mother? The leaping of her heart, the self-restraint to stay with the group of girls by the picnic table when the flashy, black sports car pulled into the parking lot and the passenger door flung open as David unfolded from the front seat.

David, the man of her dreams. The person who occupied her very last thought before she fell asleep, whose name was on her lips when she prayed, who was as familiar to her heart as her own parents and siblings.

Even more so.

Tanned, lithe, laughing, he was everything she could ever want. It was so much deeper than the appearance, of this she was positive. It was the quality they had always shared, the delight in each other's minds, the way he spoke, his eyes shining with pleasure at some new and exciting discovery, some book he had read, an incident in the field or woods. It was the shared childhood that had blossomed into much more, a pure and innocent love between two young people long before they knew what it was.

And now, there was this vast difference in their way of life. Both parents were members of the Amish church, both baptized into the faith, but with far different expectations and ideals.

This divide loomed before Anna now. The distance between them was only a few hundred feet, if that, but a yawning chasm stretched in front of her, the wrenching knowledge that her parents would never bless this union. Dave simply did not check off all the boxes for what they wanted in a man who would marry their daughter.

She felt a rebellion so raw it took her breath away.

She sagged down on the bench of the picnic table, the weight of her life gone awry, her parents steering the vessel that contained her. Was it right for a mother and father to decide whom their daughter should marry? Was it done in this day and age?

She looked up, infinitely weary, the sadness in her eyes a pool of unfathomable depth. At that moment, David walked away from the group he was with. His eyes searched the small group of girls and found her, the gaze that tore at his heart.

There was nothing else to do but go to her. Without caring, the direct goal was to do something about the sadness in Anna's eyes, the aura of unhappiness surrounding her.

On he came, their gazes locked. Both were breathless by the time he reached the picnic table. She stood, he reached out to shake her hand. Immeasurable, the look in his eyes, in hers.

"Anna."

"David."

"It's Dave now."

They both laughed. He dropped her hand, looked around, before putting his hands in his pockets.

"So . . ."

She nodded, found his eyes. Like coming home, bound to him in a circle of knowing there was a perfect place that took away all her doubts and insecurities, every anxiety about the future. He cared for her, still, as she cared for him. The separation they had endured had only proven to strengthen the bond between them.

"So . . . how are you, Anna?"

"I'm . . . okay. Good. You know, living my life."

A self-conscious laugh to hide the surge of emotion, the lump that threatened to cut off her words, the sob that tore at her throat.

Oh Dave. Dave. Do you have any idea the misery of my indecision? The gray, uncharted waters of my existence? The pleas to a merciful father to show me right from wrong? What is this between us? Pride? Lust of the flesh? A carnal attraction to the beauty of one to the other? Always at the center, like the black clouds of a tropical storm on the horizon: my parents' disapproval of you. Like roiling water against rocks, this alone is shaping me, molding me into the image they need and fully expect.

"Yeah, me too. Growing up."

He laughed again, a self-deprecating sound.

"As in?" she questioned.

He shrugged his shoulders. "Bunch of stuff."

A cramp seized her stomach, a sickening wrench of fear.

"What are you saying?"

"Oh, I dunno. Just stuff."

Immediately her thoughts churned. So many things out there, the drugs and the alcohol, the wild parties, the girls, it was all real, a part of life that had to be faced, withstood, and finally denounced.

"Do you have to be with the . . . Indians?" the name of his group.

"No. But my brothers all were. Just sorta . . . you know, did what my parents figured I'd do. They think the Cardinals are too . . . well, self-righteous."

"Yeah. Well, I dunno. My family is different than yours."

"I know. Should that keep us apart?"

Her heart skipped and fluttered and left her light-headed. The strength left her body, her knees like jelly. She could not face him, so great was the euphoria at the thought of being with Dave every weekend. To share his exuberant, happy life. To listen to his accounts of ordinary, mundane things he painted in vivid verbal tones. The joy that was David, not Dave, but her David.

"I don't know."

The milling crowd of youth played a variety of games on the brilliant September day, the white clouds like remnants of white fabric woven into the sky; the grass a rich, vibrant green; groups of trees with the maple branches bearing the beginning of color; the youth in various shades of every color imaginable coupled with the traditional black aprons, trousers, and vests.

And on the bench, by the pavilion, stood the lone couple with the weight of indecision bowing their heads, Dave leaning forward, his elbows on his knees, examining the cement floor, Anna's shoulders hunched.

Then in a low voice, she said, "Why couldn't you join the Cardinals?"

"For you?"

"Yes."

"I could, I guess."

Shy, afraid of what she had suggested, Anna fell silent.

"I'd have to dust off my horse and buggy. Getting around in cars gets addictive. It's easy to do."

"No doubt."

Then, "I'm only nineteen. It's not fair to make you wait till I'm done with my *rumschpringa*."

"It's fair."

"Why don't you join my group?"

"My parents would never approve."

"My best friend Wayne is interested in this girl over by Georgetown, and we could go around with them. You know, just hang out for a while. We'd be together every single weekend."

In the end, he gave her his cell phone number, told her to call, leaving her stranded with her insecurities and a plethora of anxious questions that threatened to capsize the small amount of confidence she possessed. She watched him leave, the black sports car in reverse, the low throb of the costly engine. She knew with a young woman's intuition that they were worlds apart.

Didn't true love require sacrifice? If he loved her in the way she loved him, how hard would it be to give up the cars, the weekends with Wayne, and the youth who were with a faster crowd?

And if he didn't?

She spent her days and nights questioning God, weighing the balance of what should be done in a situation that seemed beyond hope. To bring her mother into the maelstrom would tip the scales to the usual refusal to accept David. Oh, her admonitions never sounded like a storm—they were always smoothed over with polite kindness, the lukewarm words as artificial as the silk flowers in a vase in the living room.

Or were they?

Anna believed deep down that, in spite of her love for David, her parents cared tremendously. They only wanted what was best for her and saw nothing good in an attraction to someone they deemed unworthy. And here was the underlying struggle. Here is where the tempest lay. Was it fair, this judgment of David?

Anna looked at her mother with eyes clouded over in misery. "What is it, Mom, that you so do not approve of David?"

There. It was out. The question that snaked across a room on too many occasions, stuffed away, closed, simply too laden with portent. Anna had never before found the courage to ask the question, and so it had grown steadily bigger until there was no easy flow of words or feelings, only a stiff politeness, a forced smile, kind words.

Her mother's back was turned for a long moment. She did not reply. When she did, there were tears in her voice.

"Anna, it's not really disapproval. It's . . . we just want better . . ." She stumbled, stopped.

Anguished words from Anna. "Better what?"

"Anna, his family. The way they . . . well . . . just are. I know, I know."

Anna opened her mouth to speak.

"Let me finish. We simply have a different set of morals, of values and rules. Eli and Rachel are extremely liberal in their way of raising children. Yes, we are all Amish, but I fear for the *loss-heit*. Our ideals for you are to be married to a person who has been taught to love the Lord, to have morning devotion, to expect high morals from his children. Godly young people are so needed in the Amish church, and for change to occur, we need to start in the home."

Anna sat, her head bowed. "But what do Eli and Rachel do that you don't like?"

"This is hard, Anna. Really hard. To come out and say exactly what is wrong sounds harsh. Judgmental. And I don't want to be that way. I only want to protect you from a future of unhappiness."

"Mom, how could I? How could I be unhappy with David? I love him. There is no one else for me. For two years I have tried to become interested in others. I have truly tried."

"You're too young to date."

"At eighteen? Really, Mom?"

She was dismissed with a wave of her mother's hand, who then

turned her back to see to the tomatoes. The conversation was officially over.

Anna moved in an aura of hopelessness the remainder of the day.
She called David's cell phone and heard only the confident, clipped
tones of his message.

*Oh, David, is that really you? Has the world encroached to draw
you into its greedy maw?* She pictured him carousing and drinking.
Or worse.

As fall turned into the bitter winds of November, Anna became even
more confused, weighing obedience, the right for her parents to judge
Eli and Rachel, disobedience and its consequences, like pebbles rattling in a gourd, the constant harassment of guilt.

Would love overcome all these obstacles?

They talked regularly now. Two or three times a week she sat outside in her father's office, after nine o'clock when her parents were
sure to leave her alone. If they knew, they never let on. They simply
allowed her to use the phone to call her friends without question.

And so their story began.

Anna and David took up where they had left off, uniting their
hearts and minds with long phone conversations, sharing lives, enjoying one another's company in the way they always had.

Anna's parents noticed the difference, and were glad. Finally,
after the first two years of *rumschpringa* they had their Anna back.
She smiled, laughed, twirled around the house in bursts of energy,
loved her sisters, and joked with her parents.

She was waiting. Waiting on David.

With no doubt, he would settle down and join the church after he
gave his life to Christ. He wanted to do it the right way, confess his
sin, and become a new person—born again.

Anna thrilled to hear the passion in his voice. He would be as
committed to his religion as he was in all things in life. He would win
over her parents and make them see what a fine young man he was.

CHAPTER 6

And then, unexpectedly, he asked her to begin dating regularly, bringing a swarm of questions and insecurities as frightening as the stinging bees.

Yes, yes, her heart sang, *but . . .*

What about joining the church? What about driving his horse and buggy? What about her parents?

It was cold in her father's office, the gas heater turned to low, the bitter winds of January moaning about the building, driving wisps of snow in a cloud across the window. When Dave asked her, she began to shake uncontrollably. She wrapped her arms around her waist and held the receiver on one shoulder. Her teeth chattered so she spoke only to answer his questions. She had calmed herself sufficiently by the time he had run out of his outburst of words, speaking in a quiet tone of voice.

"Yes, Dave. I will accept. You know that. But I am not allowed to date until I am a member of the church. You know my parents' rules, surely."

"Yeah. I was afraid you would say that."

There was a long pause as Anna absorbed the disappointment and resentment in his voice. For a moment she was surprised. It wasn't as if her parents' wishes were news to him. Didn't he care? Did he expect her to blatantly disobey them?

Quickly, she checked the rising frustration in her chest. She just needed to stand firm and be patient, and surely he would have a change of heart. Love should overcome self-will, shouldn't it? If he loved her truly it would not be a long time. But to begin a life with her by his side, by her parents' wishes, he would need to give his life to Christ, take up the cross, and follow Him.

A wave of rebellion swept over her, then. Other girls were not required to meet these high standards, so why should she? Surely the love they had for one another would deem all of this unnecessary. Love never failed. The Bible said so.

"Anna?"

"Yes?"

"Are you there?"

"I am."

"What's wrong?"

She could not speak for the rise of quick emotion, a wave of despair, a desperation to make him understand. They knew each other so well that he could tell by her pause that she was troubled.

They were bound by the invisible ties of the heart, the mystery of a deep and abiding longing, a found treasure. It wasn't right that any parental rules or set of high standards should change what God had ordained first of all.

"I was just disappointed by your answer, is all. Dave, you know how my parents are. Can you try to understand?"

The silence stretched like a ticking bomb, fraught with portent.

"Yeah."

But he couldn't. Wouldn't. She knew by the drip of irony in his voice that he held no respect for a set of parents who required a relationship's strength to be built on self-denial, a heart given first and foremost to God.

"So, can I speak to them first?" She asked hesitantly.

A passionate volley of words, then, "You know, Anna, this is just wrong. No one in this day and age has to ask their parents to date. It's plain ridiculous and it ticks me off. Who do your parents think they are? It's your choice, not theirs. I mean, come on guys. This is America. They can't make you say no."

Anna held the receiver away from her ear, the words like thumb tacks scraping along the canal of her hearing.

"Don't, Dave. That's cruel."

"I don't care. I want you. And nobody is going to stand in my way."

No one except yourself, Anna thought, in a moment of clarity. But then she clung to the phrase she had longed to hear. "I want you," he'd said. Oh, he did, he did, as she wanted him.

To Anna's credit, she was courageous, summoning her parents to the kitchen table late one evening when her siblings were asleep upstairs under the heavy fleece comforters on a cold January night.

As always, her parents were kind, their youthful faces concerned, her mother's robe belted around her slender waist, her hair washed, a soft white kerchief on her head, the armour of prayer, the head covering.

"I have a request."

The mother knew, by the plunging in her stomach.

"Dave Stoltzfus asked me for a date."

There was a silence, a stone-cold moment of disbelief.

"But . . ."

Her mother's voice was barely above a whisper, then. Her father's eyes were shining with anger in a face as passive and untroubled as a deep pond on a windless day. His voice, when it came, was as smooth as oil.

"And your answer was?"

"I haven't given him one yet."

"Good."

Her mother leaned forward, her eyes alight with happiness and approval.

"That's so good, Anna."

Their relief was so obvious it was almost pitiful.

"You wouldn't take anyone, right? You know you have not yet

given your life to God, and we wish you would accept Christ before you take the next step."

Anna's voice was firm.

"I accepted Christ a long time ago."

Her father smiled.

"I believe it. You have proved to be an asset to the family. The fruits of the Spirit are in evidence, I must say. But now is the time to train the soul to a life of service to our Lord, to learn the articles of faith, to understand the whys and how tos of the Amish, and lastly, to be baptized into the church. It's all very serious, a big step requiring an understanding of the Spirit."

"And Dave?" her mother broke in. "He's willing to join?"

The steel in her voice barred any chance of denial, her eyes lasers of light that gouged into Anna's conscience.

"He is. I just don't know when."

"Well, I guess you know there will be no dating until you are both members of the church."

"Yes."

"Which means it will be toward the end of September, beginning of October until you are allowed to begin dating. If we allow it at all. That young man has to prove himself before we'll give our consent."

She tightened inwardly at the finality of their words, cringing at their assumption that she would follow their plan for her life to a tee. *Don't say "that young man" in that tone of voice*, she thought.

But she said nothing. Only the heaving of her chest gave away her feeling.

"We expect him to join the church, of course," her father said. "But that is only the tip of the iceberg."

He cleared his throat, smacked his lips, rubbed his hands together before he spoke.

"He is living in sin, now. I saw him in that black Mustang, dressed in English clothes at Sheetz. It bodes no good for you, Anna. It's not his fault as much as his parents'. It's almost as if Eli expects that the time of *rumschpringa* is a time to go out and do exactly what you want, no matter what. This is what we are trying to change. For the youth in our time to learn to live a godly life, to find a reasonable way to be a teenager, with a good solid relationship with their parents and with God before they are married. All this partying, getting around in cars, is not good. It only feeds the lust of the young life, the urge to be 'cool' and wild and senseless."

Her father paused, before adding the clincher.

"How can you expect Eli's Dave to be any kind of Christian husband if this is how he's living now?"

Anna faced her father, but the light in his eyes effectively lowered hers. The unbidden lump in her throat cut off her voice, so she shrugged her shoulders, let them droop, as she knotted her hands in her lap.

"We had always hoped you would pick someone from your own group."

"I know that."

"Then why do you want Dave?" This from her mother.

"You know why."

"Tell me again."

So my father can hear, she thought. *So you can stand side by side with twice the power to intimidate me. To make me change, forget who I am, forget Dave entirely because he is simply "not worthy."*

These thoughts churned until her lips opened to speak them. Realizing at the last second the consequences they would bring, she merely sighed.

"I'd rather not."

"Anna, you don't know the difference between love and lust. Dave is a very striking young man."

"Mom, I do know the difference. You know I do. Dave is all I want in life. We have been more than friends forever. I don't remember a life without him. It's much deeper than attraction."

"How can it be? You barely know one another." Her father broke in.

Anna brought the discussion to an end. She rose from her chair and glided away, the image of her parents' disappointment imprinted on her mind and heart.

Gusts of harsh winter winds flung snow against the window-panes, the bare black branches of the trees scraping against the sides of the house. Sleepless, Anna tossed and turned, as did both parents on the south side of the house in the first-floor bedroom.

Dave had the day off, the temperatures plummeting during the night, the wind picking up as the day wore on. He slept till almost ten, then wandered downstairs, his stomach growling, feeling weak and empty. He hadn't gone in with the rest of his friends to eat supper with the youth at Elam Fisher's, opting to hang out with two of the older guys who hardly ever appeared at any social gathering but merely hung around on the outskirts.

His mother was in the kitchen, ironing something, a scowl on her round face, her arm moving the sadiron back and forth.

She looked up. "About time."

Dave didn't bother answering. Unaccustomed to formal greetings, they merely made an appearance, went about doing what needed to be done, and, if it was necessary, began to speak. If not, they didn't say anything at all.

"You hungry?"

Dave grunted a reply from the interior of the refrigerator, where he was lifting lids off plastic containers and moving things aside to look for cream cheese and bacon.

"I don't know why you don't have some sort of system with the food in your refrigerator. It's like total chaos."

The sadiron stopped.

"It's like totally not all me," she mimicked, and resumed ironing, the batwings above her elbows swaying with the rhythm of the sadiron.

He hid a grin. *Funny one, Mam.*

He opened a drawer, rummaged in the bags of snacks, loaves of homemade bread, and store bought sandwich rolls.

"No bagels?"

"Nope."

"You just bought a bag of those everything bagels."

"Somebody must have eaten them."

"You."

"Not all of them."

But she probably had. They were very good.

He fried about half a dozen eggs, made four slices of toast in the broiler of the gas stove, poured a glass of orange juice, and sat down to eat. No bowing of the head, merely a scrape of his chair and a grab for the salt shaker.

His mother removed the large section of pieced quilt from the ironing board and turned it right side up before asking him what he thought.

Dave chewed a mouthful of egg and toast, swallowed, lifted his eyebrows and said, "Not bad."

"It's not?"

"Why purple, though?"

"It's pretty."

She folded it, laid it on the tabletop, put her hands on her hips, and said it was time he thought about girls, that he was old enough to start dating. She wanted to make quilts for him.

"I would if I could have the right girl."

His mother nodded. "You mean Anna."

"Who else?"

"You know you have to join up before you even think about dating her, right?"

"That's so stupid."

"It's how they are. The new and better way for the *youngie*."

She still said *youngie*. Pronounced it "yoongeh."

"But what sense does it make? I mean, come on. I guarantee you and Dad didn't go through all this crap."

"No. We dated when we found someone we were attracted to. But things were different then. And honestly we weren't prepared for dating and marriage the way the *youngie* are these days. I think the changes are a good thing."

She sliced more bread, bent to place it in the broiler pan. She was literally as wide as the stove.

"I asked Anna over the phone."

"You did? What did she say?"

"She has to ask her controlling parents."

His mother drew her mouth into a grimace.

"Uh-oh."

"S'what I think."

"Well, I guess if you want her bad enough, you'll do what's expected. I don't know."

She pulled out the broiler pan, then pushed it back in. She could hardly see how any of this could work, but she'd wait and let it play out.

Dave burst out, "It's just wrong, Mam. Why can't she date without joining up? I don't get all these requirements if we're simply two people who love each other. What's wrong with that?"

"Well, Anna's parents are very spiritual people, which is good. You could change, you know."

Dave glared at the whirling snow outside the window, shivered, stretched, yawned, and shook his head.

"Where's Dat?"

"I have no idea."

She stuffed half a slice of bread into her mouth, began pointing to the kitchen window, and rolled her eyes in the direction of the barn before swallowing.

"He's cleaning stables."

Dave grimaced. "Ugh."

"Go help him." It was a gargled direction, around another mouthful of buttered toast.

His father exercised the same laconic view of shared feelings as his mother. They both simply made no fuss. They felt that if he went down the wrong road, he'd realize it sooner or later and follow the trail back. Either that or bump his nose and learn.

But Dave pulled on his Muck Boots, a few heavy sweatshirts, and a beanie, bent his head against the biting wind, and went to find his father. The smell of layers of uncovered manure was acrid, biting. He heard the scrape of a shovel, the low whistle, the clank of the mules' harnesses as they jostled their necks.

"Hey," Dave called.

His father looked up, stuck the pitchfork and shovel in fresh piles of manure, pushed back his hat and said, "You know, whoever built this barn definitely didn't have a skid loader in mind."

Dave nodded, thrust his hands in his pockets, hunched his shoulders.

"Cold."

"Sure is. Was 10 degrees at nine o'clock."

"Need help?"

"Does it look like I need help?"

Every box stall needed to be cleaned out, so Dave went for another pitchfork, placed it against the wooden wall of the entry way, and asked which stall to begin with.

"Doesn't matter, as long as you keep cleaning."

They worked for a good hour until the manure spreader was piled high.

Dave's beanie was tipped to the back of his head. He unzipped one sweatshirt, threw it over the top plank of the divider, and mopped his forehead.

"Whew."

"Why don't you slow down a bit? You go at everything you do like there's no tomorrow. You'll wear out by the time you're fifty."

"You think?"

Dave grinned at his father. His father grinned back, pulled on his heavy topcoat, opened the garage door, and climbed up on the manure spreader.

"Shut the door till I get back."

When he returned, he was stiff with cold, his hat smashed down on his head. He backed the spreader expertly, calling directions to the two brown mules. They sat back against the leather britchment and pushed the spreader to the exact location.

"Whoa, whoa!"

When he jumped down, Dave asked him what he thought of asking Anna for a date.

Caught off guard, his father's eyes widened.

"You want to know if you should, or if it's okay if you already did?"

They laughed together easily.

"Either one."

"Oh, well. I don't know. You're sure you're ready for it?"

"What do you mean?"

"Well, you're young. There's no hurry. Marriage brings its own set of responsibilities, so just make sure you're willing to share your life."

"What about Anna herself? What do you think?"

"I guess she's a nice girl. Pretty proper. Her parents are those new-fangled ones who go by the book."

"What do you mean?" Dave leaned against the wall of the wooden stall. He pretty much knew what his dad meant, but he wanted to hear it in his words. Mostly he just thought Anna's parents were ridiculously controlling, but on some level his sharp intellect wanted to understand, to get to the bottom of why they believed the way they did, and why Anna felt she had to do whatever they said.

"Oh, you know. Everything done according to some Christian man or woman's views. Child raising, whatever they call it. They read those books. I don't know about that kinda thing."

"She's not allowed to date until we're both members of the church."

Eli's eyebrows lifted. He stuck his ungloved hands under his armpits to warm them. He opened his sack of chewing tobacco and inserted a hefty amount before shaking his head.

"Didn't used to be that way, but whatever. She's a nice girl, but I don't know about having Elias and that Barbie breathing down your neck."

Dave nodded.

"You think I should join this spring?"

"That's up to you."

And there the conversation ended, his father changing the subject to the Friesian horse sale coming up in New Holland.

The remainder of the day, Dave forked manure, his thoughts going from his weekends to Anna. He was unsatisfied with his parents' advice, and yet . . . He couldn't expect more. It was the way of it.

God and Bible reading, that kind of thing, was hardly ever mentioned. They prayed quietly, out of sight, read their Bible sometimes, Dave was sure, he'd just never seen them do it. His mother had read a Bible storybook to him when he was a child, but that was about as far as the religious teaching went. His father had no interest in reading German with the children the way many households did, but that wasn't a big deal. Dave was fluent in German. He understood the words in church and could read it well.

He learned a lot from the minister in church. Still, he felt adrift, not sure in which direction he should be going. He wanted Anna, this was certain. But to join the church, quit all the fun weekends, let his hair grow, drive the horse and buggy all over the place, hot in summer, cold in winter . . .

He thought of buying a sports car. Perhaps a Jeep. Something awesome to make the guys want to ride with him. So far, he still had not gone for his driver's test the way most of his friends did.

For one thing, he was saving money. A lot of money. His bank account was amazing, with all that overtime. Getting around with Wayne meant he didn't have to pay for the upkeep of a car.

But what was the use saving all that money if he had no marriage plans?

He stood by himself watching his father drive away with the second load of manure, his head bent against the onslaught of wind and snow, the mules scrambling to keep their footing on an incline, the heavy load of manure ungainly on steel wheels.

In his mind's eye, he saw himself at his father's age, bent to snow and ice, driving mules hitched to a steel-wheeled spreader, a member of the Amish church, a law-abiding, honest citizen who married one woman and raised a whole passel of kids, living in a box with a limited view of anything. Of everything, really. The tiny circle of life.

He would go to Creekside Foods for his groceries—no, *their* groceries. He'd go to the hardware in Intercourse to buy his tools and fencing, nails and necessities. He'd attend church services a couple of miles away, send his kids to the Amish parochial school a half-mile away. The same school he had attended all his life.

He read too many books. Was that the problem? Would he feel the same dissatisfaction if he hadn't read about so many fascinating places all around the world?

Or maybe it was his cell phone and the way the whole world opened up in a screen held in his hand. Colorful images he could view with the touch of a finger, like a magic wand.

He could search for and find the answer to anything. He read a lot about the West. It was the place of his dreams, though it was no longer wild the way things were in the Louis L'Amour novels he had read.

He saw Newfoundland, Iceland, Nigeria, Russia, and Yugoslavia. He could view the Galapagos, watch the Komodo dragon and the giant tortoises. Everything.

If he joined up and made that promise to God and man he would be expected to stay committed to a lifetime of drudgery. He would have to get rid of the cell phone, grow long hair and a beard, dress in broadfall pants and suspenders.

But he could also marry Anna then. With Anna by his side, life took on a certain hopefulness. She was truly the light of his life. Her laugh, her flashing eyes, the way she walked, the way her teeth protruded just slightly, even the way she shrugged her shoulders when she didn't know what to say.

She just filled his heart, his mind. She fulfilled a place in his life that no one or nothing else could.

He loved her.

So why should her parents' wishes throw him off track? In a sense, the compass with the needle pointing north had fallen away, leaving him with no clear sense of direction. He had tried to glean some guidance from his parents, but with only a mild, doubtful form of approval he was reeling like a drunken person, trying to stay upright without equilibrium.

Anna. Joining the church. Self-denial. A car. Crazy fun weekends. The whole world to see. A bank account that could make it all possible.

All of these things arranged and rearranged themselves in his mind until he was so weary he dropped the pitchfork and strode off into the house to shower before falling into bed and letting sleep overtake him.

Chapter 7

THE FISHER HOME LOST A SMALL AMOUNT OF THE SERENITY THE FAMILY had always practiced. Elias found himself doing absentminded things that irritated him, which turned into reprimanding Kathryn for small things that normally bothered no one. He watched Anna with narrowed eyes and imagined he saw a hardening of her mouth, a determined set of her jaw.

The long winter evenings of sharing stories, board games, and reading out loud were fractured by Anna's absence. Ensconced in her room, her legs curled beneath her, covered by a warm quilt, she read her Bible, seeking answers she already knew. Rebellion warred within her conscience.

"Honor thy father and mother." It was the creed by which they lived. It was not unfair, this sifting of David. They were merely being careful, wanting only what was good for her future, her soul.

Other girls lived and obeyed these exact same requirements. Her mother had taken the time to explain in detail the fundamental beliefs of a solid courtship and marriage. If Dave could not deny himself to live a godly life, then how would he ever understand the first basic step a man must take, which was to leave his parents, cleave to his wife, and give his life for her?

A husband was to love his wife as Christ loved the church.

But he might be able to do that. She would try him.

She would date against her parents' wishes, and with God's help, mold Dave into the person her parents wanted him to be. Her heart leaped at the thought of bringing him into her home on a Sunday afternoon—tall, handsome Dave, with his quick, bright smile and magnetic energy.

She felt sure that he would change, given enough love, patience, and time. And if not, well, then she'd know. But she had no doubt that he loved her, and she was confident that the fruits of self-denial and humility would appear given a little time and gentle encouragement.

She said yes.

He washed the dusty carriage that had been stored behind the buggy since his *rumschpringa* had begun.

He hated the feeling of actually being frightened of his horse. He wasn't prepared for the fiery spirit, the amount of muscle and power that refused to obey his commands. He had to ask his father to help him get the horse between the shafts, after which the animal reared and balked and backed the carriage into the shed wall.

When Dave became frustrated he started yanking on the bridle, yelling at the excited horse, which only made matters worse, until his father told him to calm down so his horse could do the same.

Stupid horse. Driving a horse and buggy was just dumb. A car went wherever you needed to go, and fast.

He sat in the buggy, holding the reins while the horse stood, flanks quivering, ears swiveling from being pointed forward to laid back, listening for commands. Suddenly the horse jerked forward, but then refused to pull the carriage, hopping from one foot to the other. Dave lost his temper and brought the ends of the reins across the horse's back, resulting in a high rearing, a twisting and bucking that upended the carriage, brought the front hub of the wheel crashing down on the corner trim of the buggy shed, bending it. His father lost his temper as well.

He yelled at Dave, told him never to whip a horse when he was balking, and didn't he know any better?

They worked together in silence to untangle the horse, fix the corner trim as best they could, and Dave stalked off into the house and slammed the door behind him.

He walked to Anna's house on Saturday evening. She met him on the porch, a vision in a sky-blue dress with a smile of welcome, a hand extended in formal greeting.

He took her hand and could not let go.

Here was Anna, the love of his life. Being with her made all his doubts disappear. It left only a clear path that shone its light for him to follow, through the maze of cars and weekends with his buddies, through the possibility of leaving all of it behind and striking out on his own to see the world, through horses and buggies and strict Amish customs and parents who didn't have any clear answers.

Anna was the fulfillment of all his needs.

"It's so good to see you," she breathed, her voice so filled with emotion it was only a husky whisper.

"And you. It's been a long time."

"It has. Are you ready to meet my parents?"

His eyes went to the windows.

"I guess."

She laughed. He had forgotten that sound, the full-throated bell-like sound of pure happiness.

"They won't bite."

He thought later that if they had bitten him, it would at least be honest and forthright. He had never seen quite the display of formality without feeling. He was not welcome, plain and simple.

"Good evening!"

A bright-eyed, overly friendly smile from Elias Fisher, a somber tight-lipped hello from his wife, who appeared to have been dragged by her feet to a place of disgrace.

So this is how it's going to be, Dave thought. *I'm an intruder on a calm and peaceful, well-ordered family, snatching their daughter away against their wishes.*

As the seconds ticked away, the tension increased, with Dave becoming uncomfortable, then scrambling for an opportunity to get away.

Elias looked at Dave, asked about his work.

"I'm roofing."

"Hard work. Do you like it?"

"Yeah."

"You do? I always assumed roofing work to be hard on a back?"

Did every sentence have to be a question?

"I like it. The fast pace suits me just fine."

"So you're a worker, huh?"

"I guess so."

Anna sat with her hands knotted in her lap, her back so straight she seemed to be leaning forward. He looked at her, hoped she'd help him through this, but her eyes were focused on a spot on the floor directly in front of her shoes.

This was not going the way she had hoped.

Dave swallowed. His mouth was dry. He swallowed again, hoping his Adam's apple didn't bob up and down for all to see. Anna's sisters eyed him with open curiosity, their faces so much like hers.

"Well," Anna said brightly, "I guess we'll be going."

"And where would that be?" Elias asked, his smile wide and toothy.

"We're walking to my friend Susan's house."

"Oh?"

"Yes. She's dating too."

This was seemingly the signal for the mother to assert her rules.

"Yes. Dating is a good thing. I remember our own time so well, before we were married."

Dave watched her face, as blank as an unused piece of paper. The only sign of life were her darting blue eyes, which seemed to pin everyone to their chair.

"Um, Dave?"

"Yes?"

"We have parental guidelines in this house, and we hope you will come to respect them. Anna must be home by eleven thirty, and your time alone with her will be over by twelve. The time you spend in the kitchen, of course, will be around the table for a snack, or whatever, after which you will be expected to leave."

She cleared her throat.

"This, of course, would all be unnecessary if you belonged to the Cardinals, which you don't. We are hoping you'll join."

"So I have this folder containing the rules and *ordnung* of our group, and we expect you to adhere to them. I included a book on Christian courtship. We require *total* hands off."

The ire rose in Dave's throat. His nostrils dilated, his breath came in quick, hot puffs. He shuffled his feet, glanced at Anna who seemed to have lost all color, her face as white as porcelain.

"I think we'll go now," she said quietly.

"All right. We expect you home between eleven and eleven thirty."

"Yes, Mom. I'll get my coat."

Nothing was said until she returned, slipped her arms into the sleeves of her coat, buttoned it, adjusted a long white scarf, pulled on matching gloves, and looked up at him.

"Ready?"

He'd never been more ready, but he only nodded, taking his leave as quickly as possible.

"Whoah," he said, stepping off the porch.

"What?"

"Those guys mean business."

"Who? My parents? Please don't be angry, Dave. You knew they were strict."

"It's not just strict. It's stupid. Does she really think we're going to listen to that curfew? Whoever heard of such a thing? We come and go as we please at my house. Nobody says anything."

"Your house is very different than mine."

"Yeah, evidently. Yet we're both Amish, go to the same church, went to school together all those years, and here we are."

The air was biting with a wet, frosty cold. The puffs of air from their mouths evaporated into the night air. The surrounding white fields were flecked with snow-covered houses and barns, the road a black ribbon that wound away into oblivion. Their steps did not match, his long strides crunched to two of hers. He wanted to hold her gloved hand, the way guys did when they liked a girl, but he didn't. Did gloves take care of the "hands-off" deal?

The evening was spent playing lively board games in the basement of Susan's home. Her boyfriend, Aaron Jay, was not an acquaintance of Dave's but proved to be entertaining in a childish way. The way he spoke, his gestures, seemed more like a boy of fourteen than a person, he guessed, older than himself.

Susan shrieked the affected, "Aaron Jay!" at regular intervals, which left him braying like a donkey, all his teeth and gums exposed.

Dave tried hard and realized he needed to lower his high expectations if he wanted to move in Anna's circle of friends. They were so different from his own group, who were more world wise, more in sync with the times.

Watching Anna, being with her, made it all worthwhile. He could do this for her sake.

She was simply the prettiest, sweetest girl he had ever met. Kind, quiet, but not too quiet, laughing easily, quick to get a joke, she was just perfect in that sky-blue dress that accentuated her eyes, brought out the light in them, and set off her blonde hair.

He was so in love, he couldn't take his eyes off her. He would go to the ends of the earth for her, lay down his life, whatever that meant.

He took to reading his Bible. He dug it out from beneath his magazines and books, cracked it open, and began to read.

He would learn how to be good, the way Anna was. She never talked in a negative manner about anyone, respected her parents as far as he could tell, helped her mother at home on weekdays, and seemed to be an angel, almost.

He read one of the Old Testament books, Leviticus, and got so bored he flipped to the New Testament, about Jesus' birth.

He learned all this in school, so it wasn't exactly new or particularly interesting. But he kept going, just for the sake of reading his Bible, so he would feel good from the inside out.

At work, he was his normal self. Outspoken, opinionated. He got into serious arguments with English coworkers about politics and foreign affairs he knew nothing about, then got ticked off when they made fun of him. He got up on the roof and slapped his nailer down in double quick time, flung the shingles around with jerky movements that belied his inner anger, then wouldn't speak to anyone the remainder of the day.

His boss shook his head. He'd have a lot to learn, that kid.

His father took notice and talked to his mother in private.

"*Eppas lets.*"

"Now what?"

His mother looked up from the *Keepers of Home* magazine, her fleece housecoat gathered around her, a soft throw across her knees. She had looked forward to this all day, and here was Eli bothering her with his concerns.

Reluctantly she closed the magazine, laid it aside, and looked at her husband, who had just come in from checking water pipes in the heifer barn.

"It's Dave. I'm worried about him."

"Well, whatever for? He's dating a nice girl, the one he's always wanted."

To her way of thinking, dating and marrying a nice girl was all they needed to keep them in the fold, especially the wild ones. The ones like Dave and his brother Amos, with that quick energy and temper.

"That's the problem, right there."

"What are you talking about?"

Eli came up with some weird notions, as far as she was concerned. Now whatever did he mean by that? Sure Elias and Barbie were better than most, but how could that be a problem? She lifted her magazine, kept two fingers inserted to the place where she was reading, and hoped he'd hurry up and say what he had to say, which would likely be something off the wall.

"I'm afraid they'll try to mold him into something he's not. Dave won't bend easily. He'll break out somewhere else, you mark my words."

"Well, if he likes her, he'll change. I don't see a problem."

"He'd be better off dating someone from his own group."

"See, that's why we have some of these daughters-in-law who have a hard time with submission. They aren't taught at home. Anna is taught well in all things like that. Those people are Bible readers."

Eli cast her a sharp glance.

"A bunch of stuff those people read is not what I'd recommend."

"Like what?"

"Oh, those child-rearing books. I don't go for that stuff."

"Well, maybe you should. Look at the way your boys ran around."

"They are your boys too."

Rachel lifted her magazine, pursed her lips and glared at her husband. There he went again, always had to have the last word. Her right arm didn't feel right. She lifted it, flexed her fingers, winced as pain shot through her shoulder. She shouldn't have moved that dresser upstairs, but around here, if you wanted something done, you had to do it yourself.

Too busy. Eli should let one of the boys take on the farm so they could retire. Of course, she wasn't ready for a *Daudy house*, those *anna enda* stuck to the side of the original farmhouse.

Nine chances out of ten, he'd want Abner to take over the farm, and it was not her choice of daughter-in-law, that one. Thin and pinched, eating gluten-free and swallowing dozens of natural pills she didn't need and thinking everyone should do the same.

Her daughter-in-law of choice was that sweet girl, Anna. Now there was a winner. Dave was lucky to have her.

He'd go through this roofing spree, then settle down on the farm with a girl like her. Besides, she didn't care what Eli said; this family could do with a shot of spirituality.

When they were old, Anna would always be willing to help. She would have been raised that way.

She lifted her magazine, saw a recipe for homemade taco pizza and thought how that would be something Dave would like. Although Eli probably wouldn't eat it. That man ate nothing but meat and potatoes, seven days a week if she let him.

CHAPTER 8

Winter dripped and ran into an early eager spring with lavender and yellow crocuses appearing between mounds of slushy snow like soapsuds. The air had a bite to it, but the sun did its best to remind everyone of the warmth that would soon arrive.

Dave sat in the gray construction truck on his way to work, his cell phone clenched in both hands playing a video game, seeing neither the spring around him, the receding urban buildings, or the wide highway that stretched ahead of him. His coworkers were used to his obsession with games, so they mostly ignored him, knowing that the phone was off limits after they arrived at work.

He was not in a good mood. He felt caged, hampered by the life that had been chosen for him. A settlement of Amish people so thick and heavy he could barely turn his head without running into someone he knew. Rules applied to his life like handcuffs.

This thing of dating the way Anna's parents wanted was beginning to get him down. There wasn't one thing normal or natural about sitting in the kitchen, sipping coffee he didn't want, eating brownies he didn't like, knowing both parents likely stood at the bedroom door with their ears plastered to the surface, hoping to catch a sentence they didn't approve of.

He couldn't stand either of them. The way they spoke, the way they moved in righteous circles, the approach they used to extract bits of information from their willing daughter while he bristled with resentment. He felt it was none of their business what he said or did, where they went or with whom.

But, the bottom line was still the same. He loved Anna.

She was his, and he fully planned on spending the rest of his life with her. He'd get this dating thing over with, they'd get married, and he'd move away somewhere, although there was always the home farm, and being the youngest son, he was expected to follow in his father's footsteps.

He'd thought it through. No way was he going to side with those parents.

He looked up from his cell phone, surprised to see they'd already turned off an exit and were traveling on a narrow country road.

All day, his back bent, hustling with the same speed he always did, he found no enjoyment in his work. He lived and relived the Sunday evening with Anna.

They should not have had their evening meal with her parents. He had not been in the mood to go to the youth's gathering if he had to drive a horse and buggy. He had to drive his father's horse, that bony, long-legged steed without a smidgen of style, knowing he would never be able to handle his own. If he was honest with himself, he knew he was afraid of him but told Anna he didn't want to put her in any danger, that the horse was not safe. He received a look of so much tenderness that he put his hands in his pockets to keep from touching her.

They walked side by side, sat side by side, or across the table from one another, and spoke in soft tones. They learned to know each other in the proper way, the way of hands-off courtship.

Many other young men may appreciate this craziness, he always thought to himself, but he was having a hard time with it.

The afternoon had started off on the wrong note, the way he had hung on to his resentment. For starters, why weren't they allowed to go upstairs and hang out in her room? He'd never heard of anything quite as unnecessary in all his life. Every guy knew what his girl's room looked like. But no, not in this household.

It was too cold to stay outdoors, so they set up a card table in the living room, got down a thousand-piece puzzle, and with all the sisters piling in, began to work in earnest while Elias or Barbie poked their heads in at various times to make sure they didn't touch each other.

Anna had been as sweet and beautiful as ever, in a pale pink dress that reminded him of a rose petal. She was just exquisite, as ethereal as the most perfect, the most delicate flower.

As always, he was in awe of her, the one shining light that kept him as he battled the ever-present irritation that presented itself whenever he was with her family.

Everything in their home was perfect. The house was remodeled, tastefully decorated in neutral tones, the floor swept, windows washed. The food was always delicious. They prepared and ate things like tacos and fajitas and pasta dishes he'd never tried but always found to be better than his mother's plain old Amish mashed potatoes and beef gravy with peas.

They used napkins, the dishes were heavy and white with matching silverware. No one raised their voice or spoke disparagingly. They praised each other and all those around them.

Elias had pressed a napkin to his mouth, before pinning Dave with his gaze.

"So, Dave . . ."

A long pause, putting emphasis on the wait. Like holding a kitten by the scruff of its neck, dangling.

Dave swallowed, almost choking on the bite of chicken breast.

"We're going into April here soon, which will mean communion services are coming up."

Dave looked at his plate.

"After that comes the invitation to begin instruction classes, which I believe you know, we're hoping you'll be among those who have experienced the new birth and are willing to become a member of the church, in order to live a godly life."

Dave didn't even think. He merely gave Elias the full benefit of his resentment by meeting the expectation in his.

"Yeah, well, that's a tall order. I don't know if I'm ready."

He found it deeply satisfying to see the flicker of surprise, the disappointment that followed. A soft sigh from his wife.

"We are hoping, Dave, on account of our requirements about dating Anna. You know we are bending the rules, allowing it at all. She will definitely be joining, right, Anna?"

"Yes, I will."

A smile, a light of willingness, the eagerness to please. The response from both parents as syrupy as molasses. He wanted to get up and knock over his chair for emphasis before leaving.

But it was Anna that kept him there.

He had nothing to say the remainder of the evening, which created a certain heightening of Anna's awareness, a nervous flutter of her hands, an eager attempt to draw him out. She worked on the puzzle with her sisters while he opted to lay on the recliner with some dumb magazine that mentioned God in every other sentence.

Serious doubt set in, sending his mood into a black downward spiral, a place of cold selfishness and unhappiness. Anna leaned over the puzzle and kept up the light talk as she practiced the virtues taught by her parents. Occasionally he sensed her agitation and was glad of it.

They may as well learn that he would not be molded into their perfect requirements. He knew he could not live up to their expectations, so why pretend otherwise?

When, finally, the rest of the family left them alone, Anna sat back on her side of the couch, turned her head and looked at him.

"So, what's the matter? Can you tell me about it?"

"I'm not a child."

"Right. You're not. But if you act like one, then I'll treat you like one."

That stung. He was still smarting from that honeyed, cold hard truth. He didn't know she had it in her. The nerve.

"I don't want to join church," he blurted out.

"Why not?"

"I don't know. I'm not ready, I guess."

"You won't be later, either. Give yourself up now. It won't be easier later on."

"How do you know?" His voice was pouting.

"Dave, look. My parents will not allow it. They are already giving in to us, allowing us to date before we're members. Surely you can appreciate this."

"They can't tell me what to do. They're not my boss."

"Who is, Dave? Who?"

He'd never seen her like this.

CHAPTER 9

He walked home in the cold March drizzle, the sky above erased of starlight, the moon obscured by the rain clouds. He hunched his shoulders against the wet, biting wind, thrust his hands in his pockets, thinking dark and bewildered thoughts.

He felt trapped, caged.

For the thousandth time he envied the youth in his group, where everyone hung out or dated in a relaxed way, groups pounding upstairs to a girl's room, waiting to make commitments to each other or the church until they were tired of *rumschpringa*, tired of the parties and the cars and all that went with it, including the girls' insincerity, their flirting and carrying on, with all the resulting drama.

To Dave, that was still the best way. The old fashioned sowing of wild oats until you, yourself realized there was nothing in all of this. Living a life of selfishness, reveling in self-will, was not fulfilling, and most of the youth wanted something lasting. Something deeper.

He had not arrived at the precipice, where he looked over the edge and found the alarming chasm of the way of all flesh. He had not seriously found the need of a Redeemer. Not yet.

Did Anna hold the power to keep him on her path? Should a girl be the reason for joining the church? They usually were. How could a guy become tangled in this web of loving someone but absolutely unable to stand that set of parents?

He had two solutions. Try harder or break up.

The thing was, could he do either one? He had to have Anna. She was as necessary as breathing. She was his life, his goal, all he had ever been seeking, even as a schoolboy. He could not have foreseen the exorbitant price of his love, the sacrifice that required everything.

His way of life was so different. The easiness of his days, the relaxed atmosphere. There was no hurry to grow up and make serious decisions, no panic if the wrong one was made. God wasn't someone who demanded stringent obedience but viewed the creation He had made with a benevolent eye.

While Dave was tossed from one side to the other, decisions tearing at his conscience, Anna moved in an ever-increasing aura of coming into her own. She loved Dave with all her heart, but God came before him. Obedience to her parents and the will of her Lord were perhaps being trampled under her own feet, doing more damage to her soul than she knew. Her prayers changed, her face took on a peaceful countenance, and she grew increasingly close to her mother, who, in turn, appreciated all of it, and thanked God for deliverance.

And yet their dating continued.

Aaron Beiler came to talk to Elias Fisher about organizing a trip to Texas. The youth would benefit from the experience of helping rebuild after the flood, so if they would lend their expertise, they'd get a bus or a few vans and go. Mennonite Central Committee already had quite a few workstations set up and needed volunteers.

Anna was glowing, excited about the upcoming trip to Texas, and included Dave in her plans, naturally.

Dave thought of his work, his savings, and the two weeks he wouldn't be making money. He imagined being on a bus for more than twenty-four hours, sitting with Anna and never once touching her, talking with the immature guys from the Cardinals. He wanted to see more of the country, but not like this. She could go.

He told her a few weeks later and was met with disbelief, then, surprisingly, tears.

"I don't want to go without you."

She dabbed at the corner of her eyes, delicately, with the corner of a tissue. She looked so much like her mother when she did that.

"I'm not going, so it's up to you."

"But . . . why not?"

"I'd have to take off work."

"Really? So will everyone else. It's for a good cause, Dave. Those people in Texas need help. The Lord always blesses those who help the needy."

"Well, He'll have to bless the rest of you then."

She would not beg, so she let it go, but not without the usual confiding in her mother, who drew her mouth in a straight line of disapproval, laid down her paring knife, and gave her daughter the full benefit of her undivided attention.

"Anna, you do realize that Dave is not coming up to our expectations. He has yet to show any willingness to sacrifice, and now this. Surely you are aware that he simply will not be a good husband?"

She had never spoken this directly and harshly.

"But, Mom, it's not all on him. My part is to be submissive, so if he chooses not to go, it's up to me to give in. No?"

Her mother took up the potato, began to peel, without further argument, leaving Anna wavering, again between her mother and her headstrong boyfriend, a place she had begun to question.

Did dating have to be quite so hard?

Her mother began to cut up the peeled potatoes, added water, and set the pot on the stove. She turned to Anna, her slim hands resting on her narrow hips, loving concern in a voice full of emotion.

"He has yet to make a decision about joining church. How can you trust him to do the right thing? How can you consider going to Texas without him? He needs your support."

Anna trembled from the effort to keep control.

"I'm not God, Mom. I can only do so much. I am not the one who can change his heart."

The mother knew this to be true, saw the futility of her words, and fell into silence.

The bus departed from Lancaster on a Monday morning, with Anna sharing a seat with her friend Martha, a thin, waif-like girl of eighteen who had a smattering of freckles like thrown pepper flakes and brilliant auburn hair to match. She had Lyme disease, so she tired easily and slept for hours at a time, after the excitement wore off.

Anna brought a few books in her larger backpack, so she adjusted her pillow and settled down to read.

When the bus pulled into a rest stop, Martha woke up, then waved a hand, saying "Go ahead. I'll lie here a while. I feel faint."

Anna folded the corner of the page, stuck the book in the flap of her backpack, and rose to her feet, stepping out into the narrow aisle between the seats directly in the path of a tall young man with blue eyes.

"Go ahead, no problem," he said.

"Sorry."

She hurried away, embarrassed, went to the restroom, bought a bottle of Diet Coke from a vending machine, and went back to the bus, finding Martha feeling unwell, her teeth chattering with cold.

"I shouldn't have come. I get days when I'm like this. You don't happen to have a blanket, do you?"

"I didn't bring one. I don't know why I didn't think."

Martha shivered, her thin shoulders hunched forward, her skinny arms wrapped around her slender waist.

"I should not have come."

"It's okay, Martha. I'll find a blanket."

Anna stood and surveyed the passengers that had returned to their seats before making her way toward the back of the bus.

"Does anyone have a spare blanket? A throw, or even a coat?"

Leon Beiler was from Millerstown, Pennsylvania, and had lived there most of his life. An outlying region of Lancaster, it was home to a large group of Amish. Asked to accompany a busload of the Cardinal youth to the flooded region of Texas, he accepted grudgingly but felt if he was asked, it would be his duty to comply.

The oldest in a family of ten, he knew all about sacrifice and hard work, his mother keeping up 75 percent of the workload and responsibilities, his father saddled with recurring bouts of depression, finally diagnosed with bipolar disorder. He was sent to rest in a retreat for troubled people in Ohio, returned, and was back again the following year. The boy's wages kept the family afloat; the meager four-bedroom home on an acre and a half carried a second mortgage.

At the age of twenty-four, Leon had aged far beyond his years, his level of maturity like a forty-year-old, with the maelstrom that had always been his life at home, the mother a pillar of extraordinary strength.

He had foregone dating, never actively seeking a girlfriend, in spite of having many opportunities. He was tall, blue-eyed, and handsome, his hair like a sultry night, a dark color not quite black and not quite brown. His eyes were set on each side of a nose that had a wide bridge, a pleasant mouth that seemed his best feature, with smoothly tanned skin that needed a shave every morning. Wearing a white shirt open at the throat, his gray denims tight around his hips, he struck an attractive pose.

When he saw Anna step out from her seat, he didn't really notice her as much as he did when she walked back through the bus.

She was exquisite. A rare flower.

He looked away, chided himself for allowing his eyes to linger. He was nothing to her, and anyone with those looks had to be taken. They always were.

"A blanket? Is there an extra one?"

A blanket. She wanted a blanket. Right. He had one.

He held out the soft gray fleece. An offering.

"This one okay?"

She looked down at him. Oh, it was him. She'd stepped out in front of him. He was . . . well.

"Thank you. I'll return it. My friend Martha is not feeling well."

"I don't need it."

She smiled, and he would happily have left the world, completed for all his life in the light of that smile. He watched her turn, walk away, and slide into a double seat on his side of the bus.

Well, enough was enough. He had not come on this trip to find a girl. Romance was out of the question. His mother had more to bear than any human should have the day she married his poor tortured father. The responsibility of being his mentor, raising the ten of them, besides the financial burden when he was unable to work, which was becoming more and more frequent as he refused to take medication, left Leon and two of his brothers to provide for the groceries, the monthly mortgage, and other expenses. His mother baked and grew produce for a roadside stand, which enabled her to keep some cash and her own sense of independence, but it was a hardscrabble kind of life.

When the bus stopped again, evening was already dimming the light in the parking lot of a Denny's, where all the passengers disembarked for the first hot meal of the day. Martha was feeling better after sleeping for more than six hours, sat up, and fussed with her hair and covering, saying she looked like a newly hatched *beebly*.

"You know how ugly they are when they're still wet," she said, addressing Anna with the wry sense of humor that made her so endearing.

They joined two more of Anna's acquaintances, Suzanna and Leah, both tired and disheveled, smoothing their hair, repositioning bobby pins and adjusting coverings.

Anna watched for him, knowing where he sat and with whom. She felt guilty, but shook it off.

They ordered, ate baked potatoes, roasted chicken, French fries and coleslaw, and burgers so thick they could barely open their mouths wide enough to chomp down on them. They drank sweet tea, Pepsi, lemonade, and then felt immensely refreshed.

Anna walked across the parking lot with Martha and breathed in the night air. She took notice of flying insects circling the pale light and the burst of daffodils along a stone wall. Spring came earlier in the South, so it was exciting to realize they would likely be working in warm weather.

And she experienced a sense of rightness, a settling of her troubles the way sediment settles to the bottom of a glass. A sense of uplifting, little squiggles of joy that made her skip a few steps, like a schoolgirl.

"You're happy," Martha observed.

"See those daffodils?"

"What about them?

"They're there. Spring is here."

"Whatever turns you on," Martha observed dryly.

They settled into their seats, Martha plumping her pillows before burrowing under her blanket, mumbling goodnight. She was out like a light.

Anna watched the remaining passengers return to their seats. He had not returned. She reached down for her backpack, lifted it to her lap, and dug out the book. She would read while there was still a bit of daylight. Her stomach felt pleasantly full. The doors on the bus opened one last time, as the driver called out to make sure everyone was present, then stepped back to allow him to enter. Breathing hard, his hair disheveled, laughing, he apologized for being late, then looked around for a place to sit.

"You can slide in here," little Manny Zook quipped, directly across the aisle.

Anna kept her eyes on her book, but her heart thumped unexpectedly. Oh, good grief. Now what? She felt the color drain from her face.

She'd just keep her eyes on her book, concentrating on the words and thinking of Dave, far away and working faithfully on one of his many roofing jobs. She wondered if he thought of her, if he wished he was here, with her.

"What are you reading?"

She jumped, gave a small laugh.

"Didn't mean to scare you."

"You didn't."

She handed over the book. He took it, examined the cover, turned it over, and read the back.

"You read biographies?"

"Sometimes. This one is intriguing, the doctors in Africa. They go anywhere, do anything, put their life on the line over and over."

"Is it true?"

"Yes."

"Don't you read what other girls read?"

"You mean fiction?"

"Romantic fiction."

"Sometimes."

He handed the book back and gave a small laugh.

"I'll let you go now. Read away."

He adjusted his seat and slid out of view. She turned slightly to view his profile. She felt disloyal to Dave and returned to her book.

When darkness fell, he said very quietly, "What's your name?"

"Anna."

"Just Anna?"

"Anna Fisher."

"I'm Leon Beiler."

He wanted to ask her more questions, and she wanted to hear more of his deep, confident voice. But neither one felt free to say so. She returned her book to its backpack, then adjusted her own seat, finding the reclining position much too close to him. She turned her back as best she could to shut him away, closed her eyes, and tried to relax and get some sleep.

But her eyes were still open when she heard, "Anna."

She turned her head. "Yes?"

"Who are you?"

"Elias and Barbie Fisher. Sam's Elias from Kinzer."

"Don't know them." Then, "I'm from Millerstown. My dad is Amos Belier. Sim's Amos from Holbrook."

"Don't know them."

They both laughed.

He whispered, "Tell me about you."

"There's not a lot to say. I live and work at home. My parents don't approve of me working away from home, so I help wherever I'm needed. Four sisters, ordinary life. Dating a guy named Dave Stoltzfus."

"I figured."

"What?"

"Beautiful girls always date."

Nothing had ever pleased her more. She felt a profound sense of wonder, a warm and comfortable gladness that he found her attractive.

Attractive boys always date, too.

Should she say it? She felt a sense of daring, a leap into the unknown. She knew not to say it. She knew too, that she would.

"Attractive men do, too."

How could she know the husky whisper stirred his senses, made his heart beat stronger? He swallowed, felt strangled by the tightening in his throat.

"I'm not dating, so go figure."

She was strangely exuberant. A rush of gladness.

Beneath them, the motor on the bus throbbed, the sound of air moving in the tires, creating a sense of intimacy neither one had experienced before.

"Why? How old are you?"

"I'm twenty-four. Twenty-five in December."

"That's old."

"Not too old. I'm needed at home. My father is mentally ill."

"You mean . . . ?"

Anna turned her head when he turned his. Was the aisle of a bus no wider than this? It was almost as if they shared a bed. They both reached for the lever to adjust seats, ill at ease and self-conscious now.

"He's very hard to understand or control, so he keeps being sent to retreats, places where trained counselors work with them. They try and keep him on medication. I've struggled over the years but have learned to accept what I can't change.

"I'm taking a course in Christian counseling. You know, the world is full of hurting people, and I don't mean just the worldly ones who don't know any better. It's among our people as well. I'm just getting started."

He seemed shy then, reluctant to talk about his life's work. "I'm not a counselor."

"But you will be."

"Yes. Eventually."

After a stretch of silence, the only sound the soft snoring behind them, along with the gentle hum of the motor, she gave a small laugh.

"Perhaps you should try your skills on my story."

"Go right ahead."

"You're serious."

"Of course."

So she spoke, haltingly at first, then with more ease, describing Dave at a very young age, the love they had felt for so long, the difference in their families' lifestyles.

Here he stopped her.

"Anna, that should not make a difference in your relationship. No two families are alike."

"But it does."

She could hear him shake his head.

All night they talked. Sometimes Anna cried. Once, he held her hand.

A man had never held her hand, and the sensation of large, calloused fingers cradling her own smaller ones sent chills up her spine. He meant to comfort, that was all, she told herself repeatedly, but the touch was so much more.

They were both surprised to see jagged streaks of silver light emerge in the east, as if the night's cover had been torn to reveal the brand-new breaking of another day. And for them, it was.

The light brought stirrings from the rest of the passengers, snorts and sneezes, loud stretching and yawning. Cries for a restroom.

Martha stirred, opened one eye, and said, "Whatever, Anna. Guarantee you talked all night."

"You were sleeping. How would you know?"

"I heard more than you think."

Suddenly she didn't care. She found it freeing, this knowing that anything could happen.

They were inseparable, no matter how they fought against it. He stood behind her when they came to the first work center and was there when they toured the devastation, the homes crumbling with mold, rotting in brown slime. The smell was worse than anything Anna could have imagined, but she grew accustomed to it as the week wore on.

The land was flat, the sun baking them like an oven. The residents of the town were grateful as they worked together to rid the houses of the effects of rising brown floodwaters.

Rubber gloves and masks, a men's handkerchief tied on her head, her nose sunburned and her blonde hair turning pale in the heat of the Texas sun, Anna worked with Leon, surrounded by groups of youth from home as well as other states. He did the heavy lifting while she swept, scraped, and scoured.

Talk circulated. Martha told her Becca had a hard time with her trailing that guy from Millerstown. Deeply ashamed, Anna switched to a different site, away from Leon.

She called Dave.

He was cool, aloof. When was she coming home? It was about time. She tried to stretch the conversation out longer, still smarting with embarrassment from being labeled as someone who chased men.

She talked to her mother and spoke to her father without mentioning Leon at all. She felt as if she was on the opposite side of the globe.

And she wanted to stay there.

What was home? Keeping face, holding up her pride, dating, Dave, twisting her parents' arms to keep them from freaking out about him.

She prayed alone at night seeking the face of God and the meaning of right from wrong. Dave was right for her, so she must do the right thing, and would, when she returned home.

She dressed in old dark-colored dresses, went out with a group of girls, working on houses, determined to stay with them. But she watched for him every morning. As the morning turned into forenoon and the sun rose in the sky, he still had not appeared. She tried to hide her deep disappointment, putting aside the fact that this was one of the last days before they began the journey home.

Martha had regained her strength, although she was assigned lighter work. She cleaned light fixtures or doorknobs, things she could lay on a table and sit to restore them to their former glow. She said little but watched Anna repeatedly return to a door or window, her face turning steadily more unhappy.

"He's not going to show up, you know."

Anna's face was suffused by a painful blush. She scrubbed vigorously at a wall, hid her face, and mumbled something about not caring.

Martha gave a short laugh.

"You can't fool me, Anna. You two are goners. What's wrong with you? You have a boyfriend at home. What is going on in your head? The minute you're away from him, it's like whoopee!"

Anna stood, scrub brush in hand, covered in dried slime and mildew, her eyes round above the blue mask.

"Martha! I cannot believe you."

"Well, it's true."

And then, very unlike Anna, she became unhinged. At the table where Martha was seated, she propped herself up by the palms of her hands and lowered her face to Martha's surprised one.

"You know, Martha, you have no right to judge. Dave is a different guy than the Dave I knew in school. He can't stand my parents, the Cardinals, and the rules. He resents all authority, in any form, because he never had any at home. Our dating is a constant battle of trying to keep it afloat. So stop it."

Martha lifted one eyebrow and stared back.

Chapter 10

At home, Dave threw himself into his work, with a renewed and nervous energy that amazed even the coworkers who knew he was one of the best. Spring was a time of meeting demands, and he thrived under pressure.

But beneath his energy was the unsettling awareness that something was not quite right with Anna. When she called, her voice sounded too high, her words hurried, as if she was nervous about something.

With her good looks, probably every loser on that bus wanted to date her. But those Cardinal guys didn't stand a chance, so it couldn't be that. He never saw such a bunch of childish young men, and clearly, Anna was far above any one of them. So he figured his fears were ungrounded.

But he could not sit still in the evening, even when exhausted. He paced the perimeter of his room, helped with the spring planting and harrowing, almost persuaded himself to become a farmer someday, the way he loved bouncing around on a horse-drawn piece of equipment.

Not that he liked the horses or anything, he just liked to be in wide-open spaces with buildings in the distance, neighboring farms, patches of woods, fencerows, and him in the middle. He tried to imagine every distant farm or house flattened, the land rolling in the distance the way it would have been before everybody and his aunt and uncle, cousin, or brother moved in to plant and harvest, build and carry on. This whole tourist thing was out of control, but if he wanted to marry Anna, which he certainly did, then he'd have to stay in Lancaster.

Women didn't do well leaving their families.

He'd heard his mother talk about her niece, Ida Sue, who had to move to Wisconsin to her husband's family. She was terribly depressed during the long, cold winters, so that her husband hardly knew what to do with her.

But that would be one solution, getting Anna way from those parents, although he knew it was not best, any way you looked at it.

She was coming home from Texas in five days.

It was time. He didn't know why he felt so uneasy, but he did. He tried reading, he played games on his cell phone, and he went to see his friend Wayne, anything he could think of to stay occupied.

On the last evening of their stay in Texas, Anna was clearing the table, preparing to wash dishes in the large kitchen and dining area that had been set up for volunteers. She turned to find Leon directly beside her.

"Meet me down at the corner after dishes. Where there's a taco shop."

She didn't dare lift her eyes. She merely nodded and slipped away. Her heart pounded. She washed dishes, dried them, then went to the bathroom, watched for her chance, and fled. No one observed her disappearance as far as she could tell, and if they had, it was too bad, she wasn't turning back.

Breathless, she arrived at the designated shop, looked around, then decided to go inside so no one would notice her. He was beside her immediately, appearing out of nowhere.

"Anna. Glad you could make it."

She was overtaken with a wild impulse to throw herself into his arms. She knew he would take her there with gratitude, and this was almost her undoing. Instead, her mother formed in her conscience, listing the benefits of total hands-off courtship.

It was very godly. The Christian thing to do. To abstain from all fleshly contact would only sweeten the touch after marriage.

Self-will was always of the devil, devised and orchestrated by him. Better to use restraint, obeying the will of God.

She clasped her hands behind her back. He stepped closer, looked into her eyes.

"Let's walk."

The night was magical, the water on one side, the blinking lights of apartment buildings on the other, the walkway along the river like a silver road dotted with overhead lamps glowing along each side. Pedestrians, joggers, a few skateboarders, couples seated on park benches. It was all like a scene from some book she had read, but she never imagined she would be in such a place.

The night was warm, the heavy air permeated with blossoming trees and the stale, musty odor of receded water.

Suddenly he took her hand.

"Oh, I hardly know where to begin or where to stop."

She suffered agonies. She should not be allowing this holding of her hand but could not summon the courage to tell him so.

"Look. I know you have a boyfriend, okay? And I have no right to ask you to accompany me on this walk. But I can't go home without a phone number or an address. I noticed you don't have a cell phone. A home number, something."

He squeezed her hand. He stopped, the light of the streetlamp illuminated his face. He reached for her other hand, held them both. Anna drew a sharp breath. Before she could begin the required gentle withdrawing of her hands, he lifted them to his lips and softly kissed the back of both, then released them.

"I'll never forget you," he murmured, brokenly.

There were no words to describe any of her fractured cries and outpouring of doubts, fears, words of the heart. So she stood, her hands dangling newly blessed, consecrated by the touch of his lips.

This kind, caring man who had suffered at the hands of a father who was often rendered incapable by the workings of his tortured mind. Who seemed so eager to help people, English people with no religion to speak of, even though his own family depended on him so much already. Anna had to look away.

Leon was not perfect, not in the way her own parents were. Not in the quietly rigid way.

Oh God, she breathed. So much confusion. She had to tell him what was on her mind.

"Can we find a place to sit?" she asked in a voice so strangled he could not be certain of her question.

When he didn't answer, she led him to a bench, a shadowed alcove of blossoming bushes and pine trees.

"Here."

"What?"

"I just need to talk." A pause. "Dave, my boyfriend, was my child-hood hero, the one and only person I loved with a deep, possessive love that never went away. He was all I ever truly cared about. We grew up, and our lives turned out to be directed in very different ways. Our parents are simply polar opposites. Mine are strict, expecting teenagers to be, well, obedient young people with Christian virtues. Strict ones."

She sighed.

"Curfews. No . . . well, you know, the hands-off thing. No touching."

"I'm sorry. I never thought."

She shook her head. "We're in Texas."

"I am sorry. I know there are groups of youth who believe this to be the only way. Very meaningful."

"Yes."

"Continue."

Oh, the kindness of him. The sincerity of wanting to hear what she had to say.

So she went on, describing Dave in detail, his upbringing, his brilliant, passionate mind, his nervous energy that bordered on wildness, his expressive conversations that always led to wanderlust, showing pictures, images of faraway places on his cell phone, reading anything he could find about people, places, and things.

Then, the most painful, his thorough dislike of her parents, and the ease with which he spoke of it.

"I want to say it doesn't bother me, but it troubles me more than I care to admit. You know how parents matter."

She gave a small laugh.

"They may be too strict, and well . . . especially my mother is a bit controlling, but they mean well. They are merely concerned about our souls, even if they have a narrow view of God's expectations. They are just so rigid, so set in what is right, and expect everyone else to come up to their standards."

"I gather they don't approve of Dave."

"They are barely tolerant of our dating."

Leon shook his head. "That's a tough one."

A man ran past, his arms held to his waist, his feet pounding the pavement, obviously having come a long way. They could hear the puffs of breath, the exertion evident in the way his head was held low.

An elderly couple stepped aside to make room for him, their heads swiveling in unison to watch him jog past. The man made a remark to the old woman beside him, she lifted her face to the night sky and cackled a dry laugh.

When Leon spoke he said only a few words.

"So it comes down to how much you really do love him. Love beats all the odds if it's the real thing, you know."

"I know. How I do know. But constantly battered between him and my family is not my idea of how dating and marriage should be."

"Like I said, this is a tough one."

He led her to another park bench where she sat beside him, a comfortable distance from his touch, a new reserve that occupied the space between them like an invisible disapproving person.

Her mother.

Anna's hands fluttered now, small white birds that found no place of rest. Her breath was quick and shallow, her eyes darting from street lamps to passing pedestrians.

"You may never respond if I do write a letter," Leon began. "You have to understand things about my family. We are the ones the family is ashamed of, as in, we are the poor relatives. There is no money. I don't have much. My interest in places of counseling is more than my financial drive. I mean, I do work, but much of my paycheck goes to support my family, so I'm afraid I would not be a caring provider, with my interests in counseling."

Anna became quite still, her hands folded in her lap. Finally she spoke in a choked voice.

"You know, this is simply over my head. I have to go home, sort out my feelings and . . ."

She shrugged.

He turned to her, his eyes darkened beneath the insufficient light of the streetlamp.

"A better man than I would agree. But I am not noble. I'm being selfish and telling you the honest truth. I can't stand the thought of never seeing you again. Of giving you over to someone you aren't in love with."

"But I am. In love. I mean. I have always been."

"If you were, you would have waved me off before taking a second look."

"That's mean."

"True, though."

How to describe the turmoil? Anna thought.

Denial, swift and efficient, eliminating the need to probe the uncertainty of the heart. She did not love Leon. He was nothing to her. To be away from Dave with a group of young people was like watering a dry earth of hidden longings and desires that were natural, a part of being human.

But that did not make it right.

She must continue to be a friend to Dave, the true and godly love required by her parents' rules. The love that was not fueled by the thrill of a touch, the meshing of fingers, the touch of his lips on the back of her hand.

She felt marred, used, when she allowed her mother to rise in her conscience.

Again.

She was infinitely weary, unable to decipher right from wrong. To be seated on a park bench with this young man of uncertain origin and questionable dreams, a thousand long miles away from Dave, in the velvety darkness heavy with magnolia blossoms and bluebonnet, a rich, earthy scent that seemed in favor of all those who teetered on the edge of personal commitment, of a deeper quest to know and therefore understand love.

"Leon?"

"Yes?"

"What are we going to do?"

"I'm leaving that decision to you."

"But I can't do it alone."

Gone now, the night's sweet intimacy, the moment erased by the searing voice of the absent mother. They returned, walked slowly, worlds apart, and both knew it.

Dave was ecstatic the day Anna returned. Their meeting was as joyful as he had anticipated. Nothing had changed.

But the next day he was reminded that the time to begin instruction class was nearing. Anna mentioned it, a questioning look in her eyes, hesitancy in her voice. He didn't want to talk about it. He still had a week to decide. He was annoyed that the happiness of their reunion was being overshadowed by the looming decision.

Dave lay facedown on his bed, his mouth pursed in the now customary pout, his thoughts darting down side alleys of justification.

He was too young, he had plenty of time to get married, Anna would wait. He was confident of her love, now that she was back from Texas. Those parents of hers needed to realize they could not control him. What was he? Some kind of puppet that danced when they pulled strings?

Saturday evening before the first Sunday of instruction class, they sat together on the swing by the garden, surrounded by the blooming salvia, the early daylilies and late tulips, the mixture creating a heady aroma, the fragrance of spring love.

Anna had decided that she would not ask more questions, not nudge him in the direction she wanted him to go. Instead, she would stay on the sidelines, allow him his own choices, hoping her patience and love would win him over.

When he gathered his courage and resolutely told her he would not be "joining up," that youthful irreverent phrase that was like barbed wire to her already jangling nerves, the disappointment was almost unbearable. The pain would have been more tolerable if he had delivered a smack to the side of her face.

She sat immovable, like a stone.

He made excuses, prattled like a schoolboy with undone home-work. There's no hurry, he said. We have our whole lives. We're young. Your parents don't like me.

They argued when she sprang to life, her outrage spoken in a level, well-brought-up delivery with undertones of her mother, inciting an instant rebellion in him.

"You have no idea how hard this decision is," he shot back, his voice permeated with self-pity. "If your parents were normal the way they should be there would be no hurry. And let me tell you, Anna, I'll never live up to their expectations. I'll never be good enough."

"If you are good enough for me, you will be for them," she insisted with more confidence than she actually felt.

After a long, strained silence, Anna sighed.

"Maybe we'd better just go our separate ways."

"What? You mean as in breaking up?"

He was shouting now, his handsome face contorted with disbelief.

"Dave, I seriously don't know what to do. I can't go against my parents' wishes."

"So you love them more than me."

Anna felt the rise of her despair grow into a lump in her throat that dissolved into a heartbroken cry.

"I don't know anymore. Sometimes I don't know what love is."

Dave was quick to insert his meaning. "Well, let me tell you, if you love someone, you won't try to twist them into someone they're not."

"But it goes both ways, Dave."

Her voice was a troubled wail, a note of desperation creeping in.

They sat, side by side, the way they had always done whenever they had a chance to be together.

But what was this? Two people who were clinging to a substance that was slipping out of their grasp, leaving them frustrated, helpless in their own inability to retain the love they had always had.

Eli Stoltzfus was the quiet, observant one. He knew this relationship with Anna was not working. Dave was not one to be pushed, and, in his opinion, was far too young for the meaningful step of joining the church.

He knew, too, he would be joining for the wrong reason, which was Anna.

To join the church without knowledge of his own sinful life, the true repentance and the desire to be a better person, was, in Eli's view, like an empty shell. All show. Those were often the ones who woke up spiritually later in life, were drawn away by some charismatic speaker promising assurance of salvation without obedience to man-made rules. Breaking the hearts of parents, roiling family relationships, they sold their horse and buggy, bought vehicles, dressed in worldly clothes, and attended the church of their choice.

More and more frequently, these partings occurred, with the rule of excommunication and shunning hanging like a sword between families. Although hearts healed, became soft, the realization set in that efficiently served the knowledge of love, the only thing left.

And there was love.

Acceptance brought it on wings of *die oof gevva heit.*

Self-blame the parents carried on their backs was eventually released, replaced by the much more manageable humility. Pride was dispersed, knowing their parenting skills had been less than perfect, but so it was, for all their fellow Amish to see.

Die ungehorsamy.

Shunning was held in a wide variety of differences. Where some shunned in the true sense, most allowed communication with those who had left the faith. Children returned dressed in English clothes, grandchildren sporting jeans and striped T-shirts, and the grandparents swallowed their disappointment and sadness, accepted them, hugged and gave them candy from the candy jar, keeping tears at bay.

This was the future Eli saw in Dave.

Dave was impetuous, proud, driven, coupled with a lust for life, the world and all it had to offer, an intolerance of rules and regulations. To be measured with the exacting yardstick of Elias and Barbie Fisher was, in Eli's opinion, *zu feel g'fuddad.*

Any of his other sons would be an entirely different scenario. They all had a wild streak at Dave's age, but it was manageable. Their conscience and respect to authority eventually won them over.

If Dave did join at this age, marry Anna, and try to live under the eyes of her parents, a rebellion would rise, leading him to make bad choices.

But Eli was a man of few words. He rarely shared his feelings with his wife or children. She, in turn, filled the air with flapping words like pecking birds, wearying, headache-inducing words that made him devise his own method of turning a deaf ear.

On Sunday morning Rachel made her way up the stairs, one foot placed heavily after another, the oak stair treads groaning in protest.

She woke Dave with efficient raps of the knuckles, finished with a volley of words about the morning of *die gmay noch gay*, finished with *Kamm na* and made her way down the stairs to fry eggs for Eli.

It took her appetite, the silence from upstairs. She had a sixth sense about Dave but depended on her words to guide him along. She slurped her coffee, her egg congealed on her plate, her eyes darting repeatedly to the door to the stairs.

Finally, she said, "*Hesslich*, Eli."

He was sopping up the last of his egg yolk with a corner of his toast.

"What?"

"Why doesn't he get up?"

"I have no idea."

"He knows it's the morning of *die gmay noch gay*."

"Yes."

"So go do something about it. He's not getting up."

"We can't force him, Rachel. You know he's not ready."

"There you go again, Eli, sticking up for that boy. That's all you've ever done, no matter what. I have seen it, over and over. Whatever Dave wants to do, Dave does, with your consent. How can I expect him to listen to me if he knows you don't feel the same? Spoiled. That kid is spoiled rotten, and it's all your fault."

She sipped her coffee with a liquid gurgling, wiped her mouth with the back of her hand, her small eyes glaring at him.

"He's not ready, Rachel."

"Well, of course he isn't. He doesn't have a father pushing him in the right direction. If you'd talk to him the way other fathers do, he'd be joining the church this morning. I don't know what's going to happen if he doesn't. Elias and Barbie won't stand for it. They won't allow Anna to date him if he doesn't make an effort to join, you know they won't. Then what? Then what?"

Working herself into a state of senseless anxiety, she got to her feet, removed her plate, and slid the uneaten egg into the waste can.

"There's still time," Eli said, referring to the allowed second and third time, when reluctant, indecisive stragglers were accepted.

"Oh, I guess. I suppose you're right."

Buoyed by the hope of Dave changing his mind, she rode to church with her silent husband, filling over his share of the narrow seat with her ample backside, wondering why Dan Beiler's hadn't planted their corn in that front field.

Anna dressed carefully in her virginal white cape and apron, a sign of purity in young girls, combed her hair in *die ordnung*, the expected respect to the minister's requirements, a song in her heart and prayer on her lips. She felt oddly peaceful, resigned to whatever lay ahead. She had prayed late into the night that God would change Dave's mind and stir in him the desire to begin the instruction classes with her, but then she gave it up to God, accepting His will whatever that should look like. She had slept soundly then, relieved of the burden of Dave's decision. It was out of her hands.

Her mother examined Anna's appearance, smiled her approval.

They sang "Nearer My God to Thee," for morning devotions, read the first article of faith from the booklet that provided each applicant with clear steps of what would be expected of them. They read it in English, so Anna would be able to comprehend it fully.

The German was used in class and read in every sermon. But mixed-in Pennsylvania Dutch was understandable to every youth, especially if the parents took the time to explain the rules in English.

But she didn't remember much of the three-hour service, as the reality of Dave's absence began to sink in. He could not make the sacrifice and lay down his own will for her. Or for God.

She cried alone in her room after the service, cried in the bathroom, cried when she dressed for Dave's arrival that evening. She tried to disguise her red, swollen eyes by using every imaginable lotion, then burst into tears at the sight of his handsome face on the front porch.

Dave felt worse than he had ever felt in his life, to see the distress in the one he loved. But how to explain it to her?

He simply could not see his way through, couldn't imagine himself bowing to the senseless *ordnung*.

Chapter 11

THEY WENT FOR A WALK AND RESOLVED NOTHING. THEY SAT SIDE BY SIDE and resolved less. Dave was adamant, like a brick wall.

Although he lowered his voice, spoke softly, hoped to persuade her of his own plans, nothing could change the fact that there was a chasm between them, with Anna and her parents on one side, Dave on the other.

And he had no bridge-building plans.

As twilight moved across the land, like a soft, gauzy swaddling blanket in dark colors, Anna became infinitely weary. So weary, in fact, that she could no longer abide this endless conversation that was going absolutely nowhere.

In soft tones, with her face in his direction, her eyes unfocused, she told him the relationship was finished. Done.

It was as if her words were a ticking time bomb, and the words from Dave like the resulting explosion.

"You don't love me! What relationship? This had never been a relationship. A friendship, that's it."

He stood up, started pacing, waving his arms as his voice rose.

"No touching. No hanky-panky. Not a relationship. Your mother may as well be seated between us on every date, your father in the background smiling his approval. It's unnatural. All you care about is keeping those two happy. It makes me *sick*!

"Fine. Fine. Just live your perfect spiritual little life with those two prophets and their perfect offspring, and I'll go live my life the way I want to live it."

Even then, she thought of the fluid grace of his body, the muscled intensity. He thrust his handsome face close to hers, his eyes like polished jewels.

Fierce, like a warrior.

"This would have worked well, and you know it, if your parents would have stayed out of it."

He rose above her, his hands clenched, his breath coming in hard ragged gasps. Suddenly he reached down, drew her to her feet, and in one swift motion, caught her in a rough embrace.

Later in her room, she touched her fingers to her lips. Bruised. Abused. Against her will. Or was it?

Only a kiss, the meeting of two lips, but conveying everything. Everything.

Her mother rose within her.

It was wrong. That kind of love was of the flesh. It was lust, and a deadly sin. The real love was a cultivation of the mind and heart, allowing an intimacy of getting to know each other without the interference of the excitement of the body.

But oh, what she had felt. Almost, almost she had relented, melted into his arms with all the compliance he wanted, resisted her parents and allowed him to be the leader, followed his plan.

There were tears of genuine remorse.

There were moments of real rebellion against her parents, times of longing to see his face, to be with him, and yet the invisible bond of *gehorsamkeit*—obedience—won her over.

Nothing else brought peace. Nothing seemed right. A blessing in the giving up of your own will, allowing God's will to take control. How to decipher between the two?

She navigated this river with her mother's expert hand on the tiller, avoiding dangerous currents and sand bars. Her map was the Bible, the words from her mouth a godly command.

And still Anna suffered.

Wayne drove him to the bank, where he emptied his savings, went to Duane's Used Cars, and bought a black Jeep. A two door. He paid eighteen thousand in cash, took his license from his pocket and put it to use.

He started drinking, smoked anything anyone offered him. He lost weight, became incessantly ill-humored, silent, withdrawn. His energy level reached maniacal proportions, his coworkers laughed, shook their heads. Crazy, they said.

What they didn't know about was the constant flow of uppers and downers infiltrating his system. There was marijuana, an array of prescription medication, far too much alcohol, and the intense need to rid himself of the skeletons that rattled in his conscience.

He always drove fast, recklessly, not caring whether he lived or died. After a year of erratic behavior, he became a concern even to his friends who lived as he did. They recognized the danger, that for him it wasn't simply wanting to party, to have a good time, but rather a slide into territory no one wanted to enter.

Eli and Rachel Stoltzfus were not stupid or uninformed. They knew the forces against their son. They knew, too, that he had no power to withstand the wiles of the devil, with all that determination to do what he wanted, at any cost.

They grew old, lost weight, their faces lined with care. They wept in church, sat with heads bowed. Rachel harbored a gigantic grudge against her husband, the way he would not take charge and rail against his son, set rules, and expect them to be obeyed.

Oh, it was hard. Terribly hard.

His brothers had an intervention and tried to get him the help he needed but were blown away by the fiery eyes and swift denial.

He came and went, entered the house silently, left it without a trace, with no words about where he was going or what he was doing.

Rachel prayed for God's hand to stage an end to Dave's madness. Anything, only spare his life if there is no repentance.

Eli went about his work in his quiet manner, showing no outward turmoil, but watered and nurtured his faith every day. He realized early on that God had a purpose in allowing all things to be on earth, whether it was good or whether it wasn't. God had given Dave this nature, had arranged the circumstances surrounding him, had allowed Anna and her parents into his life, so now the end result was in His Almighty power, and he could give his headstrong son into God's care.

"We see as through a glass darkly," was a verse of significance. We don't see the clear picture, only God does.

He knew his wife held the cup of bitterness against him, but there was nothing to do about that. No, he had not always done his duty, not in the conventional sense. She would not understand his beliefs about child rearing, she never had. All her mind-numbing words weren't the right thing to do either, so whatever.

Eli was a simple man, his faith as straightforward and unassuming as he was, thus sparing himself the days of fretting and arduous sleepless nights filled with the demons of anxiety.

Dave was in a bad way, yes, he was. But God knew the outcome, so he'd depend on Him, which would be a rewarding of his faith in due time.

Anna was baptized into the church, serene, quiet, obediently living to her parents' standards, a light of good example to the community. Kind and generous as she was beautiful, she hid away her deepest sorrow. Sometimes she thougt of Leon, unsure if she wanted to rekindle that Texas friendship.

Or had it merely been an attraction? Away from her parents' prying eyes, had she felt free to choose for herself?

She was never free to do that, she knew. Their choices were made in her best interests, she knew, so she gave up her life to her parents' wishes, with the assurance that it was the right thing.

Only at night, she wondered about Dave.

Talk was rampant, gossip dwelt on the worst of his actions, which justified Anna's parents' disapproval of him.

They spent a week at the lake in the Adirondacks of New York.

They rested, relaxed, shared feelings, swam and boated on the clear waters, slept well in the refreshing, dewy nights, rejuvenated, and retied family bonds.

Her mother walked with Anna on the trail around the lake, a good four miles. They talked, about Dave, Leon, everything.

Her mother appeared youthful, carefree, her face containing fragments of former beauty, like a rose that bloomed, but the petals beginning to curl and fade. She wore a sky-blue dress and no apron, a white *dichly* pinned to her head, her hair loose and wavy, so unlike the severity of her rolled hair at home on the farm.

She stopped and stared at Anna as she faced her.

"Anna, do you miss Dave?"

Spoken in kindness, it was Anna's undoing. She allowed the tears to fill her eyes, allowed them to spill over, but tried to suppress the sound of her sobs, like fabric being torn.

"Anna!"

Alarmed, her mother gripped her shoulders, her hands like two vises, turning her.

"Don't, Anna. Don't cry like that."

The flood of emotion was impossible to contain, as she sank to the floor of the forest, a fragile bird with a broken wing, an image that would be seared into the mother's conscience for years to come.

She lowered herself to Anna's side, a hand going to her back, a movement of her palm meant to console, to comfort. There was nothing to do but allow her space till she was spent.

An uncomfortable silence followed with neither one sure of the next step, like crossing a stream without knowing which rocks would stay solid, or which ones would tilt with disastrous results.

Finally, a small sigh broke the silence of the woods around them. "I do miss him, yes. But I'm not sure if it's him I miss, or the dream of having him for my boyfriend. My husband."

A sizeable branch fell from the height of a towering tree, rustling leaves and snapping twigs. Her mother's eyes found the branch as it came to rest on the bed of old leaves and rotting logs.

"Do you think for one minute he would have made a good husband?"

"For one minute" was the phrase that pushed the hot rebellion to Anna's lips.

"If he would have been given a decent chance? Yes, I do. He was never given that."

"You are wrong, Anna," her mother gasped. "Look at him. Denied one thing he wants and his reaction is life-threatening rebellion driven by Satan. And you know it."

The statement came with a sort of underlying horror, the defiance in Anna giving rise to the frightening thought that she would disobey even now, after all this time. The clashing of two minds like a broken mirror, allowing only fragments of their best selves.

"Anna?"

Her mother's voice was a plea to have goodwill restored. What had gone wrong? One moment there was genuine closeness, the next, a complete difference in the air.

It was David. It was always David.

Anna turned her face away. She lifted both knees and wrapped her arms around them.

"It's okay, Mom. I know you're right. Just sometimes I miss him so much I feel as if I'm grieving. Worse than that. He's still alive, somewhere not far away from me, and he may as well be on the other side of the world."

When she got to her feet, she walked slowly, her head bowed like an old woman, her feet shuffling, as if all the youth and vitality had been drained by the outburst of emotion. Her mother walked beside her, tightlipped and silent, justifying everything they had ever done to prevent Dave and Anna's courtship.

No good could have come of it, she reasoned for the thousandth time, the thought immediately followed by the sound of her daughter's despair. Could her love have made a difference?

"Have you never heard from Leon then?"

Anna acted as if she hadn't heard her mother, but fell behind a good hundred feet by the time they reached the house on the lake.

At the same time, Dave had come home from work, hollow-eyed from his weekend of abusing all manner of pills and alcohol.

His heart pounded in his thin chest as he slowly made his way upstairs to his room, where he flung himself facedown on his unmade bed, the sheets giving off a stale odor of perspiration and unwashed skin.

His mouth was dry, his head swollen and throbbing with the pain of dehydration and the searing sun.

One panicked thought after another chased themselves around in his head. Fragments of his life collided with images of his mother's anxious face, the voices of his brothers woven into tighter and tighter circles. His hands felt numb from slapping the nailer and dragging shingles, a job he found more and more difficult as he drove into the maelstrom of substance abuse.

He knew something had to give. He knew, too, he was on a treadmill that would never stop, and it was up to him to get off while he was still able.

He wanted Anna. Anna could help him. With that thought came the impossibly of it. He may as well be on the other side of the world. Anna existed only in his dreams, living inside his head and in his heart.

In the real world, she lived in a walled compound, heavy cement walls erected by her parents' rules. He snorted at the powerful image, his lips lifted in a sneer, which was followed by a long, drawn-out sob of weakness, then another, until his pillow was saturated by his tears.

Below, in the kitchen, his mother sighed as she put away his untouched plate, scraped the leftover mashed potatoes and gravy into the plastic *katza pennly* outside the back door. She straightened the curtain on the door, then slowly made her way back to the sink.

Oh, he was thin. Thin and hollow-eyed and creepy.

When she was alone she could let the truth wash over her, and she could bend her head with its large yellowing covering with the unclean strings that were pinned with a very small gold safety pin to keep them out of her way, and she could pray with another genuine plea for help.

Evidently, God had not yet answered her prayer, but He would in His time. She was exactly like the woman who kept begging and begging, in spite of all the odds against her. She knew, too, that she was awash in faults and shortcomings, but didn't God have mercy on sinners? Sure He did. And she prayed on.

She wiped countertops with one hand while she dug in her dress pocket for her wrinkled handkerchief. Her *schnuppy*. Kleenexes were a waste of money if you could carry a serviceable *schnuppy*.

She mopped at the copious amount of tears before replacing it, then cut herself another slice of blueberry cream pie, sat down heavily and began to eat, listening for any signs of life from the bedroom upstairs. She longed to enter her son's room, sit on the edge of his bed and ask a thousand questions, fixing his wounds with her motherly Band-Aids, but she knew she may as well be trying to soothe a wild animal at this point.

The pain was often unbearable, this burden of having failed her son. Remorse rode on the back of self-blame. It chafed her tired mind until she relieved it with dozens of questions to her husband, questions he could not answer. There was no rest, day or night, and it took its toll in aging Eli and Rachel far beyond their years.

That was the night that Dave couldn't sleep, strung out and coming down off his weekend of binge drinking and all that went with it. He was so tired he felt as if he was made of rubber, like one of those Gumby toys he used to play with in school.

He was thinking of leaving Lancaster, leaving the crowd of young men he ran with. He knew he was headed for disaster.

But where to go?

He needed a challenge, something to occupy his mind. Anything to get him away from here. He needed to forget Anna, start over somehow.

The West? Could he lose himself anywhere in the United States? And so his tortured mind turned gears, wondering, thinking. He picked up his phone, scrolled through his favorite sites, reading about vast areas that were still untamed, until his eyes burned with fatigue.

He fell into a troubled sleep knowing a certain small seed had been planted in his mind. The treadmill had not stopped, but it was slowing.

The moon arose on the still, hot night, and God saw the troubles of man the same as He had always done for thousands of years.

When Dave awoke, he headed straight for the bathroom, downing paper cup after paper cup of cold water. Then he leaned on the palms of his hands to peer into the mirror and gasped.

The image staring back at him was a skeletal version of his former self, dark, empty eyes that contained no feeling. Dave felt himself falling into a blackened abyss in which there was no return. Fear chased itself up and down his spine, and as his breathing quickened, he felt his legs go weak.

His heart thudded painfully in his chest, as wave after wave of fear and weakness washed over him. He found himself seated on the edge of the bathtub, his head in his hands, soaked in cold sweat, trembling as if he had seen the bottomless pit that was his own soul.

The realization that something had to be done was as startling as the image in the mirror, followed by a despair so deep he could not see his way out of it, ever. He wanted to die, was afraid to die, wanted away from himself and the awful creature he had become.

So much work to do, so little strength. Overwhelmed, he began to cry.

He went to work as usual, but spoke hardly a word to anyone, hiding his streaming red eyes and the fact that he mopped his face with his handkerchief repeatedly. His boss and coworkers were aware of his decline. They tried to talk to him from time to time but were blown away with a fierce denial, like steam from a boiler.

Today, however, was different. They watched warily, kept their mouths closed, stayed away from him, recognizing the turmoil on his face.

All that day, Dave's mind went around in circles. He was in a mess of his own making, and he knew it. Knew there was an insurmountable cliff ahead of him. Knew the first step was recognition.

No rehab for him. He hadn't been using that long. He could still turn things around on his own.

He had to get out of Lancaster. That was the only direction he could clearly relate to, knowing Anna was simply not possible.

Well, she was, he guessed, but on her parents' terms, with her morphing into that mother of hers by the month. She even had the same peculiar worry line between her eyes now.

No. Anna was gone. He would not spend the remainder of his life being subject to all manner of goodness, walking quietly, speaking with that holy reverence. Huh-uh. That was not him and they couldn't make him do it.

And so his thoughts spun, but now always centered on the one logical thought of leaving Lancaster. He just didn't know where he would go or how he would tell his parents without hurting them more than he already had. Likely it would be easier for them to have him gone than to have to watch him carry on the way he was now.

He went to the local library and came home with stacks of travel books. He wanted to lose himself and lose all contact with anyone who had ever known him. To test his own ability, become toughened, able, muscular, to experience new and terrible things. He felt the adrenaline course through his veins. The thought of adventure would win over the desperation to get away from all the heartache about Anna, the reason he'd wasted so much on alcohol and drugs.

To lose reality, to feel better.

Always, it was Anna and her parents. Everything was their fault.

He had done nothing wrong, he concluded. So he searched the travel books in the spirit of rebellion, without knowing where he would go or what he would do, lost to the knowledge of making any wrong choices.

He wanted what he wanted, and it was no one's business but his own.

All the books centered on the United States he laid aside. Not challenging. Well, Alaska, but he hated the cold.

More and more, he was drawn to Australia. He read everything he could find. He did the research on his phone and filled his head with images of wild and wonderful Australia.

It had everything from tropical forests to thousands of miles of beaches with gigantic waves, sharks, surfers, all of it. There was the Outback, that deserted area of grasslands and cattle stations. Huge. It was enormous.

He hid the books under his bed. Later his mother whacked around with the dust mop and knocked the whole stack out from under it. She picked one up, frowned, and shook her head. If it wasn't one thing it was another.

Now what was he doing? She shuffled through them, tired, resigned.

So he was thinking of going away. She squelched the instinct that would lead to panic, the sickening desperation of wanting to detain him bodily.

Hadn't she been through all of this before, even just leaving the house to go with his unruly buddies? Her mother's heart yearned to keep him from doing foolish things, to keep him from suffering even more than he already had with Anna.

Well, she supposed if he couldn't give in and do what Elias and Barbie wanted, then he'd have to do without her. Not that he'd ever been taught to give up by his father.

She resolved to speak to him again. Surely this would wake him up and shake him out of that easygoing bubble in which he lived.

If anyone could keep him here it was Eli, but nine chances out of ten he wouldn't say a word, merely plod on and accept it.

In frustration, she knocked a wooden plaque off the wall and watched as it fell onto the baseboard, knocking a hole in it. She bent to replace it and thought if he went away, she wouldn't have to clean his room, which was no sorrow. The boy had no sense of order or conscience, leaving those drawers open with his clothes hanging out like a pile of rags, hairbrushes, deodorant, receipts, keys, empty milk glasses, and dirty clothes all over the place. He hadn't been brought up this way. He just did what he wanted to do, with no thought for anyone else.

It likely never crossed his mind that he was creating more work for his mother. It's the way a lot of boys were. No wonder there were marriage problems. It was all about him.

And so Rachel worked, scrubbed the bathtub, shook the rugs, muttering to herself about the unfairness of life when a situation like this rendered her helpless. And she relied on her husband when they sat together to eat dinner, a hurried mishmash of leftovers with a side of reheated sausage gravy and congealed macaroni and cheese.

"What is this stuff?" Eli asked, lifted a forkful for closer inspection.

"Leftovers. Stuff."

Silence fell like a wet blanket.

"S'wrong with you?" Eli asked.

"David is going away."

"Well, that's a good thing."

"To Australia? New Zealand? Alaska?"

"He's not going there."

"Why would he have all those travel books under his bed? And you know he can find anything online. I bet you he's already looking into flight times."

"There you go again. You have no idea what he's doing. You're always a step ahead, expecting bad things to happen."

"At least I care. You don't do one thing about his life. That boy does exactly what he wants, and you would never open your mouth to talk to him."

"What would I say? You know he's in a bad way now. Maybe he needs to go to Australia or wherever you say he's going. Let him learn the hard way, then he'll have learned right."

"But if you'd try to make him give up, use discipline the way other parents do, he wouldn't need to go through this."

"Really, Rachel? You think? Well, I disagree. There is no giving up in that boy. None. He's determined to get what he wants, and Anna's the one thing he can't have, and it drives him crazy. He does anything to rebel, to act out, to get back at Elias and Barbie. How can I prevent that?"

"Talk to him."

Rachel's voice rose in desperation.

El shook his head. "About what?"

"About everything. About God and joining church and going to hell if he doesn't repent. His soul is hanging in the balance, you know it."

Eli shook his head and said very softly, "His soul is in God's hands, not ours."

CHAPTER 12

IN ANNA'S HOME, THERE WAS A UNITED FRONT. WITH ARMS AND HEARTS entwined, they faced the future as one. Delving into meaningful daily devotions, they absorbed the Word of God like a thirsty sponge, swelled and watered by the assurance of Christ's love and His power when parents worked together seamlessly.

For if they stood on the solid rock of Christ, what could go wrong?

Their cup of joy was filled, and both parents knew why, although one would not admit to the other that the fueling of this rejoicing was the disappearance of David. They shook their heads in pious sorrow when gossip reached their ears, knelt by their bed and prayed in unison for his soul, but the realization that he would never marry Anna was an achieved victory. A triumph of spiritual battle.

Anna took a job teaching mentally handicapped children. The school board members were in awe of her and her uncanny abilities with these little ones. She was gifted, knowing instinctively what they needed, when, and how.

A letter arrived from Leon Beiler.

True to his word, he had never forgotten their time together but had decided to give her space and plenty of time to make the right decision. His handwriting was precise, his prose well-educated, a letter that did not seem to be written by an Amish boy with an eighth-grade education.

She read and reread the words, held the letter to her heart, remembered his touch and the feel of his dry lips on the back of her hand.

She wrote back on blue-flowered stationery, wrote in kind, accepting words that thrilled his heart, bringing a smile to his face.

Dave did his research well, reading every article he could find, filling his head with images of Australia.

This was the land he set out to conquer. He'd lose himself in the wilds of this diverse land, test the limits of his own strength and see how fearless he really was. His interest was mostly taken by cattle stations. It was like the West times ten, or a hundred. Vast areas with so many cattle that they hired dozens of drifters, toughened men who were the characters he would become. He felt the dust from the dry land churned up by thousands of cattle, the pull of the horse's mouth on the reins, visualized a himself in a genuine cowboy hat. Every western movie he had ever watched grew larger and more romantic in his mind as he thought of the open range.

He talked to Wayne and was met with openmouthed disbelief. "You can't do that."

"Sure I can."

"What about . . . well, you know, your mom and dad?"

"What about them?"

"They're gonna have a fit."

Wayne shook his head and could hardly see how Dave could do this to his family.

"Dad doesn't care. Well, he cares, but not that much."

Wayne swiveled in his seat and faced his friend with the honesty that is only between true friends.

"What about your mom?"

Dave's eyes fell. He rubbed the palms of his hands across his knees, picked up a pair of sunglasses, put them back.

"She'll get over it."

They were sitting in Wayne's car, watching the crowd of youth at the ballpark in Intercourse. It was a hot, humid evening, but one that held the promise of fall, the way the leaves hung limp and old, waiting to be changed into the glory of color.

"So do you know about Australia? You know, this is just crazy. You can't do this. Why not Montana or Wyoming? You have to have a passport. I bet you didn't even think of all that stuff, did you?"

"Course I did."

But he had not. It had never crossed his mind. Well, he had his birth certificate, his driver's license, his Social Security card, so how hard could it be?

Dave got out of the car, putting an end to the conversation. Wayne's disapproval only egged him on.

His parents' response to his well-laid plans did not go well, with his mother alternating between tears and pleading. His father, as usual, said very little, only warned him of the danger of being alone in the world.

"You need to be smart, alert, and above all, don't be too proud to ask advice or direction."

His mother broke in with a wail.

"Now you're giving your consent, Eli? You may as well be telling him it's all right for him to go, when you know it isn't."

His father took up where she left off, assured Dave that he was doing something of which neither one approved. To do something so alien to all he had been taught was being disobedient to his parents and to God.

"This is hard for your mother and I, Dave. Won't you be able to find it in your heart to reconsider?"

Tremulous words from her husband set Rachel to sobbing and Dave to squirming uncomfortably in the old kitchen chair. But there was no giving up, no change of plans. His father recognized this in the set of his son's jaw, the light in his eyes, and the way he leaned forward and twitched his shoulders. He was like a horse tethered to a hitching rack, pawing the gravel till he dug a sizable hole.

Eli recognized the inevitable. There was nothing to do, but he spoke to appease his sobbing wife.

The brothers came, their wives pale with nerves and concern. They talked him out of it, or so they thought, and went home glad to be of help to the incompetent parents.

Dave realized there was no support, no good wishes, but he plowed through the mess of feelings and warnings like a well-ruddered boat through choppy waters. Australia was a destination, a homing in on an adventure of a lifetime.

He sold his Jeep, took a small loss, but was satisfied. He bought luggage, boots, clothes, whatever he would need in arid conditions or wet and cold.

He had narrowed down the research to a place the Australians called the Kimberly, the northwestern hump of the loneliest state.

His book on the region said it remained a sort of frontier. A frontier meant pushing into unexplored regions, which sent a thrill straight down his spine, tingling even his hands and feet. There had been a terrific conflict that dragged on for years in the late 1800s, when cattle kings burst into the region and tried to take the land from the Aboriginal people.

That was huge. Dave's eyes sparked with passion.

Man, he thought, wasn't that something? Those people were black and likely still not too crazy about the white people settling their land. He imagined real western life, but instead of Indians, there were the Aboriginal people.

Dotted with cattle stations, it was a land so vast you simply couldn't believe the aerial photograph.

So the country had been a British colony, which meant cars would drive on the left side of the road, and they'd all drink tea and speak with a British accent. That was cool.

The queen of England was queen to Australia, although she had little power in the government. The whole government deal seemed safe and ordinary, same as the United States, so he knew there were no weird rebel groups who would form an uprising and take visitors hostage the way they would in some countries. He hoped the Aboriginal people were peaceful, though.

Well, the worst of it was behind him—the telling of his plans to his family. It had not gone well, but then, he hadn't expected anything else. Really, to get what he wanted was a lesson in setting your eyes on a goal and plowing through. It was relatively easy.

He obtained his passport in less than three weeks, then set about booking his flight. Qantas was Australia's flagship carrier, meaning he could book a decent flight from New York City.

It was all done online with his Visa card, lying on his bed in the upstairs of the farmhouse in the middle of Amish country, the world at his fingertips via his cell phone. It was the coolest thing, he thought again, this seamless way of obtaining information.

He was set. He had to be in New York at John F. Kennedy International airport on October 2 at three fifteen in the afternoon. He'd ask Wayne to drive him to New York. He was pretty smart, could find his way around Baltimore and Philadelphia without too much trouble, looking for stadiums.

Luggage ready, flight booked, parents told, research done. He felt ready, fully informed, prepared to be a man in an unfamiliar world. He was physically fit, or getting better, since he'd sworn off the "bad stuff," as he called it now.

It wasn't easy, none of it. Not the night sweats or the hallucinations, the unbearable headaches and the shivering, being icy cold then burning up.

Still wasn't easy, but he'd done it. He had something else to replace the vacuum that had been the loss of Anna.

It still rankled, though. The loss rode on his mind like a burn, the inability to forgive raked across his soul, causing a quick temper, often a sour disposition, leaving him puzzled.

None of it was his own fault, either. That family simply didn't get it, that not everyone would fold up like an accordion the minute they expected it.

Even with all his plans for the adventure of a lifetime, he was often depressed, melancholic, as if a dark cloud arrived out of nowhere and dumped a ton of water on him. Well, not a ton, but enough to make him miserable.

His mother spoke to him about carrying a grudge, noticing the dark unhappiness in his face.

"Forgive, Dave. Nothing else will bring you happiness. You could have bent to their rules, so don't leave us with that burden on your back. I'm afraid you're trying to fill the space with Australia, the space that should be Christ's redeeming blood."

Dave left his mother standing in the kitchen watching him, bereft of a quick reply. He just couldn't think of anything to say, partly on account of her words being soaked with truth.

But that was the thing about being Amish that irked him most. You could have God with you without joining the church. Look at the billions of English people with hundreds of different ways of following God. They didn't have to dress a certain way or drive a horse and buggy. So what was the use? His own justification rang in his ears, even as the Spirit tugged at his heart to remind him of all he had been taught through the years, which wasn't much. But he could not deny knowing he was expected to honor the heritage of his forefathers, to remain in the faith he had been taught by his parents.

He knew right from wrong, deep down, no matter how hard he tried to explain it away. But wasn't it prideful to think only the Amish knew the right way of living? He was so used to justifying his own actions in his head that it had become second nature.

On the night before his departure, his father and mother both tried their best to be brave, to enjoy a good home-cooked meal together without the unsettling presence of arguments. Fried chicken, mashed potatoes and filling, lima beans from a late planting, with cherry pie and ice cream, two of Dave's favorite foods.

"So you're leaving in the morning?" his father asked.

"Yep. Eight o'clock."

Their eyes met, one with the light of anticipation, one with the muddled sadness of resignation.

"So you're not changing your mind?"

"Nope. Hey, stop acting like it's my funeral. You give me the shivers. I'll be back."

"I just wish you weren't going alone," his mother said.

"I can take care of myself."

"But where you're going, Dave. It is literally the bottom of the world."

"That's all right. I can't wait to see what it's like."

"Darwin? That's the city, right?" his father asked.

"Yeah. It's northwestern Australia. The last frontier."

Eli nodded, smiled ruefully.

"I hope you know what you're getting into."

"I do. Fully prepared. Bring it on!" He laughed, feeling lighter than he had in ages. This was going to be the adventure of a lifetime.

"Just be careful, Dave. Be very careful. Take God with you. Remember to pray. Mam put a Bible in your luggage. Take it out and read it whenever you feel you should. It's a good practice."

Dave nodded, but he hardly heard his father. Tomorrow couldn't come soon enough. He could hardly wait to be on the plane, away from the sad eyes of his parents, their meaningless warnings and advice. Why was his dad suddenly so intent on preaching at him? Probably Mam was badgering him again. Whatever, neither of them had any idea what was best for him at this stage in his life. They didn't know the half of what he'd gotten into over the last many months, and he intended to keep it that way. But if they did, surely they'd be glad he was making a clean break, a fresh start.

Leon Beiler came to visit Anna on a Friday evening, with her parents' consent. She was dressed in a lovely rose color, the pink in her porcelain cheeks heightened by the matching hue in her dress, her eyes like blue jewels. She ran up and down the stairs, ironed covering strings, grabbed her mother's cologne, laughed and twirled and sang.

Her parents smiled at one another, their approval making this an evening to remember. Their discipline had all been worth it, every heartache, every argument, every prayer. Here was real love, the kind they had always sought for their daughter.

Leon Beiler impressed them at first sight. His physical appearance was more than pleasing, but his quiet spirit was like a magnet to both of them.

They homed in, the way Anna knew they would, seating him at the kitchen table, serving coffee, noticing his manners and gentle confidence in the way he thanked them, smiled, answered their questions with ease.

Her mother took notice of his shirt, the way he wore his trousers, his choice of shoes. Very impressive. And when he launched into an account of his life as a counselor, her mother had entered effortlessly into openmouthed worship, her eyes limpid with approval.

Her father smiled widely, asking too many questions, which Leon didn't seem to mind in the least.

Her mother served mini tacos and dip, homemade pita chips, and a vegetable tray with hummus. She poured tall glasses of ginger ale and pineapple juice.

Anna seemed to hover on the perimeters of the kitchen table, smiling when a smile was expected, giving the right answer to a question. Relieved to have her parents' approval at long last, she willingly took second place and waited till she and Leon were finally alone.

They moved to the couch in the living room, in the soft glow of an antique kerosene lamp and two jar candles. He was seated so close she could smell his cologne, a heady mixture of spice and musk.

He turned to her.

"You are even more beautiful than I remembered."

She blushed, lowered her eyes.

"Thank you."

"Words can't describe my feelings. I want to hold you, kiss your lovely mouth, but I know what is required, so I'll do it, Anna. I'd do anything, absolutely anything in my power to have you, to hold you. I don't know if I'll ever be the same."

Anna lifted her eyes to his, allowed her love for him to radiate from the warm light.

He caught her hands, then let them go.

They talked till eleven o'clock, when the driver from his hometown came to pick him up. She was not disappointed in him, and he was lifted to heights of love he hadn't known existed. He asked her for a date the following weekend, which she accepted with gladness, reveling in her parents' love and approval.

Everything had all turned out well, just simply everything.

Until she thought of David. She knew he was going to Australia and agonized at the thought of getting him to change his mind, afraid he'd fall apart completely there. She knew him so well, understood the way he thought, the way he needed something in his life to present an almost impossible challenge. She wasn't surprised he was going, but still she wished she could find a way to help him before he left.

She could understand this veering off the beaten path. The path that held thousands, millions of Plain people from the Reformation until the modern day, all upholding the same spiritual views, the same honor to their heritage. Or nearly the same. Some drove vehicles, some drove horses and buggies, some were assured of their salvation, others only hoped they were saved. All longed for the same heaven, worshipped the same God.

David had stopped, assessed their church's requirements, and decided he could not scale the heights of the required *oof-gevva-heit*. Too high, too low, too hard.

His love for her was genuine, in his own selfish way.

Had it been real love?

Only God could answer that, only God knew the state of his soul. That was why she sat silent when her mother went on and on about the dangerous path he was on. He was, by all outward appearances, a mess. But who was to say that God had not given him this strong nature, and set about devising a plan to redeem him from himself, harnessed by the wiles of the devil?

And so even in parting, in being torn apart, she took up for her beloved man who occupied a space in her heart forever. She would never assume otherwise, never want him to leave. He was a part of her, like her own heart's beating, the pulse at her wrist ticking.

But he was gone.

And how did one go about picking up the pieces, even with the aid of one Leon Belier, the long-sought-after suitor her parents had prayed for?

Was it possible to love wholly, to love in the way that was expected of her, keeping all the holy promises with a pure heart if David, or the essence of him, stayed with her?

She would set her eyes on the goal, obey her parents, and do what they asked of her. She would expect the blessing of love for Leon, and his love for her. Even as she answered her own questions, she wondered if David had already begun his journey to the base of the earth.

He had.

After a hurried goodbye to his parents, a manly handshake for his father, an almost hug for his mother, he and Wayne were off in a spray of gravel and onto the macadam, where they picked up speed as they headed north to the airport.

He grinned, pumped his fist, rolled down the window, and howled like a wolf. He felt as if he could conquer anything, and he wanted to take on the world.

Gone were the restrictions, the folks with noses in the air looking down at him, spreading gossip, half of it lies. He was bursting out of the suffocating world of being Amish, away from everything that had ever held him back, and it was as exhilarating as he had imagined.

They talked all the way, passed cars on the interstate going at least ninety miles an hour, groaned, slowed and pulled off when the flashing blue lights and the imminent noise of the state troopers siren reached their ears.

"Aw, shoot," Wayne said softly.

Taught to be respectful, Wayne had no problem producing the required documents—license, insurance, registration. He was let off with a stiff warning, their mood dampened. They traveled the remainder of the way in a subdued mood, until they reached the outskirts of New York City.

Dave simply swiveled and rocked, twisted in his seat, exclaimed and panted and gasped, like a child at a carnival. This was all too much to take in at once.

The airport itself was a scene he would never tire of, the vast area with cars, trucks, miles of tarmac, towers, glass buildings that seemed as if they could not be real, the gigantic airliners taking off like steel birds that spewed gray exhaust fumes, climbing higher and higher into the sky until only a speck remained.

They parked, walked into the terminal, found the Qantas desk, and got down to business. Wayne watched his friend handle everything with authority, self-confidence sprouting all over him, making the girl at the desk smile in spite of herself. When he turned to walk over to him, he was jaunty, rocking from heel to toe, his face alight with the exhilaration of being on his own.

He flopped into the chair beside Wayne, the early afternoon light illuminating his face as it spilled through the huge panes of glass. For one moment, the truth hit Wayne.

He might never see Dave again. Who but Dave could experience this with absolutely no fear or foreboding? If he loved the Australian way of life, there was always the possibility of having him gone forever.

His luggage taken, they went to find something to eat, which was a true hassle, with long lines and outrageous prices. But Dave was undeterred, plowed through the crowd with his shoulders, plenty of charismatic "excuse mes" and "sorrys," patting shoulders, elbowing strangers till they found themselves finally seated in a room the size of a tennis court.

A burger with fries was sixteen dollars, a coke another four, but Dave never batted an eye. He ordered what he wanted and downed it in four bites, left a ten dollar tip, and winked at the waitress.

"I'm going to grow a beard," he told Wayne. "Moustache too."

Wayne shook his head.

"I'll never cut my hair, either. Just put it in a ponytail."

"You're serious?"

"Course I'm serious. I can do anything I want. Who's going to correct me? My mother? She'll never know one thing I do or don't do."

Wayne fell silent.

Dave kept watching the clock, repeatedly taking out his cell phone to check the time, his shoulders twitching. He drummed his fingertips on the tabletop, tapped his feet.

Wayne realized he barely heard his questions, being so engrossed in getting on that plane. In his mind, he had already boarded and was off to the place he'd cultivated, hashed and rehashed in his quick mind, until he could think of nothing else.

Suddenly, "Go with me."

Wayne stiffened, stared. "Why?"

"I dunno. Company, maybe."

"You sure you want to pull this off?"

"Why not? I have nothing to lose."

"Sure you do."

"What?"

Wayne shrugged, looked sheepish. Who was he to judge? "I just wish you'd change your mind."

"Yeah, well. I won't."

"I'll miss you."

"That's good."

"Lots of others will miss you, too. Your buddies. The girls."

Dave grinned, "Not very many of them."

"No, probably not."

They parted with plenty of handshakes and backslapping, promises to see each other again.

But when Dave walked away to go through the security line, a lone figure dressed in the way of everyone else around him, Wayne could not swallow the lump in his throat, or blink away the image of

Dave being swallowed by the world, his head held high, his shoulders squared.

He had been a small schoolboy with a straw hat pushed to the back of his head, with Anna beside him, the light of excitement in his eyes even then, showing her the amazing webbed feet of a tiny duckling, explaining the way the duck's feet helped them swim.

And she always believed him.

When Wayne reached his car, he backed out of the parking space with a sense of impending doom. He had to shake this off, he thought.

No use getting all soft and mushy about Dave. He'd be all right. Yeah, it was too bad about him and Anna, but it happened all the time. He'd get over it.

He parked his car and waited till the Qantas airliner took off, thrilled to the sound and the smoke from the burning fuel, watching as it climbed higher and higher into the sky, before he realized his nose was burning and tears were in his eyes.

He got out his handkerchief and mopped at them, but could barely see to drive for the next couple of miles.

He'd miss him.

He thought of getting rid of his vehicle, asking Sally Ann for a date, settling down. Life in a horse and buggy didn't look all that bad. At least it was safe, and made his mom smile.

CHAPTER 13

THE FIRST SURPRISE WAS THE FACT THAT THE INTERIOR OF AN AIRPLANE wasn't close to anything he'd imagined. Narrow aisles, narrow seats, crying babies and their short-tempered mothers, loud businessmen in ties and button-down shirts.

He found himself seated beside a fellow of medium height with sandy hair and blue eyes, dressed in a vivid orange T-shirt and jeans. He faced Dave and mumbled something Dave couldn't quite make out, but he didn't seem to be looking for a response, so Dave let it go.

He jumped when a voice came out of the intercom system, watched the stewardess hold up a seat belt, smelled something that reminded him of Ritz crackers and cheese.

He had always imagined being seated by a window and realized with a vague sense of annoyance that he should have taken the time to select a seat when he booked the ticket. He had done it all on his cell phone, rushing through the screens as quickly as possible once he had made up his mind to do it. At the time, he didn't think he cared what seat he'd be on; the important thing was just that he was going. Now, he was frustrated that he couldn't look out the window without leaning awkwardly in front of the man next to him.

He got out his phone, his go-to escape whenever he felt uncomfortable, drew up his bank account and followed his transactions.

Not too bad. The plane ticket had set him back a little over a thousand, which was almost laughable. It was cheap. Seriously. Amish people paid those fifteen-passenger van drivers a thousand dollars to travel a thousand miles, and he was going ten times that far for the same amount of money.

The voice on the intercom said to turn off all devices, so he obeyed, left with nothing to do but wait for takeoff.

The first stop was Los Angeles.

L.A. The real world where movie stars, directors, producers, extremely wealthy people lived and worked in huge mansions and studios. Hollywood.

Likely, he wouldn't see much, but he could add that to his growing list of experiences. His feet had touched California soil, or concrete, whatever. He was becoming a seasoned traveler, a man of the world, freed forever from the restrictions that bound him to the world of farms, narrow country roads with narrow-minded people driving their plodding horses along the same thoroughfares over and over until there was a groove hacked into the middle of good township roads.

Nope, that life was not for him. No one fully understood him. Not his family, and certainly not Elias and Barbie Fisher. Maybe Anna. But she had done no better, trying to get him to join the church for her parents' benefit. That's all it was.

There was too much to see in too little time. He entered the terminal in Los Angeles with his head swiveling in every direction, his eyes taking in every sight, sound, scent, unable to store information fast enough. It was a short layover, and he became so engrossed in people watching he almost missed his flight to the next leg of his journey. He ran as much as he could, side-stepped, apologized, shouldered his way through, listened to the voice repeating the call for his flight, threw himself into a seat, by the window this time, and grinned to himself. Now that was excitement.

He looked up to find a large middle-aged woman in a very purple pantsuit stop, arch one eyebrow, and ask if he minded if she sat here, that she couldn't take that kid two seats back.

Instinctively, Dave tucked himself to the left, allowing more room, but nodded, "Sure, sit down."

The entire right side was crammed with purple polyester, dark arms, and a huge head of black, kinky hair. She was quite beautiful, Dave decided, when she turned her head to face him and introduce herself.

"Delia Berns."

She extended a dark hand with fiery red nails, a trail of rings and bracelets. Dave shook it, his own pale hand appearing ghostly and bloodless beside the finery of her jewelry, and introduced himself.

"Now, Dave, we are going to get along. S'why I stopped here. You have a look about you. A good look. I can tell. Ain't much wrong with you."

A deep chuckle shook the mound of purple.

"Now don't you go thinking I'm too big for these seats."

She lowered her eyelids, lifted her chin.

"It ain't me that's the problem. It be these seats. Made for skinny people."

She dug in her purse for a Kleenex to wipe the corners of her eyes.

"Hoo-ee. No, whoever designed these seats didn't have big girls in mind, let me tell you, honey."

Dave couldn't help laughing, and when she saw this, she began all over again. Wave after wave of joyous mirth welled out of her, like a tide of happiness that couldn't be stopped.

"So where you off to?"

"If I tell you, you'll say I'm crazy."

"Try me."

"I'm going to Australia."

"Ain't nothing wrong with that. Where you from, honey?"

"Lancaster, Pennsylvania."

"Heard of it. You Amish?"

"Used to be."

"What? You mean you used to be but you ain't now? Ain't no such thing. We are born to be who we are."

"People change religions all the time."

"Make no mistake, Mistuh Dave. We can be whoever we want to be. But that upbringing, that culture of yours, it'll define you, whether you want it to or not. We are labeled the day we come yelling into this old world."

"I disagree."

"Well, that's all right. You got that right to disagree all you want. But wearin' that there little straw hat and going about your little farm life, being taught right from wrong in that there super conservative way is never gonna leave you. Never. No, no, baby."

She shook her head, the hair like a second skin. She smelled like flowers and some other heady scent.

"When I'm in Australia I'll be English. No one knows about my people there. So I'll just blend in."

She nodded.

"And well you may. But in that there heart? You Amish."

Dave squirmed uncomfortably, wishing she'd sit elsewhere. He had no answer, so he got out his phone, turned it on, pretended to have important business. Phones were like that, handy in so many ways. You could simply step away from a situation, turn people off, and enter whatever world you chose, easily.

"Uh-uh. No, you don't. Turn that thing off. We having us a conversation. Don't you know how rude that is?"

Embarrassed, Dave pocketed the device, glanced at her sideways.

"I bet you got a momma cryin' her heart out this minute. You a good boy, but you doin' what your momma don't want you to. Let me tell you about mine, a'right?"

Dave nodded.

"I got four boys. Good boys, every one. Good jobs, keep themselves in line, but it was struggle a hundred percent of the time. One of 'em, oh, did I tell you they daddy skipped? Ran off with the bartender. So I was a *single* mom."

She put all emphasis on *single*.

"By myself, with no education, except high school. It's a long story, but one of my boys is dead. Shot through the back by drug dealers. He was one himself. Running. He was running away. Now, I don't know if he had time to beg our Lord for mercy, but I can only beg for him now. He was fifteen. Too young, Lord, too young."

She dug another Kleenex out of her immense bag.

"I woulda died of grief myself, except for my own momma and my faith. God had a reason. That boy always did what he wanted, no one could tell him anything. Never worked much, never kept his promises, lied a blue streak. I could have gotten it out of him if he'd lived."

She paused, fastened her dark eyes on Dave.

"Now, when you get to Australia, you step on that land, sniff a couple times, and you turn yourself right around and get back home. There ain't one thing on the face of this earth gonna be good for you in Australia. That ain't where you belong. You belong with your momma and daddy, praising God in the church you were born into."

Dave flashed her a look.

"And don't look at me like that. I'm telling you the gospel truth. My boys wanted to go here, go there. I told 'em, no, you staying right here with your momma. They all I got. They ain't going nowhere. And they didn't. They have good jobs, working for the city of Los Angeles, all three of them. Good boys. Two of them married. No grandbabies yet. They are the light of my life."

Dave was irritated, mumbled, "Good for you."

"Don't give me no sarcasm, honey. It don't ride well with me, you need to get your priorities straight."

She launched immediately into an account that sounded too much like Dan Zook, the Amish minister.

"First of all, you do what your parents want. You honor them, respect them, listen to what they say. If you don't have a daddy, then you listen to your momma. That's the first one."

Dave lowered his head, got out his phone.

Over came the bejeweled hand, took it away, kept it this time.

"No, you don't. Remember I have three sons. They try this a hundred times. Doesn't work."

"The second priority? Work hard, save money, never lie, keep your word. Love the Lord and go to church."

"I can go to church in Australia."

She gave a snort, a deep one from the depth of that massive chest.

"And who's going to see that you do? Your momma ain't there. You get into that place, you ain't going nowhere to church. But mind you, honey, God will find you. He'll know where you are and what you'll be doing every second of every day. You can get away from whatever you don't like in Lancaster, but you can't get away from God. And if He look down on this Amish boy who don't belong there, He send you straight back. You in God's hands, honey."

Dave had never been quite as relieved to part ways with another person as he was when they finally touched down in Honolulu.

Suffocated by a massive hug that lasted too long, he couldn't help but inhale the flowery scent of the purple fabric. She promised to keep him on her prayer list and insisted on exchanging phone numbers before she moved off, making her way through the crowd.

She turned to wave, and Dave waved back and thought how his conscience would always be colored in purple—with jewelry.

He sat for a sober hour, wondering how things would have turned out had his own mother spoken to him like that. The thing was, his parents didn't really know what was right for him, did they? Sometimes they said one thing, sometimes quite another. They seldom agreed with each other. Now that he had a little distance from them, he could see clearly what a mess they were.

It was a relief to place the blame for his disappointments and failings on them rather than to dwell on Delia's words, which seemed to peg him squarely as the villain in his own life.

He was here now, in Hawaii for a few hours, so there was no sense sitting here wasting time worrying about things he couldn't change.

It was nighttime, but with all the lights you could hardly tell. He wondered how far from the ocean he was, so he walked until he found a sign that led to an outside deck, nodded to a few people who watched him through bleary eyes, crosshatched with fatigue.

He sat on a bench, took a deep breath, lifted his head to find the stars, caught the scent of hot tarmac, rotting vegetation with a briny, salty undertone. The air was warm and soft and immediately he felt his tense muscles relaxing. He wished he could stay a week, a month, watch the surfers. He'd seen some amazing photos online.

He stood alone, contemplating the vast, untold length of ocean the plane would be crossing. Onward, ho, he thought wryly, but felt a wrench in his stomach. Perhaps he should stay in the States, forget about going off to Australia, the way that stretch of the Pacific Ocean raised itself in his stomach.

He wasn't frightened, really, he reasoned. Only excited. He had too much time to stand here and contemplate the thousands of miles of open water. He longed for Wayne, anyone, to be with him to distract him from his own thoughts.

He paced, took deep steadying breaths, sniffed the air around him appreciatively. The sullen night brooded around him. With no one to share his last hours on American soil, he felt isolated.

He breathed again, deeply, realized he was close to tears, and blamed Delia for stirring all this up. He felt the doubts churning in his mind, his resolve weakened.

Ah, come on. The chance of a lifetime, and he was going to take it. Man up, he told himself, and got up from his seat, went to find something to eat, wished he could be here when the sun came up. There were lots of weary-looking people in flowered shirts and shorts, women wearing straw hats and a sunburn, likely going home after a vacation. A vacation was unheard of in his family. On the farm, it was all work, from season to season, the only disruptions being farm sales, horse sales, reunions in summer, Christmas dinners in winter. And those were all dull, boring events with dull, boring people. Amish people. Simple folks who didn't know any better.

He sat at a small round table, blinked, stared, blinked again, as if to clean his sight. No way, you mean Amish girls at an airport in

Hawaii? What? Four of them. Before he knew what he was doing, he'd almost upset the small table in his haste to make his way to them and introduce himself.

"Hey, how's it going?" he called out.

Startled, the girls stopped, appraised this overeager young man.

Dave stuck out a hand.

"Hi. I'm Dave Stoltzfus, from Lancaster."

They all smiled, relaxed, shook hands, and made introductions. Hannah Beiler, Sadie Miller, Barbie Esh, and Rose Kauffman. Three of them looked to be about his age, Rose was clearly a bit younger. Turns out they had saved up money for months to see Hawaii and opted to fly instead of taking the recommended cruise.

Dave couldn't talk fast enough, ask enough questions.

Were they allowed to fly?

No, but they went anyway.

Dave felt a connection to these girls and their sense of adventure, admired them for stepping out and experiencing life. He told his story.

Sadie was the main speaker, the other girls holding back. All of them were dark-haired, cousins, they said. He laughed, told them everyone was a cousin to someone in Lancaster County.

He noticed that Rose said nothing at all, merely hung on the fringes of the conversation, her dark eyes giving away nothing. She was tall, slim, in a green dress that set off the olive tones of her skin.

But he talked to Anna, Hannah, and the gregarious Barbie.

"You shouldn't skip Hawaii," Barbie bubbled. "It is the greatest place on earth. We're making this a once-in-a-lifetime experience, and we'll never forget it."

Everyone agreed, except Rose, who fastened her dark eyes on him and never said a word. It was unsettling the way she didn't say anything. He had a notion to ask her if she couldn't talk, but found those eyes to be a bit of a reproach, as if he was too talkative, too dumb to know that he shouldn't be going where he was.

"So now we're on our way home," Barbie concluded.

Dave shook his head. "I can't believe you all took a plane. Completely disobedient."

"I know, I know. We'll have to face the consequences, no doubt. Flying is *verboten* except for in emergencies. It wasn't exactly an emergency for us to go to Hawaii."

Was that a small smile on Rose's face?

Dave found himself taking in the contour of her cheekbones, the way her nose had a hook in it, but only a slight one, full lips, dark eyes that absorbed things but never let any of it go.

When he saw they were eyeing the flight schedules, he felt an overwhelming urge to draw Rose out, to get her to say something.

Anything.

He addressed her directly. "Rose is your name, right? Rosetta? Rosanne? Roseanna?"

"Just Rose."

A low voice, quiet, but clear, self-assured.

When they walked way, he watched them go. Rose fell behind, and turned.

His heart thudded in his chest. Slowly, he lifted a hand, his eyes on her dark ones. He smiled. He could never be sure if she smiled back, but he knew she lifted her hand and waved only slightly.

CHAPTER 14

Leon Beiler became a regular weekend visitor in the Elias Fisher home, traveling from his home in Millerstown to Lancaster by van, the usual route that left every Saturday afternoon and returned Sunday night. His life had indeed taken on an array of brilliant new colors, a vivid display of happiness, fueled by the fact that he had finally found the girl of his dreams. It was an unbelievable bit of good fortune, the Lord smiling down on him and blessing him with her presence.

They enjoyed the full impact of parental approval. He bonded easily with every one of her sisters, made his way to the top rank of their adoration. He learned to appreciate the finer things in life, the way they dressed, the décor and furniture in the fine house, the food they served.

Here was a gracious home, one in good taste, the children taught to speak quietly and only when necessary in the presence of strangers.

It was hard to imagine taking Anna to his home, but he knew it was inevitable, the meeting of his parents, the siblings noisy and so very active, the house too small and poorly furnished, the father absent, or if he was present, sullen and withdrawn.

Sometimes, when they were alone, he felt she was not with him in spirit, the way she absentmindedly replied, "Hmm?" when he'd asked her a perfectly clear question. He knew her mind was far away.

"You seem distracted, Anna."

Immediately, she corrected her mistake, apologized, yawned, said she must be sleepy, then did her best to make up for her glitch in manners. When this became more and more frequent, he felt her slipping out of his grasp, and gathered his courage to ask her about it.

"I'm only assuming, perhaps, but do you feel as if you aren't fully happy in our friendship?"

He feared the answer, but knew he must ask.

"No, no. I mean yes. Of course I'm happy. More than happy."

"All right. Good. I was just afraid you were thinking about your former boyfriend again. This David, or Dave Stoltzfus. You said he left for, is it Australia?"

"Yes, he did leave, in fact. My mother found out when she met Rachel at the dry-goods store. It's very hard for his parents."

He saw the color spread across her face, the brushstroke of pink.

"Was it. . . . Is it hard for you?"

"No. No, not at all."

"You're sure?"

"Of course."

Her eyes were downcast, refusing to meet his, her hands twisting a Kleenex on her lap, her foot swinging from one knee crossed over her other.

"Look at me, Anna."

She obeyed.

"Do you ever think of him in the way you used to?"

"No. Well, no. Not very often. I mean . . ."

Floundering, she raised agonized eyes to his.

"You do."

"No, I don't. Not in the way I used to. We had a long friendship, Leon. Long. We were friends as children. More than friends. We shared our whole life, had the same interests. It's just . . ."

She lowered her head.

Leon couldn't help but think of a graceful swan, the way she bent from the shoulders. She was exquisite, simply too beautiful, too cultured for him. Doubt and despair crowded his ability to speak.

She took a deep breath and continued.

"I can't throw away what we had so soon. What causes me more misery than anything else is the unanswered question of why he turned out the way he did. How much of it is my parents' fault, and did I do the right thing? If we hadn't had that ultimatum of joining the church before he was ready, would he have changed?"

For a long moment, Leon did not speak. With a counselor's trained mind, he picked up that she was, in fact, still living in the past, tormented by a lost love, unraveling the bond of obedience to her parents by wondering, thinking, hoping.

"I do love you, Leon. I do. You'll just have to forgive me if I drift into the past."

"Anna, I'm not enough, am I? If I was, these thoughts would be erased."

"No, no, you are everything I want in a man. Generous, kind, you are everything Dave wasn't. He was so self-centered. As my mother repeatedly told me, very poor husband material. I know that. But . . ."

Gently, Leon asked, "But what?"

"But he was Dave, being who he was, and that's the man I fell in love with. I would have given my life, except I could not go against my parents' wishes."

"So I'm the approved edition, and you're only dating me to win their love."

"No. Please don't say that. You are perfect for me, in every way. It's just going to take time till Dave is completely out of my system."

"I don't want to share you with him, Anna."

"You aren't. I mean, you won't."

There was a long silence, both of them lost in their own internal stuggles. Finally, he spoke again, his voice quiet, almost shaking.

"Tell me, Anna, if Dave came back today and said he was ready to join the church, would you choose him over me?"

She kept her eyes downcast, but he saw a tear run down one cheek.

"He won't," she said weakly.

"But if he did?"

There was no answer.

It was the hardest thing he had ever done, but he knew it to be necessary. He would put God to the test, and if they were meant to be, they'd be back together after she straightened out her past, or whatever it was that bothered her about the rebel she had dated.

"Let's break up for a while, okay? We'll simply take about six months, maybe a year, see what happens. I don't want to lose you, Anna, but you say you need time to get him out of your system. I think that needs to happen before we move forward together."

She met his eyes briefly, then lowered her own from the truth in his.

"All right," she whispered. Then repeated, "All right."

She nodded her head, as the impact of his words brought the relief of being alone to sort out a relationship she could only view with regret. There was no pleading, only a quick handshake and a meaningful, "Till we meet again, Anna. Call me."

She closed the door against the chill of an October night, leaned her back against it weakly, a hand going to her forehead as if to retain what had occurred.

Oh, what would her mother say?

She mounted the stair steps as if each foot was built of lead, went to part the sheer curtains and stand gazing out across the barnyard to the field of brown corn fodder, the winking of distant lights, the hum of traffic, bathed in the white light of the huge October moon.

Oh God, where are you? Does Dave see this same moon? Why did you place us on this earth together and make our hearts so entwined if we were never meant to be?

She felt a sense of relief, now, to know she would be alone, quiet, at peace.

She would have to absorb her mother's words as best she could, be prepared to digest the wrath, the indignation, knowing it would be veiled in righteous verses from the Bible, the handbook she carried like a shield.

The Bible was precious to Anna as well, and she turned

to it repeatedly for answers. Could one search the Bible for self-justification, if searching in the spirit of selfishness?

And so her thoughts tumbled about, spinning relentlessly, keeping her wide awake as she gazed across the land bathed in moonlight. The moon did things to a person's thinking, perhaps. The light was soft, white, as if darkness was light and light was dark, a confusion of nature.

Sleep did not come easily, which left her tired and quickly perturbed at her job, trying to instill wisdom and knowledge into the impaired minds of four children ranging in age from four to nine years old.

It was only later in the week that she had the courage to speak to her mother, tell her outright about the breakup and why.

Her mother was at the sewing machine, putting a hem into a black apron, the new clothing necessary for the upcoming November weddings.

When Anna told her Leon would not be coming on Saturday, she turned to stone, not even an eyelash blinking.

"And what, may I ask, is the reason?"

Oh boy.

"The reason is, I am not over Dave, not completely."

"I see."

She could see her mother's battle for control, the working of her throat, the color leaving her face. For a fleeting moment, Anna took pity on her, as if she had betrayed them both.

"And what keeps you thinking of Dave?"

"I don't know, Mom."

"Surely."

The word held every condescension in the book. As if she couldn't believe how dumb her daughter was, really.

"Why do I keep thinking of him? Why do I, Mom?"

Her voice was louder now, a mixture of anger, confusion, exhaustion.

Slowly, carefully, Barbie pushed the chair away from the sewing machine, raised her heavy eyelids, then lowered them to half-mast, giving her daughter the full benefit of her superiority.

"You know that our flesh struggles with the will of our Lord at all times. You must place these two men in the proper context. Dave is the one your carnal body desires; Leon the one who is the will of God. It is that simple. It's black and white. There is absolutely no gray area, no question. We were very patient, waiting for fruits to appear from Dave, which, as you well know, were not forthcoming at all."

Here her lips took on a decided curl.

"He wouldn't even join the church for you, and as I have often said, that was only the beginning of refusing to give his life for you."

"But . . ." Anna began.

"No."

"Listen, Mom." Suddenly she wanted to poke holes in all of her mother's confident superiority. "Did you know that Dave followed all your rules? He never touched me, not once . . . in that way. Leon did."

"What are you saying?"

"He did. In Texas." She paused for effect, then felt a twinge of guilt. "It was before hands-off was discussed."

"And you allowed it?"

"For a short time."

There was a pause, then a piercing gaze.

"I don't believe you about Dave."

"Believe what you want."

Clearly feeling as if she was losing control of her daughter, she told her that breaking up with Leon was the biggest mistake of her life, and if she would go her own way again, then she would only live to reap what she had sowed.

Later her father echoed her mother's words, but doubled the guilt and fear by saying she had already lost the blessing God had bestowed by her obedience, and there was only the world and her self-will to be set before her, a bitter reaping of the flesh.

The next few months were some of the hardest Anna would ever experience. She wrestled with her feelings, worried about Dave, missed Leon, endured the constant disapproval of her parents, prayed that God would make His will clear to her. One night, when she again could not sleep, she opened her Bible to Proverbs, the book filled with wisdom and advice. Her eyes landed on Proverbs 13:12: "Hope deferred maketh the heart sick: but when the desire cometh, it is a tree of life." She certainly felt like her heart had been sick for a long, long time. But was Dave really her heart's desire? If he were to appear in her room right then, would he be like a tree of life? Something had shifted within her over those months of desperately seeking God's will. She realized that she no longer craved Dave's presence the way she had for so much of her life. She still cared about him, yes, but if she was really, really honest, she was tired of worrying about him. "God," she prayed in the silence of her room, "Dave is in your hands now. I can't help him. Only you can. I am letting go."

A wave of relief washed over her, and almost immediately her thoughts turned to Leon. She knew, with a clarity she had never before experienced, that he was who her heart longed for. She slept soundly then, resolved to write to him first thing in the morning to tell him of her decision. If he would have her back, she would be his.

Leon had walked through his own valley during those months, but never once did he waver in his hope that Anna would one day be his bride. When he received her letter, he was so overwhelmed with gratitude that he knelt right there by the mailbox to offer thanks to God.

He took Anna to his home in the countryside, close to Millerstown, a small house nestled in farmland with a mountain in the background. His mother had done her best to present a decent house, the windows sparkling, the floors swept and mopped, the porch scrubbed, the children clean and warned to mind their manners.

But it was threadbare, from the old aluminum siding on the house to the couch in the kitchen that sagged in the middle, with tufts of white stuffing protruding from the worn arms. The kitchen floor was torn, in many places, the paint chipping off the long bench along the wall.

There was the sad oppression of an absent father, the children becoming boisterous at the supper table, and the mother's words unable to remedy the situation.

But the food was good and Anna felt a restful ease in their home. The mother's eyes were so much like Leon's, with the warm light of love and acceptance, the eyes of a person who has suffered and won the battle against self-pity or martyrdom. Anna liked her immediately and even more so as the day went on.

They went for a long drive in his horse and buggy, something they had not yet been able to do, always using her parents' team. So it was exciting to be introduced to his horse, Flash, and view the interior of his carriage. Upholstered in gray, with a sleek lacquered switch-box glove compartment built on the dash, plastic mats at her feet, a light dust robe, the carriage was more than she expected.

She felt at home, traveling the roads of his childhood, seeing where his acquaintances resided, noticing his horsemanship, reliving the relief in her mother's eyes when she'd told her she'd be traveling to see Leon and to meet his family.

To have a second chance at love was a gift, she decided. She was bathed in the light of Leon's devotion, all her feelings for Dave shrouded in the fog of distant memory.

He was in Darwin, Australia.

Coming off the plane disoriented, fatigue dogged him like a leech. It was hard to get his bearings, having no one to meet him, not one acquaintance who could show him around the city.

The time was fourteen and a half hours ahead of New York, so he'd lost a whole day somewhere, and today was actually tomorrow, which was so confusing he couldn't even think about it.

Everywhere there were people, which he was getting used to. He barely noticed them anymore. He had joined into the sea of humanity, blending in like water.

He collected his luggage, was swept along with the stream of people through the customs line, and then followed signs to an information desk. So far so good. The woman at the desk was very helpful and found him a room above a small restaurant to rent for only seven dollars a night. She started to write down the phone number of the place for him, then gave him an assessing look, realized he was totally out of his element, and called the owners herself to tell them to expect him. Dave was too tired and too grateful for her help to feel irked by her pity. She wrote down the address, gave him a booklet on Australia, pointed him to the car rental area, and sent him on his way.

But at the car rental kiosk, he realized he had completely overlooked a vital bit of information. He was unable to rent a vehicle without an International Driver's Permit, an IDP, which was only valid in conjunction with his own driver's license, which had been revoked on his second speeding ticket at home The first time he'd been caught he was only going 80, but the second time, at 110, the cops meant business.

This man behind the desk wasn't joking, either. He carried a chip on his shoulder the size of a two-by-six, breathing down his nose at Dave, spouting an accent like rusty rainwater without an inch of patience. He told Dave to get a taxi and stop wasting his time.

"But I need to get to the outback," Dave shouted, watching his whole dream melt away with this arrogant man holding the blowtorch.

"Yeah, yeah. They all do." He leaned his head to the right, raised his eyebrows and said, "Next!" Waved his left hand with a snort.

Dave clenched and unclenched his fists, trying to calm down.

"How do I get there if I can't drive?"

"Find someone to take you."

There was nothing to do but move away, looking behind him at a disgruntled peanut of a man. *I could lift him off the ground with one hand*, Dave thought, which gave him the confidence boost he needed to lug his bags outside and figure out his next move.

There were taxis everywhere, so he threw up a hand, without

results. He tried stepping off the curb, throwing out an arm. Nothing happened. The drivers looked right at him through their windshields, but not a single one stopped. He was thirsty, the air so dry it was like breathing dust. He kept stepping off the curb, waving, even yelling "Hey!" He felt sheepish when a passerby gave him a dirty look, but he called out even louder for the next one to stop. He was rewarded by one almost standing on its front end, the brakes applied so hard, a screech of tires and an expert swerve into a small parking space.

Dave wasted no time getting into the back seat, gave the driver the written address, and was whisked away into a stream of fast-moving traffic, deposited in front of what appeared to be a small pub.

He paid the driver, tipped generously, and stood with his two large pieces of luggage, looking up to the second story of the brick building, hoping there was a decent room behind those cracked windows and peeling windowpanes.

He hadn't counted on feeling quite so alone. He'd been here for four hours and couldn't remember one friendly face.

What was wrong with people?

He picked up his luggage and shouldered his way through the door, turned to meet a middle-aged woman with a girth the size of an inner tube, her white apron buried in rolls of pink uniform.

"You need help, hon?"

He almost cried at the "hon."

"I rented this room for a week?"

He gave her the slip of paper with the address.

She took it, read it, and waved a hand.

"Right. This way, love."

He wanted to hug her, tell her he loved her too.

He followed the wide backside up narrow wooden stairs, marveled at the agility with which the large woman navigated the steps. She stopped two doors down a poorly lit hallway, all dark paneling and brown carpeting, but it smelled of mothballs and strong soap of some kind.

"Right here you be, love. AC controls on the wall, towels in the bath. You got yourself a bargain. Where you from?"

"Pennsylvania. United States."

"Aha. Don't know much about Pennsylvania, but you have a clean look about you. Well, it's good to have you. I hope you'll enjoy your stay."

"Thank you."

"You need anything, ask for Wendy. Wendy Iggins. I own the place with my husband, Perth."

"Thanks."

She smiled, reached up and patted his cheek, and Dave felt mothered, immediately pleased to know there was one person in this vast city who would look after him. For a fleeting moment, he missed his mother with an intensity that startled him. But just as quickly, he pushed the feeling aside, embarassed by his own sentimentality.

He opened the door, which was as dark and heavy as the paneled hallway, and was met by the soft glow of a shaded lamp on a stand beside a bed covered with a red quilt, a brown blanket folded neatly along the bottom, and pillows appearing substantial. There was a dresser, also brown, with a sizable mirror hung on the dark wall behind it.

The shades were drawn, the curtains hanging heavily beside them. *Dark, everything dark*, Dave thought, but it was clean and comfortable, so he had nothing to complain about.

The bathroom was so small he couldn't imagine turning around in it, but there was a shower, a commode, and a washbasin with a shelf to set his necessities on. It was tiled in dark brown marble and he smiled to himself, thinking if he ever built a house, it would certainly be painted white.

He was too tired to unpack, so he grabbed what he needed, showered in lukewarm water, and fell into bed. He slept for fourteen hours straight, woke up confused, ravenous, and eager to begin his tour of Darwin, the northernmost city in Australia.

The food was good, although a bit bland. Every dish contained meat or potatoes, with plenty of grilled choices. He met Wendy's husband, Perth, a towering middle-aged man with small narrow-set eyes, a bad haircut, and dentures that clacked around in his mouth.

He obtained more information from Perth than if he'd bought his own handbook. He gave his seasoned opinions freely, his manner direct, his voice like rusted wheels.

"Now, you get my old four-wheel drive, you don't need no license. You get out there in the Outback, nobody's gonna stop you."

Dave was hesitant. He didn't want to end up in some Australian prison.

"I'm not sure I want to try it alone."

"Well, if you don't, you're smart. Things can go wrong. Your vehicle stops on you, you ain't got enough water, your phone got no service, you're in bad shape. Ain't nothing to mess with out there. Plus, the air conditioner is broke. You'd have to get that fixed. It gets hot like you can't imagine out there. And we're comin' off the dry season, which means it'll be going into the wet, so it can dump on you. Flash floods, walls of water in ravines. October to April. Storms can be pretty bad. So whyn't you fly out?"

Dave shrugged, bit off a piece of steak, chewed, swallowed.

"I have no idea where I'm going."

CHAPTER 15

With the persuasion of Perth and Wendy, Dave did buy the old Toyota SUV, a rusted vehicle not quite silver and not quite gray. He decided to put off fixing the air conditioner, promising Perth he'd stop at a shop before heading out of town (which he had no intention of actually doing). He leaned in under the hood, helped to reinforce every working part, change the oil, clean the spark plugs, listen to every bit of information he could gather about going into the Outback. Vast. Huge. He couldn't begin to fathom the miles and miles, thousands of them, with nothing but scrub brush, dry grass, and desert-like conditions. There were rivers, cliffs, and what they called ocher ranges, named for an earthy clay colored by iron oxide. He wanted to see all of it.

He planned on visiting Alice Springs first, then he'd go from there.

Perth raised an eyebrow, reared back, and stared, openmouthed.

"What?" Dave asked.

"Alice Springs? Are you kidding me?"

"What?"

"You better realize, this ain't no small distance from one place to the other. You got a long ways to go."

"How far?"

"Oh, lemme see."

He lifted his face to the sky, squinted, drummed his fingers, then spoke slowly.

"I'd say fifteen, sixteen hours. On the highway. You can take 87 or Route 1."

"On the highway? Me without a license?"

"You can't get there on foot."

Dave thought about the whole idea of going sightseeing in the borrowed vehicle without a driver's license in a foreign country. There were risks, but absolutely nothing life-threatening, so why not? He began to relish the thrill of living dangerously, something he had always longed to do. Precaution and safety were for, well, safe and cautious people, and he was not one of them.

So he paid Perth for the battered Toyota, the amount setting him back fifteen hundred dollars, but that was all right. He was still in good shape.

Petrol, water, food, clothing, blankets, a pillow. He checked off his supplies, then listened as Perth told him about the "buildup," the oppressive weather pattern before the wet season, when the storms dumped between fifty and sixty inches of water. Dry riverbeds, gorges, any cleft in the land filled up with a torrent of rushing water, and it was dangerous, so it was best to stay close to the highway, which had its own set of perils, especially at night.

"Any old creature comes out at night and walks across the road, so I wouldn't travel too much then."

"What kind of animals?" He pictured cuddly koala bears and small marsupials.

"There's always the cattle. Buffalo. Horses. Kangaroos, donkeys."

Dave felt the rush of adrenaline. Those big animals were no threat. If the land was as flat and treeless as he imagined, he could see those animals miles away.

"Then there's them road trains."

Perth shifted the toothpick in his mouth, spat, squinted, hooked his thumbs in his belt loops, before telling Dave the road trains were truck convoys. Eighteen-wheelers with several connected trailers totaling 170 feet long.

"They barrel right along. Takes them a long time to stop, and they take up most of the road. They'll run you right off, so give 'em space. You need to respect those guys."

A quick flash of irritation in Dave. Who did they think they were? He had as much right to the road as anyone else, so he wasn't afraid of anything.

He'd drive straight through to Alice Springs, find out all he could about these Aboriginal people, the ones he'd read about, and why they were pushed out and now lived in and around this place called Alice Springs. From there it was into the Outback, until he could be hired on for a cattle drive. Or to care for sheep, it didn't matter.

He felt ready to meet whatever the country had to offer. He'd lose his identity, his heritage, everything he'd ever been taught, and forge a trail fueled by this necessity. He'd get rid of Anna and her parents, the *ordnung* of his childhood and teenaged years. His physical condition was primed by his roofing job, the unbearable heat and humidity in summer, the cold wind that sliced through his coat like a knife in winter, his fingers numb with it. His back and shoulders were toned, sinewy with hardened muscle, his legs like stone.

So he'd drive this old vehicle, fly down the road with the windows down, the radio on as loud as possible, freed from all restrictions, out of his parents' sight, out of the sight of anyone who cared what he did or didn't do, how he was dressed, whether he shaved or brushed his teeth or changed into clean clothes. He could face the whole Outback with his own strength and fearless mind.

Bring it on, he thought. *Just bring it on. Let's see what I'm made of.*

Wendy hugged him, wished him well; Perth clapped his shoulder with his enormous hand, told him to be careful.

Dave was so eager to be on the road, he barely acknowledged their goodbyes, his eyes flicking from their faces to his vehicle, mentally going over his stash of supplies, his phone charger, cash, plenty of water, enough food for a week at least.

Perth eyed the horizon, took in the air heavy with portent, the flat air sucked of the usual amount of oxygen, as if a giant hand had reached down and taken most of it. He told Dave to head for high ground if a storm approached, even if it was miles away.

"Sure, of course." Impatient, Dave opened the door of the vehicle and slid behind the wheel, slammed it shut behind him, and grinned up at them both.

"Hey, thanks for everything. See ya."

And he was off.

The air rushed past, the sun an orange orb of pulsing heat, the sky so blue he'd never seen anything like it. All was clear and good, a good omen, like God was smiling down at him.

By the time he reached Katherine Gorge, he was hot, thirsty, and running out of gas. The air around him was so oppressive, so intensely hot and heavy, he felt as if he was underwater. He struggled to breathe as he pulled off by the side of the road, trying to keep the panic from creeping across his chest. Even on a roof in the middle of July, he had never felt anything close to this.

All around him, there was nothing but dust, weird trees he knew were called ghost gums from a guidebook he'd read, and all manner of odd grasses, bushes, and spiky growths he couldn't name. Everything was covered in dust, as if there was a giant blower with a never-ending supply spewing out of it, settling on every available surface before moving on, then replaced by more. He had not seen a kangaroo or an emu, not even a strange lizard or marsupial of some kind.

But there were the gorges, a rift in the otherwise empty land that seemed as if the earth was split open by some great shift, and never put back together the way it was before.

He drank thirstily, water running down the sides of his chin, into the neck of his T-shirt, before thinking of conserving any of it.

He took a deep breath, replaced the cap, set the container back in the vehicle, before turning to lift the can of gas.

On his way again, he wondered how long a person could drive on this level road that stretched out like an endless ribbon. When he got to the horizon, there was only more horizon, always the same, no matter how hard he pushed the Toyota. His eyelids drooped, and he remembered being unable to fall asleep, waking much earlier than normal with no idea what he would encounter for the rest of his life, which kept him awake until it was time to get out of bed.

One of his favorite songs was on the radio, the one that always reminded him of Anna. Angrily, he reached over to turn it off. Even on another continent she was with him.

That thought pushed him to a new decision. He was not going to Alice Springs before heading inland to the cattle stations. This driving was more than he'd bargained for, this bleary-eyed inertia that had him hanging open mouthed over the steering wheel, completely at the mercy of his thoughts, which were always punctured by images of Anna, sooner or later.

No, he couldn't keep this up. Too much time to think. The sun was sliding farther into the west, the air around him only intensified by its heat, the dust filtered by the rays of its descent. He pulled off by the side of the road again to study the map, finding his exact location, the best way to the nearest cattle station, which was, by all accounts, another day of driving.

He'd check his phone, use his GPS. He leaned back in the seat, tapped on the screen, then snorted with impatience. No service again. He jumped up on the hood of the Toyota, then on the roof, and tried again. Same thing.

Well, nothing to do but resume his journey and hope to find the proper route before nightfall. They'd told him it wasn't safe to drive at night, but if he slept a few hours and was up to it, he'd keep going. He hadn't seen a single animal so far, so he wasn't worried.

Headlights approached. He would have been glad to speak to someone, anyone, about his whereabouts and the best way to the first cattle station. It was still partially daylight, so perhaps he could flag this person down. He stepped out.

For a long time, he watched the distant headlights and realized it was a large truck, then realized the full extent of the approaching convoy.

A road train.

It approached at breakneck speed. He stepped back and got into his vehicle. The deafening roar of the diesel engine grew as the huge apparatus approached. Black smoke poured from the exhaust pipe of the monstrous cab. A hiss of hot air, dust and sand, the scent of rubber and oil and hot metal. The driver waved, and he was gone, trailed by five more trucks trundling along at a speed Dave could only estimate to be close to a hundred miles an hour.

He drove on, peering anxiously into his rearview mirror. The sun slid behind the scrub brush, sinking the world into a light that was not daylight but close to nightfall, an odd phenomenon that wasn't twilight at all, the way it was back home.

A chill raced up his spine. He dreaded nightfall and wished for a hotel. A house, another human being. He realized his need for anyone to be nearby, someone to talk to. He hadn't bargained for this isolation, this setting apart from all human contact. For the hundredth time he wished for Wayne. All of this would be so much better with him.

Darkness brought relief from the heat, but he had never been anywhere that it was so completely black, the night like a suffocating sock. He could barely see his hand in front of his face. Rummaging around in the back of the Toyota he realized his first serious oversight.

A flashlight.

Oh, his phone. His phone was his flashlight. He almost giggled with relief. He found his cache of food. He had to be content with the peppery beef jerky and hard, brown bread and cheese, washed down with tepid water that tasted like copper. All around him the night stretched on, only the sound of a few tired insects screeching to cut the absolute silence.

He shivered and couldn't believe how chilly it had become. He settled his pillow into a corner of the vehicle, spread the thin cotton blanket over himself, realized he'd forgotten to take off his shoes, and sat up, annoyed.

Then again, perhaps he should keep them on, he thought, remembering scorpions and snakes. Poisonous ones. He sat, undecided, when he heard footsteps.

He froze.

Definitely, someone or something was walking on the hard road. He held completely still, his ears strained to hear the footsteps.

There.

A clacking sound. Hooves.

He turned the key in the ignition, pressed the button to put up the windows, locked the doors. He went over the list of animals in Australia. Cattle, sheep, buffalo, donkeys, nothing threatening, he didn't think.

Quite suddenly, he had the overwhelming sensation of being observed. Turning to glance sideways he was face-to-face with a huge, glistening black nose and the protruding eyes of an enormous cow, which was immediately jostled away by another face, then another.

Hairy black sides scraped along the window, hooves clattered on the road, wet noses slimed across every window. An entire herd descended on the helpless Toyota with Dave trapped inside.

Tips of massive horns scraped across the left back window. Dave's hand went to his mouth, his eyes wide. He watched, helpless to change anything. He was simply sitting in their path, and they had no intention of moving around him without checking everything out.

Stupid cows.

He raised his fist, banged against the windshield, yelled until he was hoarse. It made no difference to the sea of cows streaming past.

There was one consolation, the thought of a station nearby. How many miles did these cattle roam?

An ambitious bull bumped the hood, then came around to the passenger side, tilted his head, and efficiently rammed a horn the size of a baseball bat straight through the window. It shattered it in a spritz of glass that sprayed across to where he sat.

Dave yelled and yelled and thought of starting the engine. But he couldn't move the vehicle, so what was the point?

The broken window contained shards of spiked glass scattered across the seat like pieces of ice. The cold air outside now seeped in through the broken window.

He caught the distinctive, sweetish odor of cows, a scent he would recognize anywhere. He watched in horror as a face was pushed through the jagged shards, breaking them off like icicles.

Dave yelled and punched the face, which resulted in the quick withdrawal of the animal's head.

Something had to be done. He turned the key in the ignition and revved the motor, hoping to chase them off, or at least give them a reason to detour around him.

It worked. They were moving away.

When he was sure they were all gone, he opened the door, got out to inspect the damage, and to finish cleaning up the glass. Afterward, he spent the miserable remainder of the night trying to stay warm and decipher all the strange groaning and clucking and slithering noises that made their way through his exhausted consciousness.

The light through the windshield woke him. It threw him immediately into a frenzy, fighting off the thin blanket, sitting up, blinking, rubbing his eyes, his shoulders and neck cramped and aching. He could smell his feet through his hiking boots and wool socks. He lifted an arm, sniffed, and thought it could only get worse, with no water for miles around, likely.

He touched his jug of water for comfort and ran a finger across his teeth. He couldn't waste water to brush them.

He ate dried fruit and a package of crackers, some Australian ones he thought must surely be made of birdseed and oatmeal, after which he could only think of pancakes with butter and syrup, two dippy eggs and a slice of scrapple fresh out of his mother's cast-iron pan.

Well, onward ho! He thought wryly, running his tongue around his teeth to remove all the seeds, wishing for a toothpick.

Checking the map, he saw he saw a road branching off the main highway nearby and guessed the cattle had come from that way. It was a gamble, but when he got to the road, he turned onto it, his tires bumping onto the dusty dirt dotted with potholes.

The air streaming through the broken window was like a blow dryer, one of those handheld devices Wayne used to dry his hair, spewing hot, dry blasts that made it easier to use that gel stuff he bought. Wayne was meticulous about his hair and proud of his looks. What would he say if he could see Dave now?

Dave tilted his head to the rearview mirror, dug out some hard yellow clumps from the corner of his eyes, and laughed out loud.

This was the Outback, not prissy Pennsylvania.

A few hours later, he was so hot the sweat trickled down his back and ran off his face. Grime and dust caked to every moist surface, his tongue thick and dry. He reached back over the seat to find the water jug, twisted his back too far to the right, and jerked the steering wheel, sending the Toyota off to the side and into deep red dirt.

He yanked the steering wheel to the left and the Toyota fishtailed back onto the hard surface. He breathed out slowly, shaking his head. That was a close call. He'd have to be more careful.

It was midmorning, and he hadn't seen one other vehicle, nothing.

His eyes felt as if all the dust was swimming around inside his eyelids, creating a paste. He reached for his sunglasses, set them on the bridge of his nose, relieved to find the glare diminished. He should have thought of this sooner.

On he drove, clumsy with his hands, eyelids half-closed, his breath slowing as he relaxed. The hum of the tires on the hard surface lulled him into a semi-wakeful state that seemed perfectly safe yet allowed him plenty of awareness. He lost track of time and miles, and simply sat behind the wheel and allowed the Toyota to take him forward.

To where he wasn't sure. He was simply moving along a route that would eventually take him to water, he hoped. That, or the awaited cattle station. He was overtaken by a need to talk to someone, get his bearings, learn how long until he could reach any place inhabited by people. Anyone. Black, white, or brown. Any person who would talk to him, laugh with him, tell him where he was and what he could do to be hired on at the nearest station.

Man wasn't meant to be alone. Everyone needed a friend or a wife or something. This was ridiculous. He tried humming, then singing, but his throat was so dry and his tongue so thick and caked with dust, his voice cracked and broke on the first line.

He turned on the radio, got nothing but a mishmash of voices that jumbled around in his head, then an even line of static.

He tried his phone and almost ran off the road again.

The sun beat down on the roof of his vehicle. The air that came through the window sizzled with heat. He had to find water to wash the grime. He could feel his feet, slick inside the wool socks, and could only imagine the gross odor.

Something had to give. He couldn't take this heat. It was furnace-like, unnatural. He'd die, likely. He envisioned the rusted frame of the Toyota, his own bones bleaching in the sun.

Why were there no other vehicles? He wondered if this was normal, or if half of Australia had fallen off on account of some earthquake.

Half asleep, hitting deep holes in the road, his teeth clacking every time it happened, he decided to take a break, lie down in the shade of his vehicle and take a nap.

He was asleep the minute his head hit the pillow. He woke up to find the sun had edged halfway up his legs, his face soaked with sweat, his T-shirt stuck to his upper torso. He ran his tongue around the outside of his mouth, the dust turning to mud. He tasted the grime, gagged and swallowed, staggered to his feet and reached for the plastic jug of water, lifted it and drank greedily.

The water tasted like the plastic jug, as warm as soup.

He ate more of the bread, some dried fruit, looked at the unnamed piece of fruit Wendy had given him, and decided he wasn't hungry enough to eat it. It looked exactly like a horse dropping on the road back in Lancaster.

He started off again, felt refreshed, upbeat, singing out loud some old song from school about working on a railroad.

He loved that song. He always sang it too loud and too enthused until the teacher frowned at him and the upper-grade girls glared and sniffed. Then he sang even louder to make them mad for sure. Anna smiled at him when he sang like that.

She always approved of him, no matter what he said or did.

She loved him so much. She always had. Not that it made one bit of difference to her parents. The old bitterness crept into his heart, spread through his well-being until he felt sickened, handicapped by this remorse, this longing for what might have been.

They would have been the perfect couple. She would have supported him and loved him no matter what he chose to do, just the way women were supposed to. He would have opened up her little world, broadened her horizons in so many ways.

He thought this same thing, over and over, with no other voice of reason to correct him. Not his mother, or Wayne.

He thought of the encounter with the dark-haired girl named Rose. Dark hair and eyes simply did nothing for him. There was no real beauty in that, not even close to blonde hair and blue eyes like Anna's. That Rose had looked back, though, and answered his wave.

That was sort of romantic, like blowing a kiss.

Well, he wasn't getting involved again, ever. Likely Rose had a set of parents with grim expressions and suspicious minds who would fall over in a faint if he as much as talked to their daughter. Or breathed the same air she did, for Pete's sake.

And suddenly he found himself crying, sobbing hysterically, his mouth drawn back in a grimace, as the ragged sounds came from his throat. He couldn't see to drive, helpless to stop the heaving of his chest. Since there was no one to see or hear him, he heaved and sobbed until he was emotionally spent.

Later, after he had found a miraculous clump of wallaby grass and baobab trees with a trickle of water draining into a stagnant pool called a billabong, he stopped his car and got out, stretched, reached into the back for a set of clean clothes and a towel.

When he removed his shoes, he howled in disgust, setting a flock of pigeons into flurried panic. The water felt like paradise, so he scrubbed and washed, brushed his teeth and hair, wore only a pair of sandals, stuffed his shoes in a garbage bag, and threw away the offensive socks.

CHAPTER 16

Aₙₙₐ OPENED THE SPIGOT ON THE AIR LINE AND STARTED THE WRINGER washer for Monday morning's laundry, eyeing the piles that dotted the floor of the laundry room like small mountains of soiled clothing.

Her mother was still in bed, with a new daughter nestled beside her in the king-sized bed with the quilted white headboard, her face a serene image of accomplishment.

They'd named her Esther Faith, after Queen Esther in the Bible. The fifth daughter, and all was well, so who were they to ask for more? A son would have been welcome, too, of course, but daughters were a blessing, they reasoned.

Anna quit her job, then, at her mother's request, backed by her father, whose primary concern was his wife. She was older now and needed her rest, so Anna was needed at home. Besides, wasn't it about time to think of putting a quilt in frame?

There might be a wedding in the future, they teased.

She would smile, wrestle with the unexplained despair that followed the thought of putting that quilt in frame.

She threw in a load of whites, sheets, pillowcases, her father's white Sunday shirt, absentmindedly watched the swirl of Tide, fabric, and water, the forward and backward motion of the wringer, punctuated by the sound of the air motor that drove the machine. She added a capful of Downy, swished with her fingers, then dried them on her apron before turning to enter the kitchen to start on the breakfast dishes.

Leon had left at eleven last night, the driver showing up a half-hour earlier on account of the weather prediction of rain that could turn icy. She wondered now where he'd heard that, the way there was a stiff wind from the northwest with brilliant sunshine.

He had been more than attentive, asking her question after question on the future, wanting her input on what he labeled a truly intimate relationship with Christ. He spoke on topics they discussed at the meetings, seeking her opinion on different possibilities of teaching the troubled youth among the Amish.

His eyes glowed with the inner passion he reserved for this cause, his burning ambition to help anyone who veered off the path of normalcy into the maw of depravity, describing in detail the extent of the sinner and the consequences of his actions, wrecked homes that were efficiently demolished by the wrecking ball of his actions.

At first, she was enthused and gave her opinion freely, which he generously considered, always praising her insight. But halfway through the evening, she was just tired. Tired of listening to the low class of society, tired of the endless rounds of solutions, the whys and how comes and what nows. She wanted to shout and tell him to shut up. Stop, please stop.

But of course, she was far too polite and stayed attentive until he finally left, then fell into bed in a stupor of unsolved problems with Leon in the middle.

For she loved him, she told herself, over and over.

Love was kind, patient, did not need its own selfish desires, would always want what was best for him, be a competent helpmeet in his work. After they were married he would devote more of his time to her, and if there were children he would be an amazing father, the way he was to all his younger brothers and sisters.

He was the father figure in that family, the leader, the problem solver, the one his mother leaned on.

So what was wrong with her?

She had done much better in the past, had prayed and read her Bible, found clear direction, and basked in the love and approval of her parents, finding everything she needed in Leon's adoration.

Yes, they had hit a slippery slope a while back, but their love had grown stronger from there. Dating was like marriage: you had to work on it. Love didn't always come easily.

But it had in the past. Love was in the air around her, in every breath she took, coloring everything until it shone.

With Dave, love had been different, but then, perhaps there were different kinds of love and you only loved like that once. And if it was taken away, it would never come back in the same form.

She loved the Dave of her childhood, not the rebellious Dave of her teenage years, the one who created the abyss between her and her parents.

No, it was not Dave that kept her from loving Leon the way she should. With Leon, marriage was an awaited event, but if her parents dared mention it, she felt depressed, unhappy, which was only rebellion.

Wasn't it?

She dried all the dishes, stacked them neatly in the cupboard, swept the kitchen, and went to sit with her mother, who was on the recliner, a clean sheet spread across it, a soft blanket across her lap.

The baby was sound asleep on her shoulder, the thatch of bland hair like peach fuzz above the pink blanket.

"Can I get you something?" Anna asked.

"My throat is scratchy, as if I'm coming down with something, so lemon and honey would be nice. As hot as possible."

Anna hurried to bring her required drink, then asked what else she needed. Her memory foam pillow, before settling down on the glider rocker.

"You want me to take her?"

"Sure."

Anna held her newborn sister, marveling at the perfection of her, the perfectly symmetrical eyes, the soft button nose, the peaceful puffs of breath as her little chest rose and fell.

"Soon it will be your turn, Anna," her mother smiled.

"Not yet, Mom. I'm way too young to get married. There's still so much time, isn't there?"

"Not really. Leon is older. He'll ask you for next fall."

Anna nodded, turned her head to kiss the side of the baby's head. She smelled like baby shampoo and lotion, the most delicious smell in all the world, surely.

"You don't act very thrilled."

Anna could not think of an honest answer, so she merely caught her mother's gaze and held it. She shrugged her shoulders, let them drop, then murmured, "How am I supposed to feel?"

Her mother didn't reply, simply waved a hand and laid her head sideways on the pillow Anna had brought.

She felt guilty for a small moment.

Why couldn't she give her mother the answer she wanted so badly? Would she always allow her words to ignite the smoldering coals of her resentment? If this was the way she'd go through life, she'd only be making herself miserable. But somehow, she could not stop it.

She finished the laundry, pinned it to the wheel line in the blustery air, her hands reddened and chapped. She mopped the laundry room floor, set the boots and shoes in a straight line, hung up a few sweat-shirts, and stood gazing across the lawn.

Everything was perfect, as always. The lawn service guy had put on the last application of fertilizer, ensuring healthy growth in spring. The chrysanthemums were cut, the hostas clipped, box-woods trimmed to perfect cones. The holly would be bursting with red berries, the arborvitae already showing new growth from the trimming in August.

Her mother had done all of it herself, then had a near painless birth, smiling to the rest of the family as they gathered around the beautiful king-sized bed in the early morning sunshine.

Her father opened the cow stable door, and one prized cow

after another made its way down the small incline to the barnyard and beyond. The Holsteins were very white and glossy black, their tails docked, their backs spread with fly killer. Anna knew the milk house was spotless, floor scrubbed, stainless steel bulk tank gleaming, windows spotless. There was plenty of money in the account at Susquehanna Bank in town, even with depressed milk prices, the acres of tomatoes and peppers making all the difference.

Elias Fisher was known for his produce, always the biggest and best, certain buyers looking for his vegetables and paying top dollar. Anna was proud of her father's accomplishments. She loved to pick tomatoes and peppers, grade them, and pack them in cardboard boxes, working side by side.

Leon would not fit.

This thought may as well have been written in red letters on the side of the barn, for both of her parents to see. He simply was not concerned about money, or whether he worked, or what the amount showed on his paycheck. His passion was counseling troubled youth, and as far as she could tell, he was not a paid counselor yet.

His home was clean and well kept, but very humble, which did not seem to bother him in the least. In the same way her palatial home never fazed him. She wasn't sure if he even took notice of her surroundings.

So would her parents accept a son-in-law who was not concerned about getting ahead? If she lived in a small rental property and lived frugally, which is what her life would undoubtedly turn out to be?

On the next Saturday evening, he brought up the subject of his possible plans for their future, gesturing with his hands, the way he always did when he was excited about a good idea.

"So, if and when we get married . . ."

He grinned at her.

She laughed, punched his arm. He held her fist, then slowly released it.

"We'll move to my home area, with my counseling job and all."

"We will?"

It was still far away in the future, way out there where she couldn't see even the beginnings of it, so she could easily kid around.

"We will," he laughed. He said soberly, "I don't have any money."

"None?"

"Hardly."

"Oh well."

An answer as dull and lifeless as she felt inside. He rambled on about the Hertz place a mile from his own, and she thought, Hertz. Isn't that a rental company? Hertz Rent-a-Car or something, and giggled.

He took that as a sign of her happiness. His eyes turned liquid with love and adoration, telling her she was his whole life, all he would ever need.

Wasn't that exactly what Dave always told her?

Yes, she loved him, and would be content with the Hertz place.

Her mother had always told her that being frugal was a virtue, a godly gift that worked well to please the husband. Not that she practiced any of it herself, with all the latest furniture and beautiful things, but then, her father had inherited the farm, and there had always been money, so Anna supposed that made a difference.

"So I'll be living in your valley?" she asked, with a bright smile.

He seemed shy, overtaken by a sense of his own humility.

"It's in the future."

And the conversation came to a halt, abruptly.

At the Eli Stoltzfus home, they made plans for big changes. With Dave actually carrying out his plans of going to Australia, which may as well have been to the moon, in Rachel's opinion, it was time to think of giving the farm over to one of the boys.

Eli had always enjoyed woodworking, so it would not be hard to find a job in one of the numerous woodworking shops that dotted Lancaster County. He looked forward to retirement. He'd always imagined his youngest ambitious son to be the one who would carry on the family tradition of tilling the soil, but the way things appeared now, that would never happen.

They'd talked it over, lingering after supper, discussing the best way to go about it, both agreeing that Abner and Naomi were the best candidates to run the farm.

And so family negotiations began. They started a Daudy house on the west side of the property, where the old oak tree spread its shade across the pasture. Rachel wanted nothing to do with being attached to the main house, saying it was much too close to her daughter-in-law's business.

"But that's how it's done. It's cheaper, and when we need help in our old age, someone will be close by," her husband argued.

"I don't care how it's done. I'm not doing it that way. I'll be a built-in babysitter, maid, yardman, gardener. You know Naomi likes nothing better than running the roads, and that's exactly what would happen."

She crossed her arms and pursed her lips and glared at her husband, and he thought he'd better build out on the west side of the pasture with a gate between them.

Dave had not called, never as much as left a message. Eli knew he wanted it that way, but it worked on him, this disappearance. It was a kind of death, never seeing him, knowing he was somewhere under this same sky, this same sun and moon and stars, but never being certain he was all right. If only he wasn't so brash, so passionate and quick in all his decisions, never considering advice.

Sometimes when Rachel became moody, the house became silent as a tomb. Eli knew she suffered the same fears and lack of faith as he did. Often, he wanted to go to her, comfort her, let her know they were in this together. But he knew his wife so well; she wanted to suffer in silence, so he left her alone.

He thought if children only knew the pain, the unshed tears, the cloud of uncertainty they brought on their parents, like being hastened to an early grave, they'd straighten themselves up. Wasn't that the term his father had always used?

Schicket euch. Behave yourselves. And when he spoke in that rumbling voice, those heavy eyebrows like a roof over the gimlet eyes, they knew to straighten up, that if they chose to disobey they could expect serious consequences to the tune of a good whipping in the woodshed.

Things had changed over the years, with this thing called child rearing. He still didn't approve of those books. How could one person tell another how to raise children? He simply didn't get it. Every child has a different nature and is raised in a different environment. Who do these writers think they are?

But he thought perhaps he had a bad attitude about it, with an *ungehorsam* son running around in Australia.

Why Australia, he asked himself for the thousandth time? Why couldn't he have settled for Wyoming, even Alaska?

He was just so overboard, going way beyond most children's sense of what was normal. Even as a small child, he'd never played nicely with other children. They always knew when a child came running, terrified, a face full of sand clinging to his mouth and eyes, that David was the culprit. He rammed his trike into wagons and scooters and other riding toys, upsetting a visitor's children and laughing about it. He rode his scooter faster and farther than anyone else, drove a team of mules when he was six years old, killed garden snakes soon after that.

Eli shook his head as he sat at the kitchen table drinking coffee, imagining his outspoken son's foray into the Outback, which, as far as he could tell, was nothing but a desert. Ah, it was a sadness, this constant worry about his well-being, about the state of his soul.

He thought of the prodigal son living among the swine before he woke up and realized how far he'd fallen. And how would Dave ever wake up and realize this was not what or where he wanted to be?

Well, for sure, he could always let go of his worrying and allow God to deal with his son, but that was challenging as well.

It was just plain hard.

For the first time in his life he was unsure of having done the right thing raising his children on such a long leash, or, if he was honest, no leash at all. It had worked all right with the older ones, but it seemed with Dave . . .

Where was he at this moment?

He had to get to work and shake off these dark thoughts that kept him awake at night.

Rachel slapped the reins down on the horse's back as he walked uphill, his head stretched out till the neck rein was taut.

"Come on, Charlie," she called through the raised window, then lowered it and clicked it shut.

Charlie swung into a tired lope, jerking the buggy up the small grade with every step. Rachel opened the window again, slapped the reins even harder, before clicking the window down.

She shouldn't be driving Charlie anymore, the way he was half dead by now. Old as a horse can get. What was he, twenty-six? Some cows ran better than Charlie. But if she drove Rex, that spirited black monster, she'd end up in the ditch or side swiping a car out on Route 340, or worse. Her arms weren't strong enough to hold him once he decided he wanted to go home.

She pulled on the right rein, to keep Charlie off the road, allowing a stream of cars to pass on the left. Most people were nice about horses and buggies on the road, but occasionally, some impatient teenagers would pass with a roaring engine emitting black smoke from the exhaust.

Ach, she was glad Dave didn't drive that Jeep around anymore.

So *ungehorsam*. She was always afraid he'd have a wreck, the way he had no fear. He was aggressive now, the way he'd been as a child. Him and Anna. How cute was that? *Ach* my. And now everything had gone so horribly wrong.

She felt the sting in her nostrils, the prick of tears in the corner of her eyes, the regret for what could have been always *schpeiting* her.

They had been so perfect together. In fact, they were the most handsome couple she'd ever seen, and now she firmly believed she'd had *hochmut* in her heart. That's why it had all gone wrong. She'd told the Lord over and over she was sorry, and she felt forgiven.

But still.

It wasn't funny, dealing with this heartache. And now, on the way to her sister-in-law's quilting, she dreaded the pitying glances, the questions that shone from inquisitive eyes, but never asked.

Ma dut net so.

Simply good manners, this refraining of asking questions. It was kind and merciful and allowed her to be an ordinary mother who took part in the conversation, laughing and joking as if nothing was amiss.

When she turned off the narrow country road and pulled up to the small barn on her brother's property near Intercourse, she was glad to see him step out of the house and make his way down the steps to help her unhitch.

"*Vell*, Rachel!" he greeted her.

"Elam! *Vee bisht?*" she asked.

"Can't complain. Can't complain. If I did, would it help?"

Rachel laughed. "No, it wouldn't."

"You still driving Charlie?"

"Of course. Our other horse isn't fit."

They unhitched, one on each side of the shafts, loosening the snap that held the britchment, then working the traces loose from the singletree, inserting them into the britchmen, where they hung securely while the horse was stabled. Elam reached under the front seat for the halter and neck rope, then turned to slip Charlie's bridle off his head.

"So how's everything at your house?"

"Empty."

"I bet. Hear anything from David?"

"No."

"Not once?"

"No."

"Maybe he doesn't have service."

"That's what I tell myself."

She followed her brother into the barn, watched as Charlie lowered his head to drink from the cast-iron watering trough.

"Your barn looks the same way it always has. As clean as a woman's kitchen."

"Oh, now, come on."

They shared a laugh, and she turned to the buggy for the rectangular Tupperware container filled with oatmeal raisin cookies, peered through her bifocals to look for horsehair, then bent her head to blow across the yellow lid before taking the corner of her apron to wipe them off.

"*Gals-houw*," she muttered.

Elam reappeared, watched Rachel snort about the horsehair on her container, and felt a pang of pity. She was so strong, so outspoken and in control, he knew this could not be easy.

"Rachel."

She looked up, saw the sympathy, and lowered her eyes to keep the rush of emotion in check.

"*Ma halta aw.*"

Few words, but filled with meaning. The kind of words that coated your heart like a soothing balm, took away the loneliness and despair, allowed you to know that someone cared a lot more than you ever thought possible.

She turned and nodded, before walking away, and he watched her swim in his vision that was obscured by tears.

She was greeted warmly by the circle of women seated around the square of quilt that was stretched firmly, pinned to the fabric, and stapled to the wooden frame, a sight that always brought joy to Rachel.

She just loved to quilt. Even more, she loved to talk and quilt. She was soon seated on *de vikkle side*, the side where the frame could be rolled after it was quilted, so the women would be able to quilt another foot or more, before rolling again.

Rachel was a competent quilter, and was proud of her ability to stich even, fine stiches, and finish very quickly with her portion.

Talk rippled along the quilt like flowing water, fractured only occasionally by a laugh, or an exclamation, a call for thread or a needle. Someone had forgotten their small scissors, so Malinda, Elam's wife, hurried to the sewing machine drawer to find one.

Talk mostly centered around Dan and Katie Beiler, whose twin daughters had been born at Hershey Medical Center, and were both GA positive. The genetic disorder glutaric acidurea was cropping up more and more, with both parents being carriers.

My oh, they said. My oh.

De arme dinga. The poor things. Three years on special formula created at the Clinic for Special Children, they were often hospitalized for flu symptoms and fevers.

Oh, it will be all right. At least they can outgrow GA. But think of the stress. You know a high fever can damage all their motor skills.

Not all of them.

Did you ever see a child damaged by GA?

Yes. Well?

There's not a lot left.

Ach, we didn't used to hear of such things. It's the end times.

Puh, everyone thinks the end times are always close. I remember when my aunt Mary went to the first drive-through at the bank and had a fit conniption, said the end can't be far off. That was, what? The sixties? Seventies?

Fooftzich yawa trick.

No, it's not that long.

A loud call from the kitchen. "*Kommet.* Coffee break."

Everyone bent their heads and quilted as if their lives depended on it. No one wanted to be the first to head for the kitchen table loaded with pastries, coffee, tea, hot chocolate.

"*Kommet!*"

Rachel pushed back her chair, said if no one else was hungry, she was, and proceeded to fill the biggest mug with coffee, carefully load a paper plate with two raisin cookies, a chocolate mint bar, salsa and sour cream with a pile of tortilla chips, and two carrots with ranch dressing.

The carrots were only to be polite. Let the others eat all that celery and cauliflower, those sour orange segments and fresh pineapple that looked green, really.

Oh, she hated fresh pineapple, the way no one really knew when that thing was ready to be cut up, and it wasn't one bit ripe. Like eating bark off a tree. She could stick her tongue out at the thought.

Rachel enjoyed her coffee break immensely. She felt the love and companionship swell inside of her. Oh, this was so precious, being Amish, living together, understanding one another so well.

She felt the hurt for David as keenly as the cut of a knife. She had to endure the conversation about Elias Fisher's Anna dating that Leon Beiler, from Millerstown. That was some sad family, the father so tormented by his illness. They could hardly see how this would go yet.

But we'll see, they said. We'll see.

CHAPTER 17

H IS PHONE WAS USELESS.

All his attempts at reviving it, climbing on the roof of the Toyota, and now he climbed even higher, scaling the slippery bark of some weird looking tree, holding his phone out and up.

Nothing.

So he had no GPS, no phone if he needed help, his water was low, and he had about five or six gallons of petrol.

He spread the map in the shade of his vehicles, and with the point of a ballpoint pen, traced his route. He'd traveled close to four hundred miles, maybe four fifty, but by all appearances, he had another five hundred till he reached cattle and sheep country.

He swallowed, felt the tips of his fingers tingle with nerves. He didn't have enough gas. At thirty miles to the gallon, he'd be lucky if he made two hundred miles. Surely there was civilization that was not marked on the map. There had to be.

Well, he'd calm down, get his bearings. To spend the night here by the water, surrounded by trees and scrubby-looking bushes was a shelter of sorts. At least he wasn't out on the main road being run over by the monsters called road trains, or the wandering herd of cattle that had no respect for windows in vehicles.

This was actually kind of pleasant. He should have a nice little one-man tent, build a fire, cook something.

He smiled, set about digging a hole for a campfire, set out the blanket and pillow, brought the sack of food and the plastic water jug, the stack of paper cups. As the sun slid downward, there was plenty of shade.

There was a high whining sound.

He stopped, sat back on his haunches, listened. Out of nowhere, a black cloud of insects whined and hovered over the water, then landed on his hand, arms, face. Every inch of exposed skin was a feast to these small black flies.

He slapped and danced and yelled, but wasted energy he needed to build the fire, to collect firewood and dry grass.

The flies swarmed around his head, settled around his eyes and the corners of his mouth. He spit and clawed at his face, rubbed his eyes and rubbed the flies into them, causing a burning sensation that never left.

He got out his phone, wanted to Google these flies to see what they were and what, if anything, there was to do about them. But of course, no service.

He got the fire going between spitting, wiping his face, waving at the air around him, wondering how he would ever survive the night if they were like mosquitoes and navigated the air in the dark.

He thought of the broken window, and groaned. He should have brought a roll of duct tape and some plastic.

The fire leaped and crackled, which was comforting. The rising smoke helped to keep the worst of the flies at bay, so he'd sit here and keep the fire going a while. He wondered if this water hole called a billabong would host a pile of different animals at night, the way it was in Africa when all those lions and elephants came to drink.

Here there were kangaroos, that was about it, and as far as he knew they weren't aggressive. Yeah, he'd sleep outside, here by the fire. No reason to cram his long legs into the vehicle.

The fire threw splashes of light into the twilight, illuminating the scrub brushes, giving them the appearance of hairy monsters.

He became aware of scuttling, a rustling, rasping sound as small creatures slithered and ran. He knew there were snakes of all kinds, the desert death adder the most poisonous, but with a fire, he felt comfortable.

Lizards, the one called thorny devil, were all over the place. These strange little creatures could survive anything.

His thoughts always went to Anna as nighttime closed in.

He thought of the devil lizards and survival, as he had survived loving Anna, like an angel she was, and lost her to her parents.

But he had survived. He was doing all right, even if it meant going through that drug business, going English. He had become what they thought he was then. Bitterness welled in his stomach like indigestion.

So now she was sequestered in that perfect family, being the perfect daughter, dating the perfect guy. They made him sick.

Those ghost gum trees were called that for a purpose, the way they loomed out of the dark looking like some bushy haired apparition.

Anna used to wear a dress that wasn't really pink and not quite peach colored that turned her skin to a shade just like it. Her cheeks turned only a shade darker, which made her look unnaturally pretty, like a doll. All the stuff women smeared on their faces couldn't come close to her natural beauty, that was certain. He hoped that boyfriend of hers would appreciate her the way he had. And yet, at the same time, he couldn't stand the thought of him gazing at her.

A high yipping sound made its way into his conscience. Dogs.

What? All he needed was a pack of dogs after him with that window of his jeep busted out.

He added more brush to the fire, his ears straining to hear the fractured barking and yipping. Then he remembered he'd read about wild dogs called dingoes. Australian dogs like wolves, except smaller.

Nothing to worry about. Likely more like a fox.

The fire burned to coals.

His eyelids drooped, and he swam into subconscious, the blissful place that precedes falling asleep, the sound of dingoes and slithering creatures fading away, leaving him in an aura of perfect rest.

Anna. There was Anna!

What in the world? Anna!

He tried sitting up, reaching out, calling her name, but he was tied. Tied to his blanket by strong ropes, ropes that chafed and burned. Becoming desperate, he twisted and turned, strained against the binding ropes. Kicked his feet and opened his mouth to yell in protest.

Anna came closer, a vision that glimmered like a jewel, a small smile on her face. And then she disappeared.

His cry woke him.

He lay drenched in sweat, sand clinging to every part of his body that was uncovered. He was shaking as he sat up and covered his face with his hands.

She had not been here at all. Regret, then remorse so strong that he groaned in protest.

Well, he didn't know where this had all come from. Probably just overtired. Perhaps he was hallucinating, he didn't know.

But he was left with a sense of longing for Anna so strong he felt weakened, helpless.

The dawn brought a dense humidity and a blazing ball of sun that was already unbearable by midmorning. He kept checking his water supply, pulled out his map to carefully trace a route, then sat back on his heels, gazing at nothing.

He realized he was in trouble. To turn back would be admitting defeat; to keep going risky business. Being on these back roads was far more dangerous than traveling the well-paved highway where an occasional motorist or barreling road train would stop if he needed help.

Should he retrace his route or push on?

He ate dried fruit, dry granola, and a beef stick, not quite hard enough to be like the beef jerky in the United States and not like beef bologna, either. It was good, but he decided against eating another one.

He drank water sparingly and supposed he'd swallowed a dozen of the bothersome black flies. He decided to toughen up, let them buzz and settle where they wanted, seeing no relief the farther he'd get into the Outback.

He threw sand on the fire, shook his blanket and pillow, packed everything in the back of the Toyota, and started off.

He was glad the engine sputtered to life immediately, wondering what he'd do if it didn't.

Back on the road, such as it was.

Narrow, packed with holes and small ravines, bushes and clumps of grass spread at random, with vast areas containing nothing but the reddish sandy soil, as level as the surface of a table.

The road stretched before him, the sun seemed to push the Toyota into the road, burning the arm that hung out the window.

He fought back the panic that roiled his stomach, pursed dry lips to whistle, and bent to turn up the radio. He fiddled with his phone, threw it angrily into the glove compartment, before thinking what a joke that worldwide service was.

By noontime, his gas was down to half a tank, with a small reserve in the plastic red can in the back. Nothing changed around him, nothing.

He was hoping to find a bit more grass, some scattered trees, anything to give him hope of civilization. He found himself chewing on his lower lip, his hands clutching the steering wheel till the knuckles showed white, the sweat on his palms making it hard to steer.

The way this road was going, turning into little more than a wide cow path with holes like moon craters, he'd be fortunate to be able to keep going. Many of the deepest holes weren't visible, the sand that blew in constantly giving them the deceptive appearance of not being there at all, which made the Toyota fishtail its way out when he accelerated.

His eyes darted from left to right, then bore through the dusty windshield, watching for these holes. He knew to stay alert, calculating. It was relaxed, sloppy adventurers that got into trouble. People who assumed everything would be fine.

He had always been fearless, so now there could be no difference.

He'd rode his scooter father and faster than anyone else, was good on a skateboard, and snowboarding a breeze, all that stuff. But he'd never had to be alone like this. This solitude was harder than anything he'd bargained for.

Anything.

The road stretched ahead of him, the Toyota dipped and swerved, the sound of the engine lulling him into a stupor. His eyes felt as if all the flies had settled into them, his mouth as if it was stuffed with cotton. He ran his tongue around his dry cracked lips, reached for his water bottle, and took a few sips.

The heat was almost alive, dancing and shimmering on the horizon, causing a sense of delusion, as if the sparse bushes and clumps of grass were jumping up and down.

He glanced at the needle on the gas gauge. A bit below half.

He thought of the many images in the comics he'd read of the skinny caricature on hands and knees, gasping, the sun in rings above his head. Would he turn out like that?

A sense of dread replaced the panic, the assurance of the inevitable.

He topped the Toyota, reached for the map and opened the door, went around to the front of the vehicle and spread it across the hood, his hands shaking.

Surely the cattle stations would be on the map. The line he had drawn snaked downward from his starting point, Darwin.

He knew he was somewhere in Australia's Northern Territory, which seemed to be bigger than the whole world. He felt no beginning and no end, only the everlasting red desert, sand, gorse bushes, and clumps of grass he'd figured out to be wallaby, porcupine, or kangaroo grass.

What else would you name anything in this empty stretch of the world? How could cattle survive? Or sheep for that matter?

The heat on his back was searing, the humidity like warm fog. At home in Lancaster County, if there was heat like this, usually a thunderstorm cleared the air sooner or later.

They called this the Buildup, which he took to be atmospheric pressure building up to produce the massive storms that dumped torrential rains on the dry earth, resulting in flash floods that were even more dangerous than the heat. He sighed, looked around.

He had no choice.

The only thing to do was to keep going until his gas ran out, then stay with his vehicle or walk. His only hope, he realized, was to meet another vehicle, anyone on horseback, even a stray cow. Anyone or anything to lead him to other people.

He had never taken other people into consideration. Not really.

At home when he woke in the morning, there had always been his brothers, and when they married, there was his mother hovering between stove and refrigerator, making his breakfast.

His mouth watered, thinking of the bacon, egg, and cheese sandwich she'd always had ready wrapped in aluminum foil.

Why had he never appreciated it?

His father in the barn, his classmates and teacher, his friends when he was with the youth, always he'd been surrounded by people.

If only he'd reckoned on being this alone, which was proving to be unbearable. He needed people around him, living, talking human beings who gave and took words and thoughts that tumbled around in his head like clothes in a dryer at the laundromat in town.

In summer, when there was a week of rain and no way to dry the piles of laundry, his mother would call a driver and head to the laundromat, the Sudsy Bubble, packing the van with the different styles and sizes of clothes hampers and clothes baskets, her box of Tide, Downy fabric softener, and a small Tupperware container of quarters. He would accompany her on this mission, help carry the hampers, embarrassed to be seen with piles of soiled clothing, afraid someone would smell the cow manure and sweat. When his mother bent to stuff the frontloaders with clothes, she'd inevitably drop underwear, which he'd scoop up as fast as possible, glancing hurriedly behind his back, hoping no one saw them.

When the washers were loaded, chugging the white soapsuds

against the glass, she'd give him a handful of quarters to buy a snack from the vending machine. He loved the cheese popcorn the best. He always bought a Pepsi, ice cold and so refreshing with the small bag of cheese popcorn.

His thirst was monstrous. The thought of a cold Pepsi almost made him sick with longing, the hum of the washers, the tumble of clothes in the dryer, the women folding clothes, all seemed to edge in his mind like a razor.

Where had that thought come from? The laundromat.

Guaranteed he was losing his mind, bit by bit. He thought he'd seen Anna last night, which he knew was only a figment of his imagination, or a nightmare, he couldn't be sure which.

He hummed along with the radio after he got back on the road.

He guessed it must be close to lunchtime, as hungry as he was and the way the sun hung straight overhead. He didn't feel like opening the glove compartment to check the time on his phone.

Useless device.

He had to meet some form of life. He had to. A sheep or a cow, even a kangaroo or a lizard. He gripped the steering wheel, felt his head throb with anxiety and frustration.

Why had he ever thought he could take on the Outback?

He could not begin to fathom the emptiness, the vast, level nothingness of this world. Coming from Lancaster County, with its congested roadways and back-to-back farms and houses, industrial buildings and roadways, the hustle and bustle of life, this was not something a modern-day guy could prepare himself for.

He was comforted by the honesty of his thoughts, for some reason. He'd made a foolish mistake, this he knew, and that in itself brought up the sharp reality of his situation and the intensity of his desire to bring the whole thing to an end.

But how?

He couldn't retrace his steps, or his tire tracks, he thought a bit wildly. An image of a brown world with only one set of tire tracks, a small puff of dust rolling behind it made him laugh out loud.

So here he was.

A few hours later, he ran out of gas, the engine skipping, sputtering till the Toyota drifted to a stop. He put in the rest of the gas in the red can, tilting it and shaking the can up and down to get the very last drop into the tank, before replacing the cap and turning methodically to set it in the back of the vehicle.

He placed both hands palm down on the tailgate, propped himself up by his arms, hung his head between his shoulders, and exhaled. He straightened, squinted into the distance. His fate was in God's hands. There was no hope for him unless someone traveled this road.

He felt a mild irritation at Perth Iggins. Why he hadn't warned him more? Why he hadn't supplied him with more gas? He'd simply sent him out completely unprepared, but thought better of placing the blame solely on his shoulders. He'd said he was going to Alice Springs, then changed his mind.

He blamed his cell phone carrier too. Stupid people. Claiming worldwide service. Ha.

He drove slowly to save gas and watched the road ahead until his eyes burned. The heat shimmered in the distance. He caught a flash of movement.

"Hey!" he yelled, stamped on the brakes and was out of the vehicle before he realized what he'd seen.

He stopped in his tracks to see a large grayish, reddish-brown kangaroo leap an unbelievable jump that cleared the road completely, then go bounding off between the dry scrubby bushes with a grace and agility he hadn't known existed in any animal.

"Wow," he mouthed slowly.

He sighed, returned to the Toyota, and started off. Strangely, the kangaroo had given him hope, as if he was no longer quite so alone. To exist, the animals all had to have water, so there must be something nearby.

He drove with purpose, now, stepped on the gas, and leaned forward to be sure to take in all the sights. He would miss nothing.

His teeth were jarred in a resounding clack, he was thrown against the windshield up over the steering wheel, before the vehicle came to a sudden halt, leaning on its nose, the two front tires embedded in a deep culvert that had been blown shut with dust and sand.

Dave sat back, grimaced, rubbed his chest where the impact of the steering wheel had bruised him.

"Ow," he breathed.

He felt his forehead, checked his fingers, but there was no blood, only the throbbing where he'd hit the glass. Lucky it didn't break.

Slowly, he climbed out, stood back and ran a weary hand through his hair. Here he was, stuck as tight as a peg in a timber-frame hole.

He scratched his head, rubbed his chest, checked his forehead again before sitting down in the middle of the road, giving in to the profound sense of being completely alone in a situation he couldn't control.

He blamed Perth, and Wendy, then Anna and her parents. He blamed his own parents for not raising him the way they should have. He blamed his teachers and the ministers and the whole Amish church, and last of all, he blamed God, in a way.

God could have stopped him.

He allowed his anger to control him, stomped around both sides of the vehicle clenching and unclenching his fists. He drew back his right leg and kicked the front tire as hard as he could, hurt his foot, raised his face and howled at the sun, his teeth feeling the heat of it.

He had a shovel. A small one, but a shovel.

He threw off his T-shirt, flexed his arms, and set to work.

Every angry shovelful was replaced with the dry sandy soil. The faster he worked the less he accomplished. To be able to back out of this culvert, he needed long sturdy planks to support the weight of the vehicle. Sweat poured off his back, ran in rivulets down the side of his face, dripped off his nose.

This place was not meant for human beings. No one could survive in this unbearable weather. He lowered himself to the ground on the shaded side of the vehicle, put his head in his hands, spat out a black fly, allowing half a dozen more to nestle in the corners of his mouth.

The handbook said to stay with your vehicle, you could not make it on foot if you were lost.

How did they know?

He couldn't sit here and die, either.

He raised his head, watched a few heavy dark birds circle overhead, allowed himself the chilling realization that they were vultures or buzzards of some kind.

"I'm not dead yet!" he shouted to the sky. "Git!"

He drank a small portion of water, ate more granola, and another beef stick. He wished for yogurt and cold, creamy milk straight out of the bulk tank in his family's milk house.

The small amount of food helped him think rationally and buoyed his spirits. He spread out the map, but had no clue on which road he might be. The nearest town, or clump of dwellings, was much too far away to go on another half tank of gas.

How far could a person walk if he had food and water? A hundred miles? Two hundred?

If he made twenty miles a day, in ten days he'd have gone two hundred miles, which would bring him to civilization, surely. If he stayed here with the Toyota for a week, ration the food and water, would someone come along?

He weighed his options on the scale of his own common sense, evaluated his food and water, and was racked by indecision. To stay was to trust God to send someone, to walk would be to trust himself and his physical prowess. Or maybe not. Who knew what God would throw at you around the next turn?

He doled out his food. Maybe another week, at the most. His water was even less. To carry all this would zap his strength more than if he simply sat here by the Toyota, but that he would not be able to do. He'd lose his sanity, watching down that long stretch of road.

For the hundredth time, he tried his cell phone.

No service.

He thought of radios, helicopters, small airplanes. The hand-book said the well-to-do cattle station owners all used small planes for a quick transport across the many miles that separated them. He hadn't heard a single plane.

His stomach lurched.

Perhaps he was so far out of line that he was thousands of miles from anyone, not just hundreds, the way he thought he might be. If he was, his fate was sealed.

The somber specter of death rose before him, too awful to con-sider. He needed to get out of here, and he needed to do it now.

He stuffed his backpack, tied his two remaining water jugs around his shoulders in the rolled-up blanket, put the white cloth in the window of the Toyota to signal help, and set off on foot, placing one shoe in front of the other, propelled by determination and not much else.

The rest of the day was spent doing just that, stopping only to shift the awkward pack of water jugs, or to take a drink. He realized the importance of staying hydrated, but it was necessary to ration the small amount of water.

The scenery stayed basically the same, except for an occasional streak of yellow earth, an unnamed bush or tree, sometimes an arrangement of odd rocks or placement of stones.

Mercifully, the sun lost some of its power as the evening wore on, which gave him renewed energy. He could feel the blisters forming on his right heel. His wool socks slid inside his soaked shoes.

When it was too dark to continue, he stopped, unrolled his blan-ket, spread out the jugs and the backpack, before listening to the night sounds of scurrying creatures, which seemed to unnerve him even more without the Toyota.

Everything he ate was coated in flies, so he figured he'd have a small amount of protein, anyway. They didn't bother him as much as before. Seemed like a person could get used to anything.

The night turned cold. He shivered in his thin blanket, rolled from side to side to stop the constant goosebumps, slept fitfully, but was too exhausted to wake fully. The stars hung so low at one point that it honestly felt as if the sky above had been lowered thousands or millions of miles.

In the morning, he thought he heard the low throbbing of an engine. Laying as still as stone, he strained his ears to hear, then gave up.

He was soon back on his feet, his socks and shoes dried and comfortable, the sun already climbing the blue sky to its full potential. He stopped under a baobob tree at noon, fell into a deep sleep, and was awakened by the distinct throb of an engine, the crunch of sand and small stones. He leaped to his feet, crashed through the scrub, waved his arms and cried out, screaming and shouting, jumped onto the middle of the road and waved his arms above his head like scissors.

"Stop, stop! Oh, come on. Come on! Look behind you!" he shouted, until he was hoarse.

The roiling dust cloud rose up, became smaller and smaller until it was only a speck that he could barely discern, his hope of being rescued disappearing along with it.

CHAPTER 18

Rose Kauffman was the daughter of Sam and Linda Kauffman from way over close to Ephrata. Her full name was Rosanna, but she went by Rose to shorten it.

She was twenty-one years old, therefore she was allowed to keep her own wages, decide where she wanted to be employed and what, if anything, she wanted to accomplish in life other than being a wife and mother, the ultimate goal for every young Amish girl.

Or most of them.

Rose was the unusual specimen of the female tribe, as her best friend called their group of girls. Rose had very little to say.

Ever.

She simply thought words were far too many and far too cheap, that half of all things girls said were absolutely unnecessary. And she'd never met a young man she liked well enough to hang out with more than a few times. She drifted in and out of different groups of youth and became bored with all of them.

Nothing interested her much. Sports were boring; once you'd been to one singing, you'd been to them all; guys always said the same dumb things; girls were mostly unbearably silly. So she often stayed home on the weekends and read books.

She read like a starved person eats food—voraciously. She devoured heavy classics, geography, books on plants, health, and romance, historic novels, biographies, and modern-day politics.

Since no one else was particularly interested in any of this, she kept it within, and went about her life and traveled to Hawaii with an older group of girls who were far more entertaining than the younger ones.

She got in trouble for flying.

Her parents were so *aus-ga-botta*. They had never imagined any of their children to be quite as adventuresome. They suffered through her quiet confession in church and reprimanded her afterward.

This was not to be done again, ever. She promised, felt humiliated, then shrugged it off.

It had been worth it, she figured, because now she had gone far beyond reading about a place as exotic as Hawaii. She had actually touched the leaves of the gorgeous flowers and smelled the air thick with fragrant blooms so lush it took your breath away. She'd viewed volcanoes and swam in a clear turquoise sea, snorkeled and ate all manner of delicious food, stayed at a house that hardly seemed to have doors or windows, with deep hammocks on the front patio beneath the fronds of a palm tree.

And she had met someone.

With all the books she'd read and all the accumulated knowledge stored in her dark head, Rose hadn't known what it would be like to meet a guy who intrigued her.

She had to look back. She had to wave.

And now she was surrounded by a deepening sense of gloom, a mysterious feeling of having been discovered and having discovered something herself.

And he was off to Australia to live. To be English. Had been English at the airport, for sure.

My, he was cute. Tall, well built, his white shirt stretched across his chest, his brown hair with streaks of blond cut just right, the intensity of his eyes, the well-set nose and mouth, the bright grin.

She couldn't stop seeing his face in her mind's eye.

Her mother, a tall thin woman of forty-five, noticed a subtle change in her, but overlooked it. After five daughters, navigating that messy swamp was not for sissies.

Especially this one, who simply did not follow the pattern of normalcy, which was to laugh and talk and giggle with girlfriends, to weave her way in and out of crushes on boys, just like the simple ordinary behaviors of all her girls.

Mysterious, that's what she was. Those huge black eyes like dark, inexplicable pools.

Rose worked at a restaurant simply called the "Town Diner" in the town of Ephrata. As she was in life, so she was in the workplace. Quiet, mysterious, her dark looks a magnetic draw for most men's eyes. If any one of these hapless admirers as much as tried to flirt, their ardor was puffed out with the efficiency of a fire extinguisher disguised as a cold hard stare.

She'd worked there at the Town Diner for more than five years, so she was one of the best waitresses. Coupled with her ability to help out in the kitchen, she was priceless to the owner. But she just had no spark, no personality, he thought. An occasional smile, all the right "good mornings" and "have a nice days," but never a spark of friendliness or an interest in anyone else's personal life.

Her coworkers called her Chocolate Chip: dark hair and dark personality. She shrugged it off and went on her way.

And now she couldn't stop thinking of Dave Stoltzfus in Australia.

She read all the books she could find on that specific country, winced as she read about Darwin, and figured she'd never see him again as she read about the kind of country he would be living in. But still, he stuck in her mind.

Anna was growing closer to Leon.

They shared a love of helping others, especially when it came to troubled children. Leon thrived in his work environment, constantly talking of this person or that, the circumstances surrounding the case, and the lack of skilled Christian counselors.

Her parents were more than pleased with their new baby Esther, a true gift from God, sat together on the couch and cuddled and cooed, both fond of the helpless newborns that needed their care. Leon reminded Anna over and over how blessed she was to have this wonderful set of parents.

And Dave faded into the background again, until he became like a gray sheet of parchment paper that fluttered only occasionally in her memory.

Dave sat beside the road, a sunburned, unshaven man whom his parents would barely have recognized, even if it had only been a short time since his departure. The days of being alone had taken a toll on him.

His water seemed to be evaporating in spite of having the lid screwed on tightly. He drank no more than he needed to be comfortable, which was too much, according to what was left.

He kept going, placing one foot in front of the other, his eyes constantly searching the horizon, the land that stretched out before him with seemingly no beginning and no end.

It was hard to fathom the lack of vehicles or any sign of human activity. Surely there was more going on than this. He wondered if there had been an obscure fork in the road, an unseen divide he had missed somehow.

Something, some town or cluster of people, someplace where there were signs of habitation had to be along this roadway.

But there was nothing. Nothing but the heat of the sun, the scraggly bushes and occasionally odd-looking tree, clumps of grass that stuck up like an old man's whiskers, an occasional rock, and the ever-worsening road.

By nightfall, he knew his situation was becoming very serious. He had enough water for one more day, which meant he'd be thirsty and still walking under this life-draining heat from the fiery orb that, unbelievably, was the same sun that had always shone on him in Lancaster County.

It had always been a friendly sun, the giver of light and warmth and essential for all of the verdant growth of that region. Here in the Outback, it was not a friendly sun; it was frightening.

And now he faced another night of cold with only the soiled blanket he slung across his shoulders. He decided to build a roaring fire, a large circle of heat and light, enabling anyone within a few miles, anyway, to see there was something or someone out here.

How could a region this uncomfortably hot be turned into this bone-chilling refrigerator at night?

With the heat of the fire, things turned hopeful, after his daily ration of dried fruit, beef sticks, and a few swallows of tepid water. He thought of a cold glass of fresh-squeezed lemonade tinkling with ice, a burger from McDonalds, a chicken leg the way his mother fried it.

He wondered if they ate chicken at these cattle stations, or if it was all beef all the time. If he had ever got there.

He stirred the fire with a long thin branch, gazed into it and thought about Anna and what she would do if he died. They wouldn't know for a very long time, perhaps ever. Maybe all that would be left of him would be a few bleached bones in the sun.

Dying was serious business.

Was he ready? All the sermons of his boyhood came to remind him that he wasn't. He didn't think he'd go to hell, really, but he wasn't sure God knew him well enough to take him to heaven. He just felt numb about death. Detached, sort of.

He understood this thing about Jesus dying to save him and all, he just never really felt like the story included him. He always figured he'd join the church someday, although he still didn't get why you had to join the Amish church to get to heaven.

Honor thy father and mother.

He surely wasn't an honor to them the way he'd carried on in Lancaster, all the craziness running with the wild group. Out here, he couldn't do any of that, so that was a step above his former self. Besides, he wouldn't be who he was if it wasn't for Anna's parents. He still couldn't stand the thought of either one of them.

As long as you were perfect, and did exactly what they wanted, they loved you. But if you didn't, well . . .

And he was not one of them, and never would be.

But Anna still followed him around, and that's exactly how it was. He couldn't get away from her.

Sparks flew up into the night sky as he jabbed viciously at the burning brush. These fires never lasted long with this skinny stuff, but it was better than nothing, he guessed.

His head felt as if someone had bashed him with a baseball bat, his temples throbbed, and one eye jumped in its socket. He watched wryly as the steam rose from his wet socks draped across a sort of mini wash line he'd created from sticks.

Those socks were disgusting, but without them he'd have blisters even worse than he had now. He thought of wearing only sandals but was afraid of the death adder, that poisonous snake that would spell certain death, not just the possible death he was facing now.

There was a chance he'd make it, he hoped, but it would take a total miracle.

One thing was for sure: you couldn't imagine the Outback. You couldn't even begin to visualize the heat and the desolation, the lack of things and people and noise and actions, the constant movement he had always known.

It was just dead out here.

His eyes grew heavy, his shoulders sagged with weariness, and the last thing he heard before falling asleep was the barking of the dingoes and the bleating of a sheep.

He rolled over, his body stiffened. He blinked, lifted his head to free both ears.

He had heard a sheep. The soft baa-a.

He waited, his heart pounding. If there were sheep, someone or something had to be guarding them, didn't they? Perhaps it wasn't dingoes he'd heard.

He strained to hear, praying there were real domestic animals close by, but there was only the distant barking now, a distinctive yipping he had come to recognize.

Like a person near death, hallucinating, dehydrated, he'd only imagined the sound of a bleating sheep. His shoulders slumped as he relaxed, and the most indescribable despair rolled through him, wave after wave of knowing he was not going to make it back alive.

This is where he would die.

His mouth trembled, honest tears formed in his eyes.

I'm sorry. Mam. Dat. I'm sorry you'll never know what happened.

The image of graying elderly parents, siblings who would never truly know why or how he had simply disappeared.

Oh God, I'm not ready to die. I'm young. I want to stay here and live the rest of my life. I'm not done at all.

He wept.

As he entered the quiet zone before a deep sleep, he heard it again.

Decidedly, there were sheep or goats or some creature that ma-aed or baa-ed, that distinctive small baby cry, that high bleating sound.

He sat up, his heart pounding.

Closer now. These animals were closer.

He heard the breaking of branches, small hard hooves on stone.

He leapt to his feet. His first instinct was to run through the night, capture a sheep, and cling to its neck, recognizing it as the savior it was.

Wildly now, he rummaged around, threw sticks and brush on the dying coals, and called out to the sheep.

"*Shippy! Shippy!*" He screamed the Dutch word for sheep.

He dashed madly into the dark, crashed into a heavy gorse bush, and was flung to one side. He found his footing and ran heedlessly calling out for the sheep.

Finally, he stopped. Breathing heavily, his chest heaving. He stood in the arid night, realized the futility of his mad dash, and turned to make his way back to the small red dot in the distance.

His campfire, the only thing that would bring him a small sense of comfort.

He flung himself on his blanket, raised his arms across his forehead, and stared at the stars above his head, trying to think rationally.

He knew he'd made a mistake leaving his vehicle, but then, what difference would it have made?

The passing motorist, that was what. They would have stopped, looked around, waited for someone to appear. He would have been helped, somehow.

He fell into a restless sleep, waking occasionally to feel the stickiness of his tongue, his lips cracked and dry, a burning need for water rearing its hideous visage in his dreams.

The cruel light in his eyes was unwelcome in the morning. The realization of his plight was like a heavy weight on his chest, pressing him down into his thin blanket.

Oh God.

He groaned His name repeatedly, without being aware of it. He only knew his whole being cried out to the God he didn't really know or understand, but lived with an image of the "Good Man" planted into his consciousness from the time he sat on his father's knee in church. There was no one here in this uninhabited land, this land of heat and flies and sparse vegetation, this land that could take all your false courage and self-worth, wring you out like a wet rag, and throw you aside to deal with your own lack of knowledge, fear, stupidity, remorse.

If only he'd stayed in Lancaster County and listened to his father. His parents became icons of light and sweetness. He'd always thought them as a bit bumbling, especially his mother, lumping her way through her days with all that weight and lack of energy, but he wished for all her common sense now. Her nagging. That voice that rose and fell and swished around his ears before taking off again.

He sat up, rubbed his eyes, drew the palms of his hands down over his face. He glanced at the blackened remains of his campfire, realizing the futility of lighting another one.

He was so thirsty.

He got to his feet, upended both water jugs, felt the few tepid drops that did absolutely nothing to ease his thirst. He tossed one, then the other to the ground, before sitting down on the sandy soil, his forearms flung across his upraised knees. He ran a hand through his hair, then raised his face to gaze off to the horizon.

That looked like a mountain, he thought, before he really took notice. A line of dark clouds rose in the distance.

What?

He got to his feet, shaded his eyes, strained to see the black formation. The Buildup, they called this season.

Wryly, he thought how timely this was, the oppressive humidity, the scorching sun that was exactly that, a weather pattern that was stacked against you, after which there would be rain and cooling temperatures.

If that bank of dark clouds would actually turn into rain, he would survive, wouldn't he?

All morning he watched the western horizon, watched the clouds drift, build, and go to the north, then disappear. His thirst turned to an agony, a clawing desperate need for water that threatened to take his sanity.

He found he did not have the strength to walk, so his only hope was to stay here by the side of the fissured and dented road, hoping someone would come by.

If the heat had been unbearable before, it had turned into a living, breathing dragon with tongues of fire now. The perspiration rose on his forehead. He was losing precious hydration.

He settled beneath the tallest bush he could find, attached his thin blanket to shade him, lay on his back and closed his eyes.

So this is where they'd find him, then. Someone would, eventually. A strange calm crept up and surrounded him.

Suddenly, the hot brassy light of the sun was snuffed out. He raised his head, blinked.

What?

It was still morning. He didn't know if he'd lost his mind or not. Perhaps the whole day had gone by and he'd passed out or something.

He crawled out, got to his feet, reeled, and righted himself before everything turned black.

At first, he thought he was at home, back in Lancaster County, in the shower. He gasped, turned his head to one side, then the other.

He was being pummeled by pinpricks of rain, rain that fell from the black rolling clouds, driven by a whining roaring wind.

Cold hard pellets of rain.

He sat up, crawled out from beneath the sparse shelter, turned on his back and opened his mouth to allow the drops to fall like nectar into his parched throat.

It was not enough.

He cupped his hands, licked the palms of his hands, got to his feet to open the water jugs, expose the undersides of the lids, anything to catch precious life-giving moisture.

Lightning sizzled through the air, so static with power his hair stood on end, followed by an immediate deafening roll of thunder that was three times as hard as he'd ever heard back home. And Lancaster had some awesome storms.

No matter, now. He was saved. *Thank you, God. Thank you. I sure appreciate this.*

He was wild, maudlin, drinking from the undersides of the lid before there was any real accumulation, his tongue finding every dent to lick the last remaining drop before turning to upend the second lid and tilt the jug itself to allow the small stream of water to drain across his parched tongue.

Thirst was a clawing, vicious animal that lived in your gut and raked your insides with misery. It stuffed your head with cotton balls, your mouth screaming silently for relief.

Three days, you had out here. That's it. Probably less.

He sat in water, it streamed off his body, dripped off the end of his nose, blinded his eyes. The lightning snaked across the sky, the air clenched like a waiting jaguar, before the deafening thunder rolled across the sky. He found himself rolled under the thorny bush, curled into a fetal position, the tops of his fingers stuffed into his ears.

There was an alarming amount of water, now. The jugs, the lids, everything was full. He drank, swallowed greedily, then turned his head aside to throw up everything he'd ingested before taking up the lid and drinking again.

He didn't know how long he'd sat under the small shelter because he had no idea of time. He became aware of the torrents that fell from the sky, the surface around him turning into a shallow creek.

There was no letup from the lightning or the thunder that careened around in his head and echoed in his chest. He felt its force even in the soles of his feet.

He stood up to see how much water was actually accumulating, shading his eyes with palms down to keep the water out. He was on level ground as far as he could tell. But he'd read about walls of water descending in gullies and low places, wiping out whatever lay in its path.

This was a cruel land, a land without mercy.

Days of torrid sun and life-threatening thirst replaced by another flood from the days of Noah and the ark, by all appearances.

Should he move on? Was he in a low place? He didn't think so, but had no idea how to tell, with everything deceptively level.

He shivered, the sluicing water on his body creating another level of discomfort. He needed to walk, to get some warmth into his shaking limbs.

He gathered up his meager stash, groaned under the weight of the sodden blanket and the filled water jugs, and started off, sloshing through increasing amounts of water.

His shoes pushed through it, then his ankles.

He stopped and looked around but had no idea where to go to find higher ground. He was afraid to leave the road with no phone service, no one to call in case he became hopelessly lost, which is what would occur if he traveled away from the road. Not that his phone had any battery left at this point anyway. He'd kept it charging while in his car, but once the gas ran out, that was that.

His legs were tiring as the current of water increased.

A sizzle of lightning struck a small round tree close by and sent an electric current through him. It was then that he realized the extent of his plight.

He was a sitting duck.

Here I am, I guess, God. Do with me what you want.

And still the storm raged on.

Walking made a difference in his body heat. The shivering subsided, and his energy increased. The current of water had thinned, which made every step easier, and for that, he was grateful.

When the wall of water came roaring out of the gorge, it slammed into him with the force of a truck, which is what he thought had hit him, until he rolled and tumbled, completely submerged in a vast, stinking world without oxygen.

Ironic, his death. After dying of thirst, he was being shaken in a huge washer until he drowned.

The will to live was fierce within him, the passion with which he viewed the world sparked, caught fire, and lent strength to his legs.

He kicked like a frog, scissored his arms, desperate to free his lungs from the tons of water that caved in on him. He strained to breathe, his lungs on fire, tumbling around and over before he let go. Swallowing water, he cried silently, tried to let out a scream from deep within his soul.

He slammed against a hard object, spun away from it like a wet rag doll. His head burst through the surface. He gasped, retched, choked, filled his lungs with lifesaving oxygen before being pulled under to the netherworld of death and drowning, a place that judged you harshly, without the intervention of grace or mercy.

So this is what hell would be.

Doomed, with a remorse that sucked away all the mortality with which God had blessed him. Foolish. He had been so foolish, throwing away the love of his parents, his siblings, Anna.

Oh, Anna, my love.

He struggled with every ounce of his strength, always straining to merge from the roiling pressure of being swept along by this freak wall of water rushing through this arid land, after almost dying of thirst. He felt himself weakening, unable to hold his breath a moment longer.

He breathed in, swallowed water, his desperation renewed as he felt wave after wave of nausea, the sensation of being finished, before everything blackened with a hard crunch.

CHAPTER 19

In the northwestern bump of the loneliest Australian state, in a region called the Kimberly, the aging couple had reaped the rewards of their bold pioneer spirit, having pushed through the region decades ago to settle along the Adelaide River, building one of the area's most successful sheep and cattle stations, the land reaching from craggy ocher ranges to dry grasslands for thousands of acres.

The region had always been known as the Top End, and that was where Bob and Darcy Kel still made their home. Sunburned, gaunt and craggy, they resided over the enormous house and outbuildings with keen eyes sunk deep into leathery faces, observing everything, hearing with unimpaired ears. Their son Watson and his wife Sallies, Sal for short, resided in the same house with their four unmarried sons and one daughter, and a host of immigrants they called "blowins," who came and went with the seasons, or lack of dedication, whichever came first.

Staunch Roman Catholics who attended Mass as regularly as the dawning of each new day, fiercely loyal to the clergy, in awe of the Vatican in Rome, they took their religion seriously, praying with wellworn rosary beads, calling upon their God for every need.

They had no use for any other religion. The Catholic Church had stood for thousands of years, represented the largest group of Christians, so everything else was considered chaff, as far as they were concerned. Proud of their heritage, strongly independent, they were who they were and if others didn't agree with them, that was too bad.

Every sheep station had a name of its own, so identification came easily. Broghurst, as the massive station was known, grew into and remained one of the most profitable establishments in the region, managed by Bob, Watson, and a group of loyal and hardworking Aboriginal people.

The barns were long, wide, and low, with corrugated metal roofs, a jigsaw puzzle of shearing sheds and holding pens, lambing and sick sheds, all managed and operated by the four sons and lone daughter, Ammie. She rode, roped, herded, tended to the dogs, cared for stray lambs rejected by the mothers, and never thought of staying indoors or learning any womanly skills from her mother. As far as she was concerned, there was only the vast area known as Broghurst, the animals and each new day that taught her more about nature, the workings of the station, and her skill at driving sheep.

Small, compact, with a riot of brown curls and eyes to match, she moved through her days with the intensity of a half-grown cat, her large brown eyes missing nothing, joining every foray into the dry grassland in search of the sheep, either on horseback or by ATV. She preferred horses and owned two outstanding riders named Kanga and Roo, which was a never-ending source of teasing from her four brothers, Ron, Matt, Will and Ty. The names rolled efficiently off the tongue, taking up no more time and energy than was absolutely necessary, same as everything else on this efficient station.

The bevy of short-legged Australian cattle dogs named Bo, Bev, and Bob milled underfoot with gaping mouths and quick darting eyes, waiting for commands to speed into the "bush," which is what they called the Outback.

The house on Broghurst was three stories high, with massive front pillars and low windows with wide wooden shutters on either side. Built with wood, painted yellow with black shutters, surrounded by massive gum trees, silver wattle trees and flowering acacia bushes, Eucalyptus grew everywhere, lending its distinctive odor across a

green lawn mowed to perfection by the head gardener, Null. Darcy
planted roses from the time the station was built. She transplanted,
clipped, and sprayed till the odor mingled with eucalyptus became
the heady scent of a place far removed from the Australian outback.
Now, in her eighties, she still moved among her "rosies" with pruning
shears and liquid fertilizer.

The Buildup was hard to tolerate, so she stayed indoors except
in the early morning, or after the heat of the day gave way to crisp
evening air. They had installed central air-conditioning only recently,
giving a rush of cool, dry air from newly installed vents surrounding
many of the rooms, providing comfort for both Bob and Darcy. No
matter how Watson scoffed at this unnecessary luxury, he sought
the cool interior of the house quite frequently when the heat became
unbearable.

Heat and dust and flies. That was the order of everyone's life on
Broghurst in the dry season, after which came torrential downpours
that produced millions of wildflowers in every color imaginable.
Saltbushes grew to epic proportion, nurturing the livestock with their
salty tasting leaves.

Their lives revolved around the seasons and the animals, the nearest town a good two hundred miles to the east.

Stragglers were not uncommon. Drifters who ran small rusted
vehicles until they died, then made their way on foot, putting their
lives into serious jeopardy in the dry season. Each one was welcomed,
his worth considered, more often than not given a job, which never
(or hardly ever) lasted longer than a few weeks, sometimes months.

The first storm of the season was predicted that Thursday. Darcy
sat in her floral recliner with lace covering the arm pads, her feet
encased in L.L.Bean moccasins resting on the upraised footrest
as the weatherman pointed to the map of Australia. The television
was a new flat screen mounted on the wall, shipped all the way from
Darwin, a modern marvel. Darcy loved her TV, the only source to the
wide outside world she knew existed and still loved.

Bob ambled by with a mug of steaming tea, lowering himself

carefully into his leather recliner, balancing the mug with a steady hand and narrowed eyes.

"Storm," Darcy said, pointing her chin in the direction of the TV.

"Aye, yes it is. About time."

He took a long time getting his tea situated on the coaster, then reached down to pull on the lever to bring up the footrest.

"Someone let Watson know?"

"He knows. He has his cell phone."

Bob nodded, picked up his mug, squinted and sipped, replaced it, sighing deeply before watching the flickering screen. He fell asleep almost as soon as he laid his head to one side, snoring softly, the accompanying sound the rhythmic clicking of Darcy's knitting needles.

In another section of the house, along the back where the kitchen was located, Sal was rubbing peppercorns and salt into a fat, marbled roast of beef, listening to the local news from the sound system in the corner of the ceiling. Tanned, short and stout, she resembled an older version of her daughter, Ammie. Her face was round and pleasant, with deep lines etched along her eyes like carefully folded paper.

Watson wanted her to have a cook and a housekeeper, but she would have none of it, in spite of knowing that cost was no problem. She didn't want another woman in her kitchen or cleaning her bathrooms, snooping into drawers and living in the same house. Servants, or "help," the word used nowadays, were not necessary. Not as long as she had two capable legs and arms.

She stopped rubbing the peppercorns to listen, pursed her lips and drew her eyebrows down in concentration.

"Ah, yes," she murmured. It was the end of the "Dry."

Seasons were broken between the "Wet" and the "Dry" and understood and accepted by everyone on Broghurst as a necessity, a way of life that rippled along like a well-contained stream.

The sheep and cattle traveled for miles, especially in the dry season, foraging on clumps of grass and low bushes, finding water in the billabongs that dotted the arid land. A windmill and a large galvanized tank watered all the stock in the sheds and surrounding area.

Sal estimated the storm to hit by Friday afternoon, which was from twenty to twenty-four hours away. She thought of Bob and Darcy. The roads would be impassable through much of October and November, so she hoped they'd remain in good health.

They had the Cessna, but still.

In the evening, all nine of them gathered around the long sturdy oak table, the chandelier above their heads gleaming with a thousand points of light. They bowed their heads, followed by Bob's rumbling "Father, we thank Thee," the first four words of a long dialogue that only served to whet their appetites.

Ammie stole a look at her grandmother, who winked broadly. Dimples appeared on her cheeks as she smiled back. A frown formed on her mother.

The four boys dug in, brown-haired, brown-eyed, and brown-skinned, in various stages of growth and development, their appetites appeared to be the one thing alike in each one.

They never ate during the day. After a hearty breakfast washed down with thick mugs of strong tea, they disappeared for the day, to return in the evening, their stomachs rumbling, hollow eyed with hunger.

Watson, the father, was below average height, but built like a wrestler, all compact sinew and muscle, his brown eyes twitching. He was all energy and an explosion of getting ahead, every word and maneuver counting.

"Storm's coming," he said, after the grandfather had intoned all of the lengthy prayer. There was no answer, only heads nodding as they passed dishes and wolfed down the first mouthfuls, bread torn into chunks and stuffed into mouths without butter.

"Hogs," Ammie said loudly, elbowing Ron.

There was no answer to that, either.

Silence hung over the table, broken only by the scraping of forks on porcelain and tea slurped from heavy mugs.

"It will be a good one, by the report on the TV," Darcy said, wiping her face with a napkin.

"Hope all the blow-ins are close to high ground," Watson answered, shaking his head.

"Ain't no use tryin' to warn anyone. They come out here anyway."

"Stupid people."

"Oh, you know. It's the pull of the Outback. Buy an expensive SUV and have yourself a little adventure."

Seasoned veterans of the bush from a young age, they had no patience with half-dead drifters and their empty water cans, eyes hollow with the horror of poisonous snakes and howling dingoes.

When the rain came, coupled with thunder and lightning, no one seemed to think it was extraordinary. It was the beginning of the Wet, so if it rained fifty or sixty inches in the coming months, it was all right with them. Sheep and cattle could fend for themselves, and the grass on Broghurst would be bursting out of the soil, providing food for all the livestock.

Water slammed against the window screens, the wind sucking them in and out and flinging rain in bucketfuls against the windowpanes.

Spouting overflowed, sending sheets of cold rainwater into the shrubbery below, where it collected on small leaves until it was weighed down and parted in the middle. Fat black crickets dragged their half-drowned bodies across stones glistening with rain, slipped and were swept away by gushes of water from the downspout.

Horses kicked and whinnied, tore up the paddock with their hooves as they galloped around and around. Cattle bowled, sheep bleated, slipped the quagmire and fell like sodden dust mops. Barn doors crashed and slapped against the frame as hinges loosened, until the boys ran from the house, raincoats flapping against their Wellingtons, one hand smashing the leather hat to their heads, followed by the father, yelling something unintelligible, before lowering his face and plowing through the torrent like a bulldozer.

"What?"

"Lightning hit at Wilshore! House on fire!"

"We gotta fix this first!"

For neighbors were neighbors, even if the distance between them was sixty-five miles.

"Make sure there's petrol."

"Which vehicle?"

"Take the Land Rover."

Through the maelstrom, the men plowed through, piled gasping and dripping into the truck designed with these elements in mind.

Ammie wanted to go but was refused.

Visibility was bad, but not so bad that the wipers couldn't make a way, swishing on high, raking sheets of water from the windshield. After a heated argument about the river, an ear- splitting crash of thunder rocked the vehicle on its tires.

"Turn back, Pap. Turn back!" Ron shouted, his eyes bulging like white eggs, his mouth wide with fright.

"We'll be all right," Watson shouted.

But no one could cross the river. They got out of the vehicle, stood in the wind and the downpour, watching in horror as the brown sluice of water rushed across anything in its way, uprooting eucalyptus bushes and flinging them along as if they were pretzels. The bridge shuddered with the force of the rolling thunder, the sizzling lightning its predecessor.

There was nothing to do but get back in the vehicle and turn around, sliding across deep gullies already carved out by the onslaught. Watson shifted gears, turned the steering wheel one way and then another, peering through the driving rain till they reached the portico at the big yellow house.

"This whole vehicle smells like a wet dog," Matt growled, disappointed at missing out on the excitement of a house on fire.

"Well, git. Git out."

Lots of jostling, shoving, with Matt being deposited unceremoniously on the rough flagstone. They all laughed at the ensuing yelp of outrage, then sobered when there was a hysterical screech followed by a pounding on the door, and fruitless yanking of the handle.

"Open up. Guys, I'm serious!"

They complied, all eyes following Matt's shaking finger to the drowned, bleeding figure huddled in the corner of the carport.

"Oh man. Don't they ever quit?"

"This one's in bad shape."

Eyes wide in their sockets, a ghostly face streaked by rivulets of blood that had been washed away, fresh blood following the rivulet before.

His mouth worked. He grimaced. He waved a hand as if to keep them with him. A hoarse croak escaped his throat.

By now, everyone was out of the Land Rover, staring openmouthed.

"Help."

A gulping, swallowing sound. Another frantic fluttering of the hand.

"Good Lord!" Watson breathed.

"Help me. My . . ."

A hand fluttered to the forehead, before the apparition keeled over in a dead faint, a soaked, filthy pile of torn clothing and matted hair.

"Heave-ho!" Watson shouted, and each son came to the rescue, supporting an arm or a leg and shuffling into the side entrance before depositing him on the cold ceramic tile floor.

"Get Mom."

"Blankets."

Blankets, a heating pad, whiskey, smelling salts, everything was done calmly and in order. This one had a serious head wound. The way that blood was pumping there wouldn't be much time. They couldn't take the Cessna up in this.

Lightning crackled, lit the windows in bluish white triangles, before the entire house was shaken in the teeth of the rumbling thunder.

Sal was quick, efficient, raising his body to a forty-five-degree angle, applying red pepper flakes, a tourniquet. Her hands examined the battered body, finding more cuts and alarming bruises, but nothing too serious.

He moaned, opened his eyes, stared without focus. He turned his head from side to side, grimacing in pain.

"Poor bugger."

"Definitely a blow-in."

"Green as fish gills."

"Hand o' God he's alive, boys. Now shut up. Give him some space."

Sal sat by his bed in the upstairs guest room, waking him every hour. She could only guess at his head injuries, but figured a concussion was the least of his problems, so she'd keep him from a prolonged sleep.

By morning, she'd found out his name was Dave Stoltzfus from Pennsylvania, and he'd gotten caught when a gully washer emptied into the Adelaide River and spewed him onto its banks like Jonah of old, half-drowned and clobbered on the head.

She fed him broth, which he heaved up in one roaring sound, then let him sleep. He'd be all right, she reasoned, and went off to her own bed for a few hours of much-needed rest before making breakfast for the crew.

Dave slept fitfully, waking to bouts of pain so intense he squeezed his eyes shut as tears seeped out from beneath the lashes. He dreamt of voids, black holes with no beginning and no end, of being hurled through outer space, his clothes snagged on five-pointed stars. He saw Anna in a white dress, followed by the black-haired girl in vivid shades of red. He saw the sun turn orange, then red, and back to orange before it bled all over his pillow.

He woke, felt the pillowcase. His fingers came away sticky with his own blood.

For a week, he laid in bed, visited only by Sal or Watson. The boys had no interest in another drifter, and the parents said he was far too young and too handsome for the likes of Ammie.

Flirty, she was, so there was no taking chances.

He drank sips of greasy beef broth that strengthened his spirits. He learned to enjoy the hard Irish soda bread, black and dense and life-giving. He also learned of his first serious mistakes: that he didn't purchase a cell phone with an Australian carrier, and that he failed to stay with his vehicle no matter what. A vehicle will be spotted long before a human alone. And one should never prepare for one destination before changing your mind and heading in another direction. Likely he'd have made it to Alice Springs. And his water and petrol supply should have been doubled.

Dave could only nod, feeling pangs of real humiliation almost like sorrow. He never smiled or laughed, the remembering of his ordeal too raw to allow any real emotion. He thanked Watson and Sal over and over but declined to tell them of any plans.

On the seventh day, he shaved, showered, brushed his teeth, and got dressed in a clean set of Matt's clothes, his ankles stretched out of the too-short jeans, the T-shirt straining at the seams. He was gaunt, hollow-eyed, and bruised, but as tall and as handsome as he'd ever been, albeit with a new light of self-discovery and a calm reassurance of his future.

He was going home.

Ammie fell in love immediately. She followed him from paddock to paddock, describing every aspect of the lonely life on the station in the Australian outback. Her brown eyes were liquid with worship. She begged him to stay. The four brothers were impressed with his strength once he was fully healed, and they offered him the best horse if he'd try his hand at ranching.

The brown land erupted in a verdant display of wildflowers and grasses so heavy they hung in clumps like small bowing children. The humidity lifted, leaving clear, gorgeous skies and crisp nights.

Dave learned to know the workings of this immense operation.

He recognized the people for what they were, hardworking Catholics who were as embedded in their own faith and traditions as the Amish.

But all he really wanted now was to board a plane and return home, the place where he truly belonged.

He used the landline and called his parents' number, leaving a message at the sound of the beep. He choked up when he heard the recording: "You have reached Eli and Rachel Stoltzfus. Leave a message." No "thank you," no "have a nice day," only the necessary information.

"Mam, it's me, Dave. I'm in Australia, somewhere in the Top End, a place they call the Kimberly. I'm at a cattle station with the Watson Kel family. I'm coming home soon. Call this number so we can talk."

Rachel was irritated that evening. Irked at the eyeglass place in town, she went to check her messages. Surely they'd be calling about whether she still had a warranty on that cracked lens.

What was wrong with those people?

It was not over a year since she had those eyeglasses. She had the receipt to prove it, so they could just go pounding around all they wanted on those computer keys. She had the paper receipt with the date on it.

When Dave's voice came through the receiver, she threw it down and shrieked like a much younger woman, bent to retrieve it and began weeping with abandon.

She clenched her skirts in one hand and ran the whole way to the barn to find Eli, gasped and clutched at her dress front, wept and talked and carried on until her husband feared heart failure from stress and excitement.

They returned to the phone shanty in the backyard together, Eli blinking back the tears of joy, watched his wife dial the international digits with shaking hands, before hearing the "Hello?"

It was an Australian accent, and for a moment they felt disappointment sweeping in, but then the phone was quickly handed off to their beloved son.

"Oh my, David. Is that you?"

More weeping followed by loud honking noises from the folds of Rachel's handkerchief. She pocketed it, blinked, and composed herself before listening closely.

"Are you coming home, then? When? Oh, when, David? A couple weeks? You feel you owe it to them? David, you don't owe those people anything. They just did for you what anyone else would do."

She listened, shook her head, then handed the receiver to Eli, listening to his gravelly voice as he spoke kindly, encouraging him to come home as soon as he felt the time was right.

Yes, yes, he understood. Of course he owed them. Sure. Sure. And hung up with a smile for Rachel.

"He'll be home. Just give him time."

A full year passed before they heard from him again. It was a year of anxious messages he never returned. A year of aging, withering beneath the weight of having a son who lived as an Englisha in Australia.

A year of changes and hard work, building the Daudy house and having a son take over the farm. Rachel lost weight and part of her mind, she told her friend Malinda, building that house and watching her overeager daughter-in-law hire someone to rip out perfectly good kitchen cabinets and replace them with white ones. White. She would regret that yet. Those kids, yes, she was so upset she called her grandchildren "kids," would have fingerprints and knicks in that paint before a year was over.

But she never said a word to anyone else. She kept the peace and appreciated her daudy house, with its small space and plenty of time to call a driver and run to Walmart.

Eli got a job at the cabinet shop on Appleway Road.

She packed his lunch every morning with all kinds of small Tupperware containers filled with fruit and pudding, egg salad for his sandwich, and seven-day sweet pickles to go along with it. His favorite pretzels too. Utz thins.

They planted trees, hired a landscaper to put in a small yard, at a *schrecklich* price. Rachel lamented every cent they gave that man, saying her poor mother would have a fit if she was alive. But Eli scoffed at her frugality and said he wasn't going to break his back raking that stubbly soil. Why not let the landscaper putter around in his tractor?

Rachel had an awful time of adjusting to the little house. The big farmhouse was still hers, in her own mind, and drew her like a magnet. She honestly tried to stay in her own house, but found herself at the daughter-in-law's door quite frequently. When Daniel came to her door and spoke hesitantly, asking her to please stop going to the house quite as much, she was devastated but put on a brave front and didn't set foot on that porch for ten days. Well, ten and a half if you counted that last Thursday forenoon.

It was so true what her mother said. Children walk all over your heart when they're older. They sure did. Here was David on the other side of the world, and she guaranteed the longer he stayed there, the harder it would be to come home. If he didn't call soon, she was simply going to sit in the middle of her kitchen and have a nervous breakdown. She simply had too much time on her hands.

She hardly had a garden. That little postage-stamp-sized one hardly contained enough vegetables to feed a few rabbits, but then, they didn't need very many canned goods, either. You could only eat so many pickles and red beets when you were in your sixties. Peaches and pears sat on the can shelves and turned brown on top. Eli wouldn't eat them, anyway.

Oh, she wished David would come home to eat up all those peaches and pears.

Chapter 20

In June, when the yellow peace lilies bloomed and the pink climbing rose blossomed on the south side of the house, Leon asked Anna to marry him. He got down on one knee and won her heart with his earnest expression, his dark good looks, and his kindness.

She said yes.

They planned a lovely wedding for the last week in October, after council meeting and communion. As was the tradition, four hundred and fifty guests were invited on the most lavish invitations her mother could find. In silver, white, and gray. Her colors were coordinated by her mother as well, the silver for the little sisters and the nieces on his side, gray for the bridal table waters, and the bride would wear navy blue with the traditional white cape and apron. There would be silver and white on her eck with a few understated touches of navy blue.

The food would be amazing. Nothing was too lavish for Anna and Leon, the pride and joy of her parents' hearts. Approval was the driving force behind all the generosity, the eagerness to comply with all Anna's wishes, and the need to have Leon included and welcomed in the family.

A fine Christian son-in-law. What more could they ask for?

Caught up in the whirl of wedding plans and dreams, Anna was fulfilled, her life finally free of indecision and anxiety. She no longer thought of Dave and could barely remember his face. Instead, the face of her beloved Leon meant more to her than all the love she had ever felt for her former boyfriend.

Leon was a paid counselor now, working full-time at the Homestead, a facility for troubled teenaged boys. His dream became a reality then, and he rented the small house close to Millerstown, planning to carry his beautiful bride across the threshold, embarking on a journey of love and devotion that would last for the remainder of his life.

He didn't have much, but they didn't need much. Love would provide for all their needs.

Only sometimes, when a sleepless night kept her from her much-needed rest, the questions without answers cavorted through her head like mischievous elves bringing a sense of something gone awry, some Y in her path she had never fully understood. Why did God do the things he did? Why had he allowed Dave to be so headstrong? And why had he allowed him into her life from a very young age, allowed the adoration to rise and grow in her heart, only to have him torn away?

She always consoled herself with the fact that God had provided Leon, in spite of having taken David away, which was His kindness and mercy.

She would always fall asleep with the consolation that David would never return, and if he did, he was nothing to her. She never thought of him at all, ever.

October was a whirl of activity, writing and rewriting wedding lists. They tilled the garden and sowed tillage radishes. They trimmed and mulched hedges and shrubs, and planted white chrysanthemums in pots on the patio and in flower beds. They gave a fresh coat of white paint to everything that appeared even slightly worn. They fertilized the lawn and mowed, clipped, and trimmed it until it looked like a green carpet.

They prepared an immense new shop a few months before the wedding, large enough to easily accommodate the four hundred and fifty guests. Relatives came to help. Leon presented Anna with a clock, the traditional engagement gift. She accepted it with a bright smile, hung it on the wall in her beautiful room, and never admitted that it looked cheap and shabby and out of place. Her mother positioned wall sconces on either side, so that helped.

For Leon did not have a hefty bank account, nor did he make wages that were considered substantial, so Anna was given a lecture by both of her parents and presented with a booklet on finances and the virtues of saving money for the husband's benefit. Of which her mother knew or practiced nothing. But still.

Anna had known from the day she met him that he had no idea about expensive things, name brands, the class in which the upper circle moved and lived. She would embark on this new journey, learn how to save, to be content with what he provided, and never complain, the way the booklet described.

They were married on a bright October day, with the sky dotted with white clouds like clumps of cotton balls, a fair breeze, and the sun's warmth so that guests could sit in clusters beneath the stately oaks.

Leon's father attended, calmed by his antianxiety and depression medication, his mother serene and appreciative of her new daughter-in-law.

Eli and Rachel Stoltzfus were among the guests as well, Rachel cooked the creamed celery with Eno's sie Leah, who used far too much vinegar, in her opinion, but then, if she said anything she'd be shunned for the rest of the day, so she kept her mouth shut. That's how Leah was. Had always been. She knew best in everything, from quilts to shoe measurement, paying hundreds of unnecessary dollars for those stupid arch supports she wore, claiming her back went out if she didn't wear them.

In Rachel's opinion, her back was always out, as was her head.

But they'd been friends forever, sitting beside each other in church for more than thirty years, their children attending the same school.

So why ruin a good friendship trying to change the amount of vinegar in cooked celery? Some things just weren't worth it.

Rachel was happy for Anna that day, she really was. She looked radiant, as always, and her darkly handsome groom was a perfect match.

Yes, God smiled down on this couple indeed, so she sat on the bench with the other church ladies and sang her heart out on the old German wedding songs, a boon to her spirits.

She tried not to think of David, far away in Australia, the *ungehorsam*, the rebel, the shame of their existence. How would she feel if her David was the one who stood beside Anna? Tall and so handsome.

That Leon was all right, she supposed, but what was up with his crooked haircut on the day of his wedding? But she brought her thoughts back into the harness of her Christian upbringing, jabbed an elbow into her friend Leah's side, turned her head, and raised an eyebrow. Leah was singing so loudly it rang in Rachel's ears like an annoying bullhorn, so she leaned back and watched as she poked a finger along a German line of words.

Rachel sat back, sang heartily in tune with everyone else, stopping only to help herself to yet another handful of the homemade sour cream and onion potato chips. She should actually be eating celery dipped in salt, but there was no flavor at all in a stalk of celery except for the salt, and it was bad news for heavy women.

She wiggled her toes inside her serviceable black shoes and felt her toes swelling at the thought of salt. The celery looked nice, though.

After lunch they cleaned the tables, washed the dishes with soapy water, dried and put them back on the tables with vases of celery, including the leafy tops set every few yards along the lengths.

Mints, bowls of potato chips, with plenty of water and coffee helped to make the time as pleasurable as possible. Rachel eyed the rows of folding chairs where the family, relatives, and friends sat being served all manner of fancy dishes.

There were steaming platters of shrimp, kebabs, soft pretzels with cheese dip, small strombolis or pizza roll ups of some kind. Glasses of tea or cider or punch, she couldn't tell.

Well, she was out of it, not being a close relative. None for her. And she was not the groom's parents, the important mother figure, so there was no shrimp for her. A sadness enveloped her. She felt her throat tighten at the thought of being a church lady making celery on the day Anna was married.

Leah handed her a mint Life Saver wrapped in cellophane. Rachel shook her head. Let her chew her own Life Savers. She hated those things. Like chewing deodorant.

As a bride, Anna was radiant, in every sense of the word. The radiance came from true happiness, the wellspring of joy that kept cropping up repeatedly throughout the day.

There were no more days of indecision, no more nights of wondering, of hoping, of wishing things could have been different. They were bound by the law of God and the law of the state of Pennsylvania. Till death do us part. In sickness and in health.

She was bound to Leon with an ordained, invisible rope that could never be cut except by death. There was no divorce, no getting out of this contract.

And she had no reason to think she would ever want to. She loved Leon with all her heart. Her love was sufficient to see her through the good days and the bad. Well versed in the ways of marriage by the many Christian writings her parents supplied, she felt prepared as she gazed at the beloved profile, the patrician nose, and the dark hair cut a bit longer on one side than the other.

They moved to the Hertz place in Millerstown after they worked for weeks repairing, painting, and cleaning up. Anna smiled brightly when her mother asked if they'd mentioned the state of the linoleum to her landlord, or if this was the way they would live.

"Why, Mom, of course not!" Anna chortled.

"You mean, you won't ask?"

"Why would we? This linoleum is just fine. I'll put a rug across the torn spots. No problem."

She took a secret delight in her mother's spluttering, watching the battle of what she should say and what she wanted to say move across her face.

Mother, this is what you wanted for me, she thought. *I chose the one you approved of, now keep approving for the remainder of my time here on earth.*

Was it still, then, a form of rebellion? After all this time of submission, of Christian obedience, why now this secret gladness at her mother's discomfiture?

Her mother took the linoleum in stride, got down on her hands and knees and scrubbed the cracks with a brush, waxed it with old fashioned Jubilee kitchen wax, laid the expensive rugs from Bon-Ton on top, stood back and surveyed the makeover and was pleased with the result. It was amazing what a bit of paint and some costly furnishings could do.

Anna had the best of everything. The best sewing machine and cabinet, the large refrigerator, the highest-quality stove, the living room suite from Good's furniture in New Holland.

They groomed the yard, plowed a small garden, with Leon observing the work ethic of his new bride's family, amazed at the transformation in a month's time. By Christmastime, when the holly berries peeped out from between the spiked, waxy leaves, the Hertz place resembled a cottage that could easily have appeared in a magazine.

Snow fell in January, covering the small house with a clear layer of white flakes. The woodstove in the basement provided heat, the windows glowed with the yellow light of flickering candles, and Anna and Leon expressed their love and appreciation daily, the way the book instructed them.

His counseling took up much of his time and thoughts. He brought his black leather briefcase home, did his paperwork in the evening at the kitchen table, Anna in a chair beside him, leaning on one elbow, a foot tucked beneath her.

The problems with which he dealt every day were massive, a mountainous trail that doubled back time and again. Yet he remained dedicated, inspired by his work, taking on problems too monumental for one human mind to comprehend.

They shared their feelings, sitting side by side on matching recliners, their feet encased in warm slippers, a lap robe surrounding Anna. The house was old, the many cracks around the loose windows allowing plenty of cold air to leak through. But the cheerful woodstove lent its heat, and the days moved by in quick succession.

It was when the woodpile became low, the wood in the basement all gone, that Anna felt a slight twinge of consternation.

He had mentioned the fact that he needed to order a load of logs to be cut and split, but so far, nothing had materialized.

The propane bill had evidently not been paid, either, with the alarming amount of two hundred and seven dollars for . . .

Hmmm.

Two months. Last month's bill had not been paid.

When she approached him in a quiet voice, he raised his eyebrows before he kissed her, lifting her off the floor in a playful hug, and asked why a month's bill was important when they had so much love to live on. Anna responded with a bright smile of appreciation, laughed a small laugh of acceptance, and the incident was over.

A cold front moved in from Canada the last week in January with a stiff wind that moaned eerily around the house, sent snow skittering across rooftops and whirling off the tops of drifts until perfect snow dunes lined the fields and roadways. Anna went to the basement to stoke the fire and found only six pieces of wood. She piled three of the heavy chunks into the stove, made meatloaf, green beans, and a potato casserole for supper, and thought surely there was more wood somewhere—perhaps Leon had stashed some elsewhere. The thermometer hovered just above ten degrees all day, but as evening fell, it plunged to the zero point.

Leon breezed through the door, all the whirling white and cold

outside, bringing his bright face and happy smile, the perfect anec-
dote from his day already spilling out of him.

They ate amid his accounts of the day. He did not comment on
the food, seemingly unaware of what went into his mouth, so Anna
wisely bided her time until she haltingly asked about the wood supply.

"Oh my goodness!"

Down came the palm of his hand on the table top, rattling the
dishes.

"I clean forgot to call Bill Stoner. Shoot."

He turned sideways in his chair to gaze out into the heavy darkness, his expression unreadable.

"How many pieces did you say?"

Anna told him.

He clucked his tongue, said that wouldn't hold till morning, so
he'd make a few phone calls. Anna shivered as she washed dishes,
took a long hot shower to warm up, then cuddled in a fleece blanket
with a good book, listening for the arrival of some firewood.

There was a lengthy banging and thumping in the basement, but
as far as she could tell, no one drove a truck to their house. Leon
emerged red cheeked and said he'd procured enough firewood for a
few days, till Bill Stoner would bring a load.

In the morning, Anna awoke to a freezing cold bedroom. Leon
leaped from the bed, ran down the basement steps, and back up
again.

"Fire's out," he chortled as he dived under the covers, reaching for
her as he shivered.

Aghast, Anna asked if he didn't want to start it now, as cold as it
was.

To love her husband in the knowledge of his easygoing ways was
no small accomplishment, but love him she did, just as the book said.
Eventually there was firewood delivered in a pile outside the basement door, which was paid eventually, but only after the irate Bill
Stoner knocked on the door a number of times.

Leon was completely immersed in his work. Every evening at the supper table, it was all about his day of counseling, his approach, the end result. But seldom did he ask for her input anymore, and rarely did he ask about her day or how she was doing.

Look for his strong points. Play up his best accomplishments. Forget his faults and weaknesses. She struggled to practice everything she had read about being a good wife. So soon the relationship shifted from a normal ebb and flow to one that was pooled solely on Leon, who thrived in the light of his own halo, his world infused with his own sense of being a light to others, a benevolent care giver to those less fortunate.

Money disappeared, bills went unpaid.

By the time summer arrived, Anna was well versed in the ways of stretching a pound of ground beef, of driving to Aldi with her own horse and buggy to buy a month's supply of groceries with an unbelievably small amount of cash.

Trips to see her family in Lancaster became fewer and fewer, so Barbie would consult Elias, asking if he thought Anna was being spoiled if she went to visit as often as she could, never mentioning the ever-deepening fear that things were not the way they seemed.

On one such trip, when her mother and sisters came to visit, Anna decided to make pizza sauce with the abundance of tomatoes from her productive garden. Anna cared for the lawn and garden the way she had been taught, so Barbie's praise was effusive. She did notice, however, the lack of ferns on the porch and any arrangement of ceramic or clay pots filled with geraniums or other annuals. There were a few marigolds and petunias in the garden, a long row of spindly zinnias sprung from a pocket of seeds, but no flowering perennials or shrubs.

"No flowers on your porch?" her mother inquired.

"No. It . . . well . . . I just didn't this year."

"I could have brought you some from the greenhouse on Oak Road."

"No, it's all right. Maybe next year."

They washed the tomatoes, removed the stems, quartered them, and set them to cook. It was when her mother went to the pantry for the required spices that she stood for a moment longer than was necessary.

When she turned, she could not face her daughter. Instead, she went to the stove, stirring the tomatoes with arms gone weak.

"Where are your spices?" she asked in a brisk voice.

"Above the stove to your left."

Later, her mother inquired if there was a financial problem. Anna hesitated, then decided against whatever it was that she was about to say.

"No. Not really. Leon is very generous with the recipients of his counseling sessions. He gives to the Homestead as well. It's all right. Mom, you know you have always taught me to be supportive of my husband's choices, which I take very seriously. I have everything I need. We live extremely . . . well . . . there's not much to live on. But it's fine, really. Leon is a wonderful husband in every other way."

"Why don't you work? Get a job somewhere? Take in sewing?"

"Oh no. Leon is hard against women working outside of the home. He says if women lived on the amount their husbands allotted them, they'd be living biblically."

Her mother gave her a long stare that gave away nothing.

"Well, the Bible also says a husband will praise his wife for the acre she buys and the goods she sells in the marketplace."

A small smile, a shaking of the head.

"It's all right, Mom. Really. I have learned to appreciate the way of his family, as well as my own."

There was a long silence, rife with unspoken words. Words that may have been comforting, supportive, or in the case of pure unadulterated honesty, wrought with the chaos of denial in both of them.

So they left them all unsaid, canned the pizza sauce, cold packed, labeled it, and took it down to the cellar to the jar shelves. When they passed the woodstove, Anna retained the nightmarish last week in January but spoke not a word to her mother about the wood.

As time went on, they looked forward to their baby, which arrived six weeks early and was hospitalized for a defective valve in the heart. They named him Mark Andrew.

Small and easily upset, Anna called on all her resources to get through each day and night. Leon was a loving, doting father, supporting her with his gentle advice, doing his share with the night feedings and diapering, seeing that she got her rest.

The outpouring of gifts, the donations of money, the company that flocked to the little house was astounding. Leon was a much-admired person of great skill at his calling, an outstanding member of the Amish church, with his loyal, supportive, and certainly beautiful spouse. The hospital bill was taken by the deacon, voted in church, and paid with the plentiful alms that accumulated each year.

Anna regained her strength, albeit with a pale face that resembled porcelain, a drawn, pinched look around her full, laughing mouth, a certain sadness that veiled the spontaneity of her youth.

When her mother spent a few days after Mark Andrew's birth, there were plenty of stiff moments.

To bring disposable diapers was a well-meaning gesture, especially a box that size, and to have her generous gift frowned on was not taken lightly.

"What's wrong with cloth diapers?" he asked, smiling into his mother-in-law's shocked gaze.

"Oh, come on, Leon. Surely you know they're a thing of the past?"

A question, but one that held clout.

"Not in my house. I'm not going to spend thousands of dollars polluting landfills. Do you know how long it takes a disposable diaper to break down in the soil?"

"No, I don't."

Spoken brightly, with bared teeth replacing the smile.

"After you're dead and gone, part of that Pamper will still be here."

The mother did not appreciate being compared to a Pamper, nor did she like the idea of her own decomposing bones, but she hid this all away in an extremely efficient manner without honoring him with a reply.

Turning to the baby, she began to coo, picked him up and carried him back to the living room recliner, where she settled herself and began rocking and humming as if she could remove the obstruction of cloth diapers by the force of it.

But cloth diapers it was.

Kept in a plastic five-gallon bucket of Diaper Pure water, the diapers were rinsed, twisted, placed in the churning wringer washer, and hung on the line, a row of snow-white diapers that flapped and danced in the breeze like silly maidens in long white skirts. Anna found tremendous fulfillment in washing those cloth diapers, an honor to her husband's way, a peace that passed her understanding.

He was a good husband, she told herself repeatedly. A kind man who took good care of her and their small son. He accompanied her to all his doctor visits, and was good about paying the bill, eventually.

Anna learned to become less agitated about unpaid bills, recognizing the need at the Homestead, and moved around her house with an aura of contentment.

Her father and mother were supportive of her choices and did not interfere in their married life, aside of an occasional quick retort from her mother.

His family seldom visited, his father often away for months at a time, or unstable when he was with his family. His mother was sweet and efficient, after bringing groceries, or a loaf of homemade bread, a cherry pie, or chocolate whoopie pies.

It was on one cold, rainy October Sunday morning when Leon and Anna traveled to Lancaster County to attend services at her parents' house that all the underlying frustrations came to a head.

Her mother had spent hours planting orange chrysanthemums, digging borders and mowing the lawn to perfection, the way she always did before the entire congregation arrived that morning. The sun had set in a blaze of glory, highlighting the orange mums, the beige color of the siding, and the faux stone on the porch. She was very pleased with all her labor and thought fondly of the appearance of her house and its surroundings.

Rain drummed on the roof, tinkled down through the spouting, washed out the fresh mulch, and soaked the newly mown carpet of grass. Things definitely were not going her way.

Leon was as unaware and as relaxed as always, lingering over his second cup of coffee, laughing and joking with his father-in-law. And then Mark Andrew had a very healthy bowel movement directly into the cloth diaper, which escalated up his spiney little back and down his legs.

"What smells?" she shrieked quietly.

"Oop. Here, Mam," Leon laughed handing over the smelly little boy. Anna laughed, hurried off to the bathroom, wondering what she would do with the little trousers, the only ones he had to wear on Sunday.

Her mother hovered, washed everything in Tide, watched her daughter perform the humiliating chore of prewashing the diaper in the commode before whisking it off to the laundry room to soak in a tightly covered container.

Leon made the serious mistake of telling Barbie she smelled, whereupon she turned on him and yapped like a Chihuahua about using cloth diapers, which was all right for him, living in the nineteenth century, but what about his wife, washing out that mess in the commode?

Leon's face fell. He called on all his gleaned knowledge about what it takes to love the unlovable, but things were a bit strained for the remainder of the weekend between him and his mother-in-law, who remained purse lipped for quite some time.

CHAPTER 21

HE HAD WANTED TO GO HOME. HAD MADE PLANS TO GO, TO RETURN TO the old home place and honor his parents' wishes. But somehow Dave had never quite gotten around to it. He wasn't sure if it was the homey atmosphere of this Australian cattle station, if it was the challenges he faced very day, or if all those brothers seemed more like blood brothers than his own back in Lancaster County. There was an easy camaraderie, an ebb and flow of joking and laughing, taking life as it came toward them, with no care in the world of what anyone thought of them, no judgment of their comings and goings, and certainly no dress code.

A pair of shorts and a thin shirt or sleeveless T-shirt. Boots or sneakers. Every snake in Australia is poisonous, or almost, so how was a person to tell the difference? Better to wear ankle high boots.

He turned lean and brown, sinewy with muscle and strength he never imagined. He learned to ride a horse with so much ease it was like being attached to it. He wrestled calves and learned how to shear sheep. He rode a four-wheeler, learned how to drive a cattle truck, ate copious amounts of beef, and acquired a taste for mutton.

He loved old Bob Kel and his wife, Darcy. Their heads were full of family history, of the Kel folklore when their parents and the parents before them moved into the region.

Weather ruled their lives. To plan a day was one thing, but to actually do it was another. Along with Bob and Darcy's predictions, the weather forecast from the large-screen TV was the most important information in the house.

And, finally, how much did the girl, Ammie, have to do with his staying?

Small, compact, with a riot of curly hair untamed in spite of the ever-present hairband she used to secure it, her skin browned and freckled, her large eyes alive with her love of Australia, and all the challenges each day presented, she was, before long, the light in his life.

At first, her worshipful gaze was a thing he automatically avoided. His teaching lived on in spite of the denial of it. She was an English girl, and Amish boys were strictly *verboten* to have anything to do with them. Friendships cropped up here and there, even a clandestine relationship occasionally, but they all knew it was not allowed by the parents or the church, which, really were the same thing.

And so he ran from her, at first.

He found himself comparing his relationship with the Kel family to his own family. He'd always gotten along well with his own brothers and sisters, and his parents as much as any rebellious teenager did, but there had always been restrictions on feelings, hidden love, hidden anger, the right answer given to the question thrown out. There was a code of respect, a proper decorum you didn't cross. Much like the *ordnung*, there were things you did not say or do if you wanted to keep things running smoothly.

Here with the Kels, there was an open jumble of honesty. No matter if it was displeasure or praise, it was spoken in the voice of blatant truth. Dave found himself wincing on occasion, when fistfights broke out over trivial matters, such as whose fault it was that the gates had not been secured at a certain time, the forgotten shot of antibiotic to a sick horse, or the rolling of the best four-wheeler.

The climate was a never-ending source of wonder for him. The seasons varied with such tremendous variety, from a life-sucking desert climate during the dry season, to torrential downpours and earth-shaking floods accompanied by thunder and lightning the likes of which he had never seen. What he had experienced on his solo trek into the Outback was only a prelude to what he met in the following year.

The only difference was the safety of a home, of human beings who were seasoned Australians and knew the rules of life in the Outback.

Dave's sense of adventure, that spontaneous passion for danger and excitement, was fulfilled beyond anything he could have imagined. He fit into the well-oiled wheel of Broghurst like an extra spoke that tightened its efficiency. He was smart and hugely energetic, and they elevated him to foreman before the year was out.

The Dry was his favorite season. The dust, the heat, and the flies. Riding endless miles with Ammie by his side, lithe, tanned, her hat hanging by the length of rawhide attached to the brim, her eyes surveying the scrubs, behind trees, beneath clumps of overhanging grasses, and often, those eyes were trained on him.

They were rounding up the cattle on one of the farthest reaches of this vast station, having enough supplies for a week, if need be. Ty and Matt had taken a fork in the road, planned on meeting up with them later, leaving them to spend the night alone.

Was it by design?

Dave was aware of the whole family's approval of Ammie's infatuation. He knew, too, he'd be welcomed into the family with open arms, an embrace that would bind him to this beloved family and all the days of excitement and danger he loved.

He'd lost his past, he told himself repeatedly. He never thought about Anna and all that mixture of stupidity and rebellion he'd gone through.

He supposed she was married now, which was okay with him. He was doing well on his own, but often wondered how things were going at home. He questioned his hesitation to place a call, leave a message.

Why didn't he? For one reason, he didn't want to stir up feelings of remorse in his parents, and didn't want to hear the admonishment that was sure to come. He didn't feel like being reminded of his many failures.

Failure to commit to the church, failure to bow to Anna's parents in order to win her, failure to stay home and take on the farm, failure to marry a decent girl and keep the thread of tradition that moved among families like an invisible tie.

He thought long and hard about religion after he attended his first Mass. The church was magnificent, the priest resplendent, his voice rising and falling with the ancient sacred prayers, completely incomprehensible to Dave.

Candles flickered, old wood gleamed, gold shone from carved moldings and domed ceilings. Light shone through traditional stained glass that illuminated Jesus in Gethsemane, on the cross, with a sheep in the crook of his arm, dressed as a shepherd.

He watched babies being baptized, thought it quite useless, but was touched by the sincerity of those surrounding the infant. He thought about baptism after that, then got into old volumes of Catholic history he procured from Bob and Darcy's library.

He immersed himself in this for weeks after, his inquisitive mind darting down one unknown alley, then another, doubled back, gleaned information from so many sources, all building up to the knowledge that this really wasn't what those first Christians had in mind, was it?

So without realizing what was happening, he was always learning, exploring, justifying his own existence, trying to find a way that would be right for him to stay in Australia.

And he did fall in love with Ammie that night, if physical touch with abandon can be called love.

They rode out together in the morning, bound by a new closeness, their happiness complete, their life before them with all the sunshine of boundless possibilities.

Ammie was beyond being bound by earth, her spirits soaring like the eagle that rode the warm currents of air swirling above the vast, untrammeled land. She was free to love Dave, unhampered by rules or restrictions, her acquisition blessed by her parents and brothers.

As time went on, he considered marriage, a home of his own, but could never quite acquire a sense of happiness.

He spent his days without thinking of the future, spent all his time with Ammie, learned to know her as well as he had ever known Anna. Where Anna had been conventional, withdrawn, hiding true feelings of attraction, Ammie was a gift of free-flowing words and feelings. Her love was a benediction, her happiness infectious. She was always moving, laughing, talking, a whirlwind of tanned, freckled beauty with riotous curls that blew in the ever-present wind.

The family began to wonder when the announcement would be made, bringing up suggestive questions whenever they were together.

Late one evening, lingering over a large roaster of beef and potatoes, Ammie seated beside Dave, Ty watched both of them with a secretive smile playing around the corners of his mouth.

"So Dave, when is the big announcement coming?"

Dave looked up, a cautious look pinched his features.

"What?"

"You know."

He felt the heat creep over his face, kept his features arranged in what he hoped was impassive.

"Ain't it time you two was engaged?"

Once, when he was twelve, Dave had caught a bird, a small, round bird that hung around the perimeter of the vegetable patch. He built a spectacular home for it, made from chicken wire and two by fours with a rubber sheet for a roof. He fed the bird berries and grass, nuts and seeds and fat juicy grasshoppers, but he could never stop it from its relentless journey of going back and forth, back and forth, as it sought its freedom.

His father told him it was a bobwhite, and that he should release it, as it likely had a mate. He'd heard the distinctive call from beneath the wild raspberries at the edge of the garden. The bobwhite died in the end. He'd come out to find a small pile of brown feathers huddled in the corner, as if the bird had walked itself to its death.

This was how he felt. Trapped. Trapped in a vast expanse bigger than he could have imagined. His beloved Outback closed in on him until his throat constricted and the blood pulsed in his veins, producing the dark color in his face.

He found Ammie's eyes on his, the light of worship, of ownership that brought him an intense longing to flee.

Like the brown bird.

The evening ended with light banter, a crema cake served with cups of strong tea, a loving look from Bob and Darcy, and one he could not understand from Sal.

She caught him in the kitchen, confronted him with all the ferocious squawking of a mother hen. "You know, sonny, you can't have your cake and eat it, too. You do right by this girl. She loves you and you're not running from her. You hear?"

Dave nodded. Kept his eyes averted.

"Look at me."

He did and his gaze was the first to drop.

He spent days, weeks, sorting through his feelings. He really thought he had been through with his past, but did anyone ever completely shake off the upbringing of his youth? How did one go about being English without dragging along the guilt of having been Amish?

What was the difference between guilt and traditional values that stuck like unwanted burrs to socks and pants legs?

He finally concluded that perhaps none of it made any difference. He simply had a feeling of wrongness that was like building a tower of wooden blocks that leaned slightly, and you knew the fall was inevitable.

He didn't really love Ammie in the true sense of the word. It had been more of a giving in, of pitying her too much to say no. In any other circumstance, he might have avoided her advances, but he had been lonely, her devotion comfortably inflating his ego, coupled with the brothers' avid approval.

But how to disengage himself?

Dave's existence became complicated and peppered with indecision. Days on the farm when life was full of comfort and without the searing regret of hurting his parents seemed like a mirage, an oasis of the mind.

He thought of his excursions on the pony cart with Anna, their times of fishing on the Pequea Creek. He found himself heaving with sobs of what might have been, his pillow wet with tears.

He remained bound to Ammie during this time, working side by side, his body lean and muscular, his skin tanned a deep bronze, his face taking on the craggy handsomeness of a wealth of experience, having survived the heat and drought, the hailstorms and wind and floods of the Outback.

He had experienced love and loss, reveled in rebellion and the audacity to leave, to fly into the great blue expanse of sky to the ends of the earth. It showed in the set of his mouth, in the deep color of his eyes, the strength in his neck and jaw. He had always been a handsome young man, with the smooth good look of his youth. But now his face was arresting, a singular poignancy of expression that only served to enhance his well-proportioned features. His hair remained long and wavy, shot through with streaks of blond, the look most hairstylists endeavor to achieve, charging a hundred dollars or more, with far lesser results.

He found himself being distracted, no longer caring about the success of the station, or the turn of a good profit from year to year.

He knew each time Sal and Watson rolled home in the Land Rover, a cloud of dust billowing behind them, their faces wreathed in smiles, that they had been to town for a visit with the accountant. A large bonus would follow. His bank account was lined with these profits, for which he was grateful, but he knew, too, that it was just another reason for the parents to put more pressure on a commitment from him.

So where was God in all this? He wondered about the God he grew up with. The One he had cried to when his life hung in the balance. Did He care whether he stayed or if he went back home? Was it okay to turn Catholic? It wasn't that much different, was it?

Well, he'd leave it to God, at any rate. He was not sure about anything, so he'd bide his time and see what happened.

He realized he was a fledgling doubter. His thoughts went one way, then the other like waves of the sea. A doubter is unstable in all his ways, the preachers used to say. He always visualized a bucking horse, bucking and kicking, unseating riders just to be, well . . . unstable.

As he felt most of the time.

When Sal told Dave there was a message on the phone for him, her voice was unusually soft. "You'll want to listen to it right away," she said, giving him a sympathetic look.

He picked up the phone, pressed the voice mail button. It was Mam and she was crying.

"I don't know if you're even there anymore," she said between sobs. "But your father . . ." here there was a long pause, during which Dave could hear a sort of whimpering. "Dave, he died. He's gone." And that was it.

For a long moment, Dave stared off across the room, seeing nothing. It was only when the living room coffee table took on a life of its own that Dave realized the blurry movement of the wood was the tears awash in his squinted eyes.

Oh, Dat. Dat. My father.

There was a hand on his back.

"You okay?" Sal asked.

Dave nodded.

He had to go back. His mother. All his brothers.

Everyone. Anna and her parents. Uncles. Cousins. The whole lot.

He turned to go outside, to be alone.

Ammie followed him, put her arms around him and murmured endearments, held him as he heaved with sobs of remorse.

She told him he had to go.

"You'll be back, Dave. You love it here. I'll be waiting for you, waiting till you come back to me, okay?"

So great was her unselfish love, the confidence she placed in their union, that she helped him book a flight, pack his things, find suitable clothes to wear on the return trip home.

She kissed him, held him, spoke of her undying love, which was followed with many more hugs and words of comfort, hand clasping, and good-natured thumps on his back.

"See ya round." From Ty.

"Git back soon's you can."

"Stay long enough to comfort your mother, okay Dave?" This from Darcy, her old eyes swimming in tender sympathy.

He left amid waves until the clouds of dust obscured them all and there was only the brown dirt and scraggly bushes surrounding them. He hadn't called home to let his mother know he'd be coming. He told himself there wasn't time, but he knew that was ridiculous. He knew he owed her an explanation for all the times he hadn't returned her calls, for not coming home when he said he would before. It would be better just to show up, to make amends in person.

At the nearest town, they got into the small Cessna, a two-passenger lightweight plane that flew him into the afternoon sky and whisked him away.

He gazed down on the awesome distance of this still, dry land that stretched from one horizon to the other, dotted with gum trees and kangaroo grass, eucalyptus trees, endless dust and red ocher ranges, billabongs.

He marveled at his own suffering, his close proximity to death, his lack of experience, the stupidity of abandoning his vehicle. So easily, he could have succumbed to the heat and the drought, been washed away and drowned by the ironic rush of far too much water, when all he'd wanted was enough to quench the biting, clawing thing that was his thirst.

Involuntarily, he snorted.

The pilot, an old grizzled man of almost eighty years old, slanted him a derisive look of impatience, then went back to his control panel.

"You see that thar river?"

Dave's eyes swept the area below, but couldn't see a river at all.

"No."

"Well, it's dry now. But you can see where the water will go, when them storms hit. Looks like a worm. There, to your right."

Dave shrugged, pretended to see what he should.

"You know, that's what happens to blow-ins. They git caught."

"I should know," Dave answered, and set to the telling of his story, resulting in one delighted cackle after another, much thumping of his palm on his thighs, accompanied by head shaking and exclamations of wonder.

"You know, folks is green. They ain't got no experience. They just full o' themselves. This land is something to reckon with."

Amen to that, Dave thought, but only smiled and nodded.

Darwin was much as he remembered, the same beautiful city with many buildings that never spoke of the realities that lay on the outskirts.

Dave still harbored a sense of regret about not viewing the ocean or the tropical regions, but he could not bring himself to the assurance that he would return. First, he had to face the demons that had driven him from Lancaster in the past.

His stomach lurched as the stark reality of his father's passing hit him with the force of a blunt object. Oh God. It was a bad dream from which he could never wake up. His father was dead.

His quiet, easygoing father, who walked around the farm and accomplished a great deal with a minimal amount of effort, taking life as it rolled by, never losing his temper, or his good humor. And now he'd never be able to say goodbye, to tell him he shouldn't have gone away.

His father would have told him not to worry. Everything was fine. He was forgiven. Some boys just have to experience stuff, learn the hard way it would all come out in the wash.

"It's all right."

Dave could hear his father's voice. How often had he used this simple phrase? And how often had it done just that? Set everything right.

He walked the streets of the city in the dense night air thick with wheeling insects around the streetlamps and talked to his father, begged forgiveness, and cried. Over and over, remorse overtook his ability to return to normal thoughts, only to be bludgeoned by reality as unforgiving and cruel as any torture device.

On the plane he slept fitfully, jammed against the window, a large, rather brutish fellow wedged in the seat beside him, who snored openmouthed or ate a prodigious amount of broken pretzels from a bag with British logos. It was like being seated beside a horse with a never-ending supply of shelled corn.

At one point, he was elbowed, and the bag of pretzels shoved under his nose, followed by a set of raised eyebrows like two black caterpillars. He shook his head and was ignored the remainder of the way.

Disembarking in the still tropical evening of Hawaii, he found something to eat, some kind of fish and a drink that tasted like bug spray. He thought wryly of his brother Mark's description of weak Kool-Aid.

The beauty of the island did nothing to comfort him. He paced the tarmac, sought the stars and the languid breeze of the date palms, felt the thorns of his father's death in his soul. Bruised and battered, emotionally drained, the last leg of his journey home was rife with dark sorrow and pitiful attempts at self-justification.

Placing the blame on Elias and Barbie Fisher was like a helium balloon that had been inflated for months. Limp and weak. It just didn't seem as if it was the proper way to continue.

Sure they'd been strict, exacting in their way of thinking, but he could have gone along with it. He could have had Anna if he would have complied.

Remorse is a terrible thing, and for Dave, alone in his plane seat, it was excruciating. Pain and fear and wishful thinking, coupled with what might have been, the hindsight as painfully brilliant as a welder's flash.

Oh God, he kept groaning to himself. *Please, please God. If you're there and I still qualify, would you please consider my plight? If only I wouldn't have been quite so hard-hearted.*

He found no solace in his attempts at reaching forgiveness. There was no light at the end of the long dark tunnel that stretched endlessly in front of him. But he had set foot in the beginning of that tunnel, and no matter how terrifying, he was going to see this through until he saw some sort of light, some semblance of understanding why God did what he did.

He returned home with his long sun-shot hair, his tanned face that had aged beyond his years, still dressed in Australian clothes, the true figure of the lone prodigal come home a few days too late, with nothing to sustain him except remorse and sorrow.

CHAPTER 22

ELI STOLTZFUS HAD BEEN A MAN OF SOME RENOWN, WITH HIS ORGANIC crops and his tendency to create friendships with everyone he met. So when the old gentleman who owned the Town Diner heard of his demise, he ordered a vast array of pastries and dinner rolls to be baked with special care and taken to the funeral. He wanted to pay his last respects to a trusted old friend, one who kept his restaurant supplied with a steady stream of the best tomatoes and peppers and onions available.

He hoped to continue purchasing the same vegetables from his son who had taken over, but he highly doubted he'd be quite as pleasant as Eli himself.

He chose Rose Kauffman and Barb Lapp to accompany him to the place of the deceased, to help unload the trays of dinner rolls and to show respect by having the Amish girls by his side. Barb told him they would both need to be dressed in formal black funeral attire, that she wouldn't set foot on that property in this blue dress and white apron. Rose only nodded her agreement, dressed in black and accompanying her boss to view the deceased.

While standing in line, she heard the low murmuring of one woman to another, about how awful it was for Rachel, having to bury her husband without the comfort of her son from Australia being present. They clucked their tongues and shook their heads, dabbed forlornly at eyes brimming with sympathy.

Rose bit down hard on her lower lip, her eyes dark pools that stared above the heads of the gathering crowd dressed in black. Was this Eli his father? Dave Stoltzfus.

He would not be back for the funeral, they said. Did this mean not in time for the funeral or he would not be returning at all?

Either way, it was nothing to her. She had to stop constructing this air castle in her head. She shook hands with the family, felt a distant pity for the disheveled weeping mother and widow, then stood at the open casket and looked down at the deceased man and felt nothing at all, only a need to step outside into some fresh air.

She went back to work the following day, efficiently setting aside every thought of Dave Stoltzfus and his ill-timed comings and goings. Too bad if he wasn't able to see his father buried. After all, he could not have been all that beloved or he wouldn't have taken off for the far reaches of Australia.

She'd done her research, holed up in her room at night, surrounded by the quirky objects she loved. Her room wasn't in tune with the styles that came and went, the colors and fabrics, the ornate bedroom suites from Amish furniture makers. She liked furniture that spoke of past lives. Babies born, lovers huddled, children bouncing, girls weeping into pillows for lost loves. She owned an old brass bed, bought the best mattress she could find, and covered it with white sheets and an old quilt she found in her grandmother's cedar chest.

She liked wind chimes and old sundials, an artist's rendering of a waning moon above a stark forest, willow branches stuck in concrete vases. Books lined one wall of her room, a chalkboard another. She wrote poetry and erased it after it came into being.

She knew the region called the Kimberly was unlike anything he would have imagined. She feared for the unknown youth's life. Labeled with too much audacity, passionate about dreams that would undoubtedly disappoint him, he was meat for the Australian cleaver.

He took a long time paying the driver. When he could no longer stall his way out of the vehicle, he stepped out, squared his shoulders, and walked to the house.

Small. It was so small, so cut off from the big farmhouse and the surrounding prosperity of cows and crops in the fields. Huddled by a growth of old deciduous trees, the little house seemed to apologize for its existence, as if it was the reason for its master's death.

Of course, his mother was not alone, two days after the burial. He spied MaryAnn, shaking a rug from the side porch, swinging it over the white railing before making her way inside.

He steadied himself with a deep breath, stepped up to the door and rapped gently. MaryAnn looked once, then twice. Her mouth opened and closed, opened again.

"Dave?"

Clearly puzzled, she seemed to shrink into her black dress.

"It's me."

"Seriously. Dave. It is you. Oh my. Come here."

Hugs from MaryAnn were a usual thing, but after his years of hurting her by his wild ways, they had stopped entirely, so it was only now that he realized how much he'd missed her.

"Mmm," she said, patting his back. "You came after all. I told Mam you would be here."

She stepped back.

"Mam! Come look who's here."

An older version of his mother appeared, accompanied by a gasp of disbelief and a rumbling to life of every sob and hiccup she could muster, coupled with a shower of tears from red rimmed eyes.

"Oh, dear Lord. *My Gott im Himmel.* Praise be!"

She gathered him into a soft, messy bind of heavy arms that smelled of the fabric softener she used, a bit of Yardley's soap, and the odor of bacon.

He allowed himself to be duly hugged and patted and fussed over, before wiping his own eyes, swallowing, and grinning sheepishly.

"Your hair!" MaryAnn shrieked, wiping her eyes.

"Don't worry about his hair. He's here, he's alive, and I'm so glad. Come. David, let's sit."

They told him how his father had passed away. He had not felt well that morning, complaining of an upset stomach. She'd cooked a dish of Cream of Wheat instead of scrapple and eggs. He took a long nap after lunch, then said he felt better. She asked him to see Doctor Richards, but he said he'd be all right.

She found him later that afternoon on his recliner, his work shoes put neatly on the rug in the laundry room. He was still warm to her touch, so it hadn't been long. No sign of a struggle or pain, merely a last breath as the massive coronary stopped his heart.

She'd gone to Centerville for groceries, and found him. His last words to her were, "I'll be all right."

As he was, now. All right. Gone to a much better place, she said.

Dave shook his head. "He shouldn't have left without knowing where I was, or if I was okay. That must have killed him. It's my fault that he died."

His eyes bore the misery of his self-loathing, the blame he picked up and carried like an unwieldly anvil on his square shoulders.

"Dave, you can't think like that. He knew his heart wasn't good. He just didn't realize how bad it actually was."

"But he worried. Wouldn't talk about it," Dave murmured.

"Oh. I think he trusted you. You know, there was a time when I think he was even proud of you, to be able to do something so unconventional. Many more of our people think about experiencing things the way you did, but no one really tries it, except you. And I know he chuckled about this more than once with that old restaurant man."

His mother broke off, looked at the clock.

"Oh, MaryAnn, those plastic trays. We have to have them ready when he gets here. They're in the basement over at the house."

"I'll go."

MaryAnn got up and went through the door, leaving him alone with his mother. She placed a hand on his knee. Their eyes met. They shared their grief in one long, understanding look, and Dave felt the shift in his own world of pain and loss and bitter regret.

"It will be all right," his mother said, a small smile sliding into a lopsided grin, before she burst into a fresh outpouring of sorrow.

Dave bowed his head and wept with his mother, the look in her eyes giving him strength to place one foot in front of the other, moving on through the dark tunnel of remorse, searching for the light that would guide him to forgiveness.

A knock on the door.

Dave watched his mother move across the kitchen, the usual hitch in her step worsened in the years he'd been gone.

"Yes, those trays?"

He heard the low plangent voice.

"Dave, would you please show this girl where the basement is at the house?"

"Sure."

Dave wiped his eyes, took a deep breath hand went to the door. His mother stepped aside.

She stood on the bottom step of the stoop, her eyes wide. Her hair were the shade of a moonless midnight, her eyes fringed polls of liquid coal.

She recognized him immediately and guessed he'd come home too late for his father's funeral. He looked exactly the way she had imagined him, after the years of experiencing a climate and terrain no one here could even imagine. His hair was shot through with sunlight, his skin the color of a wet acorn. He was a beautiful man, a man of her dreams, her forbidden air castles. His eyes were soft from having wept, the eyelashes separated from the moisture. His lips were parted, perfect teeth showing a slash of white.

Neither one could break the stunned silence, although their eyes recognized each other.

Finally, he spoke. "You're . . . that girl."

"I am. We met in Hawaii."

"We did."

Another silence, another long look, drinking in every detail of facial feature and expression.

"The trays?" she murmured.

"Oh, that's right. The trays," he said, and followed her as she turned. They walked to the other house in an awkward silence. They found MaryAnn wrestling the large trays up the basement steps, not impressed at the lack of interest in the sister-in-law banging pots and pans in her kitchen.

Dave laughed, reached for the blue plastic trays, and loaded them in the back of the minivan. He closed the door and turned to find her watching him, her eyes giving nothing away.

"You'll be going back."

A statement, not a question, as if expecting the worst would keep her from the unbearable truth that he would, after all, feel the pull of the Outback.

"No. I don't think so."

A small uplifting at the corners of her mouth.

"I'll be working at the Town Diner in Ephrata."

"Every day?"

"From nine to five."

"I'll be there."

He sat in the glow of the September evening, seated at the old oil-cloth-covered table, square now that every leaf was removed and stored in the pantry. The kitchen was small, like the table, but the oak cabinets were polished to a gleaming hue, and the floor was a good grade of Congoleum. The golden light shone through the double windows to the west, picking up the fresh luster on the beige walls and illuminating the calendar with a portrait of Belgian workhorses.

Dave swallowed hard, toyed with a water glass, before he began to talk to his mother. He told her everything, starting with his dislike of Anna's parents, the love he had to forget because of them.

"David, now stop. Sometimes things just aren't the way we like to think. You had a choice. You chose to leave her on account of her parents' rules. So therefore, you are not to be pitied. It was not Elias and Barbie's fault that you went to Australia and wasted all that time and money, or that your father died while you were gone. You can't shift the blame on someone else, which enables you to be a poor martyr, which you are not.

"David, listen. In the garden of Eden, Adam shifted the blame on Eve, Eve threw it off on the serpent, and to this day that's how we are. Human nature resists taking the blame all the time. Only you, David, only you could not give into their rules, and you gave up Anna because of it."

Dave stared at his mother. He'd never heard her talk this way. Not in this reverent tone of voice that seemed to come from somewhere else, like a preacher who knew what he was talking about. His own mother. His soft, obese, wrinkled unambitious mother who ambled through her work, waiting for the delight of the day—her recliner, a good book, and a cup of coffee. His mother was not exactly a stronghold in the family, more of a necessary item that made meals and did laundry. She was fussy, always talking, but none of her words settled into your conscience, probably because there were just too many of them.

And here she was with these words of truth that stung his heart, actually made him feel as if he was the one who had done something wrong, not Elias and Barbie.

He raised the flag of one last attempt at victory.

"But they're so self-righteous it isn't even funny. They think their whole family is absolutely perfect. And there she went and married that no-good counselor. Seriously . . ."

"That is not for you to say. That's God's territory, not yours. If they are, then God will set things right, not you going around trying to fix things by nursing your wounds in Australia."

"It was worth it."

"Was it, David?"

"Of course."

"Ach, you're so young and so impetuous . . ." Her voice trailed off.

Dave stared at his mother. Impetuous? He didn't even know she knew that word. He felt as if he had never known his mother at all.

"Mam, do you think Dat knew he wasn't well?"

"He complained of chest pains. The heat was awful hard on him this summer. He had no interest in his work at the shop. It was as if the life went out of him after he gave over the farm."

Dave shook his head, the accustomed regret rearing its hideous visage. "I should have been here. He could have kept on farming."

"Well, you weren't. You were far away in Australia. It is this way now, Dave, and the Bible says anyone who puts his hand on the plow and looks back is not ready for the kingdom of God.

"It's over. Done. Anna is married, and you have your own life to *fa-sark*."

Fa-sark. It flowed so easily from every Amish mother's lips. To take care of. They took care of a large amount of children, of huge gardens and houses. *Fa-sarking* things was a way of life, a duty they performed without thought for themselves or their discomfort when long nights with crying babies became their lot, or days of near 100 degrees and a garden over run with vegetables ripening on the stalk.

There was no air-conditioning, no temperance against the elements. You did what you had to do, which was bend your back and haul in the beans and corn and tomatoes and *fa-sark* them in a kitchen with the thermometer already approaching ninety degrees.

When the heifers broke through the fence, you helped your husband *fa-sark* that too. You *fa-sarked* the problem of little Mary being unable to learn the German alphabet in a day, the way the teacher prescribed, among many more issues that cropped up in daily life.

Dave watched his mother go to the stove to replenish her coffee. The expanse of her hips always amazed him, the way she moved around the house on feet that appeared much too small to support the expanse of skirt and apron above them.

But he looked at his mother with new appreciation. Here she was, stranded on the island of widowhood, still strong, still *fa-sarking* an issue that raised its head so soon.

The issue of her *ungehorsam* son, whom she still loved and tried to nudge into the path of righteousness.

But, what, exactly was righteousness? To return to the fold? To be Amish? To do what your parents wanted? Or was there a deeper pool of spiritual guidance of which he still had not broken the surface?

There was the girl, Rose.

To come home, begin a relationship, get married, work on a rooftop in the congestion of towns and super highways, cities with sprawling suburbs, riding to work in a pickup truck towing a trailer. Was this what it meant to be Amish in Lancaster County?

There had to be more. He was not ready to take up where he'd left off.

The wilds of Australia filled a spot in his soul that satisfied him, the vast untrammeled beauty and terror of perfect days and horrifying storms, of drought and floods and all the tempered beauty of the perfect days with the sky an azure dome with clouds like white cotton candy that floated just above reach.

For a fleeting movement, all this longing crossed his features, leaving a deep, dark scowl of remembering. He was caught in the middle of two different lives, the search for forgiveness to Anna's parents like a giant hook that left him dangling over a deep gorge.

Did he have the ability to make the right choice?

"Mam," he said suddenly.

"Hmm?"

"How can I be happy here, back to my old roofing job, in the same old, same old . . .?" He shrugged his shoulders.

"You need a girlfriend. Someone to love. Someone to share your life and make it interesting."

"That's not all I need."

"Why of course not. It is an unspoken fact that you need God. But you already know about God. You were taught that from a very young age. So you are blessed. But each one of us needs to deal with his or her own need for a personal Savior. It doesn't matter how much we have learned as children growing up in a Christian home. But a good start is learning obedience."

Dave scowled. "And how does that figure in?"

Obedience was always a hard obstacle. It brought out a natural rebellion from someplace within, a place that he had never taken the time to remedy.

Oh, plenty of his siblings would try to help him on his journey of self-discovery, he was sure, but they wouldn't be able to help.

"Oh, well, it just does. The fear of God is the beginning of wisdom, you know."

"So He's some mighty being sitting up there ready to throw me into hell if I don't listen."

"Dave, stop."

Consternation crossed his mother's round features, a darkening of her countenance.

"Well."

His famous pout after that.

His mother sighed. "Dave, we're both tired, and it's time I go to bed, okay?"

With that, she heaved to her feet and cut the conversation short, leaving him to stare into his coffee cup.

At midnight, he regretted all that coffee. He rolled from one side of his bed to another, rearranged his pillows, pulled up the covers and kicked them off, lay on his back and stared at the ceiling, listened to the crickets and katydids until he thought he would surely lose his mind.

He didn't care if Katy did or not.

So here he was back in the same old groove. Different house, his father gone, completely wiped off the face of the earth. His own father was dead.

This sentence was imprinted on his heart like a hot brand. He never had the chance to tell him goodbye, or to tell him he was sorry. The only comfort was the fact that somehow, he knew his father understood him.

He was not really okay with his travels to a distant country, but yet he was, in his own way. Dave knew his father never experienced the deep heartache of his mother, thinking so liberal. His father left a dull pain, but a bearable one, now that he had time to allow himself the privilege of reminisce. To remember their time in the barn, doing chores, laughing at the same things, always understanding the same point of view together. His father's passing left him with the comfort of their bond too.

The biggest missing piece of the puzzle was why he was so hesitant to pursue the dark Rose. Surely it was more than coincidence that she would turn up at his mother's doorstep the same day he arrived home. But there was Ammie—and Anna.

CHAPTER 23

Anna heard of the passing of Eli Stoltzfus and wanted to go to the viewing with her parents, to pay her last respects to Dave's father. But funds were low, as usual, and Leon had an important interview at the Homestead, so she gave in and later talked to her mother about the entire procedure from start to finish.

Elias and Barbie Fisher were named as *fore-gayer*, or organizers of the whole funeral, along with two other couples from the church district, so she could fill in all Anna's questions.

Yes, Eli looked nice in his coffin, so peaceful and natural. He had always been a nice-looking man, indeed. And Rachel had certainly taken it well, for the shock she must have had, but then she had always been a strong woman, for sure. Anna had extracted the information about Dave not being there in a roundabout way that would have befitted the best counselor.

So he had not come.

Was he dead, like his father?

All the remembering overtook her with the strength of a tsunami, washed her along as the powerful current of a denied love, helpless to disengage herself from its grip. Where was he? Did he know his father was dead?

Caught in the helplessness of her inability to contact him, to comfort him, she realized the futility of her separation. It wasn't right or fair or decent to be cut off from Dave by her marriage to Leon.

She held little Mark Andrew to her shoulder, rocked back and forth in agitation, her lovely face darkened with the luxury of allowing herself to know how much she still cared. To comfort him would be all she would ever require from life. To touch him one more time, to be the one to hold him when he received the word of his father's passing.

Oh, Dave. My beautiful Dave. Why did I love the way I did? Why were we denied what we had between us?

She stopped rocking, sat very still. She literally checked reality, shook herself free of this adulterous longing. This spiritual breaking away from marriage vows that were sacred.

Forgive me, God. But this secret longing was one luxury she could afford, remembering the one happiness she could always obtain in quiet moments such as this.

She kissed her baby boy with great tenderness and thought how strange it was that she loved Leon even as she still carried Dave in her heart.

Leon was the one God gave to her, and for this she would always be grateful. His kindness and compassion were gifts, his love true and steady. His inability to manage finances was a source of irritation, of course, but no one was perfect. The hardest part of their union was the near-constant preoccupation with his work, the troubled people he dealt with on a regular basis. Anna felt secondary, a wife who bore him a son, cleaned and cooked and washed, supported him 100 percent of the time, and rarely had needs of her own.

But she was taught to be a helpmeet.

Puzzling, though, this latest trend. Leon was having a difficult time accepting the fact that most of the troubled people were caught in all manner of painful situations, sins beyond anything he knew was possible in Plain homes justified by the Amish way of life. Outwardly righteous, inwardly eaten by sins of the flesh. Why do we Plain people need these places of counseling?

For a time, Anna consoled him by saying Amish or not, there was a way of the flesh, and sin was orchestrated by the devil, and he was like a lion, stalking around, seeking whom he may devour.

She felt like a true helpmeet.

Anna's life was filled with the care of little Mark, keeping the home neat and tidy, cooking nourishing meals, making new friends, and learning to fit into a new community of Amish folks who all came from Lancaster County or neighboring ones. If Leon had a few doubts, it would pass, she told her mother, and she went outside to blow leaves with the new backpack blower they had received for a wedding gift.

The day was sunny, brisk, and cool, with barely a breeze to disturb the piles of crumpled brown oak leaves she set on fire. The smell of burning leaves coupled with the warmth of the October sun and its accompanying brilliant blue sky took away every melancholy thought or longing, and she found herself humming, whistling soundlessly with the sound of the gas engine by her ear.

She saw the brittle roses, their heads drooping at summer's end, the hosta that needed clipping, and boxwoods that would have to be trimmed into rounded contours. It would be best for the snow sliding off in winter. She finished with the leaves, then pushed the mower around the yard, before going to check on the baby, who was still sleeping peacefully.

Tiptoeing back outside, she closed the door carefully and looked up in time to see Leon's driver return from work. She greeted him with her usual bright smile, disappointed to see the pain on her husband's visage.

"Oh dear, Leon, is something wrong?"

"I think it's a migraine, Anna."

He shouldered past her, slammed the door, went into the bedroom without speaking. She found him spread-eagled on his stomach, and no amount of quiet persuasion could get him to speak.

She heard Mark's shrill squeal from his crib and hurried out, closing the door gently behind her, her stomach already roiling from the stress of this unexpected turn of events. She had never seen

Leon quite so upset or so blatantly unresponsive to her questions. Something very serious must have occurred at work to bring this on.

Suddenly, she despised the Homestead and all its fractured men. Grimly, she changed Mark's diaper without the usual talking and the kissing of his little stomach, causing him to eye his mother with a quizzical expression. But her thoughts were far from her baby.

The Homestead took too much away from Leon.

When his headache subsided after a lengthy nap, she approached him on this subject, which was met with a vehement denial.

"No, no, Anna. You truly do not understand at all. To be helping the afflicted is allowing the living waters of Christ to flow through me. It restores my soul. It really does. My job is my life, and I am constantly blessed through it. I would wither up spiritually if it wasn't for my job. It's actually a calling, like a ministry to me."

He would overcome his doubts, he said. Her words helped him tremendously. Everything would be all right.

And she believed him.

But when the cold winds blew that second winter and she started a fire in the good woodstove in the basement, and all the smoke poured out of the stove door, and she realized too late that the chimney was clogged, and the pile of firewood would not be enough to keep them warm till Christmas, she spoke to her husband in gently clipped tones of admonishment.

Yes, his life was his job, his job was his life. But he also promised to give his life for his wife, according to his marriage vows and the Bible, so come on, she said. Her house filled with smoke, a buildup of soot in the chimney, his head in the clouds of the Homestead. No, enough was enough.

Her reward was a cold house and stone silence for days, throwing her into a maelstrom of feelings that bounced between remorse for having opened her mouth in the first place and justifying her actions in the name of necessity.

The chimney remained clogged. Anna heated the house with the gas oven turned on, and a propane heater from a corner in the living room that glared its brilliant orange eye like a baleful antagonist, a reminder of her harsh words spoken out of turn.

He raved, then. He paced the floor and yelled at her, threw out his hands in jerky movements of infuriation, then went to the shed for a ladder and the rope with the chimney-cleaning attachment. She heard him thumping around on the roof and felt an emotion bordering on disgust.

That night, when he reached for her, she succumbed to his advances, but lay crying quietly afterward, the sickening thought of him carrying his father's genes like circling wolves, penetrating her heart with a deep and abiding fear.

The Homestead was no place for her husband. She recognized that he had changed drastically in a few years.

Oh, dear God in heaven, she prayed. *Please help my husband.*

Another visit from her parents set things right again.

Leon was in an effusive mood, benevolence dripping from honeyed sentences.

Her mother walked with her to survey the perfection of the garden, put to bed with a healthy cover of tillage radishes, the rosebushes mulched and trimmed, the hosta clipped. She spoke approvingly of the neat borders, the raked leaves, the way she she'd done the boxwoods.

"Good job, Anna."

High words of praise from an exacting mother kept Anna's well-being afloat for weeks. They sat around the kitchen table and played Monopoly with the younger sisters, ate popcorn, and drank hot chocolate, the small drafty house well heated with the roaring woodstove in the basement.

Her parents traveled home with the satisfaction of having married their daughter off to a kind and caring man. What were earthly goods compared to the love and joy between them?

Dave could not summon the will to go to the restaurant in Ephrata. He was not sure why, but day after day went by and he was content to look for work, check into the cost of building a dog kennel, dabble in helping his brother on the farm.

He dialed Ammie's number, repeatedly, always pressing the off button before it was completed. He felt himself adrift, lost in a world without an anchor. He did not want to return to his old roofing job; he simply had no heart to be crouched on a nine-by-twelve pitch slapping a stapler or nailer until he felt numb in his brain. He didn't care about money. He still had plenty.

He didn't want to buy another vehicle or get in with the old crowd again. It was a time of retrospect, of wondering where he had taken a wrong turn in the road, or what was missing in his life.

He often wondered what kind of man this Leon had turned out to be, whether he treated Anna well or if he was as smarmy as he figured.

And still he did not go to the restaurant.

Alone, wandering around, Christmas crept up on them with a fresh layer of snow. His mother set out the red jar candle with the faux holly berry wreath, disappeared for days at a time, and came home laden with huge plastic bags, her eyes snapping with excitement.

"I'm spending your inheritance, Dave," she trilled.

Dave looked up from his book, grinned half-heartedly.

"It's so good to come home and find you in Dat's chair," she said, through a throat thick with emotion.

Dave nodded, returned to his book. He needed to check the library for the second book in this history of World War II, a subject that never failed to fascinate him. If the people around here thought he was a bad person for having gone to Australia, leaving his father to die alone, they should meet some of these characters. He wasn't anything close to the evil doings of some of these guys.

He rose to his feet, stretched, then went to the refrigerator for a slice of sweet bologna and some American cheese, which he rolled into a log, bit off half and began to chew. He opened a cabinet door and found a sleeve of Ritz crackers.

"Who was your driver?" he asked.

"Marty."

"Is he busy?"

"Why?"

"I need to go to the library."

"Take the team."

"Too cold to let a horse stand at the hitching rack."

"Blanket. That's what they're for."

"I'll call Marty."

She was always trying to get him to go away with his horse and buggy, which held no thrill for him at all. Too slow. Too much bother getting that harness on, backing that unwilling horse between the shafts.

Later, he made his way between books, shelved in alphabetical order, or in categories. Confused at the way these volumes of history were shelved, he stopped, leaned left to find the silhouette of an Amish girl seated on a low stool, her black sweater the only thing he could identify.

Curious, he made his way forward, stopped short and turned toward the shelves of books when he saw she raised her head, revealing the white covering.

He said, "Excuse me," before he pushed past her and made his way along the aisle between the heavy columns of history.

She looked up, but he didn't see her puzzled expression. He was wearing a black hoodie, with the hood up, so a good ten minutes elapsed as he searched for the author he wanted.

From time to time, Rose Kauffman checked out the tall black figure in front of her, and thought perhaps it was him, but no, it wasn't. He wouldn't be in the library in the middle of the day, would he?

She was here to check out a book she needed to win an argument with one of her coworkers, the big know-it-all. She didn't care if he had Google or whatever, he had it wrong when he said it was Adolf Hitler who started World War II. She found exactly what she was looking for and said out loud, "I knew it."

The hooded figure turned toward her, surprised.

She kept a finger on the page, and looked straight into Dave

Stoltzfus's eyes. One hand lifted in dismay, her mouth opened, then closed.

He pushed back his hood, stood looking down at her, his eyes crinkling at the corners as a wide grin spread across his face.

"You knew what?" he asked.

"Nothing. It's nothing."

With that, she rose to her feet, turned, and disappeared. He hurried to the end of the aisle, looked right, then left, but could find no trace of her.

He stopped, his brow lowered. Well, now. She had the guts to just go stomping off like that. He had his share of touchy girls. You could never know what went on in those pretty heads. If you said or did one thing wrong, or if you didn't do anything, they ended up with their nose in the air. She had black hair and almost black eyes anyway, so that did absolutely nothing for him.

He liked the blonde girls. Or the ones like Ammie, all freckles and curly hair. He went back to the bookshelves without success, finally admitted defeat, and made his way to the front of the library where the information desk was located.

"Can I help you?" the white-haired lady asked sweetly.

"Yes."

He gave her the title of the book he was looking for. She tapped his information into the computer with gnarled, arthritic fingers, then turned to him with keen eyes, as alert as a sparrow's.

"Checked that one out only minutes ago. Sorry."

"Thanks."

She probably had that book. She was seated in the exact space he was searching. A stab of irritation shot through him. Testy women. He was never getting married. Imagine living with that.

He started toward the front door, the massive oak one with side windows and an old fashioned transom with blue and yellow squares of crinkled glass. If he ever built a house, he'd search the world for a door like this. Even the knob on it was worn copper, set lower the modern day standard ones.

"Hey."

He turned to find her in the magazine room, seated on a tufted hassock with a magazine draped across her lap.

"I have your book."

"So?"

"Come back in a week and I'll return it."

He nodded, planned on being curt, but was strangely curious about the magazine draped across her knees.

He pointed toward it with his chin. "What are you reading?"

"Why do you ask?"

Dave grinned, turned to go.

She called after him, "Antiques."

"Cool," he called back, and let himself out the door. Now what kind of girl would be reading up on World War II and antiques? She certainly was not like any other girl he knew, worried about shoes and dress fabric and the color of their rooms. You even had to drive a certain horse these days, either a Friesian or a Dutch Harness or a combination of both.

A high-stepping Friesian being the equivalent of a Ferrari. Huh, he thought. I'll never be Amish, for real. It's so dumb.

A few weeks later he hadn't returned to the library and had no desire to finish reading the series. If he could only find a job he cared about, he'd be much happier.

Christmas had come and gone, the spirit of joy and giving passing him by completely. He had never felt more alone than he did surrounded by throngs of siblings and their offspring. They brought only a vague pressure of guilt, not having bought a gift for anyone, not even his mother. His sister's endless chatter was an annoyance beyond anything he'd ever encountered, which left them to tell him he must have come home from Australia with Australian burrs stuck in his gears, then went off in a huff and left him to himself.

He decided to try working with his brother, hanging drywall and finishing it, but hated the job so much he quit after a few weeks. Who wanted to eat drywall dust all day? It was enough to give a person chronic lung disease.

He tinkered around in his father's small workshop, found he had a knack with the router and shaper. He made a cabinet door, then two. After that he built a cabinet, sanded it, painted it tavern gray, and wore off the edges. He showed it to his mother, who threw up her hands and exclaimed her surprise.

"It looks as if it comes straight out of *Country Living*."

He thought of the magazine draped across Rose's lap.

His sister MaryAnn bought it on sight, gave him 100 dollars, and ordered two more.

He dived headfirst into endless books on woodworking and toured an array of serious cabinetmakers and furniture shops.

He thought of Rose's interest in antiques and wondered about crafting some replicas of old dry sinks and pedestal tables. Would people buy them? He was surprised by how much he wondered what she'd think.

Eventually he made his way to Ephrata with his friend Wayne, who had joined the church and was dating Leah, a petite girl who would give him nothing but trouble for the rest of his life. But you didn't go around saying things like that to your friends.

He saw Rose waiting on a table along the back, but sat in the booth opposite Wayne and drummed the tips of his fingers on the tabletop. He watched her finish the table, turn to another one.

Dressed in purple, with those dark hair and eyes, she was the color of a bruise. Very fitting.

He grinned.

"What?" Wayne asked.

"Oh. Her."

He tilted his head in her direction.

"Oh, Rose. You know her?"

"Not really."

"Well, do you or don't you?"

"I told you. No, I don't."

"You'd like to."

Before he could answer, Wayne called her name, waved her over.

"What?" she asked, in the low, unexpressive way.

"Do you know this guy?"

"We've met."

"Is that all?"

"Look. I'm busy. Sheila will take care of you."

He left that day without a chance to tell her about his furniture-making abilities. Without any conversation at all, really. So he went back one day in February, when the days were cold and gray, the air biting with the wet cold of coming snow, the sky lowering and pewter gray.

He seated himself strategically, at a table he knew she would be serving. She had no choice but to bring that little tablet over and stand at his table.

"Hey."

Low and quiet.

"How are you?"

She shrugged. "Okay I guess."

"Sit down."

"I can't. I'm working."

"How long?"

"Closing time."

"When's that?"

"Half an hour."

"Good. I'll order. I'll take you home. I want to show you something."

"How? How will you take me home?"

"My Ferrari."

She laughed. Low, soft, the way her voice sounded.

"You don't."

He laughed. "A Friesian. Same thing."

"Oh."

She looked amused, but her eyes darted nervously to the kitchen, to the front door.

"What can I get you?"

"Coffee, for one thing. Uh, I don't know. Cheeseburger? Everything on it." She scribbled furiously, then left without speaking. He had no answer if he could take her home or not.

She brought his coffee, threw a few creamers on the table and moved off. He thought of Ammie's absolute devotion, thought of the huge difference between this silent aloof girl and the warmth and vibrancy of his girl who was so far away now, both in body and in thought.

She surprised him when she brought the cheeseburger and slid into the booth, facing him squarely for the first time ever. He was surprised as well, to find the dark brooding intensity of her eyes framed by the heavy lashes, the olive tones in her skin, with the smattering of freckles across her left cheek.

He felt clumsy, uncovered. His cheeseburger lay untouched as he stumbled for the right words.

"I'm . . . I started making small pieces of furniture."

He sipped his coffee.

She raised one eyebrow, her dark eyes giving nothing away. If she would have encouraged him with a "Really?" or a "That's great!" it would have been so much easier, but with only a long, dark look and no comment, how was he supposed to continue?

"I . . . you know, wondered what you'd think of the colors I'm using."

"You're using color?"

She may as well have asked if he was spreading icing on his furniture.

"You know, old colors. Antique ones."

"Oh. Why do you think I care?"

Ouch. No wonder this girl was still single.

"The magazine on your lap at the library."

"Hmm."

He started on his cheeseburger. He had not the faintest hope of coming close to being impressive at this point, so if he got mayonnaise all over his mouth and lettuce between his teeth, it didn't matter.

"Do you have pictures?"

"I do."

He slid over, made room for her as he brought out his phone. She leaned in and he struggled to breathe. She smelled like food and some kind of soap, like shampoo in a fancy bottle.

"This is the first piece."

No comment. What did he expect?

"It's pretty primitive," he mumbled.

"Go on. What else did you make?"

"These."

"Hmm. They're not bad. What is the color?"

"You can't tell on my phone. You'll have to come see my shop."

"What is the color?" she repeated.

"Tavern gray."

"Cool."

He finished his burger, pushed the plate away, raised his cup and his eyebrows. She slid away and filled his cup, giving him a wide smile that was so genuine he scalded his tongue with the hot coffee.

Her coworkers peered from the opening to the kitchen and raised their own eyebrows, shook their heads in disbelief before high-fiving and placing bets on the chances of Miss Doom and Gloom procuring a boyfriend.

"She smiled," Sheila whispered to the cook.

"She also raised that eyebrow, which does not bode well."

"The poor guy. She has about as much warmth as a Sub-Zero refrigerator in excellent working condition."

CHAPTER 24

Dave experienced days of struggle, however. Wouldn't any friendship with an Amish girl turn out the same as things had with Anna? The unexpected loomed before him like a dire prediction. That, and the guilt about Ammie.

To be bound to someone as closely as he had been, then travel thousands of miles away leaving her to sort out her feelings without as much as a phone call, was cruel, and he knew it. But he could not bring himself to make that call.

Australia had made a man of him, challenged him to every extreme of his physical and mental strength, so why was his cowardice all that remained?

Too chicken to call her. He despised himself for his weakness. So what had he gained, really?

The most monumental struggle was the looming decision he would have to face. To ask the aloof Rose to be his girlfriend would eventually bring the inevitable. The joining of the church. The giving up of all worldly pleasure. To cut his hair in the *ordnung* and basically live a mundane life bereft of thrills or excitement.

Did he have to drive a horse and buggy in order to get to heaven? How come billions of people the world over drove cars and got away with dressing and doing whatever they felt like? Or didn't they?

There were hundreds of versions of Christianity. Churches dotted all across the land, their spires reaching to the heavens, and each one was just a bit different than the other, but all believed in God and His son, Jesus.

Seriously. Why did he have to be born into this seventeenth-century thing? Old-fashioned, traditional, never changing, on and on, plodding through the decades, placing one black shod foot in front of the other without ever wanting to do anything else.

And so he began attending church services all over Lancaster County. He dressed in his white shirt, homemade broadfall trousers, his matzo, and his black hat, hired a driver, and listened to an array of ministers who conducted their services in English.

He sat in Mennonite services, in Baptist and Lutheran, and the Church of God out on Route 283. He read his Bible and came to the conclusion he could justify his actions or condemn himself, it all depended on his attitude.

His mother watched her son's turmoil with eyes still filled with the grief of her husband's passing. She spent her nights with intermittent wakefulness, praying in broken whispers for the son who had come back to the fold and was bashing the gate with his passionate spirit, the sense of adventure that drove his restlessness. She longed for Eli, his calming presence and his easy words. She had never realized before how much she had leaned on him, even if his easy flow of words were usually ruffled by her cares and anxieties.

Dave had already lost interest in the furniture making. She badgered him about getting a job. He needed to give himself up to something, construction, welding, shop work.

The morning was brisk and cold, the shop fire out, the furniture making come to a halt. Mother and son sat at the breakfast table with coffee cups half empty, the small kitchen rife with the smell of frying bacon. The winter sun was weak, tepid, as if the gathering clouds were draining it of its power.

He set his coffee cup in the sink, turned to go.

"So where were you last evening?"

His mother, large and florid of face, her dress the usual navy blue, her hands clasped across her stomach.

"Oh, I went to some church thing they had in the basement."

"What church?"

"I'm not even sure. That big stone church in Lancaster."

"In the city?"

"Yeah."

"Why do you keep putting yourself through this, Dave? You do not belong in that church basement listening to a speaker who doesn't hold our views or values. You were born Amish; it's where you belong. You'll break my heart, and it's already broken by your father's sudden death."

Tears welled, spilled over. She reached into her pocket for the ever-present wrinkled *voddags schnuppy* and dabbed at the corners of her eyes before honking into it.

Dave sighed and let himself out the door, the cold like a slap in the face. He hated thinking of starting a fire in the stone-cold stove in the dusty little shop, working on yet another stupid little table that no one really wanted but fussed over just to make himself feel good.

Whatever.

He crumpled newspaper, threw in a few sticks of kindling and held a lighter to it, watched the small flame lick greedily at the paper. He slammed the door, shivered, gazed across the landscape at the brown fields, and thought how the seasons came and went and nothing ever changed in Lancaster County.

That meeting last night had been interesting, for sure, until the subject of pursuing a career came up. How did one pursue a career if one only went to eighth grade? Get your GED online and go from there.

To what? Schoolwork was tedious, so he imagined high school and college would be no different. The only bright spot had been the glowing, laughing Anna, seated at her desk with her bright blonde head bent over her schoolwork, handing out her sweet innocent smiles to his starving soul.

If he could only see her, just once. If he could see she was truly happy with that husband of hers, and had a good life, well, then, perhaps he could move on. More and more, the thin realization of his miserable existence centered on thoughts of Anna.

Anna in school, on her scooter, driving her pony. Anna mowing grass and waving at him, sitting on the creek bank waiting for the red and white bobber at the end of her line to disappear below the surface. Anna in ninth grade, shy and a bit intimidated meeting the other ninth graders from other church districts.

She lived in his subconscious, and there was no way around it. He was doomed to live with this malady of the heart for the rest of his days, to wander the earth with the weight of this great love and the accompanying terrible remorse.

He went to Ephrata to the Town Diner, simply on account of being starved, he told himself. He'd been on the road all morning, looking for work, trying to show his mother that he was listening to her words. It was true, what she said. He needed to give himself up.

Die oof-gevva-heit. A daily dose of Amish life. Giving yourself up.

But every office held the same lack of charm, adventure, and purpose. Every shop contained a dull future made up of repetition.

If he could only get past his mother's tears, he'd hop on the next flight to Australia, take up where he left off with the sunny Ammie Kel and her loving family, but he could not do it to her. She was his mother.

He saw Rose across the room, but she was fully occupied, so he sat at the counter, cleared his throat, leaned in and drummed the top with his fingers. All the waitresses were busy.

What was this? They needed more help.

Here she came, her dark eyes on his face, her mouth compressed into angry impatience.

"What?"

"You need more help. I've been sitting here for five minutes."

"It wasn't even close to that."

"I'm hungry."

She pointed to the blackboard with the daily specials and left with the coffeepot. He watched her go. She walked as if she carried a chip on her shoulder. Two or three, really.

Before he could order, the space beside him was filled with an enormous presence dressed in a plaid shirt. The odor of diesel fuel was so strong he could almost visualize it floating on his coffee. He'd not order any, that was sure.

The large head swiveled in his direction, then back again.

Rose returned, raised one eyebrow, her tablet poised.

"Are you serving breakfast?"

"No."

"Come on."

"Eleven." She turned toward the clock. Eleven oh five.

"It's not much past. I want pancakes."

"You can't have them."

His eyes met hers, exchanging hostilities. He saw the challenge, she saw the need to get him out of her head. Disappearing for weeks on end, showing up just when she'd seen the futility. Nobody messed with her heart. Nobody.

"What else is good?"

She shrugged.

"Look, I'm busy. Order."

A loud guffaw from the massive plaid shirt, the shaking of the gray hair.

"You two know each other by any chance?"

That was how Dave met Gary Lawson, who owned a logging company, worked locally, but mostly in Maryland and Virginia. Dave didn't remember what he ate, didn't remember ordering. He ate the food as if it was sawdust, and listened with rapt attention to the man beside him, who painted a colorful portrait of danger and adventure far beyond anything Dave could have imagined in homely Lancaster.

"So what do you think? David? Is it Dave?" the man asked, wiping his wide face that had a surface like fallen bread dough, with wrinkles and fissures and discolored blotches of leftover summer sun.

"It's Dave."

"You ever run a chainsaw?"

Dave shook his head, wished he had run one sometime in his life so he could qualify.

"Never?"

"Nope. I can't recall."

"Are you strong?"

"I like to think I am."

They parted on the parking lot with a handshake, Dave with the promise of a new job, one that just might be everything he had always been looking for.

He needed a cutter, but also someone who could drive a skidder and a loader. The thought of cutting trees in an untamed wilderness, driving huge equipment down steep slopes, the roar of eighteen-wheelers with diesel smoke spouting into the sky, shot adrenaline through his veins.

Here was a brand-new undertaking, a thing unforeseen, unexpected. To learn how to fell those trees using an enormous chainsaw, to stomp through the woods parting underbrush like some Paul Bunyan of old, was exactly the challenge he needed.

His mother shook her head, predicted dire things.

Did he know how many accidents occurred in the woods? Her Uncle Levi *iss um-komma*—died—in a logging accident. It was dangerous work that took all the strength from a man.

He barely heard her words.

Someone picked him up at four o'clock in the morning, the wide dual-wheeled pickup truck with a fuel tank and logging equipment thrown in the back, mud and dirt and streaks of salt and calcium from the roads making it impossible to find color. The interior was covered in dirt and gravel, a plethora of coffee cups, fast-food wrappers, discarded napkins, soda cans, wrenches, nuts and bolts, old wrinkled T-shirts that had been white at one time, smashed candy bars, and things Dave couldn't explain.

Gary Lawson roared out of his mother's driveway, past the silent, dark farmhouse, causing Dave to wince slightly, but he couldn't ask him to tone it down on his first morning. He drove as if the road was his alone, the motorists who shared it only a minor annoyance.

Dave found himself on the edge of his seat, his eyes shining with anticipation, half listening to his driver's account of past hired men and their tepid attempts at becoming an experienced cutter.

Dave had no doubt in his mind that he would become one of Gary Lawson's best. He had it in him. Anyone could tell him what a roofer he'd been, the long hard days in the saddle in Australia, the sheep shearing, surviving the flood. Yes, he was capable.

When he limped into the Town Diner on Saturday forenoon and glanced at the clock with bloodshot eyes, Rose barely recognized him. His hair was long and unkempt, as if it needed a good shampoo and a comb.

His clothes looked slept in, filthy. A strong odor of diesel fuel wafted up from his blackened hands.

She felt the despair, then. If anything, he was more attractive than he had ever been. Would this craziness never end? She had never remotely felt an emotion half this powerful about anyone, and had certainly not planned on continuing with this one, but what was a person to do if he evoked these feelings of . . . Of what? She wasn't sure.

She only knew she wanted to be with him, listen to his stories, wait for the exclamation points that would punctuate every sentence, find the intensity in his eyes. But she had determined he would not hurt her.

She stayed away as long as possible, before coming to stand at his table, tablet poised.

"Hey."

"How are you?"

"Good. What do you want?"

"Everything."

A lift of one eyebrow.

"Aren't you going to ask me about my new job?" he asked, his teeth a flash of white in his grimy face.

"Not now. Can't you see I'm busy?"

"Sit down with me."

Her look made him want to crawl under the table and apologize for sharing space on the earth with her.

"Please order."

"Okay. Three pancakes, three eggs, sausage, bacon, home fries and three slices of toast. Coffee and apple juice."

She scribbled, nodded and left.

He smiled, watched her go. Happiness coursed through his veins. He felt his life shift on track.

She brought his food, set it before him with no comment, and left. He smiled again.

When she returned with the coffeepot, he looked up, and smiled. She allowed herself a small upturn at the corners of her mouth, followed by a hesitation, a few seconds of staying.

"You don't have time to sit?"

She surprised him with a lithe movement, folded herself into the opposite side of the booth, the coffeepot between them. Dressed in red, with the black apron, the black hair, and the dark eyes, she was the opposite of the fair Anna.

Anna had been open and friendly, always smiling, always sweet with her words and actions. Her blonde hair was like an angelic halo, one that brought out the good in him.

How could he keep from comparing the two?

Springtime arrived in fits of rainsqualls and teasing sunshine. Mud was a logger's nemesis. Mud bogged down heavy equipment and made entry into low places impossible. They erected temporary bridges with heart-stopping anxiety as they watched the tons of steel and rubber tumble across.

Dave was covered in mud, soaked through, his face and hands barely recognizable, his eyes alight with energy and excitement.

He could drive that skidder anywhere. He could handle a chainsaw with skill and precision, had learned to drive wedges with a sledgehammer, had experienced the satisfaction of directing where the huge trees would fall, crashing through the branches of smaller ones to hit the earth with a resounding crash.

His work fulfilled him. For the first time in his life, he felt as if he had truly found his calling. If a job could be a calling, he thought wryly.

He loved his work. It was so simple. Quitting time came too soon. All the cruelty of aching muscles, abrasions and deep cuts were like a mosquito bite, only an annoyance, part of the job.

He felt himself a man, drove himself to the limits he set for himself then went beyond that, raising the bar time after time.

His hourly wage escalated, then changed to an amount per load of logs, which set a fire beneath him. He equaled the most skilled cutter, then passed that mark and went on to the next.

Anna lived about seventy miles away, in the humble rental cottage with her young son, her loving husband, and a future that stretched before her.

Her happiness lay in contentment, in making do, in supporting her husband's work, and above all, in raising their children, a constant source of joy.

She looked forward to the warmth of spring, the renewal of life around her a metaphor for the new life stirring within. She hoped for a daughter, knowing she would have a lifelong friend, but another son would be as welcome. She pictured two small boys playing together.

Leon was still wrestling with the downside of being Amish. He searched his Bible long after Anna had gone to sleep in the evening. She spoke not a word of her husband's struggle to her parents. They were secure in their relationship with him, so why stir up trouble? Let sleeping dogs lie, she reasoned. No use riffling calm waters.

She went home with a cheery smile, a sunny disposition, rife with tales of her idyllic life in Millerstown, exactly the way she had always been taught. An honor to her parents, looked upon with favor wherever she went, Anna moved in the Christian circle of love and inspired all those around her.

The bottom fell out of her self-made container of perfection when Leon came home from work one evening with a ravaged expression, got down on his knees, and laid his head on her lap.

"Anna," he said, and began to cry, a broken sound of great sadness.

"Leon. Oh my, Leon. Whatever is wrong?"

She drew him into her arms, where he lay weeping until he was spent, then told her that he had reached a crossroad, and to be honest with himself, he had to leave the Amish church and all their rules and regulations behind, move on into a church where he could worship freely without being bogged down by a man-made *ordnung*.

The weight that settled on Anna's chest that day never completely lifted. The ensuing turmoil, the announcement to her adoring parents, the visiting of strange churches, and her own inner struggle was her undoing, and she slid into the deepest recesses of despair.

Leon repeatedly told her, in order to follow Jesus, she must be able to leave father, mother, sister, brother, as the Bible taught.

"But why Leon, why? They are believers. Why must I leave them if they do believe in Him? Are you quite certain you are not misled, husband?"

There was no reasoning with him. His eyelids at half-mast, he patiently explained the way of the Lord, to go out and preach the gospel. So how could you do that without your own form of transportation?

She countered with the Amish way of being a light to the world by blooming where you are planted, being a helper in the community, a blessing among your peers. She was torn between her husband and her family, one arm extended to the husband, the other to the parents.

Her mother begged and pleaded. Her father nailed Leon with Scripture of his own, handpicked his own weapons, and backed him into a corner, with his wife egging him on. Anna sat in their homely little kitchen and held her words, thinking this was all wrong, so wrong.

This was not what God had in mind for the Christian church. But in the end, she accepted her parents' bitterness, their empty eyes and sad expressions, clung to her husband, changed her way of dress, and went with him to apply for a driver's license.

They sold the horse and buggy, and a 2006 Dodge now stood in the driveway. They sold the gas appliances and replaced them with a secondhand electric refrigerator and stove.

The Amish ministers were patient and kind, waiting close to a year before the family was excommunicated, as they obeyed the teaching of the forefathers.

Eventually, Leon found another job, being unable to continue at the Homestead, it being an Old Order establishment. He was a youth counselor at Christian Day School, and a good one. Anna made new friends, named her daughter Adelaide, and slowly rediscovered a sense of peace and contentment.

Rachel heard all this from her friend Leah, who sat beside her after dinner at church, spoke in a voice only a decibel above a whisper.

"And, get this, Rachel. They say Anna doesn't even wear a cape dress the way most of those women do. I pity her mother."

"I don't."

Leah reared back, aghast.

"Why do you speak in such a way, Rachel? I would not have thought it of you, at your age."

"My age? Age has nothing to do with it and you know it. I have always spoken my mind and plan on continuing, thank you very much, Leah."

"Well, being a widow and all, I would think you would want to stay close to *unser Gott*. You know, not talk about people. Life is very serious with your husband dead and gone." Leah pursed her lips with her own sense of exalted righteousness. Rachel slanted her a look.

"And how would you know, with your own husband still alive and well?"

"Oh now."

She clapped hand on Rachel's generous knee, gave it an affectionate squeeze. Rachel took this as a good sign that the soil was fertile for her bald honesty, the only thing she knew and practiced.

"I don't care what you say. Elias and Barbie need to learn that life isn't always under their control. All that perfection. They may as well tumble and get roughed up a bit, cause it's bound to happen to the best of us."

"It sure did happen to you, didn't it? With Dave. My oh."

Pursed her lips and shook her head, her eyes closed in reverence. That really brought out the rebellion in Rachel.

"Dave is doing very well. He loves that new job of his. He comes home filthy dirty, tired, and happy."

"It's not a job for Amish."

Rachel bristled. "And why not? What's the difference? On a roof out in the world among English people or in the woods with nature?"

"Oh yes. I guess you're right."

Here Leah's husband Joe made an appearance, raised his bushy eyebrows at his wife. She caught sight of his face, nodded and started the lengthy task of saying goodbye to her close friend.

"Are you sure you have a way home, then?"

"I told you I walked."

"You walked? Well, all right then. I guess you'll be all right. Okay, then. All right. Will I see you this week? Call and leave a message if you want to. We should go visit Amos sie Katie over on the pike. You knew her grandson has heart problems, right?"

Rachel nodded.

"You knew that. Okay. All right. All right. I must get my shawl and bonnet. Did you wear one this morning?"

Her eyes fastened on Rachel's round face.

"Yes. It was chilly."

"It was chilly, wasn't it? All right, then. Bye."

Rachel watched her lumber off, her narrow belt pinned crookedly over her *leblein*, that small, rounded swatch of fabric that was centered between every black apron. The mark of being Amish. If she'd use a small mirror to see her back when she pinned that apron on, it would help.

She sat alone, staring at the door, thinking how very nice it would be to have Eli come tell her he was ready to go. The realization that he really was gone was like a cruel blow, yet again. Sorrow was like a cloying vine, it kept growing and never relinquished its hold.

She had to work on giving herself up to her lot in life. If Leah said "all right" one more time she would have pinched her arm.

CHAPTER 25

Dave's job brought new responsibilities and very little time to think about other things, which was just as well. But as the summer wore on, he began to think of his future and felt as if something was missing in his life.

He was lean and brown, the muscles in his back and shoulders sculpted like those of a weight lifter. There was not an ounce of spare flesh on his body.

His face thinned, his eyes fell in their sockets, framed with the stress of the excruciating labor.

He would not quit, however. The drive to excel was like a bellows, puffing rapidly to fan the flames of his greed to accomplish more and more.

He heard it from his mother.

"You know that dark-haired girl you liked?"

He looked up from his plate.

"Who? Rose?"

"Whatever her name is."

"What about her? How did you know?"

"She's dating Marcus Beiler."

Dave swallowed his mouthful of macaroni and cheese, swallowed again.

"Is she? Who told you?"

"Who do you think?"

Dave nodded. "None other than the Amish media, Leah."

"Mm-hm."

Dave shook his head, laughed ruefully.

"Well, there goes another one. I just can't seem to catch any of them."

"You don't try very hard."

"I had a real girlfriend in Australia. Sometimes I still miss her. I should just go back again, take up where I left off."

His mother shot him a look of reproach. A comfortable silence followed, broken only by his mother's soft sigh.

"So how much have you figured out yet, going to all those churches?"

Dave grinned, then turned serious.

"You know, Mam, I have to hand it to you. You gave me an awfully long rope with which to hang myself. I don't see much sense in doing anything different than what I was raised. At least for now. You're alone since Dat passed on, and why would I pile sorrow on the grief you already live with? As long as the church allows me to drive that skidder and use the chainsaw, I'm okay with having a driver haul me around. I'm just not ready to join up yet. I thought I'd ask Rose, but the timing was never right. She's not very easy to approach, anyway. She scares the tar out of me. Anna was so different. She was sweet and sunny and filled with light. You know how she was."

"Is. She didn't die," his mother corrected him. She reached out and broke a slice of Swiss cheese in half and stuffed it into her mouth, followed by a long slice of green dill pickle.

"She has died more than either of us will ever know."

His mother crunched the pickle in her teeth, her jaws working contentedly.

"She must have given up so much to leave with Leon."

Dave slid down in his chair, his thumbs hooked in his trouser pockets, his eyes hooded, reclusive. Yet he could not bring himself to talk about what had happened in her life. The silence dragged on between them, until he sat up, reached for his water glass and drained it.

His speech was guttural, tight with emotion, when he spoke in a voice that dripped with bitterness.

"They chose Leon for her. I wasn't good enough."

"Well, you weren't back then. Perhaps now that you're older . . ." Her voice drifted off.

"She's gone, Mam. You know that. I know it. The best I can do is wish her a good life. She will, you know. It's in her nature to be happy, to rise to any occasion." He shook his head, as if the mere thought was hard to believe. He yawned, stretched, laughed.

"I can't believe I'm sitting here talking to you about all this. I would never have done that a few years back. I was way too cool."

Rachel chuckled, reached for the remaining slice of cheese, as Dave knew she would.

"I'm too cool for you, that's what."

They laughed together, and he went to feed the horse and talk to his brother out at the farm.

On Saturday morning, he woke early, stretched, and lay in bed with his hands crossed behind his head. Now that Rose was dating, there was no need to get all dressed up to go to her workplace, but since he needed a chainsaw file and bug spray, he'd go to Lowe's and get his breakfast at the diner.

He wondered if she was pleased with Marcus, if she'd be any happier to see him. That dark brooding look out of those black eyes was enough to make his knees weak, so how could he ever hope to have asked her for a date? Marcus was a bigger man than he was, for sure.

And, too, he still carried Anna in his heart. A thorn that caused pain, perhaps, but a presence he still could not deny.

Oh my sweet, sweet beautiful Anna.

He dressed with tears in his eyes, his fingers fumbling to close the buttons on his shirt. He drew a comb through his hair, ran the sides of his fingers across his teeth and clattered down the stairs to find a note written on yellow tablet paper.

"Went to town. Be back soon."

She should have told him.

But he found his way to the diner with old Marty Burkhart, sat at his usual table and waited till she came to take his order. He looked around. The tables were really loaded, the noise deafening as each party tried to speak above the other. What a fiasco. He'd never be able to ask her the questions he needed to ask.

Needed? The sense of urgency was a grim awakening. Now where had this sudden intensity come from? He realized he was becoming quite desperate, annoyed at all the diners and their ridiculous chatter.

And then she was there, face flushed, eyes snapping.

"You're still living?"

"Yeah, I'm here."

"Where have you been?"

"Around. Logging."

She nodded, looked over her shoulder.

"Quick. It's crazy in here."

"I want to ask you something."

"Fire away. But hurry."

"Are you happy now that you're dating?"

A puzzled expression drew two lines between the black wings of her eyebrows.

"Who am I dating?"

"You know. Don't play with me."

"Who?"

"Marcus Beiler. Amos Belier's Marcus."

"I'm not dating him or anyone else."

"What?"

"Serious."

Wave after wave of gratitude washed over him, a hurricane at sea that threatened to wipe away any composure he had maintained when she came to his table. He felt himself lifted to great heights, borne by the power of the clear light ahead of him. He broke through the tunnel he had unknowingly been navigating.

There was a light of God's love, the warm rays of His mercy and understanding. His understanding was so brilliant. Dave closed his eyes momentarily.

He felt blinded. Dazzled.

He had not known he was stumbling in darkness, or felt rejected by life. He'd merely found a job in which he could lose all thought, drive himself to the limit, and set God handily on the back shelf. But here He was, in the form of this quiet, brooding dark-haired girl who was very clearly somehow meant for him.

He was awed by the power of His direction.

All this went through Dave's thoughts in a moment. The beauty of God's knowledge was the still small voice of His Spirit, come to visit him in the middle of a very noisy, overflowing restaurant in Ephrata.

When Dave looked at her, his heart shone from his eyes, his smile so genuine it took away the stony reserve Rose had built around herself.

"That's a relief."

"Why do you care?"

"Look. Rose. We need to talk sometime, okay?"

"Not now."

"Where do you live?"

She inclined her head. "Over toward Lititz."

"Can I call you?"

She hesitated. "Yes."

"May I have your number?"

She nodded, but did not move away immediately. Instead, she paused and looked into his eyes for the first time. There was mystery in those dark eyes, but there was also the beginning of access into the story of her life.

He called her that evening. Their conversation lasted approximately one hour and forty-five minutes. In the remaining time between the forty-five and fifty minutes he asked her for a date.

A real drive clear over to her house with his Amish horse and buggy kind of date.

She said yes, and he cried, later.

He wallowed in tears and sobs, releasing the pent-up hurts and frustrations, the rebellion and inability to conform to Elias and Barbie and Anna. He cried because he walked away from his vehicle in the arid Outback and very nearly lost his life while he was saddled with hatred and unforgiveness. Because he still hadn't made things right with Ammie, hadn't ever contacted her after he left.

He realized he was among those who stood at the foot of the cross and was sorry for all his past sins and that there was enough blood shed to save him, same as everyone else.

And he cried even more.

The night was mild, scented with roses that needed trimming, the arborvitae bushes hosting the unwieldy growth that straggled across them. Their fragrance reached his bedroom window along with the smell of mown hay and an essence of the clear, dark pond surrounded by bulrushes and dotted with lily pads. The chugging of the frogs was in harmony with the incessant monotone of the pronounced fact that Katy-did, whatever it was that she actually did.

Sleep completely left him. He could hardly believe the warm beauty of the summer night, the week that stretched before him like a path so bright and beckoning with the promise of a life changed for the better. There was purpose and understanding, victory over the bitterness that repeatedly dragged him under, leaving him confused and disoriented.

To comprehend forgiveness was a gift in itself. That was the one ingredient that had been missing half his life. Forgive himself for being unable to accept the rules that had been set for Anna. Forgive himself for not being there for his father. Forgive all his past sins, the parties, the fast pace, the blindness that drove him to substance abuse.

"For God so loved the world, that He gave His Son." The verse went on, but it had never meant anything until now. It pulsed in his veins and brought discovery and understanding. He truly believed God sent His only begotten Son, and all you had to do was believe and all the missing pieces of life's puzzle would fall into place.

Joining the church was no longer the heavy weight he had always imagined. This was what he wanted to do now, to be baptized into a body of believers, to be a joy and a balm to his grieving mother. He wanted to embrace his brothers, tell his sister MaryAnn, shout out to the whole world that God loved everyone, that Jesus was on the cross. He really had been there. And he rose victorious, and so could everyone who believed.

For the first time in his life, it was all right that Anna had married Leon. God loved them too. This was his path, and this was what God had intended way back when he stood on the threshold of damnation.

He shivered, but was comforted by his first real attempt at a prayer that was saturated with love and acceptance.

Their first date was a time of overcoming his own fear and awkwardness, a time of practicing the newfound confidence in God and his leading.

Rose was not Anna. This he discovered the first hour. She was quiet, content to maintain a conversation, not lead it, so before he realized it, he was talking incessantly, saying things that weren't proper for a first date.

Her home was a small brick ranch house set beneath a few pines, with a growth of shrubs, the usual Amish housewife's profusion of summer flowers, a clothesline that ran on a wheel attached to the small barn, a large well-kept garden, a few outbuildings all set beside a sleepy country road.

"My parents are retired," she said.

He nodded, followed her into the house to greet them, and was rewarded with a firm handshake from a tall, dark-complected, white-haired old man with a genuine grin of acceptance. His wife was small, a bit round, with the same dark eyes and graying hair.

She looked up at Dave and said, "Well, hello, young man. So this is who you are."

He asked Rose what she meant by that, and Rose shook her head, laughed, and said she couldn't take responsibility for everything her mother said.

He fell in love with her dry sense of humor, her endless knowledge of books and places and things. Her brooding eyes came alive with interest when they discovered they'd read many of the same books.

"So why do you read so much?" he asked.

They were seated on the back patio in the soft waning light, with tall glasses of mint tea. The air was warm but not uncomfortably so. Crickets of late summer chirped beneath the patio, grasshoppers whirred in the garden, and small moths and mosquitoes circled the birdbath set in the begonias.

The home was so ordinary, so comfortable and unassuming.

Dave felt a sense of home, of belonging that he had never experienced at Elias Fisher's. There was no need to be pretentious, to watch your manners or your words, to sit properly and smile widely and aim to impress the hovering authority.

These people were common, middle-class Amish who had always worked at menial jobs, never owned a farm, never "got ahead," but who carried the aura of contentment, satisfied to let others build palatial homes or buy that second or third farm. They had raised a small family, lived on a modest income, and that was fine with them.

Dave had noticed the magazines strewn around the recliners. Not the normal publications other Amish families received in the mail, he thought, which explained Rose and her insatiable appetite for books. He looked forward to long conversations with her father.

She leaned back, clasped her long slender fingers around her knee, looked at him to answer his question.

"I just love to read. It's simple, really."

"Don't you run around much?"

"You mean on the weekends with the group I belong to?"

"Yeah."

"I do. But . . . it's boring. I have a few good girlfriends, but their endless chatter about stupid things really gets to me. The books they read, their view of the world goes no further than their dress fabric and what's new at Kohl's." She looked at him. "I'm sorry. That sounds *grosfeelich*."

"No, no. I know exactly how you feel."

"You do?"

"Yeah. It's easy to become bored."

"I've often thought about being born Amish. It really hems you in. If I was English, I'd further my education. Go to college, probably go to graduate school."

"What would you study?"

"I have no idea. Something. Actually, I'm just saying all this to impress you."

He laughed, enjoying the playful challenge in her eyes.

There was no curfew. The parents retired about ten o'clock, the lights blinked out, and they were left on their own. They lit a fire in the firepit, made chocolate and peanut butter s'mores, drank strong coffee, and talked about every single thing they had ever lived through. Or so it felt.

Midnight came and went. Reluctant to end the evening, Dave kept making excuses, saying he didn't have church, and she didn't either. Church services among the Amish were held every two weeks, and this was an "off" Sunday.

She was fascinated by his Australia stories. She loved hearing about the hard work, the weather pattern, the Kels. But she became unsettled when he spoke of Ammie.

"You need to call her. That's not right to leave her without hearing from you. I don't care if she is an English girl that ran after you."

He blushed to the roots of his hair, felt terribly chastised and deeply ashamed. The following week he did what she told him and made that phone call, hearing the voice of the past, his energetic, sunny Ammie.

He apologized, said he got tangled in his Amish culture, could see it would never work to go back to Australia.

"Then why didn't you call?"

Her voice carried thousands of miles and stung him efficiently.

"I'm sorry. I was being a coward."

"Worse than a coward. You're just like all the other blokes. They come and go, don't give two hoots about girls like me. You better never come back or my dad will beat your boots off."

Click. The whirring of dead reception.

He felt really rotten the following day, chiding himself mentally. It was Ammie, but it wasn't just her. How many hearts had he trampled on, too selfish or too scared to treat them with any kind of meaningful care? When it came down to it, hadn't it been the same way with Anna, with his parents, with pretty much anyone who had ever cared about him? He wrote Ammie a long letter of apology and told Rose that he'd done so. He had half hoped that she would praise him for doing the right thing finally, but she made no comment, just searched his eyes with her own, as if trying to gauge whether she could trust him. It made his heart sting, knowing she had every reason to second-guess their own blooming friendship.

A new problem arose in the form of Rose laughing and talking to the customers at work, having woken from her self-inflicted brooding.

The truth was, Dave was everything she had dreamed he would be. She was crazy about him. She loved his grin, his eyes that danced with the fervor of life, his hands that were so calloused they did not feel human. She loved the way he dressed, his trousers low on his hips, the expensive shirts, and the way he cut his hair. To be so in love was an awakening, a blessing from the God she had learned about at her mother's knee, the Jesus and his disciples in the Bible storybooks. She had never experienced any major event where God was concerned, but He had always been there, received her prayers and concerns, and now, her praise.

So her eyes shone with a new light, her smile flashed, and the men at the diner responded with long looks that Dave found unacceptable.

He told her about it, when they were driving the twelve miles to his sister MaryAnn's house one evening in late summer.

"Oh, come on, Dave. It doesn't mean anything. I'm just happy."

"Well, some of those men are too happy, and you know it."

"Well, maybe so. But no one is serious."

"I am."

She stared straight ahead, watched the easy, light-footed trot of this beautiful black Friesian. His Ferrari. She grinned. She loved Dave's sense of humor, his knowledgeable way of talking. And now he was jealous, and she could not hide her pleasure at his self-imposed misery.

"You're serious about what?"

"You. I don't want you flirting with those men."

"I'm not flirting, Dave."

"Yes, you are."

That was unfair. Her temper flared.

"Think what you want, but I am not a flirt. I don't want those men's admiration or any other attention. You're just sitting there with your childish jealousy. I didn't think you were that stupid."

Dave bristled, his retort sounding harsher than he intended. "You didn't used to be that kind of girl."

"You want to know why I am now? Because I'm happy I found you."

That statement turned the tide immediately and threw a whole new light on the reason for her dancing eyes and wide smile. His heart pounded, wondering if he should try to kiss her. That had been quite a statement, almost as if she'd told him she loved him.

Wow.

He glanced at her. He drove with one hand, slowly drew his arm up over her head to rest on her shoulders, his hand drawing her close to his side. His heart beat so loudly his eyes clouded over and he could barely see to drive. The close proximity of the buggy was a perfect haven for young love.

They had held hands sometimes, but he had never ventured further into the world of physical closeness. Thoroughly burned by his past relationship with the dear love of his life, forced to accept convictions that were not his own, and then having ventured too far with Ammie, in what he now recognized as lust, he floated in indecision, hesitant to talk about it with Rose.

She did nothing to make it easier, the way she sat on her side of the buggy without leaning in. He had a hard time driving this way, felt awkward and foolish, so he slid his arm along the back of the seat and placed it in the normal position, holding the reins.

There was an uncomfortable silence, which neither one knew how to alleviate, so the moment passed, and normal conversation resumed.

The truth for her was that she had never been in a close embrace with a man and certainly had never been kissed. She desperately did not want Dave to suspect this, so she had no intention of leading him on, before they discussed it, at least.

What if he found her repulsive? What if the English girl still held a piece of his heart? No, it wasn't worth the risk.

MaryAnn noticed a stiffness, a sense of unease between them. It ruined her evening, being receptive to all manners of moods and feelings, always thinking the worst about any given situation. So when they called it a night before eleven o'clock, she was hugely relieved, fussed up a storm to her laconic husband, and went to bed without sleeping, got up and flounced on the recliner to spend a miserable night.

Dave was simply a constant cause of worry. If he wasn't whacking around in unfit terrain with that piece of equipment he called a skidder, he was dating girls who looked like models and didn't really want him all that much.

Rose was gorgeous, like her name. A dark rose. So reserved and elegant. Willowy, like an exotic princess. Likely she could have anyone she set eyes on. Not that Dave wasn't a catch, but still.

He seemed red faced and downright bumbling when he was with her. Rose made him feel that way, she guaranteed.

Why couldn't he be normal like his brothers? Content to marry a normal girl and settle down to a normal life? It was exhausting, always worrying about what would happen to him next.

CHAPTER 26

LEON QUICKLY MOVED UP THE RANKS OF THE CONSERVATIVE CHURCH THEY attended, his zeal to be a true servant of God taking him to the poorest neighborhoods in the surrounding cities in Pennsylvania. As he had always done, he gave most of their income to the poor, the suffering, the addicted, which left Anna to get a job or be evicted.

She never spoke of this to her parents, who were supportive now, after the initial hurt of having a daughter leave the fold. They still had a deep-seated respect for Leon, and as the months wore on and they heard Anna's stories of his work in the church, they felt justified, secure in the choice they had made for their daughter.

Anna went online, received her GED, found a job at Mission for Jesus Elder Care Center and secured a reliable babysitter for her children. She found solace in caring for the aging people who were left to live their lives in the keeping of strangers. Her soft heart was warmed by the menial tasks of being responsible for their comfort and well-being.

They called her Angel, and she deserved every ounce of praise she received, moving in and out of rooms with her pastel-colored dresses that reached to the floor.

It was only after the shift was over, and she drove the battered little Subaru home, her children dirty and disheveled after the babysitter's lack of care, as her hands gripped the steering wheel till her knuckles turned white and her nails bit into the palms of her hands, that she allowed tears of frustration and weariness to course down her wan cheeks.

Hidden from her parents and Leon, maneuvering through the traffic on 283, she was truly in touch with who she really was, which was becoming harder and harder to decipher.

She was tired, that was all.

Her love for Leon was still there, but it was only her teaching that supported it. "Wives, love your husbands in the Lord." It was burned into the soul of her existence, and she remained obedient to every admonition.

She never spoke ill of him, even if the financial responsibility was sometimes overwhelming. She learned to cook with even less, to buy all her clothes at Goodwill, praised God for yard sales and the kindness of well-to-do people who allowed her to fill a grocery bag with items for a dollar. The old house was cold in winter and hot in summer, but she still kept it neat and tidy, the garden weeded, and the lawn mowed. She canned and froze vegetables late at night, smiled at her husband as he sat peeling peaches after the children were in bed. Her thoughts were not always in the same kitchen, but in her past, when life had been joyous and, if not carefree, at least easier to handle.

The conclusion that God wanted her to be here with Leon was restful, and she grew in grace and servitude. When he asked her to go to the city of Lancaster to minister to the poor, she agreed readily enough, found someone to keep the children for one Saturday, packed a cooler with food and drinks, looked over the pamphlets Leon had printed and slid a bundle into her own purse in order to stand beside her husband to distribute them.

They chose the corner of Evers and Conyer, a busy thoroughfare that brought the pedestrians and buses that deposited all manner of humanity. The day was warm, so Anna soon rid herself of the white sweater she had donned that morning.

Behind them was a deli owned by an Indian man who allowed

them out of the goodness of his heart to be there (or because he knew he couldn't do anything about it anyway).

They stood side by side, Leon and Anna, handing out the religious literature, saying "God bless you," over and over, occasionally able to witness to someone who seemed to be hungry for the Word of God.

A large dual-wheeled truck slowed, swung into a narrow parking space, the door flung open before it came to a sudden stop. Anna stepped up with a pamphlet, a warm, welcoming smile, with Leon behind her.

The smile slid away. Her face froze, and the color drained away.

"Anna."

Confused, Dave stopped directly in front of her.

She still looked the same, still harbored that inner light, the blue eyes unforgettable as always.

Anna felt as if she was caught in the crosshairs of her own honesty, the truth that was buried in many layers of traditional teaching, of parental obedience and fear of being counted among the *ungehorsam*.

She lowered the pamphlet. It fell from her nerveless fingers.

Dave's eyes were alight with recognition, the light drawing her own eyes as sure and as intense as a laser. Gladness crowded out every other emotion and crippled her need to lower her gaze.

As if in a trance, she reached out both of her hands, palms up, as if asking him if it was okay to be here at this moment, caught in this grip of rekindled friendship and caring and remembering. He stepped forward, gripped her hands in his own blackened calloused ones, and the world disappeared.

There was only the two of them. David and Anna, young, carefree, walking home from school on a golden autumn day when the maple leaves lay in a thick yellow blanket by the side of the road and sun shone on their faces like a benediction.

Leon cleared his throat. "Someone you know?"

"I do know him."

Her voice was barely above a whisper. Dave took a deep breath, dropped her hands, turned to Leon. He seemed to shake off the dream that shrouded his vision.

"Your husband?"

"Yes. Leon, this is Dave."

They shook hands. Anna looked from one to the other.

Dave was in heavy work clothes, his large hands blackened from his grip on chainsaws and logs, Leon tall, thin, and pale, his dark looks as handsome, but without the robust vitality.

"Nice meeting you."

"And you. Would you be interested in the love of Christ?"

Leon handed him a pamphlet with a wide smile.

"Thanks." He stuffed it in his trouser pocket, turned to Anna.

"I wish you the best, Anna."

"Thank you, Dave."

There was a long pause, an intense exchange that left Leon an imposter, and Dave turned on his heel, forgot to buy the drinks and snacks he had intended, reentered the truck. Gary Lawson pulled away from the curb and roared away, leaving them both standing in a black cloud of diesel exhaust.

Anna sighed, watched the truck disappear into the dense jumble of fast-moving traffic, her shoulders hunched slightly, her face the color of the unsteady sky.

Leon clapped a hand on his wife's shoulder, drew her close to gaze intently into her face. He shook her gently.

"Anna, my love. Are you all right?"

With a huge effort, she raised her eyes to his. Bright with unshed tears, he mistook the gleam for the light of freshly rekindled love, and smiled.

"So fortunate, Anna, so fortunate for you to have escaped the talons of the hawk. He looks the way you have described him, a wild and strenuous man. He would drain the life from you with his electrifying ways."

Anna nodded. Drained of all desire to change anything, she

merely bowed her head and accepted Leon's words. Yes, yes, she nodded.

But he had come. She had held his hands. What they had would never vanish completely. She would always know there was a place she could find the remembering, the special times they shared, the flame of a love that outlasted life here on earth. And he knew this too. He did. She had seen it in his eyes.

She would be a good wife to Leon, with a pure and wholesome love she would share with him, the kind that bloomed where God sowed the seed on fertile ground. But when she rocked her babies or washed her dishes, the song that burst from her lips would be the bright joy of remembering the knowledge that they both were led along paths that were very different, but designed by God for reasons neither one would ever fully understand. They did love, had loved, but it was not meant to be.

Was this, then, a tragedy? She thought not. She would live till God chose to end her days, and only He would know what inner peace and happiness controlled her life. The future was not bleak, but held great promise to do what she set out to do. Obey her parents' wishes in the best possible way, in spite of being different.

She could still love them, return on a regular basis to spend time with them, show her gratitude and appreciation as best she could.

She inhaled deeply, lifted her face to smile at Leon, and stepped out to hand two young girls a glossy tract that would point them to the way of the cross.

Dave's encounter with Anna left him shaken. He slept little, ate sparingly. To see her on the street corner doing evangelical work was something he could not have prepared himself for. He'd heard they left the Amish, but . . .

Why had God chosen to allow all this?

He wanted to visit her home, sit at her kitchen table and talk to her. *Tell me your true feelings. Tell me why you married him.*

Tell me you love me. It was always me, Anna.

But in the end, he chose to pour out all his feelings to Rose.

They were seated on the sofa in the living room late one Sunday evening. His face was dark with an unnamed emotion, his words a quiet monotone that held no interest in anything he was saying.

Rose shrank into a corner, her arms crossed.

"Why don't you just go home?" she asked abruptly, wrestling with the fear of this being the evening when he'd tell her he was no longer interested.

Confused, he'd say. I'm confused. Which was to say he'd found someone else.

To her horror, he began to cry. Thinking he was kidding around, she sat up, ready to stalk off, but found the choking breaths to be genuine sobs. She sank back, shocked into silence.

"I'm sorry," he choked.

She said nothing.

"It's just that . . . you're going to think I'm completely unstable."

"Try me," she said in a whisper.

So he did. He told her everything, which was quite an amount of territory to cover, including the insecurity, rivers of self-doubt, and the long mountain range of his rebellion against Anna's parents.

A mountain that was erased time after time, yet appeared in all its impossibility to forget at other times. Self-blame is sometimes never conquered, in spite of a person's most honest efforts, which eventually will create a humility of sorts, he finished quietly.

She listened without comment.

"What do you think, Rose?" he asked into the silence.

"I think you have never gotten over this Anna."

"Oh, but you're definitely wrong. I have. She doesn't mean anything. She's married."

"She is, outwardly. But you still carry the past around with you."

"No." He shook his head vehemently. "God took it all away."

She disagreed. "She's still here."

There was nothing he could say to set her right.

Their breakup lasted two weeks, in which he discovered the desolate misery that blanketed his existence, suffocating him with every breath.

He struggled to understand what he was supposed to do, before his mother got tired of witnessing her son moping around the house like a dog with mange, set him down and took matters into her own hands.

"All right, out with it. You broke up, right?"

He nodded miserably.

"What for?"

He shrugged.

"Oh, don't give me that. You know why. You think I don't, but I do. You saw Anna. Well, young man, let me tell you. You can choose to drag her around with you and wreck your own and everyone else's life, or you can let go of all that once and for all. The bottom line is giving up. You were never much of an expert. She's married."

"She's not happy!" he burst out.

"And how would you go about making her happy? Of course she is. I've told you before Anna will always be happy, no matter where life takes her. Now you wake up and appreciate Rose and get over yourself."

With that, his mother bent her back, picked up the clothes basket and called back over her shoulder.

"I'm tired of washing all your oily clothes. It's time you joined the church and got married."

He went to Rose's house and knocked on the door. Her father opened it, grinned, and stepped aside.

"She's in the shower. You want some coffee?"

Dave nodded. They spoke easily, sipped coffee, waited till the bathroom door opened. Rose stopped. In a red dress, a towel around her head like a turban, her eyes wide, she merely looked at them without speaking.

"Coffee?" her father asked.

"No, I'll be back."

They talked, then, far into the night, sharing insights on the past, hopes for the future, and the futility of lost love.

"Obviously it was not meant to be, so we're going to close that box and seal it," he finished.

"We are? You mean, you are."

"Me?"

"Of course. I wasn't there back then."

Suddenly, she lifted herself off the sofa in one graceful movement, stood above him and reached out with both hands. In the dim light of the lamp, her eyes were huge and dark, unfathomable.

He got to his feet, their faces locked.

"I wasn't there, Dave, but I'm here now."

Softly, with all the grace of a woman in love, she stepped closer, lifted her arms, and slid her hands to his forearms.

"I don't know what is wrong with you, trying to listen to Anna's parents to this day."

And she stood on her tiptoes. Her hands went to his shirt collar and tugged ever so slightly, tilted her head just so and brushed his lips with her own. She was like a beautiful dark flower, scented with an unnamed fragrance of hope and a brilliant future.

He gathered her slender body against his, sought her soft, willing mouth, and claimed her for his own, forgiven, found, loved, assured in that moment and for many more.

Rose was his equal, his love, his heart's desire.

Anna may have occupied a place in his heart, but Rose was the one who would stand beside him in the force of life's storms.

She leaned back in his arms, her eyes gathering him into her life, saddled with all of his insecurities and lack of faith, the past that would sometimes rise up in front of him, but steadily lose its power as the years came and went.

"I'm sure, Dave. I will never let you down. I love you more each passing day. I'll take you in spite of all you bring with you."

"Like what?" he asked, smiling into her eyes.

"Everything. Everything I will always want or need in a man. You."

The moon hung in the sky that night, a king to the myriad of twinkling stars, illuminating the little house that was truly home to a love that had finally found the two hearts that belong together.

The End.

GLOSSARY

Allus schtruvvlich–Unkempt

Anna enda–Other end

Aus de school–Out of school

Aus-ga-botta–Disappointed

Beebly–Chick

Bleivat aus de grick.–Stay out of the creek.

Dat–Dad

Daudy–Grandfather

Daudy house–An extension built onto a house for elderly parents to live in after their children's family takes over the home property.

De arme dinga.–The poor things.

Dess leave–This life

Dichly–Kerchief

Die gmay nemma–Having church in one's home.

Die gmay noch gay–Joining the church

Die oof gevva heit–Giving up

Die ungehorsamy–The disobedient

De vikkle side–The rolled side

Dote. Sie sinn all dote.–Dead. They are all dead.

Eck–Corner table

Englisha–A non-Amish person.

Eppas lets.–Something's wrong.

Fa-sarked–Looked after

Fooftzich yawa trick.–Fifty years ago.

Fore-gayer–Organizers of a funeral

Gals-houw–Horsehair

Ganz allenich?–All alone?

Gehorsamkeit–Obedience

Grosfeelich–Arrogant

Hesslich–Really

Hochmut–Pride

Kamm na—Come now

Katza pennly—Cat's dish

Kommet—Come all of you (plural)

Iss um-komma—Has died

Leblein—A small, rounded swatch of fabric centered on a black apron

Lieve leut, voss doot eya sneckst?—Dear people, what will he do next?

Loss-heit—Liberal thinking

Ma dut net so.—You don't do that.

Ma halta aw.—We will pray.

Mam—Mom

Mammy—Grandmother

Matzo—Suitcoat

My Gott im Himmel—My God in heaven.

Oof-gevva-heit—Giving up

Ordnung—Literally, "ordinary," or "discipline." The Amish community's agreed-upon rules for living, based on their understanding of the Bible, particularly the New Testament. The *ordnung* varies some from community to community, often reflecting the leaders' preferences and the local traditions and historical practices.

Rumschpringa–Literally, "running around." A time of relative freedom for adolescents, beginning at about age sixteen. The period ends when a youth is baptized and joins the church, after which the youth can marry.

Schnuppy–Hanky

Schicket euch.–Behave yourselves.

Schrecklich–Scary

Schpeiting–Causing sadness to

Ungehorsam–Disobedient

Unser Gott–Our God

Vass die alte trick glesst hen.–What the forefathers left for us.

Vee bisht?–How are you?

Vell–Well

Velleta raus?–Do you want out?

Verboten–Forbidden

Vindla–Diapers

Voddags schnuppy–Everyday handkerchief

Voss Gebt mitt da boo?–What will happen with the boy?

Zu feel g'fuddad–Too much expected

OTHER BOOKS BY LINDA BYLER

LIZZIE SEARCHES FOR LOVE SERIES

BOOK ONE   BOOK TWO   BOOK THREE

TRILOGY

COOKBOOK

SADIE'S MONTANA SERIES

BOOK ONE

BOOK TWO

BOOK THREE

TRILOGY

HESTER'S HUNT FOR HOME SERIES

BOOK ONE

BOOK TWO

BOOK THREE

TRILOGY

BOOK ONE

BOOK TWO

BOOK THREE

TRILOGY

Christmas Novellas

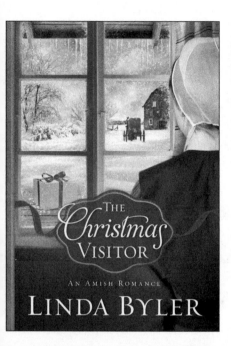

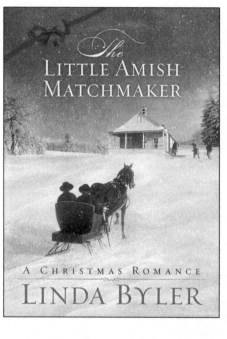

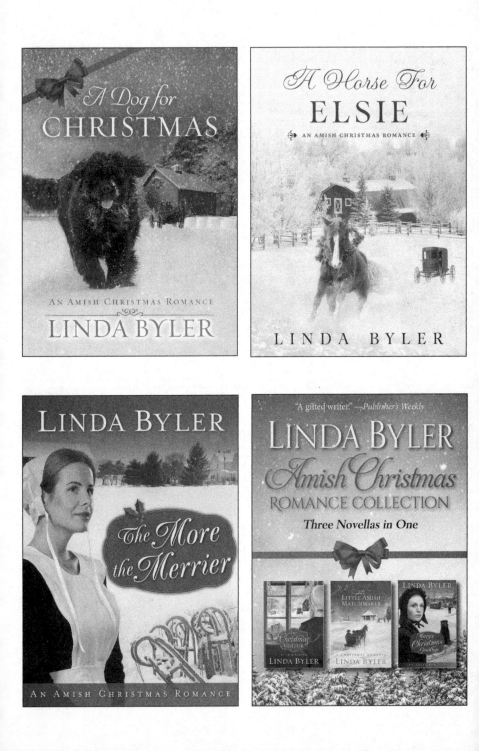

THE HEALING

A SECOND CHANCE

ABOUT THE AUTHOR

LINDA BYLER WAS RAISED IN AN AMISH FAMILY AND IS AN ACTIVE MEMBER OF the Amish church today. Growing up, Linda loved to read and write. In fact, she still does. Linda is well-known within the Amish community as a columnist for a weekly Amish newspaper. She writes all her novels by hand in notebooks.

Linda is the author of six series of novels, all set among the Amish communities of North America: Lizzie Searches for Love, Sadie's Montana, Lancaster Burning, Hester's Hunt for Home, The Dakota Series, and the Buggy Spoke Series for younger readers. Her standalone novels include *The Healing* and *A Second Chance*. Linda has also written several Christmas romances set among the Amish: *Mary's Christmas Goodbye*, *The Christmas Visitor*, *The Little Amish Matchmaker*, *Becky Meets Her Match*, *A Dog for Christmas*, *A Horse for Elsie*, and *The More the Merrier*. Linda has coauthored *Lizzie's Amish Cookbook: Favorite Recipes from Three Generations of Amish Cooks!*